CW00954050

The crowd scatte

Arkaen pulled his mare to a
But the image of the high lord ri
for a battle could only stoke the ~~fires of distrust~~
image he could build.

He rode on, the few remaining people he passed seemingly prepared for his arrival now. Anyone on the street had already lined up against the walls, eyes firmly stuck to the cobbles by the time he arrived, and he never again came across a group careless of his approach. As if some runner ahead warned every street before he turned on it. As if someone—or something—led him toward a certain goal. His muscles tightened, nerves strung for combat in the peaceful streets.

"I should turn back." He muttered the words under his breath, one hand rubbing at his bare belt loop as he turned the final corner to a broad alley that led to Brayden's home. Four men, barely older than boys, loitered in the middle of the street. Arkaen pulled his mare to a halt again, the scrape of leather on stone clearly audible behind him. "Sayli's going to kill me."

A deep chuckle from behind. "Nay, milor', I ain't think ya gotta worry 'bout that."

Arkaen half turned in his saddle to scout the threat behind him. Only two, though one was a heavy built man with thick mats of blond hair who filled a good chunk of the street by himself. That one would be tough to push past. The other boy with him, similar in build and coloring but much slighter, looked wide-eyed and terrified. One frightened child likely facing an early initiation and the leader. The four in front would be skilled enough to hold their own without direct leadership, then. Arkaen had no weapons but his wits and what he could re-appropriate. And Lasha, who wouldn't miss the fight if Arkaen needed him. He offered a grim smile.

"You gentlemen may want to stand down. I've no desire to take lives today."

Wake

of the

Phoenix

Chelsea Harper

Wake of the Phoenix is a work of fiction. Names, characters, places, and incidents are the product of the author's imagination or are used fictitiously. Any resemblance to actual events, locales, or persons, living or dead, is entirely coincidental.

For my brothers, Bryan and Chris, who told me when I was eight that I could be good at writing even though I was just a kid. And for my seventh grade English teacher who planned a writing retreat for my school when she realized I didn't know how to find and shadow an author for my career day assignment. And for the author who did that retreat and told me:

"There's no such thing as a professional writer. Only published and unpublished writers."

I hope he knows how much it meant to an eleven year old little girl to hear that her writing was just as valid as his, if not yet as polished.

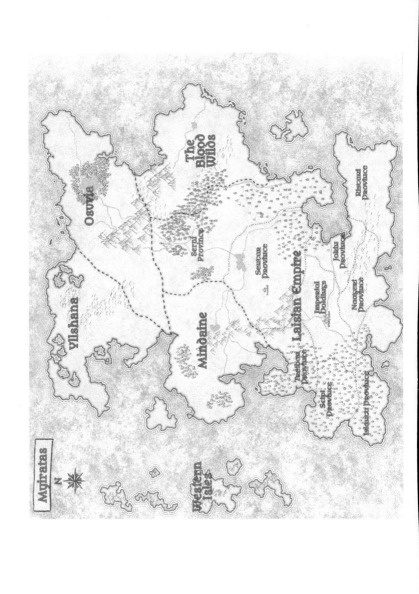

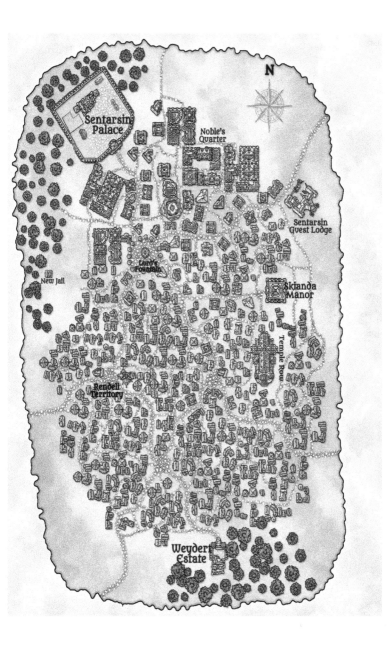

A lady never interrupts matters of state. She guides them from the shadows behind her husband's chair.

— *High Lady Katrivianne Istalli Sentarsin*

Prologue

Saylina Sentarsin paused by the heavy wooden door into the lower lords' council chamber, noting the voices that carried into the hall. Count Brayden Skianda's deep baritone cut through Count Jussi Tenison's nasally complaint.

"The succession is clear. Our prince has returned and is prepared to take the throne. On what grounds do you challenge his claim, Jussi?"

Saylina yanked the door open before Count Tenison could voice a reply that might forever damn him as a traitor. Three pairs of eyes focused on her, the three noblemen turning from where they had leaned over the oak council table. Skianda to her right, his brown hair wild and lean face showing a new softness. He stared down Tenison's narrow frame and bowed shoulders, on her left, while Baron Oskari Weydert watched from his seat on the far side. To the left of the high lord's chair, where only the most trusted of advisers sat. Count Skianda's posture sagged as he saw her and the hand he'd held clenched tight relaxed into a splayed grip on the table edge. Saylina pasted an innocent smile on her face and stepped inside with girlish whimsy, waving her maid in to deliver the tea she'd brought.

"My lords, I thought it might be time for refreshments." Saylina circled the room, the swish of her skirts emphasizing her careless stride. She paused by a chair placed one seat to the right of the high lord's chair. Reserved for the heir. Her youth benefited her here. Count Tenison would discount her presumptuous stance as childish ignorance. While Baron Weydert would know better, he wouldn't dare challenge her in her own home. She rested one hand upon the chair's high, cushioned back. "You've been arguing for hours now. Perhaps a new ear to hear your concerns will help you find a resolution."

"That's kind of you, young Lady Saylina," Count Tenison said, sinking into the chair behind him as if his frail legs had finally given out. "I'm afraid this matter is beyond the reach of your woman's tactics. There's a succession to resolve."

"Certainly, My Lord Tenison." Saylina sat in the heir's chair, pointedly ignoring the outraged look from Baron Weydert. "But I've been the only heir to the Sentarsin bloodline since I began my woman's moons four years past. At least, the only heir in a position to take this seat. I may have learned a few things beyond how to mend my late father's clothing." She turned her gaze to Count Skianda, the only one still standing. "Have you concerns, my lord?"

"I'm well versed in the diversity of your talents, my lady," Count Skianda replied. He waved a hand at Saylina's maid, still setting out the cups for tea. "But your maid is not privy to these discussions."

"Of course." Saylina nodded to the young woman. "If you'll excuse us, we can manage our own tea."

The maid gave a deep curtsy and swept out the door. As they'd discussed. An apparent concession to the lords' concerns, though anyone knew they'd all tell trusted servants what transpired after the morning's vote.

"Now then." Saylina smoothed her skirts, taking the moment to examine the tension of the room. Count Tenison and Baron Weydert couldn't have sat further apart, leaving Count Skianda caught between their united front. "I understand my brother's return from war has been unexpected, and my father's so recent demise a genuine tragedy. But what seems to be the concern with my brother's inheritance?"

Count Skianda drummed his fingers on the table once, taking his seat with a heavy sigh. "My Lords Tenison and Weydert have concerns over your lord brother's choice of combat brothers. He did not fight for the Laisian Empire."

"But our new emperor has laid such concerns to rest, has he not?" Saylina examined each of them in confusion. "My brother is our only legitimate heir, and he received a pardon for any crimes committed in his recent experimentation with foreign interests."

"The pardon applies to fighters." Baron Weydert spoke for the first time, his voice hard as stone. "The emperor meant to aid conscripts, who had no choice but to turn traitor on their empire. Your brother wasn't a common soldier and he wasn't born to service in Serni. He was their gods-damned general, defecting from a province loyal to our empire under your father."

"And more than that," Count Tenison added, his lined face drawn with sympathy. "Your lord brother convinced loyal troops of the empire to turn traitor and join the rebellion. There's reports of it. General of a rebel army, turncoat. There's rumors *he* gave the order to murder Emperor Deyvan's uncle."

"So what would you have us do?" She leaned forward, demanding their attention. "Oust him, when we know Emperor Deyvan treats my brother as kin? Hold a Successor's Tribune and pray Emperor Deyvan follows Sentar traditions after we've killed his friend in single combat? Who would even rule in my brother's place?"

"I hear you, Lady Saylina," Count Skianda said. "I know your brother is a good man. We all know he means well, whatever our differences. But he's returned with a conquering army and he won't send them home. Get him to send his troops back to Serni."

"I'm not sure I agree with you, Brayden," Baron Weydert said. "I don't think I can truly say he means well. Not when there's talk he murdered his own kin, also."

"My brother had nothing to do with that. Father's accident was just a tragedy of carelessness." The lie sat heavy on Saylina's lips. Someone was behind her father's death. But now she needed to secure the province. The only way to protect her people was to put her brother on the throne.

"The lady makes a good point about the Tribune, Oskari." Count Tenison. Not the ally she'd expected, but a welcome one. "Our new emperor shows an unusual preference for the Sentarsin boy. Would a Tribune even work?" He tapped a finger on the table, mumbling as if thinking aloud. "We'd have to marry Lady Saylina off first, of course, or we'd name her as an accomplice. Though she's not even old enough for a proper marriage contract. Even if we marry her out, our Lord Emperor might argue we have none of the proper bloodline left to take the seat."

"He is not to be trusted, Jussi," Baron Weydert snapped. "Our presumptive high lord is a traitor to this realm. He's only biding his time for whatever larger scheme he has in play. I'll trust his loyalty when I see it."

"My brother will always devote himself to the greater good of this empire." Saylina rose, glaring at Baron Weydert. "I'll swear it on my life. And if you call Tribune on him, I will not wed to save my life. You'll murder me beside him, for a suspected treason you can't even name."

"That's unnecessary." Count Skianda frowned at her. "Your brother has my vote, and those I represent. With Lord Tenison's we have enough to confirm his ascension even if the rest of our peerage object. This is the safest path, my lords." He fixed Saylina with a stern look. "But I do hope you'll keep him in check, my lady. Your brother isn't the same boy who ran off to war."

"He's still my brother." Whatever else he'd become, she was certain he was that. But she wished Count Skianda's words didn't ring quite so true.

Ain't no honor in taking another's meal, nor in getting what ya ain't earned. Honor before hunger, lass, or ya won't have nothing in the end.

— *Master Trieu*

Chapter 1

"**N**ia!"

The shout woke her from a light doze like a slap across the face. Niamsha Pereyra scurried out of the filthy mess of straw and rose to a crouch, smoothing her loose trousers to brush the last of the straw free. The damp stone walls and ceiling were too cramped for her to stand, but the Rendell gang she served often ignored this storeroom. And it never got cold enough for her to freeze. Her haven in the ruined noble's mansion that served as a stronghold for her... *benefactors.*

"Aeduhm's blessed arsehole." Her tongue burned with the heretical curse, her hands scrambling through the straw in desperation. Niamsha snatched a small pouch off the floor and shoved the worn strap through her belt. The door burst open a moment later.

"Where's me take, girl?" Marcas Rendell, chief lieutenant of the Rendells, filled the doorway with paunch and stench.

"Eli's a shit-suckin' coward. He split too fast and we didn' have the lookout."

Thick mats of blond hair fell into Marcas's eyes as he glared at her. Niamsha shrank back from the hit he didn't throw. He would soon enough. He wouldn't care where the real blame fell.

"I didn' ask bout Eli," Marcas said, swinging his fist into the tight space.

The blow sent a burst of pain through her upper jaw and she stumbled into the slimy wall behind her. Cowering in the straw, Niamsha hid a seething glare behind her dark brown hair. The sting of her cheek drew another retort to her lips, but she fought it back. If she looked meek enough, Marcas wouldn't force his way in to hit her again.

"Where's me take?" Marcas crossed his arms, feet spread. As if his natural bulk wasn't threat enough.

"Gotta eat, Marc," Niamsha pleaded. The desperation in her words grated against her temper.

"Ya got a debt, girl." Marcas's voice took on a terrifying calm. "Pay in coin or pay in flesh. Don' matter to me."

He glared into the closet at her. He'd come alone, but if she didn't produce something, Marcas could find someone to drag her out. Niamsha pulled her pouch free and hunted through it. A sliver of sharpened metal for a blade, a piece of mis-blown glass from her papa's shop, a scrap of paper from the temple. Her fingers found coins, and she knew without looking how much. One copper lais and two hard-won silver cails.

Niamsha pulled the silver coins out, throwing them at Marcas. "I'm not a whore."

"Ya ain' a good thief." Marcas smirked as he scooped the coins off the floor. "Ya may should think on it."

Niamsha sank to her knees as he left, rubbing at the sore cheek he'd given her. She'd meant to visit her brother, Emrys, at the temple today, but she couldn't go now. She'd gotten their mother's darker, brown skin to Emrys's paler tan, but the bruise would still show. Not that Emrys hadn't seen her bruised in the past.

Niamsha ran quick fingers through her hair to untangle it, weaving a half-braid tied with string. The rest of her hair she let fall down her back. Her papa had always complained when she wore her hair back. Not proper for an unwed girl, he would have said. She did a lot of things that weren't proper these days. A lot of things Papa's debts had forced her to do.

Another twinge of guilt made her hesitate. Her papa would have scorned the thought of his daughter skimming coins from the streets. Honor before hunger, Papa used to say. But he'd never been hungry. Not like she and Emrys before Nijel Rendell had swept her from the streets after Papa's death.

Niamsha cracked the door and checked the hallway. No sign of Marcas or the rest of the gang. Pristine stone floors, a stark contrast to the filth she used to hide her sanctuary, led off to either side as far as she could see. The stairs were a few doors down, but they weren't safe for her. Niamsha jogged across the hallway to an elegant window overlooking what had once been a fine lord's courtyard. A thick strap of patched leather hung over the side. She threw herself over the edge and climbed down the leather to its end, halfway to the floor below. From there she let herself drop. The fall, only a few feet, jarred her on landing. The few breaths she took to regain her balance stretched to an eternity as she scanned the shadowed doorways that led into the main keep. She didn't dare stay too long. Marcas wasn't the only Rendell who thought she should use her body, and several didn't plan to pay her for it.

Niamsha slipped into the streets as soon as her breaths calmed enough, a light fall wind cutting through her worn clothing. She bowed her head to blend with the few others headed to market this late. The stench of the crowd was light this morning, the sun just high enough to reach the worn cobbles of the alley. Poor day for thieving if she'd ever seen one. Too busy for an ambush, too quiet to hide, and her usual ploys wouldn't work in a street with so many wealthier marks.

Barely two buildings from the Rendell house, she saw the sign. A charcoal drawing, sprawled across a stone wall in mimicry of the child's game Papa'd taught her. X's for names, O's for money. Make a line for title or wealth. But these playing boards broke all the rules. She paused by the sketch, examining the message. Three O's on the left, each with an X overlaid. No stealing coin this day, on pain of Nijel's wrath.

The next line held three X's, the top square smeared with green and yellow. The Rogue Baron was always off-limits. But the bottom color caught her eye. Bright red on one side of the square, blue on the other. Like the banners that hung over the noble's doors on last night's job. Surely Marcas hadn't defied an order from Nijel. The ban must be punishment for their failure. Nijel considered the target too dangerous now. And he'd want someone to blame, just like Marcas.

Niamsha glanced back toward the Rendell house. Not safe, and less so if Nijel blamed her. But the temple wouldn't let her in without silver for Emrys's keep, and a ban on thieving meant death or worse to anyone who defied Nijel.

A man paused beside her, scowling at the sketch on the wall. "Godsdamned brats, defiling the high lord's city."

She ducked her head, edging further away. Orange and gold tunic, with trimming of red. Not just a man, but one of High Lord Arkaen Sentarsin's royal guards. Nijel would have her head if she hinted these warnings meant something beyond innocent games.

Niamsha slipped into a side alley, head still bowed. The third line wouldn't matter to her. Rules for the rumor mongers, not the thieves. No use learning who Nijel wanted influenced today when she didn't know the stories his people told.

She edged around a stack of barrels, moving deeper into the small space before scanning the crowd. A beggar watched the crowd with too much interest, his shoes too clean for a man without a roof. Nijel's watchers. A poor day for thieving indeed.

Niamsha slipped into the fountain square, pausing by a flower merchant to take quick stock of the crowd. Merchants, workers, and drifters, all packed in before the Lord's Fountain. She knew the central statue well enough without seeing the whole thing. A thirty-foot rendering of High Lord Arkaen Sentarsin, called The Phoenix of Serr-Nyen, kneeling in a pool of water with one hand outstretched in supposed love. The other hand poured fresh water from an enormous stone waterskin into the pool.

"Shit-faced bastard," she muttered, glaring at the chiseled, broad brow and expressive eyes that were all she could see of the stone face.

High Lord Arkaen's first round of laws on taking his seat five years ago had spanned a baffling range. He'd built this monstrosity and ordered that everyone deliver their taxes in person to his guards at the fountain's foot. No matter that meant hard workers left their jobs to meet his guard captain's hours. He tore the guilds apart, leaving her papa to fend for himself. Started a soldier training program—paid, but not enough to live on. Must think common folk had spare days to hang out in taverns.

One of the soldier recruiters stood by the edge of the fountain in a plain brown tunic with only a single patch of color on one shoulder. The tax guard loitered nearby, casting vicious looks at the recruiter. More guards in High Lord Arkaen's orange and gold lined the square, bored attention written on every face. Her only chance at avoiding Nijel's watchers. Only a desperate fool stole under the noses of High Lord Arkaen's guards. Niamsha couldn't afford to be a fool.

She wandered through the square, skimming trinkets from the edges of the tables. Most wouldn't sell for any coin, but might be worth a trade for an extra bit of food. Maybe get her a job the Rendells saved for more trusted members.

Her eyes fell on the glasswright's stall, a shiny bauble hanging from a string on one side. Too expensive to steal. But she knew the apprentice—Janne Ferndon, the worthless, clumsy-handed son of guild-master Ferndon.

Papa'd tell her to forgive. Hatred only breeds pain, and the guilds suffered under the new high lord. But Papa died. Left her and Emrys on the streets and the guild let them starve. Guildmaster Ferndon let them starve.

The chance at payback was too much to pass up. Niamsha fingered the narrow blade in her pouch and sidled up to the stall. A commotion in a large side street caught Niamsha's attention just as she reached for the piece, the cluster of figures surrounding some newcomers. She glimpsed horses. Gods-damned lords always seemed to show when she needed to avoid notice. But this was like a godsend.

She cut the bit of string as Master Ferndon's lad leaned over the stall, peering toward the street. A simple matter to weave back into the crowd, away from the stall. Now was the harder part. Walking casually with something so expensive in hand, heart pounding and ears straining for the sound of an alarm. The throng pressed tighter around her, trying to catch sight of the noble that had come to the square or avoid someone dangerous. She couldn't tell without shoving her way to a clear spot, and that would risk calling attention to herself. Besides, all nobles were dangerous. The sooner she was away, the better.

Just as she cleared the last of the onlookers, a giant brown horse charged around a corner ahead. A shout and a sharp jerk on its reins brought the creature to a stop in a flurry of hooves. Spittle dripped into her hair as she scurried back. The creature reared, shaking its head against the pressure of the taut leather straps leading back from its blood-flecked lips. One hoof lashed forward toward Niamsha. She turned so it only grazed her shoulder, but the force knocked her down and scattered her treasures across the cobbles. She cursed and scrambled out of the way. A quick glance sent ice down her spine.

The Rogue Baron himself, blond hair caught in a tight gentleman's tail at the nape of his neck. He swung off the horse and landed beside her.

"Gutter scum!" the Rogue Baron shouted. He tossed the reins of his horse aside to point an accusing finger at Niamsha. "And foreign, thieving scum, no less. Whatever boon you thought to earn from the *high lord's* indulgence isn't to be found here. Out of my way!"

He leveled a kick at her. Twisting aside in a futile attempt to avoid his wrath, Niamsha squeezed her eyes shut and pulled her knees to her chest to protect herself. A fierce, animal snarl that was at least half hiss wove through the air in front of her, adding a new tremble to Niamsha's huddled form. Nothing fully human made *that* sound. Screams sounded around her as she waited for a kick that never landed. Niamsha cracked her eyes open to peek at the scene.

A long black cloak billowed in her face. Above it, eerie, midnight hair seemed to reach out, tendrils flowing against the breeze as if looking for a living creature to catch. A strange creature held the Rogue Baron's boot in one eerily pale hand and glared with a threat so obvious it made the hairs on her arms tingle in fear. Called the high lord's demon, this creature looked too horrifyingly human, drained of color with skin scarred by holy wrath. His rage was a tangible thing in the square.

High Lord Arkaen's demon snarled again. With a shove of the booted foot, he pushed the Rogue Baron to the ground and rose with a grace that flowed like water held in a man's form. His pale, almost transparent, white skin traced with fiery lines drawn across every visible inch of his body mesmerized Niamsha. Her eyes fixed on the pulsing glow of those burning lines. If rumor was true, that glow came from the lifeblood of the victims he'd killed for High Lord Arkaen, tattooed onto his skin as a sign of the gods' fury.

They said he could smell fear. That he ate children. That he'd see your death at a touch. Foolish stories to frighten children, of course, but for just a moment Niamsha believed every wild claim ever told about the creature.

She trembled in terror, quick gasps of air the only breath she managed. The Rogue Baron's face was stricken with horror, his trousers soaked and reeking.

"Kai'shien?"

The monster before her had a soft, almost musical voice at odds with his fearsome appearance. Niamsha scooted further from the creature and glanced around.

"No, Kìlashà." From somewhere near the fountain, High Lord Arkaen's voice held a snap sharp enough to crack a whip. "You may *not* start a civil war in my fountain square."

"As you wish," the demon replied.

"If you lay another hand on any of *my* lords, Kìlashà, you'll lose it." The words hung in the air, an implied demand for the Rogue Baron's loyalty that even Niamsha could hear. And, slowly, the importance of the words sank in. If the Rogue Baron denied he owed fealty to High Lord Arkaen… For all his words, High Lord Arkaen was as close to starting a war as his demon.

The silence stretched out into an eternity, the demon poised for action the instant the Rogue Baron uttered a denial that would release him from High Lord Arkaen's command. Niamsha knew it could only have been seconds before the Rogue Baron rose. With as much dignity as he could muster in his soggy trousers and disheveled tunic, he raised his chin and turned away from the demon before him.

"I am pleased to see, *High Lord*, that you have not forgotten your oath," the Rogue Baron called over his shoulder. "A ruler sees to lower lords first, then his duties, then his succession. If there's time remaining, he may pursue his own pleasures."

He snatched his reins from the limp hands of a terrified onlooker and stormed off, head high and rear damp. Niamsha watched his retreat until he was little more than a shape among many before her trembling slowed. Only then did she notice the continued silence in the square. Niamsha looked up to meet the demon's tar-dark eyes, all black with nothing to distinguish iris from white from pupil. He watched her as if waiting for a response. Hands clammy, she turned to look behind her. An empty avenue lined by merchants, beggars, and everyone in between stretched from her place on the ground to High Lord Arkaen.

He sat on a brown horse, leaning on his saddle with light brown hair swept back in rugged, loose locks that framed his broad face and firm jaw. His lean body hid a strength that many said could best his own demon in combat, and his long fingers rested casually on the reins of his horse.

High Lord Arkaen watched her, one hand flipping a knife back and forth between two pinched fingers to catch the base on his palm. Niamsha huddled under the weight of High Lord Arkaen's gaze… focused, poised, and perhaps slightly curious. Why… Oh, gods. She was directly between him and his demon.

Niamsha scrambled to her feet, but a cool, firm hand caught her arm. Pulled forward, Niamsha froze face-to-face with the demon. Those eyes… some alien, unholy intelligence lived there. Her breath froze into a solid lump as he turned her hand over and pressed something cold and metallic into it.

"Visit your brother."

The demon released her arm with those words and walked past her toward High Lord Arkaen. Niamsha trembled, staring at the wall across from her until she got herself back under control. The demon had spoken to her. He'd helped her. Niamsha uncurled her fingers and stared. He'd given her three gold jayls. Fifteen times the worth of her two silvers. She spun around, but he'd vanished. The soldier's recruiter ran toward her, eyes wide.

"Goodwoman, are you all right?" he asked.

"Fine, sir, thank you," Niamsha replied.

"Let me—" The recruiter stopped, staring at the goods scattered around her.

Her take didn't matter now, just getting away. Niamsha shoved the demon's coins into her pouch and ran through the streets toward the holy district. Her hand found its way to her side, rubbing the heavy weight she carried. Aeduhm's grace. More money than she'd ever held at once. At the cost of revealing her theft to High Lord Arkaen's guards. And earning the fury of the Rogue Baron.

The Sernien War was perhaps the greatest failure of political discourse in human history—not for some great blunder, but for dozens of small ones. Both sides attempted diplomacy over and over, yet each meeting served only to further inflame the tensions which led to war.

— *from* An Abridged History of the Sernien War

Chapter 2

A rkaen urged his mare forward into the courtyard of his keep, Lasha a few steps behind and the shouts of angry guardsmen echoing from the walls ahead. To his right, his royal guard captain and several others argued with three *Serr-Nyen* soldiers on his left. The *Serr-Nyen* were distinguishable from commoners only by the patch of red and orange cloth on the shoulders of their tunics, each depicting a bird leaping free of flames. Arkaen threw himself from his horse, tossing the reins toward a gawking stable hand as he landed.

"Stand down, all of you." Arkaen strode forward, grabbing the closest man to pull him back. "What's going on?"

The three *Serr-Nyen* flameguard stepped back as one, each slamming a fist to their chest in salute. Arkaen's royal guards milled about in confusion, their bright uniforms a roiling cluster of discontent contrasting the stoic patience of the flameguard.

Arkaen waved his flameguard to rest and faced his guard captain. "Explain, captain."

"These traitors were demeaning our empire," the captain replied. He scowled at the flameguard leader, Jarod, a man nearly ten years Arkaen's senior with short blond hair. "This one even swears by treasonous leaders of his rebellion."

Arkaen glanced at Jarod, who stood at parade rest without a hint of anger in his features. The two others glared, but kept their hands folded behind their backs. Away from the blades Arkaen had trained them to use against imperial loyalists in the Sernien War.

"Jarod is a valued ally," Arkaen said. "I trust him with my life. And High Emperor Deyvan Corliann pardoned all the *Serr-Nyen* soldiers in return for their pledge to serve him. My flameguard are no traitors."

"A matter of opinion, kai'shien." Lasha strode past him, toward the formal double doors leading into Arkaen's elaborate keep, and cast a final comment over his shoulder. "Your flameguard are well vetted, but they hold no more loyalty to Deyvan than to his uncle."

"Kìlashà." The name slipped out, his frustration turning his words sharper than he'd intended.

Lasha barely hesitated at the call, offering an unusually human shrug as his only response. Arkaen gritted his teeth and fought back a curse. Lasha was playing a dangerous game by dismissing his concerns in front of witnesses. The guard captain reached for his blade and paused. Arkaen's flameguard showed less restraint, the soft hiss of their movements a sign they'd taken hold of their weapons.

"Kìlashà san Draego de Mìtaran." Arkaen stepped forward, between his guards and Lasha, and let his words slide into the *Serr-Nyen* accent he'd picked up during the war. An old ploy by now. The accent should hint to Lasha he wasn't angry despite the extra snap he added to his words. "Stand and answer me. What have you done?"

Lasha paused a few steps from the doors, his thin frame taut with nerves. After a moment, he turned back to Arkaen and cocked his head.

Lasha's midnight hair twisted around itself in agitation, revealing his irritation as the glow from the fiery veins on his skin pulsed once with power. The guard captain backed away, his men scrambling over themselves to escape the anger they imagined in Lasha's stance. Arkaen stood his ground.

"A necessary risk to preserve a valuable pawn." Lasha examined the *Serr-Nyen* flameguard, who had taken defensive positions on either side of Arkaen. "One of more use than your human sentries."

Jarod stepped forward to face Lasha, his eyes narrowed in anger he rarely showed. Arkaen's nerves roused and his muscles tightened for action, sending a jolt of pain from his injured—and long-healed—shoulder.

"Milord Phoenix, sounds ta me like yer dragon could use a bit of tiring out," Jarod said. "Got a bite left in him that don't suit milord's needs."

"Jarod…" Arkaen froze at Lasha's warning glance, Jarod's use of his old war title hanging in the air like a challenge.

"You propose to face me?" Lasha tilted his head as if to get a better look and stepped forward, his movements as smooth as a snake tamer's hypnotic weave. His stride hinted at the animalistic beast the *Serr-Nyen* had once believed Lasha to be before his power had marked his skin. A remnant of the man Arkaen had first met—had first loved. Before Lasha's gods transformed him from a strange, distant human into this avatar of Their will.

Jarod lifted his chin and smirked. "Ya tested me once already. Gonna do it again?"

"You were tested for loyalty. But combat prowess?" Lasha's lips flicked into a momentary smile. "A tantalizing invitation, to be sure. But my kai'shien has need of you yet."

Lasha spun on a heel and walked into the keep. The bang of the double doors sounded as a release, the guard captain waiting just an instant before he came forward to protest again.

"My Lord Arkaen—"

"Enough, captain." Arkaen scowled at the man. "I've answered your concerns. My flameguard serve House Sentarsin for as long as I rule. Accept them or step down."

The guard captain froze, his gaze jumping from Arkaen to Jarod and back. The insignia sewn onto his flamboyant uniform caught the sun as he shifted, reflecting pure golden thread. Fine enough to cost a minor fortune if he'd outfitted his entire wardrobe with the stuff. What house was this man from? Arkaen had paid little enough attention to the guards when he was younger, but the pompous authority this captain projected spoke volumes of his loyalty. Steadfast to the death, or until the formal commendations ran out. Not like the *Serr-Nyen* soldiers, who had abandoned the last of their homes and families in Serni province to join Arkaen's flameguard.

"Of course, my lord." The guard captain's gaze settled on Jarod, his fury announcing the lie in his words. "I serve my province. Allow me to escort you to your study, my lord. Your seneschal has left some petitions for your review."

"Begging pardon, Milord Phoenix," Jarod said. "I've a few points to discuss."

"I don't suffer treason in my province, Jarod." Arkaen turned a narrow-eyed glare on Jarod. "However innocent it may seem."

Jarod had to know his words antagonized the royal guards. But then, light treason was in Jarod's blood. Between Lasha's customary test of the flameguard on acceptance and the armies they'd faced together, Arkaen had no fear for Jarod's loyalties.

"Aye, milord." Jarod met his gaze with head held high. No reaction to admit the rebuke stung. He'd know Arkaen had no intention of punishing his use of the title.

"Captain, I need your men to deliver a message," Arkaen said. "Kìlashà angered Baron Oskari Weydert. Bring him a bottle of fine wine and my regards. See if he'll attend court."

"My lord!" The guard captain put a hand to his heart as if wounded. "Such a task is better suited to a servant, surely…"

"My peace with Baron Weydert is fragile enough already," Arkaen replied. "I'd far rather honor him with my guard captain's respect than insult him with a common-born servant. Go."

The guard captain scowled, offering a quick salute as he headed toward the stables for a horse. Turning away, Arkaen stepped toward his keep with a wave behind him.

"Jarod, with me," he said. "The rest of you are dismissed."

Jarod fell into step beside him, silent until they were out of casual hearing of the other guards. "Reckon yer captain don't much care fer me, Milord Phoenix."

"He'd mind you less if you'd stop hinting that you follow me for my rebellion against his former high lord."

"Ain't never known yer lord father." Jarod shrugged. "Got nothing for or against him."

"Because you didn't know him," Arkaen said. "What did you want to talk to me about?"

"Couple a the boys want to head up north, see their families." Jarod paused at the door, waiting until they'd stepped inside and beyond the hearing of the door guards before continuing. "Some talk of trouble up there."

Arkaen stopped, scanning the bare stone of his entryway as the hairs on his neck tingled in alarm. "Any news from your sources?"

"Nah." Jarod shook his head. "Just talk. Like to find some bastard claiming Serni noble's blood or some such. It'll sort out."

Arkaen's fears eased at the answer. Jarod's information network missed nothing, and it stretched from Arkaen's capital to the far reaches of the newly conquered Serni province. Deyvan should hear about the rumors, maybe even send an arbiter to resolve the claim. But any talks of war would have reached Jarod long before these rumors.

"Pleased to hear it." Arkaen smiled. "If the flameguard can wait a week, I might join them. I've friends in Serni still."

Jarod offered a rueful smile. "Sorry to say, Milord Phoenix, but that ain't like to happen. Rumor says you got enough to see to here. Them petitions ain't gonna answer themselves."

Arkaen nodded, biting back a curse. Two disasters already today, and now a pile of demands from his lower lords that Jarod's sources said would need his personal attention.

"Well, then, give your men my approval." Arkaen offered a quick salute and stepped around Jarod. "I've got matters to attend, it seems."

And gods help him if Lasha—or anyone else—started another near-war today.

Arkaen pushed into his study, the rush of fresh air warning him he wasn't alone before Lasha spoke.

"Your petition is there, kai'shien." Lasha waved at the heavy oak desk with a free hand from his slouch in a padded chair by the cold fireplace. He didn't even look up from the book he held.

Kai'shien. The term of endearment from Lasha's home made Arkaen smile. *One and only love of my life*, it meant. All Lasha's skill with his blades combined with Arkaen's own wouldn't save them if anyone translated that word. But the language was a variant of Derconian that no one in the Laisian Empire had spoken for over four centuries. And Arkaen couldn't ask him to stop using it, whatever the risk. The subtle reminder always soothed his nerves, regardless of anything that had come between them that day.

Arkaen crossed to the desk to shuffle through the papers waiting for his attention. A smile tugged at Lasha's lips, catching Arkaen's attention. That smile was too rare these days. The book was probably military theory. Lasha loved to mock human battle plans.

Arkaen's heart ached for a chance to comb through Lasha's midnight hair and trace the exotic, fiery veins that cut across his pale skin. They hadn't been able to slip away in far too long.

Lasha turned another page, running a finger down the paper before marking his place with a strip of silk. He set the book down and looked up.

"You have duties to attend beyond watching me read, kai'shien," Lasha reminded him. "See to your petition."

Arkaen turned away, stung by the reproach more than he knew he should be.

"I was just thinking…"

There was no point saying it aloud. Lasha would know already, and he'd never been much for sentimentality or regrets.

Lasha sighed. "Fate is not kind to its chosen pawns."

He offered the explanation as though it answered the distance forced between them by this plan of his. It should have been calming. Lasha rarely acknowledged the difficulty of the path he'd chosen for them. Arkaen struggled to find the words to respond, but Lasha found them first.

"I… am sorry for the harshness of my words. Human attachment is still inscrutable in many ways. How may I assist you, kai'shien?"

Arkaen smiled, leaning back against his desk to meet Lasha's dark eyes. "It's hardly true to say you didn't expect this. Your Drae'gon understand love. They mate for life."

"But it is not the same." Lasha cocked his head, considering. "The Drae'gon have not the fragility of human hearts. A Drae'gon would hear a fact where you heard a criticism of your choices. And you are using that to avoid asking the question you wish answered."

"A foolish ploy against you."

For an instant, he'd forgotten the demands Jarod had thought needed his personal attention. It had to be something more than a request to remove Lasha from the keep. Arkaen grabbed the paper off the desk behind him and skimmed the petition.

"This is the fourth request to have you removed from my personal guard detail." Arkaen flipped to the second page. Nothing new so far. Taxes were high on nobility, causing concerns for their continued wealth. The strange demon was a danger and inspired fear. Refusal to acknowledge the demands of his lower lords showed a disrespect for the residents of Sentar province.

"The seventh."

"Pardon?" Arkaen looked up. "Jarod's spies have only found *four* petitions..." Lasha had turned back to his book, disregarding Arkaen's objection. "I guess they missed some."

Lasha gave another half-hearted shrug. He assumed human incompetence in most cases, but Arkaen couldn't believe they'd missed half the complaints Jarod had them monitoring. Still, Lasha was never wrong. Arkaen examined the page.

"Count Skianda?" Arkaen's jaw fell open as he read the list of signatories. Most of these names had been stalwart supporters, and many had opposed his father for the very reasons they supported Arkaen. "Brayden has always... he'd never challenge me. 'Our province has sat too long with no clear heir, a situation which we must insist you remedy immediately given the pressures placed on the lower nobility. Refusal will force the undersigned to reconsider our support,' he says. Gods above and below. What's Brayden doing? We grew up together. He sent soldiers to Serni. He knows..."

The realization of what Count Brayden Skianda *might* know cut his protest short. His hand clenched, crinkling the petition. Lasha's gaze bored into him from across the room, demanding he voice the fear that cut through him the moment he made the connection.

"What *does* he know?"

"Nothing," Lasha said. "And he has no expectation you will do more than offer lip service. He, and many others on that list, are only trying to push you into taking a stand against those sowing dissent."

"Then maybe it's time I do." Arkaen's stomach turned at the thought. He'd have to strip his dissenters of noble titles their families had held longer than Sentar had been part of the Laisian Empire, and that meant another war. Death on a scale he'd hoped to never see again. "I can't lose the support of this many of the lower lords and retain my place as high lord."

"It is not time," Lasha replied. "Ostracize them too early and you will not have the soldiers when you need them."

"I…" The words stuck in his throat. Lasha was *always* right. Except once, and that once had almost cost Arkaen his life at the hands of one of Lasha's clansmen. His shoulder ached, no doubt with remembered more than true physical pain.

"Your visions are the entire reason we're here, Kìlashà," he said at last. "If we intend to stay and intend for me to stay in power… I trust you. Gods, I always have, but I need this support."

"You need not cater to their whims. They are not important. You need the young female from the fountain."

"*Her?*" Arkaen hated the derision in his voice. "The one person you've never mentioned before today, and only *after* you nearly started the war you've been warning against by attacking Oskari in full view of the public. Whatever her purpose, it has to wait until I've dealt with this rebellion. I can't rally the soldiers of Sentar province against an enemy if they depose me before we know who that enemy is."

Lasha shrugged again, staring at the cover of his book, his attention focused on something far more complex than those pages. His eyes deepened into the flowing, midnight blackness that signaled a glimpse into his visions. In the middle of a conversation. Again.

Arkaen threw up his hands in frustration, storming to the window to throw open the shutters. With a sigh, he stared out at his capital city. The midday sun shone down over Torsdell, illuminating the thatched roofs interspersed with stone and shingles as smoke rose from several shops across the city. For an achingly long breath, Arkaen strained to see the source of that smoke, his heart pounding as though armies stood at his gates. Chimneys, of course, and blacksmiths. Lasha's silence grated against his nerves.

"What plan requires me to push loyal subjects to the brink of rebellion?" Arkaen demanded, turning back to the room. "You can at least tell me that."

With a quick shake of his head, Lasha looked up. "If it would aid you, I would, but the knowledge would only distract from the decisions you must make."

"At this rate—" Arkaen stopped himself. Arguing with Lasha wouldn't accomplish anything. "So what am I supposed to do? I'm out of excuses for my actions without admitting that I know a war is coming. Most of my people think that war is your fault."

The statement hung in the air between them, hinting at a question Arkaen couldn't voice. What if Arkaen's people were right?

"I am not the cause of these difficulties, nor will I cause any war your people pursue." Lasha's dismissive tone would have sounded absurd from another. The very concept would have offended anyone else—or, at least, anyone entirely human. *Lasha* considered causing a deadly war as a thing potentially worth the risk, depending on the other possible outcomes.

Arkaen's fingers dug into the wooden molding of the window frame. He couldn't completely believe Lasha. Every sign pointed to his lords rebelling over Arkaen's refusal to respect their wishes. If Lasha called that a rebellion over Arkaen rather than Lasha himself, the distinction was too narrow. But, gods damn him, he trusted Lasha more than his own judgment here.

"Then what? We've been waiting five years for something to change. It has to be this woman, right?"

"Indeed." Lasha rose, taking his book from the table and crossing to the door. "Her role is complex. For now, your humans need your guidance. Soothe your lords…" Lasha's entire form froze, his body tensing as if for combat. Arkaen's hand itched for the twin war blades he hadn't worn since returning home, running a finger along the hilt of the dagger he wore beside his useless dress sword. Lasha could handle any threat, but Arkaen hated being defenseless.

"Oskari sent you an invitation," Lasha said, his voice still distant. A sign that his visions still gripped him. "It is a courtesy, but it offers an opportunity. Use it as a distraction to convince your lords you have considered their request."

Arkaen grimaced, a foul taste filling his mouth at the thought. "You mean flirt and imply marriage potential. You know I might have to…"

Lasha focused on him, intense gaze a pure black. The depth of the darkness felt almost sentient. "I dislike your pain, kai'shien, but there is little choice. Oskari is a cur, but a cornered dog is dangerous. He must be delayed."

Lasha slipped out the door before he could respond, leaving Arkaen to consider what this warning meant. He pushed away from the window to search the papers for the invitation Lasha had mentioned. Near the bottom he found it, a single card with a brief message, designed for Arkaen to lose or ignore.

By hand of Baron Oskari Weydert—

Let an invitation be offered to attend the formal reception of Her Royal Highness, Princess Prillani Kitorn, Emissary of Osuvia, to His Lordship, High Lord Arkaen Sentarsin and his honored lady sister, Lady Saylina Sentarsin. Event to be held at the Weydert manor home on morrow-eve, hosted by Count Jussi Tenison in his official capacity as Lord Diplomat of Sentar province.

Arkaen sighed. "At least Sayli will be pleased."

Never neglect the care of your Lady's Court. Properly tended,
they'll maintain the peace of your lands.

— *Lady Katrivianne Istalli Sentarsin*

Chapter 3

Saylina Sentarsin giggled over the edge of her fan, catching her maid's mischievous gaze. "Now, Caela, such rumors are beneath my dignity as High Lady of Sentar province."

"That's as may be, my lady," Caela replied, keeping pace beside her in the narrow hallway. "But I imagine it was beneath the dignity of Baron Weydert to wet his britches in the fountain square. Some things can't be helped."

Saylina choked back another laugh. Holy Thirena's grace. These rumors would be all over the city in hours. And when everyone stopped laughing, they'd find Arkaen's old comrade had put them on the brink of war. Baron Weydert didn't take disgrace lightly.

"I'll need to walk in the public gardens after noontide meal." Saylina paused at the door to her personal solarium. "And see if Count Tenison will speak to me later. He's a traditionalist, but I hope he'll see the need."

"Yes, my lady." Caela dropped into a quick curtsy, her grin still lingering on her lips. "Anyone in particular you'll be meeting in the gardens?"

"The usual."

"I'll see to it." Caela set off down the hall, her quiet laughter shaking her sturdy frame.

Too much good humor for her own safety. If Baron Weydert caught her laughing at him, it would be the death of her. Saylina stepped into the solarium, greeting her guests with a bright smile as she scanned the room. To one side, the younger ladies from minor houses sat under a delicate cherry tree Arkaen had imported for her. A cluster of more prominent, and therefore more powerful, noblewomen dominated the center of the garden, draped artfully over cushions or seated on Saylina's rose-covered benches.

"My lady." A younger woman rose from the center group, bowing her head in greeting as her pale blond hair trailed into her eyes. "My father was honored by your invitation, Lady Saylina. I'm so sorry for my father's—"

"Sit, please, Lady Camira." Saylina waved at the chair Camira Weydert had vacated, crossing the garden to follow her own advice. "We're not talking about dissent here. Your father's disagreements with my brother are matters for another time."

"Yes, my lady."

Lady Camira sank back into her seat, but her hands twisted around themselves in her lap. The sullen turn of Lady Camira's lips would taint the entire event if Saylina didn't find something to distract her guests. She cast around for a distraction. Anything to keep her ladies' minds from wandering to Baron Weydert's near-treasonous criticisms in Arkaen's fountain square. Her gaze fell on a woman several years her senior.

"Lady Skianda. How is your brother?" Saylina waved toward Count Skianda's estate in town. "I hope you'll pardon my curiosity, but I'd heard he abandoned his betrothal. Is everything all right?"

Lady Arianne Skianda chuckled. "The lass was a knave. After Brayden's money and nothing else. All the better he let that one go." Her predatory smile invited the ladies to join in her pleasure. "I imagine plenty of my fellow Sentarsi noblewomen will be pleased to hear my brother is available once more."

Her invitation pulled several sighs of relief from the group. Count Skianda still had a face to break hearts, and enough money to entice plenty of women with no interest in his looks. Saylina let the women chatter, listening to the bits of gossip and offering an opinion when required. A couple families were planning unions, though the intended ladies only fell silent at the mention of potential marriages. Tenison's eldest, if her manners and unusually sisterly attention to a younger girl from a minor barony could be trusted. Likely one of the less prominent girls, also, into a count's family. Hard to tell from across the garden.

Under the sparse leaves of the cherry tree, Lady Kyli Andriole held an energetic court among the younger ladies. A twinge of guilt made Saylina turn away. Kyli might have been well settled by now, if she hadn't sacrificed for the good of her province.

"My lady, have you any news?"

Saylina snapped her attention back to the group, smiling at the woman who had asked. "Pardon, my mind wandered. News on what?"

"About the princess," the woman replied. "The servants say she brought all the newest fashions from beyond the sea."

"I've received very little detail about Princess Kitorn," Saylina said.

A thrill of excitement ran through her at the news despite herself. Few among the imperial nobility bothered with new styles, still recovering from the horrors of the old emperor's rule.

"Her father is quite wealthy, though," Saylina added. "I'm not surprised he has connections beyond the sea. Not everyone can be so insular as my dear brother."

The ladies tittered with laughter, hiding their smiles behind fans as though they feared her retribution over her own joke. Even in Sentar province, the old emperor's reach had left enough scars to sow fear over every minor jest. Saylina's gaze trailed back to Kyli. The center of attention among a court of girls too young and unimportant for her status.

"I'm excited to see what the Osuvians have brought." Saylina grinned, letting her enthusiasm seep through. "Lady Camira, Count Tenison allowed your father to supply a location for our guest's reception, did he not? What an honor."

"Yes, my lady." Lady Camira's cheeks flushed pink. "The Lord Diplomat should have planned the event here, of course. I hope we haven't offended your lord brother."

Saylina waved the concern away. "Of course not. I imagine Count Tenison simply respected my brother's obligations. Think of the scandal if we hosted the reception in the high lord's palace and the high lord found himself unable to attend."

Several of the ladies hid frowns or sighs of disappointment at her words, but Lady Camira's nervous fidgeting eased. One potential feud resolved before it started, at least. Arkaen should have demanded the right to hold a reception for the Osuvian princess at the palace simply to avoid the tension. But he'd no doubt forgotten the princess was arriving at all. So focused on smoothing residual hostilities he overlooked a dozen concerns within his own lands.

"Speaking of your brother's obligations, my lady." Lady Arianne leaned toward Saylina, her eyes sharp. "Has he considered any proposals for furthering the Sentarsin bloodline? I hate to be so forward, but my brother has received concerning news and asked if I would pursue the matter with you."

Saylina froze, the eyes of every woman in the circle trained on her. After a few breaths of silence, she could feel the scrutiny of the lower ladies as well. Everyone hanging on her answer to the one question no one else would dare ask.

"My brother manages so many things, Lady Skianda." Saylina swept her gaze over the crowd, noting the hopefuls.

Lady Arianne herself. Her brother likely had no idea she'd intended to broach the topic. A few of the younger ladies, too enamored with Arkaen's handsome face to think about the politics involved. Lady Camira's eyes dropped as Saylina considered her. She'd given up on claiming the contract their fathers had negotiated, then. Not surprising. Arkaen had chosen a bloody civil war over marriage to Lady Camira last time.

"Kaen is painfully aware of our province's need for an heir," Saylina said. "But his duty to our new emperor comes first. High Emperor Corliann needs my brother in the south far too often for him to do justice to a new wife. He would never ask a woman to wed him only to sit in an empty palace and await his return."

Dismay settled over the two circles at her words, each woman turning back to smaller, less controversial topics. Saylina's heart ached for them. With as long as Arkaen had dangled his availability in front of his lower ladies, who could blame them for hoping?

"Your pardon, my lady." Kyli stood from her circle, dropping into a quick curtsy as Saylina focused on her. "With respect, your lord brother has been home for near three months without a summons from the capital. Surely that is enough time to do justice to a new wife. I hardly think many women have the stamina for much longer."

A few shocked snorts of laughter broke across the gardens as Saylina frowned at her. Ambition shone in her posture. But Kyli had to know Arkaen wouldn't choose her. No, her challenge was a blatant demand for attention. An insistence that Saylina grant her the status she'd sacrificed to protect the province. Guilt lingered as an ache in Saylina's throat. But she would not allow such blackmail.

Saylina let her displeasure chill her voice. "Then perhaps he is considering his choices, Lady Kyli. My brother does not discuss his bedroom activities with me, or his intent for such in the future. As is only proper."

"Of course, Lady Saylina." Kyli smiled. "But your ladies have no need to *ask* about your lord brother's bedroom activities. We were inquiring as to his wedding plans."

The rebuke stung, as much because of its truth as Kyli's tone. Saylina turned away, leaning from her chair to examine the flowers she'd planted a day past.

"When I've news of my new sister's identity, I'll inform you, Lady Kyli." Saylina plucked a flower to twirl between her fingers. "I'm sure your new high lady, whoever she is, will appreciate your concern for my brother's virtue."

Kyli sank back into her chair, regal in her poise despite Saylina's sharp words. In moments Kyli had the group giggling amongst themselves again, fluttering at her comments and vying for her attention. A true social elite. Eiliin curse her for being right. Arkaen needed to focus on securing the succession, but he seemed bent on bedding as many women as he could manage before one caught him with a wedding vow. Gods only knew what he thought he could hide behind those trysts.

"I heard she has a different man every night," a woman in Saylina's circle whispered. Several of the ladies cast knowing looks at Kyli.

"My mother said she's had three children planted and rooted them all out," another added. "Thinks she's too good for a younger son's hand. Keeps taking the brews to end the term before her child comes so she won't have to marry the man."

The ladies hid their guilty delight behind scathing rebukes of Kyli's exploits, a few giggles slipping out from the less restrained of her circle. Saylina let them gossip, monitoring those who chose not to engage. Lady Arianne again. No surprise there, especially given her brother's care for the less fortunate. Another lady, one from an old, if now unimportant, family. Her face flushed at every accusation. More concerned someone would notice her own activities than concerned for Kyli herself. And Lady Camira Weydert. A surprise there. The Weyderts weren't known for their understanding, even beyond the feud with Arkaen.

Saylina gently directed the conversation to more proper topics, casting another sidelong glance at Kyli. She must know the way her peers talked about her, but none of the disgrace showed in her manner. Strong and capable. Arkaen might never choose her, but her bloodline was old and her family had always supported Sentarsin rule. And she clearly had the loyalty of several younger houses. Perhaps redeeming Kyli's honor wasn't such a bad idea, after all.

Holy Aeduhm sent His Divine Children to guide the lands into proper worship, each with a particular fondness. While some focused on beauty or love, guiding the well-born, Istvan came to the lowest of the lands. He showed them the beauty of hard work, the glory of a product well-made, and He raised His followers above the baser folk into merchants.

— from the teachings of Holy Aeduhm and His Kin

Chapter 4

Niamsha hurried down the narrow side street, ducking under another low-hanging flag displaying the Rogue Baron's colors. More territory claimed by the baron and his allies. He hadn't expanded this far last time she'd visited Emrys. If the Rogue Baron found her in his territory after this morning, she'd never make it out of his presence, much less his part of the city. But what if the baron had taken over the temples? She pushed the thought away. No use getting her thoughts wound over a problem she hadn't seen yet. She'd seen enough already, with the demon's humiliation of the Rogue Baron over *her* safety and the high lord's guards after her. She'd be lucky to get a clean death if she got caught.

But the high lord's demon had protected her.

"Stupid girl," she muttered under her breath. "A fluke. An excuse for the high lord to make a point. He don't give a damn 'bout you."

Niamsha paused at the end of her street, the stench of recently emptied chamber pots fresh in her nose. Across the street stood her destination, one of a half dozen doors on the endless corridor that stretched to either side. But this door held a freshly carved image of a merchant's pan scales. Holy temple to Istvan, God of Merchants. Often deserted by worshippers during the day, she couldn't decide without coming here. Emrys deserved to know.

She scanned the broad street before the temple with an intensity that would have felt foolish when her papa was alive. Papa'd sent her here to study. Expensive, and if she'd known the cost, she would have refused. But the temples gave hope back then, each a small shrine that grew as each faith gained popularity and gathered more donations, many a hodgepodge of buildings re-purposed from other, less holy uses.

High Lord Arkaen ended that, as with so many other things. Holy sites should be safe for worshippers, he decreed. He saw the disparate locations and convoluted structures as evidence the religious sites needed stronger protection. All the buildings vanished overnight, rebuilt over most of a year into one enormous structure, parceled out inside for each temple. Generations of history and tradition lost to one pompous fool deciding how everyone ought to worship.

This quiet street looked safe enough for the moment, but Niamsha knew better. Thieves swept in as soon as they finished the building, pushing any good intent aside to make their own system. Holy donations made good profit, especially since His Lordship didn't choose to post guards here. Apparently the gods were less important than taxes and soldiers.

Anyone beholden to the Rendells *should* let her pass, but she'd be foolish to trust that supposed immunity. In an alley with no witnesses, who was to say which hand held the knife that ended up in the throat of an incompetent thief? Niamsha forced her hand to release the pouch at her side. No reason to draw attention to it.

With quick steps, she crossed the street and knocked, fidgeting as she waited for a response. The temple door cracked open, and an acolyte peeked out.

"Yes?"

"Here to see my brother," Niamsha said. "He's a merchanter's 'prentice."

The acolyte nodded and edged a little further outside, glancing down the long street before waving her inside. Niamsha hurried through the door. The entire process felt like an illicit sale instead of a visit to a holy site.

The entryway of the temple felt close and intimate, hung with brightly colored tapestries and rugs that seemed to smother the room. Incense hung thick in the air, perfuming every breath until a strange aftertaste lingered in her mouth. Niamsha always dreaded this visit, the acolytes contemptuous of her and dismissive of her brother. But Istvan's apprenticeships were the only option for a glassblower's child too young to have learned his father's trade. Her only shot at getting Emrys out of poverty and into a skilled profession.

A simple stone altar draped with a linen cloth sat against one wall, displaying a set of merchant's pan scales. The acolyte bowed low before the altar, muttering a prayer. Niamsha pulled her thick brown hair forward to hide the bruise Marcas had given her that morning, her fingers shaking. For the first time, she wondered if the temple would question her coins. Peasants didn't carry lord's gold, and certainly not ones who had begged the day before for more time to gather the money owed.

"Your brother's name?" the acolyte asked.

"Emrys Pereyra," she said. "I owe on his keep, but I have it with me."

The acolyte nodded and pulled a ledger down from a shelf over the altar. He flipped through several pages and paused, skimming the names. Niamsha fidgeted, fingering the pouch at her side again. She'd never had so much money on her at once.

"You said Emrys?" He sounded confused.

"Yes." Niamsha licked dry lips, her heart racing. They wouldn't have thrown Emrys out already. The priests had always given her a warning and time to find the money before.

"His keep was paid, goodwoman. This morn, for a six-moon. Says the bill was covered by a... Nih-gell. A cousin?"

"Oh..." The mangled name had to be Nijel. Why would Nijel pay Emrys's keep? They'd only met for an hour, four years back. Emrys had been barely twelve. Still young enough she'd passed him off as a child when Nijel asked her which of them could work.

"Shall I check again?" The acolyte turned back to his book, flipping another page. "Mayhap the entry's placed on the wrong line..."

"No, it's proper," Niamsha assured him. "I, uh..." She smiled, heart pounding. If Nijel had paid Emrys's keep, turning the gift down would be dangerous. "I ain't s'pected it, but it's proper. Nijel's me cousin on me mama's side, and he ain't around much. Came in all a sudden last eve and I reckon he thought to pay the keep fer us. Just need ta see my brother."

The acolyte stared at her for a long moment, eyes narrowed and hand poised over the page as he considered her claim. She fought to control her trembling and look confident.

With a last glance at the book, the acolyte opened the door, leading her down the hall. Relief flooded her, but her stomach churned in dread. Nijel's help never came for free. She'd need the high lord's coins to pay off whatever new debt she'd just gained. But what could Nijel be planning?

The acolyte stopped outside a plain wooden door. "Emrys Pereyra. You've a visitor."

Emrys opened the door and paused at the sight of her, his slim figure mostly hidden under a loose shirt and trousers. He smiled the same carefree, generous smile she'd always known, turning his pale skin and freckle-covered cheeks into the child she'd half raised since Mama'd died when they were little. Niamsha grinned, but Emrys shot a nervous glance behind him and swung the door close to block her view. Niamsha's heart skipped at the motion.

"Em, you okay?" she asked.

"Sure." Emrys nodded. "Just, uh, let's go out, 'kay?"

"Okay."

Niamsha frowned. Emrys had never taken her away from his room before, and his speech still held too many hints of the gutter speak she'd hoped the temple would train out of him. A glitter of something on his bed caught her eye as he stepped out into the hall. Was that clothing? Some dark color trimmed in gold?

"Garden's this way."

He gave her a smile and led her further down the hall. His steps were stilted and cautious, making Niamsha's skin prickle with fear. The hall ended in a set of broad doors with vines carved across the surface. Emrys pushed them open and Niamsha stared in awe at the riot of greenery.

An enormous circular room, the garden held seven distinct sectors of plants around a central oak tree guarded by a priest and three of High Lord Arkaen's flashy guards. Each of the seven gardens around the edge had a statue to a god or goddess, gilded in gold and shining under natural sunlight. The plants varied in each, from a sector of all vines to one of nothing but forest trees and everything in between. Emrys urged her forward, striding down the polished cobblestone path that snaked between each sector.

Following him into the garden, Niamsha looked up at the immense, domed glass ceiling. She could see the sky almost as clearly as if she were outside. That much glass, and that clear… She'd never heard of such a thing. It must have cost a fortune. She stopped to stare as they drew near the first statue. Marpaessa, Goddess of Fields and Family, had smaller depictions around the base. Niamsha recognized the sword surrounded by stalks of wheat as from the kingdom of Mindaine's religion, but the others were foreign to her.

"Come on." Emrys tapped a foot impatiently on the path until she hurried after him once more.

Niamsha scowled at the riot of greenery and elegance around her. The money to build this temple might have fed the entire province for a month. Maybe longer. When they reached Istvan's statue, the plump God of Merchants held his traditional scales for weighing market goods, but smaller carvings decorated the base. A lean woman holding a beggar's bowl, a strange creature holding swords with wings sprouting from his back and a dead body at his feet, an old man tending to a flock of animals. Niamsha frowned at the images. She didn't know enough Mindaine lore to know which one was their god, but the very idea of multiple religions on one altar was the deepest of heresy. Emrys knelt without comment, ignorant of—or choosing to ignore—her anger.

"Sorry 'bout the cold welcome, just…" He trailed off and looked back toward the door. "He said ya weren't comin', so I didn't expect ya."

"Who said, Em?" A trail of ice crept down Niamsha's spine. Nijel couldn't have known she'd be delayed, right?

"Yer friend," he replied. "Marc, or whatever."

"Marcas?" She heard the disbelief in her voice, rising above the quiet of the temple garden. "Em, you stay away from Marcas."

Emrys scrambled to his feet to clap a hand over her mouth, eyes wide as he scanned the nearby shrines. Niamsha stood frozen. Marcas, here? He must have known she'd planned this visit. Must have delayed her on purpose. But why? And why was Emrys so worried someone had heard her?

Satisfied with whatever he'd seen, Emrys stepped back. "Don't talk like that out here," he whispered. "Marc's been trainin' some o' the 'prentices. Just fer the last couple months, but he's got skills, Nia. He can teach ya anythin'."

"Training?" Niamsha's mouth went dry.

Emrys couldn't be learning thieving. Not here, where she'd sent him to be free of the streets and learn a proper trade. She'd promised Papa she'd keep him safe. And when had he started calling her by that bastard-ized nickname?

"I… look, I shoulda said somethin'." Emrys paced away from her. "It's just, you been bent on me getting a trade, and I don't much want one. Marc says I don't got to. He can get me in as a servant, all I gotta do is wash linens and let him know a bit of info once in a while."

"A servant?" Niamsha's face burned hot with anger. "Emrys! You'd shame Papa like that. After all he did to give us chances. To carve us a place where we could be what we wanted—"

"What would Papa think a you?" Emrys spun around to glare at her, hands clenched into fists. "His perfect little girl. I'm talkin' 'bout a safe job, with food, housing, pay, an' days off. Marc told me 'bout the house *you're* stayin' in. All *they* got's whores and thieves. Which are you?"

Niamsha's mouth fell open, her anger frozen mid-burn. Not Emrys. He wouldn't. Her own brother wouldn't accuse her of selling her body for coin. Niamsha couldn't find the words to respond. Slowly, she watched regret creep across his face. But it didn't matter anymore.

"Eiliin's damnation. What happened to you, Em?"

"Nia, I—"

"My name, Emrys Pereyra, is Niamsha." Anger made her enunciate, her voice taking on the temple schooling her papa had given up so much to afford. "Given to me by a mother who loved her Yllshanan homeland and wanted to keep it alive in her daughter. I expect the gods-damned imperials to disrespect my heritage, but you? You've already insulted *me*. Don't you dare insult our mother."

She backed away, the hurt in Emrys's eyes tearing a hole in her fury. But this… whoever this boy was, he wasn't the brother she remembered. She spun on a heel and ran out of the alcove, back down the polished cobbles toward the door. Her throat closed, tears threatening to break out of her control.

Her run drew whispers from the others in the temple, but her eyes were too blurry to see, much less care who saw her. This gods-forsaken city had taken everything. Her mother when she was just a child, her father when she should have been preparing for apprenticeship, her honor when she and Emrys had nearly starved on the streets.

A hand caught her arm just before she reached the door, pulling her off balance.

"Niamsha, stop." Emrys. He used her full name now, as if he thought that would somehow heal the breach he'd made by calling her a whore.

Niamsha yanked her arm free and turned to face him. He paused, lips moving as if trying to find the words he wanted to say.

"Yer all I got left," he said finally.

"Apparently ya got Marcas."

The words felt false in her mouth. She couldn't leave him with the Rendells. Emrys had always been a kind-hearted boy, too innocent to accept the way things had to be. The Rendells would eat him alive. Except he wasn't the boy she'd known. Not anymore. Somehow, in four years of brief visits every fortnight, he'd morphed into something she didn't understand.

"Nia, I—" Emrys cringed, but she let it go. "I shouldn'ta said that, an' I didn't mean it. Papa died and I never saw ya while we's on the streets, you out begging all day. Then Nijel took you in and I was off to temple an' I never saw ya. I ain't been through what you have. I know that. Yer looking out for me, jus'… I just want a choice."

"You think I don't?" Niamsha scoffed. But she understood. Just one chance to make her own life. Apprentice to a glassblower like Papa and work the molten beauty that had been her joy for fifteen years before Papa took ill. Her voice turned bitter at the memory. "What choice I ever had, Em?"

"That's my point." Emrys's voice jumped up a pitch in excitement. "Dontcha see? We *got* a choice now. Work with Marc, get a lil' cut, set some coins aside for later. Marc's got a job tomorrow, easy as anything. Work the kitchens and look for doors out, tell Marc. Nothin' to it."

"The Rendells ain't never gave no one a choice, Em," she warned. "I been around them. Seen too much. One little thing turns inta five little things turns inta debt you ain't never gonna pay. Stay away from the Rendells."

Emrys shook his head. "Can't. I already promised."

Niamsha cursed. That was bad. Marcas wouldn't let anyone out of a job, much less her little brother. There weren't many choices. She'd already tried everything to keep Emrys out of this mess, and still he was here. Everything except cross the long, empty balcony to the other side of the Rendells' house where the whores lived. Where Marcas and the other Rendell boys spent their nights with whichever women hadn't found a client for the night.

"Eiliin's tits." Niamsha scuffed a toe against the cobbles of the path. She could try and talk to Marcas. Get him to let Emrys out of this job. If she built up his inexperience…but no. Marcas would want something else for her brother's freedom. Something she wasn't willing to give.

"It's one job," Emrys said. "Can't be that bad. I ain't taking anything, just helping."

"Not how they work." She'd never explain it to him. Anything was a debt to the Rendells, and Emrys didn't know he was already in debt to Nijel.

Niamsha's hand slipped to her pouch, fingering the coins she'd nearly forgotten. She needed them to buy her way free of her own Rendell debts so she could leave town. No way she'd be able to outrun a Rendell debt. Nijel always collected. But how could she leave knowing Emrys was stuck here, under the watchful eyes of Nijel and Marcas? She dug into the pouch and pulled out two of her three precious coins. She'd need the last, if she had any chance of finding a way out of this mess.

"Here." Niamsha pressed the gold into Emrys's hand. "Pack your things and go. Head south, toward Aerlin, on the main road. That should let ya set up shop on yer own. Just stay clear of any guards with them coins. I'll talk to Marcas and meet ya there."

"What? Why?"

"Just go, Em." Niamsha couldn't bring herself to lie to him. "I made enemies today, and I can't stay. If I leave you here, it'll just fall on you. So go. Let me handle it."

"But…" Emrys watched her for too many breaths, as if deciding whether to argue. "Okay. A week, in the market, in Aerlin." He walked past her, head hanging, and then turned back, hand still clenched around the coins she'd given him. "Be careful."

Niamsha nodded, watching him slip out of the temple garden. Now she understood why Marcas had been so on edge. This job Emrys had agreed to… it was too soon. Especially with Nijel's ban on thieving from the noble house. Like as not the previous night's job *had* been unsanctioned, and that meant Nijel's eye on everything Marcas's crew did. No simple bribe would get her and Emrys free while Marcas was dodging Nijel's wrath.

She might buy something worth trading for her gold coin. Anything worth two lives would cost more than coin, though, and it might not matter what she found. Most days Marcas wouldn't do her a favor for damned near anything. Short of the one thing she'd never yet been forced to give. But Nijel'd chase her to the ends of Eiliin's hell to collect her debt, and Marcas would enjoy the hunt. Unless…

A master glasswright's notes would be worth a fortune. Every formula held a secret, and the guild had collected and stored each member's work as insurance against betrayal. If she could find her papa's notes, not even Marcas could refuse. It meant stealing from a well-guarded house with no time for a good plan. Stealing on a day Nijel had deemed off-limits, and targeting a well-connected merchant who might have resources to hunt her down. To reveal the Rendells to High Lord Arkaen, who Nijel so carefully avoided.

But it also meant taking something priceless from under the nose of Master Ferndon. Revenge and safety all in one. A risk, and one she'd never consider under other circumstances. One Niamsha should—must do everything she could to avoid taking. But this gods-damned city had taken everything else. If there was no other way.... She'd be damned if she'd let the city take Emrys from her, as well.

One will come to the clans, sent by the Ancient Spirits. Of the clans but born beyond them, this chosen of the Spirits will bring the People from the darkness.

— from the prophecies of the Chosen of the Four Clans

Chapter 5

Kilashà san Draego de Mìtaran collapsed into the chair by his bed, the thick cushions a harsh reminder of the foolish human opulence that his kai'shien's people required of this palace. Gold-adorned window dressings, expansive silk-covered bed, hand-crafted oak table, and a gorgeously sculpted fireplace. As if any of it would hide the stench of human corruption. Or the desperation that rose in waves of fear and hopelessness from every gaze he met and every polite chat he engaged in. He'd come—*demanded* that his kai'shien return to these people, who had scarred them both—because he desired to save them. Some days he wondered what there was to save. And on others, he met someone like *her*. Kìlashà pulled his unruly hair back from his face, the locks twining around his fingers in an echo of the near-sentience his Seeker's power had gained during the human war, and closed his eyes.

The fiery rage of possibility assaulted him as soon as he relinquished his grasp on the physical world, the mantle of the Chosen of the Four Clans of the Drae'gon. A hundred moments of time danced, flickered, and blazed behind the lids of his closed eyes. Kìlashà let the fire of his Seeker's power sweep through him, sifting through the moments to find those most likely to occur. The inferno grew, his acceptance feeding the tongues of possible futures. There. Kìlashà wound his way through the flames to the moment he'd come for.

Kaen stood before the imperial throne in Whitfaern, his high lord's scepter of rank in one hand. Deyvan sat the throne with casual authority, his broad, tall frame dwarfing the jeweled shape of the highest chair in his empire.

"High Lord Arkaen Sentarsin, you come before this throne to offer your word on my proposed law," Deyvan said. His voice boomed through the chamber, but his gaze scanned the room beyond. Everyone knew Kaen's answer. "What say you? Shall my uncle's law against the joining in house and body of any born of the same sex be allowed in our empire?"

Kaen bowed. The obsequious version he used to show his complete obeisance to Deyvan. Only used when he thought one of Deyvan's treacherous lords would reignite their war at the slightest sign of weakness.

"My Lord Emperor, our land has seen enough bloodshed," Kaen replied. "What harm in allowing a man to lie with a man, or a woman with another woman? If the gods so abhor such a union, let them see to their own punishment."

"Then the vote is unanimous." Deyvan stood and caught the eyes of the courtiers behind Kaen. "My uncle's law is rescinded."

Kìlashà let the moment fade. It couldn't happen. The possibility existed, of course, or Kìlashà wouldn't be able to see it at all. But the path was too narrow and the cost too high. His kai'shien would never forgive him for allowing so much death for that decree. No matter that Kaen desired that moment more than any other. Kaen would always sacrifice his own desires for the safety of others, Spirits-cursed saint that he was. Kìlashà smiled at the thought. If Kaen had been less honorable—or less kind—he would not be Kìlashà's kai'shien.

A vision flared, tugging at his thoughts with sharp licks of burning possibility. Time itself, warning him of a change to the future he'd studied. Kìlashà opened his thoughts to the scene.

Baron Oskari Weydert, blond hair pulled back into a ragged tail and emerald and gold cloak flying behind him in a fierce wind, backhanded the young female from the fountain. She staggered back, coughing red-tinted spittle onto the cobbles below.

"I rule my lands." Oskari snarled. "You foreign gutter rat. How dare you set foot in my home, claim ties to my family? If you've a message, it's for me."

The female—

What was her name? Kìlashà should really find her name.

—glared up through her loose hair, eyes filled with all the fire that marked her as chosen by the Ancient Spirits.

If only he knew what intentions his gods planned for her. The Ancient Spirits could hardly expect him to protect her if They didn't reveal her purpose.

"Then I reckon you'll want this," the young female replied, pulling a letter free. "But I ain't lied. I's sent here with a message for the baron from Nijel. How you think he's gonna take it, you hittin' his messengers?"

Oskari froze, eyes going wide as his hand shook. "Nijel?"

The vision went black and Kìlashà scrambled to find it again. Who was Nijel? Tongues of possibility flared and guttered, each a moment of the female's life, none the vision he sought. He pulled on the power and poured himself into it. His desperation fanned new flames to life. He dove through timelines. Sifted through hundreds—thousands of improbable moments and near impossibilities. Nothing. The vision was gone as if it had never been.

"Shethka-se, Spirits!" He flung the Drae'gon curse into the air as he leaped from the chair to pace in agitation, the walls suddenly too close. His power simmered in the back of his mind like a mockery of his own pride. There should be nothing he couldn't find with enough focus, facts, and time.

The thought froze him mid-stride. More focus. He hadn't needed an aid to his focus since the human war ended, but it would be a simple matter to brew a tragyna tea to bring his powers under tighter control. The wait would allow him to seek more information on the young female. More focus and more facts both.

With the plan came a twinge of guilt, and Kìlashà sent a silent apology to the Ancient Spirits for his outburst. His clanmother would have had his head for cursing *anyone* to time's bowels, much less the deities that had elevated him above mere mortals with Their gift of his Seeker's power. And They were not responsible for his own failure.

Kìlashà busied his hands brewing the pungent tea while his mind probed the fires of possibility for more information on the human female. First, a name. Kìlashà swept through the flickering moments of possibility and found it. Niamsha Pereyra, born of an Yllshanan native to one of Kaen's merchants. Kìlashà hesitated over the mother's timeline. The people of Yllshana didn't travel except for great need. The last had been the human woman Deyvan had been infatuated with years before. This mother's presence here might mean…

He pushed the visions away. Time enough to research Niamsha's heritage once he'd divined her purpose.

Niamsha's life was remarkably bland. Kìlashà skimmed past the mother's death, the brother's birth. Wait… he pulled the vision back and watched again. The brother was born *before* the mother died. That made sense. Kìlashà scanned forward in her life again. The boy from temple lessons was attractive. Kaen would have liked him. Kìlashà diverted down the boy's life for a few years, but he died of a lung illness. Unfortunate. He returned to Niamsha's timeline and skimmed the rest of her childhood. Nothing of note before she joined the thieves—the Rendells?—and met Kìlashà. The choices from there were too many. She would most likely do as he'd said, but he couldn't see how she got from there to the vision he'd lost, or what made her important.

Kìlashà tested the tragyna brew, the acrid, slightly moldy taste lingering on his tongue. Four or five more minutes for proper potency. He stood and paced again. Perhaps the vision that had sent him to the fountain would contain the details he needed. An instant of thought brought the vision to the forefront.

The female—

Niamsha. He knew her name now, and should use it.

Niamsha slipped through the crowd, adept at avoiding notice in all the right ways. People saw her, but they'd never remember the grubby form hunched to mimic an older child more than the young adult she truly was. Her hands acquired meaningless trinkets as she strolled, the last swipe catching the attention of Kaen's guards.

Ah. The change had occurred before his decision, then. When he'd met her, Niamsha hadn't been caught.

She broke free of the crowd and hurried toward an alley, the guard close on her heels. Both seemed ignorant of the figure shoving through the crowd on the other side. Oskari reined his war horse to a halt a scant few steps shy of trampling Niamsha, and she fell back. Oskari's boots hit the ground an instant later, his foot flying into her gut. Niamsha puked on the ground as he stepped back for another blow.

Kìlashà frowned at the scene. All the colors, from the solid gray of the cobbles to the deep brown of her hair to the emerald green of Oskari's tunic, shone vivid and firm. The sign of a fixed moment in time that could not easily be changed. And yet it had changed with a minimum of effort. Had changed even before Kìlashà intervened. Kìlashà gave himself a mental twist, adjusting the conditions to see a different version. What of that thief she'd noticed earlier in the day?

His Seeker's power flowed against the change, sluggish and difficult. There was almost no chance the thief would have interrupted her, then, and therefore any results would be minimally useful. He forced the vision anyway. She argued for a bit, still took the baubles, sold to a run-down shop on the southeast edge of town… no, she didn't encounter Oskari at all if she got delayed. The first vision was clear. Her meeting with Oskari was the key. A flash of his earlier warning. Nijel. Who *was* Nijel? He scanned Niamsha's timeline again. How was it *possible* that Nijel appeared in none of his visions?

Hesitant, he found the correct moment from the square and followed her timeline backward. The thief, her fascination with a child's painting. Kìlashà's anger burned at the treatment she received from the blond oaf, but he skimmed past. Every new person she encountered he stopped, considering all the branching options for that identity. One of these had to be Nijel, or had to be connected.

A pause at another unknown face, near two years prior. He couldn't get a clear picture. The boy seemed fleeting, unimportant. Every image too changed to have been the same person. Kìlashà's anger returned, and he dove into his Seeker's power. He *would* find Nijel. A flash of blue eyes and blond hair.

"Raeky, where we goin'?" The boy, barely four and still slightly pudgy with baby fat, his jet black hair cut close to his scalp, looked up at young Prince Raekeen.

Raekeen smiled through golden locks, pushed his cloak back, and revealed a pair of wooden practice swords hung by his side.

Kìlashà shoved the moment away. This wasn't about Raeky—a quick shake to clear his thoughts—about Prince Raekeen. The imperial prince was dead twenty-six years now. But the boy from his earlier visions… Blue eyes, blond hair. Similar to the prince whose death had started it all. The prince had few surviving relatives, and Kìlashà knew them all. But the combination wasn't rare. Perhaps his Seeker's power had gotten too tangled with his emotions.

Beginning once more, he sorted carefully through the visions available, following the exact path as before to find the moment when he'd seen the new boy. As before, the moment had vanished. He followed every path, down a dozen side alleys of the female's life and more. If she had gone to temple instead of her brother. If she'd married the brute who offered while her father lay dying. If her brother had died of the same illness as her father. Nothing, nothing, and nothing again. There was no blond-haired boy in her life. Not a single one.

Kìlashà snarled, the sound tainted with too much hiss from his human lips for true Drae'gon fury. His power coursed through his veins as a fiery heat came from his skin. Possibility raged within him, pouring through his nerves with too many moments of time. Distantly he could feel his own body, tense and rigid where he'd crouched beside the fire, but the sensation was like a memory decades old. Too much knowledge and too little understanding. What was real? Kìlashà felt himself slipping from the world. Pulled away by the river of time, hidden from the bulk of his people behind the inferno of possibility. Infinite and endlessly moving, calm and raging at once… *Kaen.*

Kaen was real. Kìlashà scrambled to find an instant of Kaen's life—*any* instant—and clung to the truth of that moment. Slowly, like the trickle of a clogged stream filling an ocean, his grasp on the physical world returned. Stiff wood under him, sore muscles, thirst. How long had it been? He forced open his eyes. Hadn't they been open when he searched this last time? Kìlashà pushed himself upright and crossed to the window, struggling to keep a sense of the present.

Grabbing the windowsill, he stepped onto the ledge running just outside. Whispered an apology. Kaen hated it when he stalked the streets of Torsdell. Said he frightened the commoners and gave the lords a reason to complain. But he didn't have a choice. They needed information. Who *was* Nijel?

Never walk out on a debt, 'less you plan on someone else paying for ya. Someone always pays.

— Thief's Code

Chapter 6

Niamsha hurried through the dim afternoon sun toward the craftsman's district, cursing under her breath. No options from her contacts in High Lord Arkaen's part of the city, and nothing to bribe or bargain from the few she still talked to in the Rogue Baron's territory. Not even for the gold that still hid in her pouch, leaving her jumpy and nervous. That left few options. Her best option, and the only thing to save her from a dangerous, forbidden theft, meant begging a favor from an old friend. A long-ignored friend who might not want to see her at all.

Far ahead a wooden sign held a crude depiction of a man with a blowpipe, the end of the carving marred with a blob that she knew was supposed to be a bit of fresh glass. Her destination. Second-best glass-wright in the city, or used to be. But the trade secrets from *any* of the city's master glasswrights should suit her needs. Maybe enough to get her and Emrys free of their debts.

Niamsha jogged the last steps and slipped into the light of the shop, pausing as the heat of the furnace assaulted her.

"What?" An older man, sweat-drenched gray hair hanging to his shoulders in thick clumps, looked up. "Nia, girl, what're you doin' here?"

"Came ta see Tressa." Niamsha planted her feet and crossed her arms, staring down the old glasswright.

He sighed, setting his blowpipe aside to stand. "Nigh on three years you ain't come by. Now you need to see my lass? She's out back, seeing to her marriage. Like you ought to." He waved her away and returned to his work. Glass was too delicate an art to let sit while he argued with her.

Niamsha strode through the shop toward the back door, her eyes drawn to the beautiful vase on a counter, waiting for a wealthy patron to collect. So he'd taken to the flattery the guild demanded for high-end jobs. Once she would have stopped to discuss the technique, but now… the guild's rejection hurt and Master Ferndon's treachery infuriated her. But nothing cut as deep as having a friend torn from her by her change in status. Thieves and glasswrights didn't mingle, and certainly not thieves who worried their gang might harm the glasswright's daughter if they learned about the connection.

The back door sat half open, Tressa pacing in the tiny dirt patch that served as her family's garden. Alone, her narrow waist a contrast to the broad frame and height she'd inherited from her father, chestnut hair flowing down her back in full, curly waves that Niamsha knew had taken her forever to accomplish. Tressa's hair was always straight. Niamsha knocked gently on the door, standing just inside the house so Tressa could see her without forcing herself into the yard.

Tressa glanced up and froze, her face lighting up with joy. "Niamsha! It's been… Come, come out!"

Niamsha stepped down into the yard. The garden looked unusually bare this time of year. Odd, since Tressa's mother loved tending it while her husband worked.

"Where's yer mama's—"

A choked sob from Tressa cut Niamsha's question short.

"I'm sorry," Niamsha said. No one recognized that blank look of grief better than Niamsha, one she'd worn too many times already. "I didn't know."

"Course not." Tressa flashed a smile, but the flat tone spoke volumes. Niamsha didn't know because she'd avoided her friend for years. And Tressa had never known why. "Mama joined Aeduhm's Eternal Feast near a year past now. Papa says it's time I move on. I've a marriage proposal today."

"He said as much."

Tressa didn't sound happy about it. Niamsha kicked a toe into the dirt, noting the dry puff of dust that kicked up. This land had lain untended since that time, and possibly longer. Had Tressa's mother been sick, like her own papa? Too many of the glasswrights in Torsdell died from illness. More than other towns, or so she heard. Niamsha's papa had been the second in as many months. The guild dismissed it, but something was wrong.

"You like him? The boy?" Niamsha asked.

Tressa's cute face twisted into a grimace, but a smile danced in her eyes. Niamsha giggled, her hand flying to her mouth by instinct to cover the sound. An instinct long forgotten before now, left over from a childhood where she and Tressa had played at mimicking the guild masters and hid their laughter from their fathers' disapproving stares. Tressa smiled, a proper one this time, with the dimples by her mouth and a slight flush to her pale cheeks.

"He's nice enough," she said, crossing toward Niamsha to stand by her side. "I could wish papa found someone easier on the eyes. But the pretty one had nothing to his name but dreams and a promise from a guild that ain't here no more. It's a stable marriage."

"That's something." Niamsha fiddled at her pouch, her remaining gold Jayl still heavy on her belt. That much gold might have bought even *her* a stable marriage. If she weren't already in too deep with the Rendells. "Better'n I got, at least."

Tressa sighed. "Papa should have taken you in. Wasn't right, letting you and Em starve. I never knew…"

The question didn't need said. Niamsha was here, and Emrys wasn't. Thank Holy Aeduhm *this* assumption was wrong.

"Got Em in at temple," Niamsha told her. The lie was slight enough to ease Niamsha's conscience. Emrys *had* been studying at the temple. That he wouldn't be any longer wasn't something Tressa needed to know. "Been getting by. Just..."

She hated to ask now that Tressa had welcomed her. Anything that involved the Rendells would poison Tressa's family, even with Niamsha in the middle. And there was no keeping Nijel out of knowing who her supplier was. Marcas she might fool, but no one kept secrets from Nijel.

"What?" Tressa glanced back at the house, but pivoted back to Niamsha. "Papa's had it rough, but if I can..." She stopped.

The last time they'd had this talk, Niamsha's pride had prevented her from accepting Tressa's help. She only wished she had that luxury now. Without Tressa, Niamsha had only one choice.

"I need help," Niamsha admitted. "I got some debts, can't pay. But the... If I had something to trade. Something worth selling." She nodded at Tressa's father, still at work inside the house. "Can you get yer papa's patterns? Makes some good glass. He's got secrets. We all did. Old guild master's got my papa's notes, but yours..."

Tressa shook her head, face twisted in a mask of sympathy. "Niamsha, I can't. He won't teach me, and he ain't had a 'prentice all these years. He's talked about shutting the shop down after I'm wed."

"But..."

Niamsha spun around to stare inside the house, fury clawing its way to the front of her throat. A glasswright's secrets were priceless. How could he take them to his grave? The old man coughed, a deep, wracking cough that shook his shoulders like a storm-tossed branch. If she hadn't been looking so close, she'd never have seen it. His eyes squinted, breath quick and shallow, and the tiniest of discoloration of his skin. The same thing that had killed her own papa. No wonder he didn't want to teach anyone his trade. The realization hit like a bucket of water. She couldn't ask Tressa for help, which meant she had nothing for Marcas.

"Could you ask old Master Ferndon for your papa's notes?" Tressa asked.

"Never much liked me." Niamsha bit at her lower lip, body tight with the desperate need to find another answer. Stealing from the old guild master was a death sentence. Or salvation with a little revenge mixed in.

"I could come with," Tressa offered, misinterpreting Niamsha's hesitation. "Ferndon's harsh, but he ain't gonna let ya starve. Not when he's got your father's skills hidden."

Niamsha shook her head. Tressa might be a useful entry plan—and it would be so nice to spend more time together—but her optimism added a potential witness. Niamsha couldn't risk anyone learning that she'd stolen the notes. A light knock came at the outer door of the house, catching the attention of Tressa's father.

"Yer husband's here." Niamsha pointed at the door and smiled, stepping away toward the back gate. Tressa had enough to worry about, anyway. "I'll convince old Ferndon. Thank ya, Tressa."

"Wait, Niamsha!"

Tressa turned as a male voice called her from inside, and Niamsha took the excuse to slip out the back gate. No choice now. The last of her options exhausted, she turned her steps toward the manor homes wealthy merchants built at the edge of the noble's quarter.

The first failure was of prevention. Emperor Laisia invited the nobles of the northern nation, Sernyii, to treat for an exchange of goods. They dressed in their finest, brought their gifts, and shared tables and secrets with imperials. On the second night of their residence, both imperial princes were murdered.

— *from* An Abridged History of the Sernien War

Chapter 7

Arkaen loitered in the courtyard of his keep, waiting for Sayli to join him. The tight-fitted doublet and breeches of his formal wear strained across his shoulders every time he shrugged against the stiff fabric. Gods-damned clothiers. This delicate red silk doublet, slashed through to reveal the orange and yellow patterns of his undershirt, was all about the effect and ignorant of utility in a crisis. And this effect...

Twisting slightly, Arkaen scowled at the loose bits of the undershirt that fluttered as he moved. A clever design that turned his outfit into an illusion of feathers and fire when he danced. Beautiful, complex, refined. A *gaudy* nod to his war title, Phoenix, that left him feeling cheap and callous. People had died for his glory.

The door to the keep opened, interrupting his thoughts as Sayli stepped out in a cluster of maid servants, sparkling gems, and full skirts. Her silver and emerald gown flared at the waist, leaving enough room to hide half a unit of his soldiers under the skirts, but her pace was quick and light-hearted as she trotted down the stairs with a bright smile.

"Kaen, you never take me to balls." She threw her arms around him in childish delight.

Arkaen chuckled into the intricately woven braids of her light brown hair. His breath stirred the chips of emerald her maids had placed to emphasize the green eyes she'd gotten from their mother.

"I rarely have such a perfect opportunity." He gave her a quick squeeze and pulled free, gesturing to the carriage. "We've a royal guest from Osuvia to greet."

Sayli cast him a sly grin. "Planning... foreign relations, are you?"

The taunt pierced through his mirth. Gods. Even Sayli acted like he cared for nothing but personal entertainment and a decent tumble in bed. Arkaen pulled the carriage door open for her, painting a gracious smile on his face as he offered a hand to help her in. He shouldn't blame her. Lasha's plan demanded he cultivate the appearance of frivolous indolence, and at almost nine years his junior, Sayli could hardly rely on her childhood memories of him. Still. She knew him better than that.

Arkaen climbed in after her, setting the bulky, basket-hilted dress sword against the wall as he settled in his seat. No use arriving with a bruise the size of his spread hand because someone thought his sword hilt should match the theme of his clothing. Sayli fiddled with her lace fan as the carriage clattered out of the courtyard, watching him over the edge as if waiting for something.

"What is it, Sayli?"

"The reception for the Osuvian princess is at the Weydert manor home, and Baron Weydert isn't exactly in your good graces." She dropped the fan into her lap, leaning back against her seat with a comfort he'd never managed in his own court attire. "What plans have you devised?"

"You said I should seduce the Osuvian princess." A hint of his bitterness lingered in the words. "The lower lords just sent another petition complaining about my policies, and Oskari didn't even bother to hide his influence this time. A foreign fling would certainly give fodder to the rumor mills."

"We both know that's a poor idea," Sayli said. "You're as like to start a war as smooth any ruffled feathers that way."

Arkaen nodded, the last of his discomfort fading at her response. "Then if we agree on that point." He stared out the window at the dimly lit streets of Torsdell. "What *are* we going to do about Oskari? All his stated concerns over province security aside, everyone knows he doesn't give a horse's ass about my virility."

"You're asking me?" Sayli batted her eyes at him with a coy smile. "Why, brother dear, I am but a shallow girl too dull-witted to be worth the political training that our mother brought to her marriage."

Arkaen scoffed at her. "You had at least as much political training as I. More, if you kept pestering my old tutors after I left. And you've always been better at this than me, even when I was *trying* to learn."

Sayli laughed. "I don't believe I saw those days, Kaen."

He chuckled with her. "Horses and swords were more entertaining." And those skills had served him well in the war.

"Yes, well…" Sayli's brows pulled together as she considered his question. "What to do with Baron Weydert depends on what he wants. You're right that providing an heir won't appease him, but you're wrong that he doesn't care about the succession."

"I've heard the rumors, Sayli, but he's not in line for the throne." Arkaen leaned back against the cushions, stretching as much as he dared in his court attire. "Only a genocide of Sentar nobility would give him a claim." He hesitated, watching Sayli carefully. "I've heard rumors he dislikes Kìlashà. Thinks I'm too familiar with a lowborn guard I met in Serni."

Arkaen studied her for any sign of a reaction. Sayli, as the person closest to him, had the best chance to discover his relationship with Lasha.

And Lasha insisted the revelation would put her at risk. Oskari's recent behavior certainly gave Arkaen reason to fear repercussions to his kin.

Sayli shook her head, a quick snap that rejected the very consideration. "No. I'd never recommend Baron Weydert as a model for proper behavior, but he's hardly that petty. Or that impulsive. Think how he handled your order on trade."

"By calling an emergency midnight council meeting and shouting at me loud enough to wake half the city?"

"Before that." She waved a dismissive hand, as if the threats leveled in that meeting had been nothing more than childish gossip. "You came home after five and a half years at war a person we barely recognized. Some demon-marked *thing* following your every step and the only explanation we got was he's a personal guard, demanding we name you high lord when you'd done everything in your power to avoid it before. And a fair share of us know Father didn't just fall off his horse into that ravine, Kaen."

He cringed, turning away to avoid her gaze. The story had been for her more than anyone. He'd long since learned to live with the guilt of lives taken for the greater good.

Sayli grimaced. "Not that I much blame you. At that point, Father had gotten..." She paused, eyes closed in a mask of the grief she'd just dismissed.

His heart ached to offer some comfort. But what comfort was there from the man who'd killed her last remaining family? Arkaen was hardly the boy he'd been before the Sernien War. Not truly the brother she'd bid farewell to so many years ago.

"But you were the rightful heir," she continued, opening her eyes to catch his gaze. "And the first thing you did after taking the throne was disrupt every facet of our economy. Declared foreigners equal to natural-born citizens. *Beautiful*, in principle, but in practice? The province's merchants built decades of trade agreements on the old system.

Foreign merchants paid higher taxes for more limited trade locations, but held a proprietary market on certain items. You offered nothing in recompense for your changes, and no nullification of previous agreements. Anyone with a multi-year contract found themselves locked into higher rates for goods no longer more expensive to produce. Do you even know how many wealthy merchants you impoverished, or how many common tradesmen you left destitute?"

"Seven hundred." Arkaen had asked Lasha as soon as he'd realized his mistake. "Give or take a few."

"Give or take a few *hundred*, most likely." Sayli hesitated, then shook her head again. "Or the tax increases. What in all the gods' names are you even *doing* with all that money? It isn't going to renovations."

"It's offering stability to the poor." Arkaen frowned at her. "Paid combat training to give them a chance if they ever need to defend themselves. And it's a minimal cost compared to Emperor Corliann's standing army, which is much smaller. The province will thank me if we ever need a defensive army."

"But why would we?" Sayli glared at him. "You've already won the war, Kaen."

This war. But he couldn't say that without dragging her into Lasha's plans against Lasha's will. Lasha swore ignorance would serve her better in the conflict to come. Arkaen turned away, staring out the window again.

"Fine." She brushed his explanations off, sweeping her fan open again. "My point isn't that your economics are ill-conceived. It's what Oskari's done. For three years he petitioned the council to refuse to implement the laws. They supported you, either from fear of your anger or desperation to seem loyal."

"Or maybe they actually agreed," Arkaen said.

"With that?" She gestured to one side toward his soldier's training grounds. "With spending thousands of gold to support your personal army? Half of them think you're planning to march south and take the throne from Emperor Corliann."

Arkaen scoffed. "If I wanted the imperial throne, I'd have it."

Sayli fell silent, staring at him with eyes wide. The threat of his words lingered, an unintended treason that Deyvan would have understood. That Lasha refused to reveal.

"I meant—" Arkaen ran a hand through his hair. Another lie for the greater good. "Not me, of course. I have no claim. If I wanted influence over imperial decisions, I'd have taken a place as our emperor's right hand instead of coming home to rule."

"But you see why they're concerned." Her voice was hesitant as it had never been before he left. "That statement alone is grounds for any of them to demand a Successor's Tribune and take your seat."

And there was her actual concern. She thought the lower lords might challenge his rule. No one had called a Successor's Tribune in more generations than he could recall. Not that Arkaen had anything to fear from the swordsmanship of his lower lords, but the principle held.

He smiled at Sayli. "Of course. Especially with my flameguard taking over so much of the family protection. But I fought side by side with our emperor. The army isn't for him."

"I believe you," Sayli said. "Or at least that you believe that. But wars are a great deal simpler than imperial politics. Baron Weydert has tried everything in his power to convince you to respect the traditions of Sentar province, and he's tried to rally support from the lower lords to challenge the incomplete plans you've proposed. When he failed at both, he lost his temper and yelled at you."

"And then undermined everything I've done in as many ways as he can," Arkaen added. "He's not a saint, and none of that answers my original question."

"I'm not sure a good answer exists." Sayli leaned forward to peer out the window, eyes sparkling as the lanterns of the Weydert estate shone down the street. "Baron Weydert may not be in line for the high lord's seat now, but with you gone so long in Serni, Father was discussing marrying me off to name a proper heir. He and Baron Weydert were great friends, and you remember how Father loved to reward his friends."

"He wouldn't have offered you to *Oskari*, though." Arkaen cringed at the thought. It wouldn't have been entirely out of character for their father by the end. "Gods, Oskari's got children our age. Maybe he meant the son? Rikkard?"

"That would be as possible now as then," she pointed out. "Far *more* possible, in fact, since you've so little desire to provide an heir. Except that Baron Weydert has made such a point of making you an enemy."

"So you think he's planning a genocide of the nobility?" Arkaen couldn't imagine it. Not even from Oskari.

"Or some strategic bribes." Sayli shrugged. "No need for war if half the nobles agree on one heir and the other half are arguing over options."

"A truth." Arkaen drummed his fingers for a moment, thinking. "Then I can't leave him in power."

Except removing Oskari for actions he *might* take would be like executing someone for voicing dissent. Nothing to give credence to claims of tyranny like denying someone the chance to accuse it.

"I need to delay any further movement toward breaking our province into political factions." Arkaen frowned out the window at the carefully sculpted hedges lining the road to Oskari's manor home. "Can you see what information you can glean from the lower lords? Try to convince the more influential ones to speak with me in the morn."

"Of course." Sayli's childishly sweet tone set his nerves on edge. "Whom shall I charm, brother dear?"

"We've serious work to do tonight."

"No reason I can't have fun, Kaen. Count Brayden Skianda just broke off his marriage contract with that merchant-lord's daughter from down south." Sayli grinned, waving her fan toward the approaching manor. "He'd make a pleasant dance partner, at least in looks."

Arkaen laughed. "Then charm him to your heart's content, though if you're planning to marry, I'd rather you picked someone your own age. Actually, for tonight, though, Brayden's perfect."

"Anything I should address?"

"Brayden authored the most recent complaint," Arkaen said. "Along with several of our allies. Check on Count Tenison, as well."

"Certainly." Sayli leaned forward to peer out the window at a carriage in front of them. "Oh, look." Her finger shot out to level at a lady and her escort. "That's a new fashion. Mindanese, I think."

Arkaen sighed, leaning back against the seat. "I'm sure it's gorgeous."

Sayli sighed. "Really, Kaen, *you* should be looking. After five years on the high lord's seat without even a bride, you're coming close to neglect of duty. Look there…" She pointed out the window again. "Several of your unwed lady courtiers are gorgeous. The Lord Marshall has a daughter, Count Skianda has a sister. Or Lady Kyli Andriole, though some others have better connections."

"You mean, have any connections left," Arkaen corrected. "Viscount Andriole is clinging to his noble's title with the last of his strength. That marriage alliance she lost was their last hope."

"That's not kind, Kaen," Sayli said, her voice heavy with hidden emotion he couldn't read. "There was more to that than you knew."

They'd signed the marriage proposal shortly after he'd left for the war. Six months after he'd come home, Kyli returned from the imperial city to a broken contract. It was scandalous of the families to have waited that long to resolve the contract to begin with.

Sayli fixed him with a shrewd look. "You know, the Andriole family has always been stalwart in their support of our reign. Perhaps *you* should aid a long-standing ally of our bloodline and wed their daughter. Restore their honor and soothe the lower lords all in one."

"I don't need you marrying me off tonight, Sayli."

They'd slowed to a crawl as the line of carriages approached the manor house. Fine ladies and their escorts never seemed prepared to exit a carriage, always taking an inordinate amount of time to gather skirts and fans and who knew what else. His army training grated against the slow pace. An enemy would have cut down a dozen courtiers before one of these ladies stepped onto the cobblestones.

Sayli scowled at him. "You have a duty to provide an heir. The rest of this won't be nearly as dire if your legacy is secure." She slapped her own delicate fan against his knee. "It's not as though you don't have the drive."

"You're my heir, Sayli." He rubbed the knee she'd hit, the dull sting a reminder of happier days when they'd played in their father's courtyard. "You've got more sense than most of the unwed ladies, anyway."

"No amount of wishing and orders will make the lower lords accept my rule." Sayli glared at him through the too-old green eyes she'd grown into while he fought a foreign war. "If I'm going to be your heir, you'd better marry *me* off."

Arkaen scowled. "My sister is not a prize mare to breed for posterity."

"Then you'll have to be a stud."

A moment of matched wills and he turned away, watching the last of the courtyard creep by. Finally, the carriage slowed to a halt before the wide, extravagant marble steps leading to Oskari's—palace. Nearly as large as Arkaen's own keep, but with none of the defensive walls or small, slit windows to protect against attack. But Oskari had never needed that.

Arkaen threw the carriage door open and stepped down, quick and efficient as he'd learned to be on the battlefield. Carved wolves sat frozen mid-leap from pedestals around the entryway, and pillars on either side of an enormous set of cherry-wood doors displayed scenes of hunting. He plastered a polite smile on his face as he turned back to offer Sayli a hand.

"Now, don't fret." Sayli grinned at him, eyes glittering with excitement and renewed good humor as she stepped out of the carriage. "I'll mingle with our friends, learn what I can to minimize any threats from Baron Weydert. You do a good job of diplomacy with Osuvia."

Sayli glided across the stone steps beside him like a child on iceblades glided on a frozen lake. Gods, she'd gotten so refined in the years he'd spent in the north. Nothing like the careless child he remembered from before their mother's death.

"And seduce some poor lass," she added. "Highborn, if you can manage, so the lower lords think you're considering marrying her."

"Sayli!" It was one thing for Lasha to callously suggest he seduce an innocent woman—Lasha's suggestion, unsavory as it was, would have come from his near-omniscient powers. Sayli was an entirely different matter.

She chuckled, ignoring his scandalized look, and stepped up the stairs in a brisk walk. Arkaen trailed in her wake, a smile teasing at his lips. Somehow, Sayli could always ease his mind no matter how uncomfortable her accusations.

The doorman cast them a false smile, broken by an instant of hesitation as he realized who they were. Stilted and formal, he turned to a list in his hand and scanned the entire thing, glanced at Arkaen again, and turned back to his list. Arkaen's temper simmered in his gut. Oskari had little reason to expect him, but no one would actually dare to leave their ruler off the guest list.

"Oh, dear," Sayli exclaimed, her tone perfectly pitched for concern. "Has your lord's clerk made an error? I'm certain Baron Weydert wouldn't have neglected our names on the list. Why, just yestermorn he was proclaiming his loyalty in front of near a hundred of my brother's subjects. As I heard, he was so desperate to make his loyalty known he had quite an embarrassing... incident."

"Now, Sayli, there's no need to exaggerate." Arkaen fought back a snicker and graced the doorman with a sympathetic smile only half feigned. "It was barely three dozen, and your lord was quite dignified." As dignified as anyone could manage, having lost control of his bladder only moments before.

The doorman hesitated a moment longer. "I… pardon, my lord, my lady. I'll need to…" He glanced behind him, eyes panicked as he looked for anyone he could call for help. He clearly didn't know exactly what Oskari expected him to do. Insult them and let them in, insult them by turning them away... Arkaen took pity on the man.

"Oh, no need to find an escort." Arkaen intentionally misinterpreted the doorman's confusion. "Sayli and I have visited often. We'll show ourselves in. Good eve."

Arkaen strode past the man before he could find the words to object, leading Sayli past the priceless doors and into a grand foyer.

Mortals, in their ignorant state, heeded few warnings from the Divine Children and many sank into greed, theft, and dishonesty. Aeduhm looked upon the lands His Children walked, aggrieved by the masses of corrupted. For the protection of His Eternal Feast, He knew such mortals could not be tolerated. He cast all who had not the spark of reverence from His sight, so that His Table might not be fouled.

— from the teachings of Holy Aeduhm and His Kin

Chapter 8

Niamsha scowled at the dark line of the newly built wall only a few roads beyond Master Ferndon's home, puzzling over the rough plan she'd devised. Too many guards to just sneak in, but they were hirelings and hirelings tended toward lazy guarding. Especially when they'd pulled the late shift. She could come in from High Lord Arkaen's newly built palace wall and offer a gold coin to look away as she slipped inside… it might work. But she'd have to be careful to bribe the right guard.

If she knew Master Ferndon at all, his glasswright's secrets would be near his bedroom. The apprentices always joked that Master Ferndon saw his blowpipe more than his wife, and she'd heard they even had separate sleeping chambers. That might be a problem, though. Niamsha had been in several wealthy merchant houses since Nijel had brought her into the

Rendells, and the one thing they all shared was a maze of corridors between any exterior windows and their bedchambers. The wealthy of Torsdell learned long ago that windows facing the street without guards under them brought more stench and thieves than pleasant eves. Well-guarded interior courtyards served for fresh air, but wouldn't serve as an exit. So, she could try to get past too many guards on the way in and slip out through the corridors while they searched the courtyard, or she could come in from High Lord Arkaen's walls like she'd planned but have no escape.

She crossed the street in a quick dart and hugged the hedge at the edge of an expansive home, trying to move only when the wind set the branches waving. With luck, that might cover her own movement.

The wind was low this eve, not enough for true cover of her creeping form, but she made the corner of Master Ferndon's mansion with no one calling an alarm. Good enough, she hoped. There, hidden in a natural hollow in the hedge, she watched the gate that led to her target's home. During the day she might pose as a delivery girl, but this late anyone coming by would be suspicious. Her papa would have taken a customer, friend, or most any other until bed, which often meant well into the night after Niamsha and Emrys slept. But someone as well off as Master Ferndon had rules. Thought he needed to keep an appearance of proper standards and piety, though she'd never seen him at temple.

But that gave her an idea. Master Ferndon's pride likely meant he kept unsightly services to times when others wouldn't see. Refuse collection, for example. Nothing to make a braggart look common like a grubby man hauling the day's meal bones, worn-out boots, and bits of broken plateware out of the house. Master Ferndon likely wouldn't risk the rubbish trader being seen in the mornings, which meant he'd be by soon.

Niamsha pulled her hair forward over her shoulders, hunching her shoulders and bowing her head. No one *should* recognize her. Not after four years among the Rendells. But she didn't dare take any chances. Faking a determined stride, Niamsha crossed the street to the gate.

"What business ya got?" The guard peered through the bars, his uniform ill-fitting and stained. A hireling, as she'd suspected.

"Here fer the rubbish," Niamsha said. The guard leveled an uncertain look, and she added another quick lie. "New, sent me ta learn the trade. He'll likely be by ta check on me work."

That should delay discovery for a bit if the actual rubbish trader came by while she was in the house. Not a good plan, but the best she could manage with no time to prepare.

"All right," the guard replied, stepping out to unhook a complicated latch on the inside of the gate. "Be quick. Master Ferndon expects a visitor this eve."

Niamsha nodded and followed his wave inside the entryway. A pause and quick survey told her all she needed. To the left, a small stable and workshop stood against the side of the sprawling wooden manor house. The kitchen would be to the right. No one put the kitchen next to the horse shit. She wandered toward the right side, scanning the small entryway as she passed around the edge. She wouldn't have wanted to try coming out this way even if she hadn't needed it as an entrance. Too many guard posts and no way to tell which ones Master Ferndon had ordered manned this eve. With a visitor on the way, Master Ferndon had likely paid for all of them to have a man inside. Master Ferndon would care more for how his security might impress his visitor than the value he got for his money.

No one loitered on the far side of the building just now, but a thin strip of light shining from under the door told her the kitchen wasn't empty. She could handle that, though. Once out of sight of the guards, Niamsha ducked into the deeper shadows beside the building and jogged around the corner, her worn boots too soft to make any noise on the ground. Somewhere there had to be another servant's entrance.

She scoured the edges of the manor, hunting for any nondescript and poorly guarded entries. Chill air cut through her clothes and the sweet aroma of glazed meats tugged at her resolve. Her stomach rumbled loud enough to make her cringe. Too long since she'd allowed herself the luxury of a properly cooked meal. Niamsha rounded another corner, huddling under the shadows of a towering oak until her craving passed. No time to dream. She moved further into the greenery to continue her search.

Finally, Niamsha stopped in a flower bed in the tiny scrap of pleasure gardens and stared at the only option. A darkened room behind a door of framed glass, exquisitely clear and expensive to make. Master Ferndon must be wealthier than she'd thought to afford a door made entirely of such clear, smooth glass. Who knew how many guards he might have inside to protect his guest, or what she might find inside that darkened room? But there was no other way in.

Aeduhm guard her. She had to try.

Niamsha slipped across the yard and pulled the bit of mis-blown glass out of her pouch. Thin enough to slide in the keyhole, sturdy enough not to snap. Like Papa had known she'd need a pick for such a door. But of course not. Papa would have turned her in himself. The guilt lay heavy in her stomach as she slid the glass into the hole and pressed upward on the inside latch. A light click and the door released. She slipped inside and shut it behind her, hunting for anything she could hide under until her sight adjusted to the deeper gloom inside. There. A darker blot by the door out into the hallway. Likely a chair and it looked large enough she could crouch by it and blend into the shadows. She darted forward.

Footsteps echoed down the hall outside just as she reached the spot and Niamsha huddled close, not daring to investigate who might pass by. The slow, measured steps told her no one knew of her presence. A blessing from Aeduhm himself that no one had discovered her yet. With a story as weak as hers, if the guard at the gate looked for her, he would know the truth far too soon.

Niamsha's breath huffed in too-loud bursts that she couldn't seem to quiet, her heart pounding as she listened to the approaching stride. Thunk, thunk. Closer, past the door, and now fading. Not even a slight pause. Not a patrol. Just someone passing by. She let out a breath she didn't remember holding and slumped against the chair. At least now she could see as well as she would manage this night.

As slowly as she dared, Niamsha cracked the door to the hall and peeked out, examining the long corridor. Enough decorative alcoves to hide in as long as no one was looking. Or walked past her. Not ideal, but then, nothing about this plan was. She stepped out, hurrying as fast as she dared and pausing at any door she found. A moment to listen for voices or motion inside, a quick twitch of each door handle to test which of the unoccupied rooms were unlocked in case she needed to retreat, on to the next. Her shoulders ached from tension by the time she found Master Ferndon's bed suite.

The rooms were dark and empty, but she searched them anyway. The main door opened into a receiving room, lushly furnished as if he expected fine visitors every day. A lounge couch sat against one wall, stuffed with something too soft to be scrap cloth and therefore expensive. He had a finely crafted low table in front of the couch. A second table, under the window, was too small to serve as a dining table. Decorative. She gave a cursory search to the room, finding nothing to indicate a hiding place.

Beyond, an empty archway led to the bedroom and an enormous, feather-soft bed that dominated the space. Large enough for her, Emrys, and Papa at once. Niamsha checked the tables on either side, the drawers filled with clutter. She hunted inside the sturdy chest by the foot of the bed that held bedding and pulled open the heavy doors to the dresser. No papers, no hidden compartments, and no satchels to hunt through. Maybe he kept them in the main room somewhere? Before she could go back and check, voices in the hall caught her attention. Master Ferndon's high-pitched whine and another, deep as thunder. Niamsha darted back into the bedroom and crawled under the heavy frame just as the outer door swung open.

"My lord, the guild will offer what support we can..." Master Ferndon's voice, pinched with years of wearing the tight nasal closure he insisted on using when visiting the guild's glasswrights at work.

"I don't want weak promises, guild master." The other voice—distantly familiar, though she couldn't place it—said. "I need to know that your guild will support my claim should anything... unfortunate happen to our liege."

"Yes, my lord baron," Master Ferndon replied. "But I don't understand. He's not ill, is he? Lord Arkaen has his differences of opinion with the guilds, but he's been mostly good to us."

Niamsha choked on a humorless snort. High Lord Arkaen had differing opinions from the guilds in the same way a rat catcher had differing opinions from rats.

"I only fear for the city, guild master. Our liege refuses to produce a proper heir, and without that security, our province faces dangerous times."

Even Niamsha could hear the lie in that. Besides, from what the street rumors said, High Lord Arkaen had tumbled enough women to have produced plenty of heirs as long as they didn't mind the brat being bastard-born. This didn't sound like a quick conversation, though, which left her trapped until Master Ferndon saw his guest out. Niamsha shifted, easing the pressure on one hip. If she was going to be here for a while, she couldn't afford to let her muscles get stiff. An ache in one shoulder made her shift again and she caught her finger painfully in a deep crevice in the floor. She bit off a curse and pulled her hand back, sucking on the injured finger. Who had damage to a floor *under* a bed?

Carefully, she slid her hand along the floor again, finding the crevice and measuring the sides. Just enough for a single slat of wood, raised slightly from the rest. She wiggled to the side, scraping her hips against the rough wood floor and the bed alike, but finally got enough leverage to pull the plank free. A thick stack of papers filled the space where the plank should have been, and the piece she held was too thin to have supported any weight. A false floor.

Niamsha hunted through the papers. She'd never properly learned her letters at temple, but she knew enough to separate the papers into different categories. Old glasswright's contracts, though she couldn't imagine what good they did now. One contract had the Rogue Baron's seal on it. Or at least she thought that was the Rogue Baron. Another had a symbol that—Niamsha gasped, shoving the papers back into their hole. Nijel had a contract with Master Ferndon. If Nijel had Master Ferndon under his thumb… but no chance to turn back now. She was already here. She sorted through the documents again, ignoring anything that didn't have the glasswright's guild crest on it, and finally found the one she wanted. Those carefully marked symbols on top were Papa's signature, but the pages themselves…

"That's not—"

Niamsha cut herself off, glancing at the door. The rumble of voices continued undisturbed and she turned back to the pages. The flowing script held little in common with the letters she'd learned. But she knew the hand that wrote them as well as she knew her own name, the scrape of her mother's quill on parchment carved into her mind. Not her papa's notes at all, but her mother's. Her heart ached at the thought of trading them to a brute like Marcas. But for Emrys, she had to. Mother would understand.

Niamsha folded the papers into a compact chunk, placing them with extra care into her pouch. The only way she could save Emrys. And herself.

Emperor Laisia laid the charge of murder against his Serr-Nyen *guests, using such pretense to send his generals north for retribution. And yet there were those among his nobility who defied him, speaking whispers of tyranny in eager ears.*

— *from* An Abridged History of the Sernien War

Chapter 9

Arkaen swept through the door, Sayli matching him pace for pace, into a burst of lively music and lights. Oskari's ballroom was enormous, with light wood paneling and marble floors covered in gold inlay. Elegant glass candle brackets hung from the ceiling every few feet, suspended on the thinnest of wires to give the room a feel of glittering extravagance. Nobles and wealthy merchants alike paced the floor in groups, gossiping behind hands or with sly looks at the subject of their news, and servants in green and gold livery lined the walls, holding trays of drinks or finger foods. A servant beside the door banged a staff four times as he and Sayli walked in, catching everyone's attention.

"High Lord Arkaen Sentarsin and his sister, Lady Saylina Sentarsin," the man announced.

The guests all dropped into a respectful curtsy or bow, the entire room poised and immobile for one moment, before the entire crowd rose and turned back to their conversations. Arkaen knew many of those discussions would now be about him. He led Sayli down into the reception, dread sitting in his stomach like a mass of cloth shoved into an open wound to staunch the bleeding. This was a den of rumor and secrets, and he'd better keep his own close. If anyone discovered who and what Lasha really was... but distraction was the best disguise, and nothing distracted his lower lords better than rumor of a marriage prospect for their high lord.

Arkaen scanned the room, hunting a likely mark, and smiled at a pretty redhead with creamy-white skin who batted her eyes at him from across the room. He didn't remember the woman's name, but she was a third daughter of a minor family. She might be a good option for the evening. Minor enough that his flirting wouldn't require pursuing a formal arrangement, but notable enough to spark gossip. Just as he turned away, considering her through the corner of an eye, her companion said something that made her bounce with excitement. Arkaen got a sudden, horrifying image of Emperor Deyvan bounding into Arkaen's war room with his standard carefree exuberance, his broad frame shoved into delicate court attire with his shockingly red beard and hair done in curls. Arkaen tried not to smirk. Maybe not a redhead tonight. He'd never be able to keep a straight face.

"I'll see to what we discussed," Sayli said, taking her hand back from his light grip. "We can meet in the morn to evaluate our successes. Do try to enjoy yourself, Kaen."

She navigated the crowded ballroom toward a group of her friends as easily as he would thread his way through the *Serr-Nyen* forest where he and Lasha had practiced combat years before. At least that was one worry off his mind. Sayli could manage their allies for this evening, especially if what Lasha said was true. Now for his part. First, to gauge the room. A merchant stood a short distance away, hands gesticulating wildly as his voice rose.

"... beasts that'll tear yer limbs off, they say."

Arkaen threaded his way over to the conversation. "I hope you're not planning to sell such things in my city, goodman." He cast a wry smile at the noble boys who had been listening to the tirade.

"Oh, my lord…" The merchant twisted his hands together, giving a quick, nervous smile. "Nay, my lord. I was only telling the boys about the north. I'm sure ya saw in the war. The beasts them Serni rebels tamed. Rumor tells they've got wolves the size of a horse they turn on outsiders and flying drakes of fire."

"I saw no flying drakes, to be sure," Arkaen said. The words might ring false if anyone ever met Lasha's clan, but such a false comparison would offend the Drae'gon themselves. And the *Serr-Nyen* had no knowledge of, and less control over, the Drae'gon. "As for giant wolves, I assume you mean the warig? Dangerous, to be sure. The fur has the thickness of spines and turns a blade better than some armor I've seen. But they're rare, wild beasts that terrorize the *Serr-Nyen* until a party hunts the lair down. No tamed pets anyone could turn against the empire."

"Have you fought one?" The question came from one boy, eagerness boiling over.

A quick scan identified the lad as the youngest son of one of his more minor lords. A supporter of Oskari's. If Arkaen impressed the lad, it would work wonders for him later. A plan formed as he grinned at the small group. These boys were all younger sons of disillusioned minor nobles. Charm these lads, supplant their fathers, and he'd have a path to stability that didn't require war.

"Indeed, young lordling. A warig caught me scouting one evening." Arkaen pulled a sleeve back to reveal a deep scar left on his upper arm. "I nearly lost my entire arm to the beast. Nasty fighters, and far faster than you'd expect from a beast their size. But it's just an animal, and steel kills it as any other."

Lasha's steel had killed the warig that ambushed him that day, but no need for these boys to know that detail. They looked impressed enough at the demonstration to speak well of him to their peers, at least, if not their fathers. The merchant frowned at him.

"I'd heard, my lord, that them Serni rebels is talking 'bout fighting again. Any truth to the words?" A hidden question lurked behind the one given voice. Over ten years back, when the Sernien War had begun in earnest, Arkaen had vanished from his father's palace here and returned a war hero at the head of a Sernien army.

"No talk of rebellion has reached my ears," Arkaen answered. "And I sit on the Imperial Council as interim high lord for Serni province. I'd imagine it's just rumors and fears."

It bothered him that these suspicions hadn't reached him through Jarod's network or Lasha's visions. Rebellion never really began until rumors had been flying for months. If someone was starting those rumors back up, it might lead to the *Serr-Nyen* doing something rash. They'd never been entirely happy with the way the war ended. A Sernien victory in name only, they'd remained a vassal of the Laisian Empire, only trading a brutal, cruel emperor for the same man's nephew. Deyvan hadn't given them a reason to rebel again, but some men didn't need a reason so much as an opportunity.

Arkaen excused himself from the discussion and wandered, trading war stories and offering assurances where he could. More than a few merchants and lower nobles shared fears of an uprising in the north, though no one above a baron's younger son seemed to know anything specific. And no one would admit to knowing more than the first merchant. Serni was talking rebellion again. Serni disliked the emperor. Serni was preparing for war. But only the lowborn, or the younger sons out of the line of succession, knew anything. Someone was spreading the news through the commoners in Torsdell and it was trickling up, as slowly as water runs uphill. No wonder it hadn't reached him.

A delicate, white-gloved hand settled on his arm as he surveyed the ballroom.

"My lord, pardon my breach of protocol." A young woman stepped around to offer a slight curtsy, her skin a deep brown, well complemented by her exquisite ruby-colored dress. "I don't believe we've been properly introduced, and my host seems to have vanished."

Arkaen graced her with a quick smile. The dress was a masterpiece of elegance, with a plunging neckline no lady in the Laisian Empire would risk in the aftermath of their former emperor. The princess from Osuvia.

"Gods above, no. Please, pardon my manners, my lady." Arkaen took her hand and bowed low over it, dropping a quick kiss on the back as he scanned his memory of Osuvian politics. "High Lord Arkaen, at your service."

The little he knew of their royal family told him this princess was likely adopted, though that was a common practice in the country. Something about pure bloodlines breeding poor rulers, such that every noble family adopted a child and named one of the adopted children as successor rather than a blood relative. He'd never understood how the system didn't result in widespread revolt of the lesser nobles, who by now should be more numerous than the commoners.

Lasha claimed Osuvia held no significance in the larger schemes of the world, so he'd paid little attention to them since it became clear they had no plans to help the *Serr-Nyen* in the war against Deyvan's uncle. Now, though, he needed to charm. An adopted princess as a diplomat might very well mean they'd sent the heir to their throne. He'd thought she was just a passing diplomat, possibly valuable for trade negotiations, not a potential imperial ally.

"May I find you a drink, my lady?" Arkaen gestured at the servants still lining the walls. "I've heard the vintage Oskari brought out for this occasion is impressive."

She laughed, a full, comforting chuckle that reminded Arkaen of nights spent in the Serni fields bonding with the soldiers he was about to send to their deaths.

"Everyone has heard that, my lord," she said. "I've had more than enough wine for the evening. What I would enjoy is a dance partner."

Her expectant pause gave him barely an instant to suppress a grimace, his nerves tightening to a hair's trigger. If the nobles saw him dancing with the Osuvian princess... well, it would spark the rumors he was hoping for. But he couldn't dismiss a foreign royal as a marriage prospect without risking a far more serious political insult than he dared. Deyvan would never forgive him for starting *another* war on their northern border.

"My lady..." Dammit. He'd forgotten to ask her name, and he should remember from the invitation, anyway. Remembering obscure names was half the job of ruling.

"Just Prillani, please." She smiled again. "I'm not nearly as important as my sister. She's the heir. Father says I kept too much of the wild heart that led my birth parents into a bandit's den."

Right, Prillani Kitorn, who had kept her Yllshanan name to honor the dead merchants she'd been born to. That was why he'd expected just a diplomat. Yllshana and Osuvia had a bloody history, and the Osuvians would never accept a pure-blooded Yllshanan on the throne, adopted child of their ruler or no. Relief flowed through him. He knew how to handle a younger daughter's infatuation.

"My lady Kitorn." Arkaen plastered on his most diplomatic, and apologetic, smile. "I'm afraid I have obligations to my people to see to. And you, surely, have negotiations with my tradesmen who travel to the far north. I'll let you return to those."

He stepped away, scanning the crowd. A rejection from him would sting, but she'd likely just think he was a bigot, and she must be used to that. Especially among Oskari's guests. Poor thing. He wished he could afford to befriend her.

There. Arkaen considered the knot of young ladies gossiping a few feet away, circling around the tall, slim figure of Lady Kyli Andriole. She watched Arkaen through half-veiled eyes, as though calculating the best time to interrupt his evening. Sayli had suggested her as a bride, but his lower lords would never believe such a contract until they saw the paper. If he spent the evening with her, it should start the rumors he needed without anyone demanding to know his intentions.

"Obligations, you said, *Lord* Sentarsin?" Prillani Kitorn's scorn spun him around to face her again.

She'd followed him. Gods above and below. What was her plan? He didn't want to offend the woman more, but he had other matters to attend to tonight.

Prillani barred her teeth in a predatory grin. "I'd love to know what *obligations* the high lord of an imperial province has at a reception no one expected him to attend. One might think you concerned about looking too friendly with a foreign neighbor. Especially given your reputation among your own noblewomen."

Arkaen scowled, catching himself only as she chuckled at his frustration.

"Of course my lady would have her sources," he said, turning away to smooth his expression into something more diplomatic. "I hope you'll believe me when I say imperial politics are rarely what they appear."

"No nation is above such a reproach." Prillani slid an arm through his, leaning close. "Let's have that dance and consider some more personal negotiations."

He tried not to cringe at her tone as she led him toward the center of the room where a formal dance was finishing a set. If anyone had overheard… but it didn't matter who was listening. The very sight of Arkaen walking arm in arm with foreign royalty drew all the attention he could have feared. There'd be a dozen or more petitions on his desk for a diplomatic alliance by the time he woke. Especially with the rumors of a Sernien rebellion. Marry the daughter of the Osuvian king, add an ally on the Sernien northern border, stop the war before it starts. Except the war might not be starting at all, and he couldn't marry.

They paused at the edge of the dance ring as the current song trilled to an end. A shuffle of feet, two dozen or more glances from the other dancers, repeated over and again as he stepped into his place in the dance line with Prillani as his partner. A moment of silence, the room poised to see what he might do. Surely the entire room couldn't be staring at him. *Someone* must have other concerns. Sayli caught his eye from her place down the row and smiled. Gods damn it all. He'd never hear the end of it from her.

The first chords of the music struck, and he stepped into the intricate weave of the dance. For a moment, he lost himself to the comforting patterns, so like sparring with a well-practiced partner. And then the first spin. Prillani glided into his grasp like a tailored glove fitting onto its intended hand. She leaned close to whisper in his ear, matching his pace to perfection.

"My father wants a trade deal with Sernyii, but their lords say *you* are their representative."

He missed a step, tripping forward and spinning her a half step too far. "Pardon?" The whisper barely escaped his lips as they parted.

The dance continued, with intricate weaves and partner swaps as his mind sped through the new information. The name she used—an old title for the *Serr-Nyen* lands before the old emperor's avarice had expanded that far north. Gods. She'd played him for a fool. Smart, though. The best place to discuss an alliance with him was in a dance. The nobles would all assume something far more personal was transpiring in those whispers, and they'd both avoid the scheming nobility that came with all negotiations. His carefully crafted reputation as a womanizer only helped the illusion.

The second spin and he fixed her with a stern look. Her eyes twinkled.

"You didn't truly think I wanted an invitation to your bed, my lord? No telling what—or who—has been there."

Arkaen smiled. "One might think you intended the misunderstanding. Perhaps intended me discomfort and concern."

She tweaked his sleeve as they paused at the end of the spin, leaning in as if to add an intimate comment. "One might think you'd earned it."

He stepped back, caught her gaze, and pitched his voice to his best sultry tone. "A fair point, lady."

The dance took them apart again, but plenty of dancers had noticed the exchange. A safeguard against prying ears. Arkaen swept into the next steps of the dance with an enthusiasm he hadn't felt since his childhood, his nerves soothed by the precise forms of the dance. Arkaen cast a smile at Prillani, losing himself to the innocence of careless dancing and the complexities of trade negotiations between friends.

A few more rounds of dancing, several whispers behind Princess Kitorn's gloved hands. The Osuvians wanted battle-quality metals from Serni's northern mountains and mutual defense against enemies. A guarantee of war against Yllshana if he'd ever heard one. But Osuvia could prove a valuable ally in the conflict Lasha saw coming. Arkaen murmured noncommittal agreement, directing the conversation toward the assets he knew Serni could afford to lose. Rough outlines decided, they lingered over a single glass of wine before parting for the evening.

Arkaen leaned against a stone pillar and watched Prillani slip away through the crowd. A curtsy here, a sly smile there. And just enough veiled glances in his direction to remind the entire room of their ploy. Before the evening ended, the entire court would be talking of his impending tryst.

A shame he couldn't let those rumors persist. If his lower lords thought he'd scorned a chance at a proper alliance with a foreign power, he'd lose the last of his power to arrange his own matrimony. He scanned the room, noting the responses of his most steadfast suitors.

Lady Skianda kept her back pointedly turned away. Camira Weydert's ever-tragic stares held no sign of wishful fancy. He'd even disheartened the younger ladies who chased him more for the fun of the hunt than a genuine desire for his bed.

Another boon of negotiations with Prillani. He owed her a great deal more than the cask of fine southern wine she'd accepted as a price for her impending heartbreak. Among the few noblewomen who still cast him inviting, longing, or jealous looks, Arkaen quickly narrowed his choices to the redhead from earlier or Lady Kyli Andriole.

He watched the redhead flirting with a young lord from a neighboring province. He'd hate to ruin that option for the girl. Kyli already had a reputation for indiscretion. He scanned the room again and found Kyli speaking with another lady several feet away. She cast him another of the quick, inviting glances she'd been throwing him all night. When he didn't look away, she excused herself from her conversation and headed toward Arkaen.

"My lord," Kyli whispered, stepping up beside him and offering a glass of wine.

Arkaen took the glass with a smile as she dropped into a deep curtsy and her hair fell forward in a rain of black locks and shining jewels. Her eyes traveled up his body as she rose, pausing for a moment at his hips before she cast him a seductive look through her eyelashes. She licked her lips in an unsubtle hint and he fought the urge to scowl at her. He should *really* choose the redhead. Kyli had plans. But there was that other lord the redhead seemed to like.

"My Lady Andriole." Arkaen glanced out at the ballroom and searched for any eyes looking their way.

A few of the less discrete gossips, but no one he really cared about. The redhead might be safer, but if he made a well-timed exit now, he probably wouldn't even have to take Kyli to *his* bed. Arkaen forced another smile and examined the pretty gems set along her neckline.

The stones had exceptional clarity for a lady from such a poor house. Lasha would love the sapphires to remind him of his mother. He pushed the thought away. He should be thinking about Kyli's breasts. Hopefully she'd think he was.

"I understand you're a frequent guest of Baron Weydert's daughter," Arkaen said, glancing back out at the ballroom. Sayli was dancing with Count Skianda. Too engaged with their plans for the handsome nobleman to notice her brother slip out. "Perhaps my lady could show me some more private attractions of the house?"

"Honored, my lord," Kyli replied.

She cast a glance over her shoulder and led him through a side door into a small hallway. She paused there, pulling him close and catching his lips in a desperate, hungry kiss as she pressed her body against his own. Arkaen let his wine glass fall to the floor and slid his arms around her waist. He returned the kiss, but his body wasn't reacting to her passion. Her figure was too soft and her desperate passion too gentle. He wanted lean muscle under his hands and a little bite against his lips. Lasha would have pinned him to the wall.

A gasp and clatter of a tray pulled him out of the moment, Kyli staggering back in shock. Arkaen just glimpsed a flash of the servant who had stumbled on them. Brown hair flying behind the slim figure, a flash of terrified brown eyes held in a too-familiar face. He'd never seen the boy before, he was sure of it, but something about the face nagged at him.

Kyli fidgeted with her dress, cheeks crimson. Gods damn it all, he would have to take her home after all. Calling this off now would just look cheap and cruel.

"My lady, pardon my indiscretion." Arkaen slid closer, running a finger across her cheek. "Perhaps this is better managed in my private chambers. Say, two hours? I'll tell my guards to expect you."

She smiled at him, a bit of her composure returning. "A fine plan, my lord."

Arkaen held the door for her to return to the reception, following at as discrete a distance as he could manage. The interruption was a boon, really. Now he had time to investigate these endless rumors out of Serni.

Proper craft is a matter of trust. Trust the glass, trust yer skills, and yer patron'll trust you. Get their trust an' you'll have anything ya need.

— Master Trieu

Chapter 10

Niamsha leaned further into the shadows of the doorway, hiding from the lantern light that spilled out of the courtyard where the Rendells were arguing in boisterous, carefree voices. Near two full days scouring this city for something to substitute for her mother's glasswright's notes. Anything else that might convince Marcas that she and Emrys weren't worth chasing. All she'd managed was exhaustion and recognition of her own defeat. But at least Emrys had a chance. He should be halfway to Aerlin by now, and the priceless notes should satisfy the debt.

Not that Marcas would honor her payment if he could find any way to reject it. He'd always wanted something she refused to give. And she couldn't trust Nijel to protect her. Even if he didn't blame her for the failed job Marcas had given her—even if he forgave the crime against a forbidden noble—she'd stolen these notes on a banned day. From someone Nijel held sway over. No, Marcas's greed was her only chance here.

Pulling on what little dignity she could muster, Niamsha stepped out of the doorway and crossed to the broad arch that led into the courtyard that had once been home. Marcas and three of his companions, each with some variation of Marcas's blond hair, blue eyes, and pervasive stench, sat on a box of goods from whatever job they had just finished, each man's neck draped in chains of gold and gems. They toasted their success with whatever liquor they'd scrounged from their mark's stores, boisterous cheers echoing off the stone walls of the courtyard. Another, larger group made a similar racket closer to the main keep.

Marcas saw her and smirked. He grabbed a flask of the liquor and crossed the courtyard, his companions watching from their place. If she tried to run before Marcas finished with her, they'd help, but most of the Rendells kept out of Marcas's way when he had his eyes set on her.

"And what *you* want, girl?" Marcas's sneer was too close, but he stepped closer still, his breath wafting across her face in a wave of stale beer and another, fouler stench she didn't care to place.

The heavy fall of costly jewelry dangled under her chin, stealing any chance she had of bribing Marcas. With this much gold in hand, he wouldn't care about her offer. Marcas loved money, pride, and a woman in his bed, in that order. And nothing else. There was nothing he'd love more than a woman who'd scorned him—who had injured his pride— forced into his bed night after night.

Niamsha swallowed a lump of disgust, hoping to force determination into her voice. "Came ta pay my debts."

Her skin crawled at the only option before her. But she couldn't run now, had nothing Marcas would take in trade, and Emrys owed a debt to the Rendells. Nijel's reach was far beyond that of a street gang. She'd seen his guards drag people before him that had fled weeks before. And Marcas would hunt Emrys for missing his job. She stared at the Rendell manor house that had been half prison and half home for four years, dread sitting in her gut at the thought of what she had to do.

"Done owing fer me own life."

Laughter echoed from behind Marcas, harsh and loud enough to catch the attention of the other group. Aeduhm's grace, let them stay away. The more who witnessed this, the higher the price Marcas would demand. Humiliating her in private would never be enough, but an audience always goaded him further.

Marcas grinned. "You ain't got that much, lass. I ain't seen the like nowhere near you."

"I got this." She pulled the final gold Jayl from her pouch and slammed it against his palm. "Ain't all, but it's a start. And…" Bile rose in her throat as she forced the words out. "You said coin or flesh. I ain't got more coin, but—"

"Nia, what're you doing?" Emrys pushed to the front of the crowd.

"Em?" Niamsha stumbled back, eyes wide as the single gold coin fell onto the ground between her and Marcas. The disbelief in her own voice cracked through her resolve, leaving her shaky and weak. "Why? I said…"

"Ya told 'im to leave." Marcas chuckled, malice echoing in his voice. "But the lad's got more loyalty than 'is rat of a sister. An' more skill, too. Brought some right good gossip from tonight's haul."

"Nia, please." Emrys stumbled forward, pushing past Marcas to reach for her arm as she backed away. "I gave me word. Ain't right to walk out on that. Didn' think you'd ever know."

"Now, lad, yer sister's made me an offer." Marcas slid a hand just inside his belt, pulling the waist loose as if he planned to force her to make good right there. "And I've a mind to take it."

"Marc." Emrys threw his hands up in protest. "That's me sister. She's tryn' ta pay *my* debt, that I ain't got no longer."

"You's a Rendell, now, boy," Marcas said. "Rendells take what they want. 'Sides, ya may have paid yer own debt, but hers ain't square."

"Eiliin curse you, Em," Niamsha whispered. The words left an ache in her throat—no worse sin than to curse her own brother—but her anger burned high. She couldn't back out now, having made the offer and agreed to pay the debt. But Marcas would never let her go, knowing how she hated whoring with Emrys in the house. "Ya shoulda left."

Marcas pushed Emrys aside, stepping forward again.

"Marcas!" A new voice, deep, smooth as water over polished stones, and accompanied by the sharp click of expensive boots, sent ice down Niamsha's spine. Nijel.

The effect was immediate. Liquor vanished from the hands of the Rendells scattered around the courtyard, and a flurry of activity sprang to life. Crates lost their lids and men dug out cloth-wrapped packages of all shapes and sizes, each man hunting for a reason to vanish into the Rendell manor house.

Niamsha watched the activity with nerves tight, hands clenched at her side. Her eyes caught on one smaller object, poorly wrapped with glints of near-perfect glass shining in the lantern light as if calling to her soul. A foolish childhood fantasy. Glass had always been an escape when Papa had been there to show her how it bent in the flame, how it danced to the right breath at the right time, turning from a formless lump into a beautiful, arcing statue, or noble's drinking glass, or ornament.

She needed that escape now. For all Nijel's kindness toward her in the past, she'd seen too much from the man for his arrival to reassure her. If he learned she'd been trying to leave the Rendells, there was no telling what he'd do.

"What *are* you doing, Marcas?" Nijel demanded, pausing beside Niamsha without deigning to recognize her presence. "We've work to do yet this eve, and you haven't even stowed our last collection."

Nijel's thin blond hair was slicked back from his narrow, boyish face and his full, red lips pressed into a tight frown. He looked almost small standing beside them, like a man not fully grown into himself, but anyone who'd worked with the Rendells knew better. Nijel didn't need

Marcas' greater bulk or decades of crime to hone the cruelty that bowed the Rendells to his will.

"The lass." Marcas gestured at Niamsha. "She came ta pay her debts. Was just discussing the cost."

Niamsha stared ahead, but she couldn't help the shudder that swept through her body as Nijel's eyes landed on her. His scrutiny left her feeling almost naked. She'd offered herself to the whorehouse, but Nijel would ask far worse if he decided she owed on her debts now. After an instant, Nijel flashed her a quick, vicious smile through brilliantly white, crooked teeth.

"Little Nisha is our ally, Marcas." Nijel turned away from her, his voice pure venom. "And she's recently brought us a brilliantly talented young man in the form of her brother. I believe you've inducted him into our little family this eve?"

"Aye, Nijel, only—"

"Then, if young Emrys is Our new brother." Nijel barely seemed to realize that he'd interrupted Marcas, his use of a plural word not seeming to include anyone but himself. He paced forward, steps measured and deadly. "Surely *his* sister is as *Our* sister. And I know you wouldn't dishonor my sister. Would you, Marcas?"

Marcas's face had gone white. "Nay, Milor' Nijel. I ain't gonna lay a hand on her."

"Very good." Nijel waved a careless hand at the activity behind Marcas. "Get our new possessions stored and see if you can get a few of our men sober. And leave the ladies of the public wing alone tonight. They've enough boorish bastards to manage without you adding to them."

Niamsha could read the fury on Marcas's face, but at least Nijel's protection spared her any expectation of sharing Marcas's bed. From anyone else, salvation would have been welcome. From Nijel...

"Come with me, Nisha, dear," Nijel ordered. She didn't dare refuse, not even to correct his pronunciation of her name. He had a plan for her or he wouldn't have intervened. No point angering him before he'd implemented it.

Nijel led her back toward the one solid, clean-swept doorway in the entire courtyard. The entrance to his study. She'd only been there once before, and she'd hoped never to return. Even Marcas was better than what she'd seen in there. At least, Marcas had been before tonight. Now Marcas would hound her in any way he thought Nijel wouldn't notice. And she couldn't leave the Rendell house now, because Nijel had taken a special interest. He'd keep a closer eye on her than she'd ever known. Not to mention the danger if the Rogue Baron discovered where she was.

"How d'ya get inta this mess," she muttered to herself.

Nijel paused at the threshold of the doorway, glancing back at her. "Now, Nisha, there's no shame in protecting your blood. A brother is a rare thing. A thing to savor if the opportunity presents itself. Which is *exactly* why I desired to speak with you."

That didn't sound like he wasn't talking about Emrys anymore, or brothers at all. Niamsha bit her tongue, unsure how to answer. Nijel led her on without waiting for a response.

The entryway to Nijel's study was actually another room, former-ly a receiving room of some sort. Now overturned benches littered the room, remnants of the days when the previous occupants fought someone decades ago. A clear path meandered through the chaos, lit with glass lanterns hanging from the ceiling. Niamsha had never seen those run out of oil, but she couldn't imagine Nijel climbing up to refill them. And no one came into Nijel's study without an invitation.

At the far end of the room, Nijel opened a plain wooden door and led her into an elegant parlor she knew too well. A single, thickly padded chair sat before a small hearth, one low table beside it for Nijel's use. On the floor, a thick, expensive rug drew the eye with its bright colors and a scatter of books and dishes lay discarded along one wall. The clutter gave her no more comfort this time than it had the last. Niamsha shuddered at a smear of red that had once been fresh blood staining a corner of the rug, faded to near-invisibility now with almost three years of age. The merchant had trembled in her arms as his son lay in that pool of blood…

"Have a seat, Nisha." Nijel gestured at a low bench beside the fireplace and collapsed into his own chair with careless grace.

That bench… he'd used it to tie the merchant's wife before her turn to pay her husband's price. Niamsha pushed the memories aside and crossed to the bench, perching on the edge. Refusal would earn her the same treatment she'd helped him deliver then.

Nijel grabbed a glass of wine and took a slow sip, watching her over the brim. She tried not to fidget. Confidence would serve her best if she could mimic it well enough. Satisfied with whatever he saw, Nijel set the cup down with extreme care and smiled at her.

"Now, dear, tell me how you found yourself in possession of lord's gold."

Not the question she'd expected, but she should have. Damned stupid, not to have considered that he'd wonder. She had a story ready for Marcas, but Nijel wouldn't believe her.

"I's headin' to the fountain…" She trailed off at Nijel's frown.

"I know you've had temple training, child," he snapped. "Marcas and the rest of his lot may be witless thugs, but you are no such thing. The least you can do is honor your father's efforts and speak properly."

"Aye, I… Yes, Nijel." Niamsha struggled to remember her schooling, so many years ago now. The formal speech patterns felt awkward in her mouth. "I was going to the Lord's Fountain to steal…" She hesitated, remembering the ban on theft. But his watchers would have told him. If he planned retribution for that, she'd already have seen it. "I planned ta… to make some coin, under the noses of the guards. Figured a few trinkets, no one would miss them and I could pay down my debts."

"A shame about your late father's finances," Nijel said, staring absently into the cold fireplace. "I hate to burden a family in grief, but debts *must* be paid. You've done well for yourself despite that. What has this to do with the lord's gold you threw in Marcas's face this eve?"

"Yes." What was she going to say? If Nijel thought she had a connection to the high lord, he might try to exploit *that*. "I was leaving, and I ran into a noble. He got mad, and I got scared an' there's a fight." She caught herself before her accent slipped too far into the gutter again. "I found it. After the fight."

"I see." Nijel took another long sip of his wine, setting the cup down with the same exaggerated care as before. "And was this altercation, perchance, yestermorn?"

Niamsha sucked in a sharp breath, her throat tight and unwilling to allow her normal rhythm. He'd already known. Aeduhm protect her, Nijel's plan was about that cursed demon somehow.

"Yes, Nijel."

"Indeed." Nijel nodded, as if he'd confirmed a verdict he already knew. "That settles a delicate matter nicely. The noble you encountered was a patron of mine who expressed vehement disapproval over the, as he put it, foreign gutter scum wandering the streets of this fine city. I've no love for bigots and I take rather personal offense to his description of such a fine, well-spoken young lady. I think it's about time I reminded him of his place. I'll need you to deliver a message."

Niamsha nodded, hands ice cold at the thought. Nijel's messages were rarely on paper, and only a fool would miss the insult intended by sending the very person who'd angered the Rogue Baron to deliver such a message. Whatever relationship Nijel had with the Rogue Baron, it wasn't friendly.

A sharp knock at the door interrupted them. Nijel cast a glance over his shoulder, a slight frown marring his boyish features.

"Yes?"

The door slammed open and two of the Nijel's thickly muscled guards dragged a trembling man into the room. Niamsha turned away as they dropped him by the cold fireplace. She didn't want to know what he was about to do.

"Ah, is this him?" Nijel asked.

"Aye, milord."

"Very good." Nijel rose, a flicker of movement in the corner of Niamsha's vision that she couldn't ignore without closing her eyes. "Good sir, I believe we had an agreement. I supply you with unusual goods for your travels at a reduced cost and you spread the words I want spread to the ears I want to hear them."

"Yes, Nijel, I—"

Nijel's hand swept across the man's face with a sharp crack, the sound hanging in the air as the man fell to the ground.

"I haven't given you leave to speak, sir." Nijel stalked across the room to a cabinet on one wall, pulling the door open to consider a series of long, narrow objects inside.

Niamsha didn't have to look to know what the cabinet held. Fingernail shunts and narrow blades for making shallow cuts to bleed the target just a little.

Nijel ran a finger across one blade. "Now, what I heard is that you attended a rather impressive party this eve." Nijel turned back to the room, the blade in his hand and a predatory smile on his lips. "One that attracted all the most influential members of our fair city. And that at that party, you spoke rather indiscreetly about matters intended for the ears of the lowborn only. Why, I even heard that your indiscretion brought those matters to the attention of the high lord."

"Nay, Nijel, I ain't said a word. I swear!"

"What did you tell him?" Nijel stalked across the room, one hand clenched in a fist around the narrow hilt of the blade. "The high lord is a very delicate case. I need to know every word you said in his presence."

The merchant scrambled across the floor, but the guards stood between him and the door. Niamsha shuddered, holding as impassive an expression as she could manage. Nijel wasn't as easily goaded into violence as Marcas, but he saw compassion as a weakness and strove to drive it out when he saw it. She didn't want any of this man's blood on her conscience.

"I's talking to the boys, like you said." The merchant held his hands up to stop Nijel's fury. "Told 'em 'bout the wolf beasts and the fire lizards. Ain't my fault the high lord heard more."

"Don't lie to me." Nijel swiped the narrow blade across the merchant's cheek, drawing a thin line of blood that seeped down his skin. "If this were the fault of anyone else, you wouldn't be here. Tell me *everything*."

"That's all it were. I swear!" The merchant's voice spiraled up into a screech, cowering at the feet of the stoic guards that had dragged him in.

Nijel stared for an endless, strained breath. "A pity." He sighed. "You were such a useful commodity, and I paid so fairly for the use of your tongue. But, as I can no longer trust your word, I've no further use for it and will reclaim the property I purchased."

The merchant squirmed, trying to slip out as the guards grabbed his shoulders to hold him still. Nijel leaned forward, the blade held ready. Too much. She couldn't watch anymore without doing something, and nothing she did would matter. Niamsha pulled her knees up to her chest and squeezed her eyes shut, shaking as the screams from the man turned into something unintelligible.

"Take him away." Nijel sounded as calm as a beggar skimming scraps from the trash. As if cutting a man's tongue out were a common, everyday task.

She knew better than to open her eyes. The casual chat was for his guards, and until they'd left, the merchant would still be here. Still bleeding on the rug and begging. But he couldn't beg now. Niamsha shuddered again, clenching her arms around her knees.

Nijel's boots clicked on the floor as he paced toward her. "Sadly, I believe his son already left with our latest goods. That'll be a debt he owes. I'm sure he has some assets that can be of use to our organization."

The scrape of a heavy body being dragged out of the room. A soft clunk as Nijel set the dagger down. Niamsha cracked her eyes open. Nijel still had plans for her.

"Such unfortunate business." Nijel wiped his hand clean on a strip of pure white cloth, tossing the resulting bloody mass into the fireplace. "Now, to your message, Nisha. I'll send an introduction for you to deliver. You're to serve my ally as a personal servant. A manservant of sorts, except…" He gestured at her body with a rueful smile. "And you'll report his every action to me."

"I ain't gonna." Niamsha shook her head, the words slipping out as she stared at the floor and the blood of Nijel's latest victim haunted her vision. "Rogue Baron don' like me anyhow. I ain't gonna spy on him."

Nijel froze in his casual steps across the room, his entire form tense. "Now, Nisha, dear." He considered her through narrowed eyes. "I have no desire to see you suffer, but I'm afraid you do owe me a great deal of money. I'll collect on *your* debts one way or another." He reached out to lay a finger on the blade he'd used on the merchant.

Niamsha's heart pounded, the sound pulsing in her ears so she could barely hear anything. Nothing but thud, thud, scrape of the blade against wood. A shout, carefree, from outside. Emrys. Rendell debts were family debts. If she didn't pay, Nijel would collect from Emrys. The Rogue Baron would kill her. But Nijel would do worse.

"I ain't got no knowledge o' serving no noble's house."

Nijel smiled. "Not to worry, dear. My ally will understand the purpose of your presence. Just watch your speech. Can't have gutter slang in a fine household." He waved carelessly at the door. "Go on, now. I'm sure you've things to say to your brother before you leave, as you can't return here once you've begun. I'll have proper instructions delivered in the morn."

She rushed out the door, shoulders trembling and one thought on her mind. Emrys. She had to get him out. She had to convince him to leave.

The Serr-Nyen *abhorred combat. With their highest nobility under fierce guard in the imperial capital, the remaining leaders
yielded their lands after only a few skirmishes with imperial
might, offering their fealty in return for peace. And so it was that
old Sernyii died and the imperial province of Serni was born.*

— *from* An Abridged History of the Sernien War

Chapter 11

Arkaen turned over, rubbed sleep out of his eyes, and reached for the
pitcher of water he kept by his bed. The sharp rays of morning sun
pierced his head and gave him a pounding headache to match his roiling
stomach. Dark wood paneling on his bed chamber walls gleamed in the
early morning light. He groaned at the pain and shifted on his thick,
feathered mattress.

A soft sigh and gentle caress of his thigh reminded him why he'd
drank so much last night. Kyli Andriole. Kyli in his bed reminded him of
the incident at the fountain, which led his thoughts inevitably to Lasha.
Damn Lasha for sending him hunting this tryst. For demanding he hide
their love behind casual sex. Arkaen slipped out of bed and Kyli's hand
slid off his ass, hitting the bed with a thump.

"I'm a bastard," he muttered, staring at the tousled black hair splayed
across his pillow.

Lasha would praise the distraction he'd created. No one could claim Arkaen wanted Lasha when he'd just charmed a foreign princess and fucked Kyli, and if he'd gotten Kyli with child, he'd end up married. Well, he'd end up on the run from the whole gods-be-damned empire with Lasha scolding him the entire way for not being more careful. Arkaen ran a hand through his hair, thick and grimy with day-old sweat, and sighed.

"Milord?" Kyli mumbled the word into his pillow.

Arkaen scowled. He'd hoped for a moment to bathe before putting on his gentleman's face. He took a long drink of the water he'd poured himself. Lasha kept insisting it helped after a night of heavy drinking, though Arkaen hadn't yet seen an improvement.

"Pleasant morn, my lady," he purred at Kyli with a forced smile.

He sank down onto the edge of the bed and reached out a hand to brush her hair back from her face. Kyli scooted away from his hand with wide, terrified eyes and clutched his silk sheets to her breasts. Arkaen frowned, a trail of ice running up his spine. She was self-conscious *now?* He'd seen every inch of her last night, and she'd seemed perfectly happy for him to see it.

Perhaps she'd had more wine than he'd realized. Arkaen took a quick sip of his water and tried to remember how the evening had gone. Had she been too drunk? Gods, what if she had been? Any number of willing ladies had climbed into his bed, and he'd casually used them to hide his attachment to Lasha… but they'd always been aware of what they were doing.

Arkaen forced words past a lump in his throat. "Are you well, Lady Kyli?" What would he do if she *had* been too drunk?

"Yes, my lord." Kyli stared at his bedcovers and her voice dropped into a tense whisper. "Just overwhelmed by my lord's attention. Perhaps I could have a moment to compose myself?"

Arkaen hesitated. He didn't want to tell her no when she was so obviously distressed, but he could hear the lie in her words. And the fear worried him more than anything. He glanced out the window and decided.

"That's horseshit, Kyli, and you know it," he said, dropping all pretense. "If you'd like me to put some clothes on, I'll happily oblige, but let's not play games. What's wrong?"

She blushed a rather pretty crimson at his coarse language and pulled the covers a little closer, but he saw her shoulders relax. So she wasn't afraid of *him*, at least. Probably. Arkaen's tension eased a little, but only a little. If her fear wasn't directed at him, she likely expected her father would disown her for risking this night. Kyli might think she could talk Arkaen into a marriage contract, but Lord Andriole would know better. His gut twisted in guilt. He should have found another way. Kyli stared at the covers, shoulders trembling. He could almost feel the tension running through her.

"I'm well, my lord." Kyli's smile, flashed up from her downcast eyes in too-feigned coyness, held all the joy of a funeral. "I only fear…"

Her unfinished words loomed over them, more like abandoned scout towers than hidden concerns. Arkaen set his water down and scanned her posture for any clues as to her intent. All a mix of signals. Batted eyes and artfully smoothed hair a contrast to the clutched sheets and tight muscles. Still flirting, but frightened. Desperate to make her gamble work, most likely.

"I've said, we both know you're not all right," he said. "First things first. Would you be more comfortable if I dressed?"

"Oh, no, my lord, I—"

"Kaen," he corrected. "You've no need to 'my lord' me in private after last night."

She blushed again and shot him another glance, but her eyes shimmered with unshed tears and he could feel her wanting to talk to him. Arkaen waited for another moment while she decided how to respond.

"I think so, Kaen," Kyli said.

She pronounced his name as a hesitant murmur, as if she wasn't sure he'd really meant it. Arkaen nodded and leaned over the edge of his bed.

He suspected Kyli had agreed to buy herself time to plan her story while he picked out an outfit. If so, she was about to be sorely disappointed.

He pulled out a travel pack from under the bed and dragged a worn pair of leather breeches out, sliding into them with comfortable ease and twisting the laces into a quick knot. A loose undershirt followed, and he slipped it over his head, letting it fall into place as he turned back to Kyli.

"Better?"

She nodded, her eyes sweeping over him in an appraising look that reminded him how comfortable she'd been with his body the night before. He suppressed a grimace. Mimicking passion was difficult while drunk enough to dull his senses. He didn't trust himself to maintain the ruse while hungover. Arkaen settled back on the bed beside her.

"We'll start here." Arkaen fixed her with a look he hoped was comforting enough to overcome the harsh words. "We both know you had a plan last night."

Kyli hesitated, and her gaze skimmed over him in overt invitation. She reached a hand forward, as if to protest. Gods, if he'd been wrong, he was going to look like the most callous ass.

And then her shoulders slumped. Her lips twisted into a gorgeous, perfectly sculpted frown.

"I'd be a good wife." No hope in her voice. She didn't expect him to agree. Not really.

Arkaen sighed. "I'm sure you would. But I don't need a wife, and you deserve someone who actually wants to marry you."

"But he's…"

Kyli looked away, her hands dropping to her lap in defeat. The sheet slipped down from her shoulders, revealing a swath of her chest. Arkaen slid closer, taking one hand in his own. The sheet slid lower. Just below her breasts.

"He's what, Kyli?"

She lifted her free hand to pull her hair back. The sheet fell to her lap. Frantic, she snatched her hand away from him and pulled the silk up again, cowering under it as if he'd slapped her.

"Gods," he said, voice quiet in sudden understanding. "The scars. You know I saw them already."

The deep, crisscrossed patterns of old wounds that marred her stomach, back, and legs had been perfectly visible in the candlelight last night. The gods knew he'd spent plenty of time in a position to see them. He reached a gentle hand out and pulled the sheet away. Kyli wrapped her arms around her stomach. As if anything could hide the damage.

"I'm not used to a man wanting to look at me," Kyli whispered. "After, I mean."

Arkaen nodded, a grim smile stealing across his lips. He knew enough to recognize a souvenir of Bloody Emperor Laisia. The bastard had been a sadist of a special breed, and stronger men than Arkaen had fallen under his cruelty. Kyli was far from the only one to bear a physical reminder of the old emperor's rule.

Arkaen hunted for anything he could say, silence between them a shared agony as his mind wandered to the jagged tears that covered most of Lasha's skin. Hers were more precise. The work of a torturer's blade and not claws. But not the torturer. Deyvan's bastard of an uncle would never have let another hand touch someone he'd chosen for his... pleasures.

Fury stirred in the pit of Arkaen's stomach, working up through his body to clench his jaw. Arkaen followed another scar with his eyes. A blade, placed just so as she endured Bloody Emperor Laisia's bed. He could practically see the moment, though he'd never seen the chamber in Whitfaern where it had happened. Deyvan had burned the palace to the ground.

Arkaen's regard made Kyli tremble, and he slid closer still, laying a hand on her cheek in comfort. Kyli looked away, her face pale again and her shoulders tense. There was more damage to her psyche than her body. He suspected that had come later.

"Who cast you off for having survived such a tragedy?" he asked. His voice was deadly calm.

"My lord, I—"

"Kaen." The bite of his anger slipped into the correction.

She stared at him. "I... but..."

"You're not the first to use me for their own ends, and you won't be the last." Arkaen fought to keep his temper under control. "Who cast you off?"

"It's not the lord's fault." Kyli's defense was immediate and desperate. "His Imperial Majesty did what he did. A lord can't be expected to accept a ruined lady."

Arkaen caught her chin and forced her to look at him. Her eyes were wide and her skin trembled beneath his hand. Gods. How many years had his lords rejected her for that bastard's cruelty?

"You, Kyli Andriole, are not ruined," he snapped.

Kyli pulled away and stared at the covers again, but he could see her thoughts churning. Finally, she glanced at him and sighed.

"I was engaged to Rikkard Weydert."

"Which is why you know his sister so well," Arkaen added.

That also explained why Oskari couldn't have betrothed Rikkard to Sayli while Arkaen was away at war. Technically, Kyli had been attending imperial court and the marriage contract held. Everyone knew what attending court meant under the old emperor, and no one had tried to help her. His hand twisted a corner of the sheet into a furious ball as if moving of its own accord.

"It wasn't Rik." Kyli's eyes spread wide with concern.

"Oh, no, this has Oskari written all over it." Arkaen scowled. He'd be damned if he let Oskari get away with such treatment. "Should have let Kìlashà kill him."

She gasped at the statement, but Arkaen ignored her and slid back off the bed. He could no longer tell if the pounding in his head was borne of wine or anger. He couldn't have let Lasha kill Oskari. Not if he wanted to avoid war. The contract would have contained a faithfulness clause, they all did, and that meant Oskari was technically within his rights to terminate it when she returned having clearly had… relations. If he killed Oskari for destroying her life, he'd just make a martyr for his dissenters to rally around.

Killing Oskari wouldn't even resolve the issue. Kyli's honor was long since tarnished in the eyes of her peerage.

Arkaen paced to the window. "Should have killed him."

"My lord?"

He spun around, correction sharp on his tongue, and bit the word off. She deserved his wrath least of all.

"I've a private bathing chamber through there." He nodded toward the door beside his bed, fighting for a calm tone. "Take your time. I'll call for some breakfast."

Kyli hurried into the other room, obviously unsure what his anger would mean. He stalked to the door and yanked it open, calling the three servants draped against the far wall. Heartless curs. Making bets on which lady would walk out his door, probably. They all pushed off and came forward at his call. He sent one for food, another to call Oskari to court, and the third to announce to his lower lords that he'd be late. He'd make morning court when Kyli was ready, and not before. His courtiers could damned well wait.

Kyli's fear, still lingering in the room even without her present, grated on his nerves. As if he'd ever harmed an innocent in punishing the guilty. Dozens—hundreds and maybe even thousands—of faces swirled in his mind, soldiers fighting for their homeland against rebellion in the north. Lives lost to his blade. Or Lasha's, or Deyvan's armies. But he'd targeted no one directly unless they'd earned their fate.

Arkaen pulled Kyli's dress from a chair and dug out her undergarments and corset, placing the undergarments just inside the door to his bathing chamber. The delicate blue silk dress Kyli had worn last night he laid over the back of a chair. Then he paced the room, bare feet too soft on the polished wood floor. The smooth boards, stark contrast to the torture she'd endured, fanned his anger higher. He'd *never* harmed innocents.

But there were commanders—men and women just doing their jobs, but doing them too well. Too good to let live, though they treated the *Serr-Nyen* villagers, their soldiers, and their prisoners all with equal respect. But that was war. Collateral damage for the greater good. Bloody Emperor Laisia had been a scourge on the land. His death had been worth any cost.

"This isn't war." He mumbled the words under his breath, the measured sound a reminder of the control he needed so desperately. This wasn't war, but it damned well would be if he killed Oskari. Even if the bastard deserved it. And he did. But Arkaen's soldiers didn't.

A light knock at the door. Arkaen spun toward the sound, one hand slamming into the door frame in pent-up fury he dared not release. He drew a long breath through clenched teeth, held it for a count of ten, and opened the door. Sayli raised an eyebrow at him, her hair perfectly curled into a demure style and her jasmine-colored gown finely pressed.

"Having a rough morn, brother dear?"

"Get out." Arkaen's temper was far from forgiving this morning, and Sayli's hedging over Kyli's circumstances put her in harm's way.

"Kaen, we've matters to discuss." Sayli crossed her arms and leveled a stern look at him. "And I can't leave a room you haven't properly allowed me into yet."

"This is not a morning for political games, Sayli."

"Well, this is the only morning we have." She pushed past him and into the room, taking quick note of Kyli's dress, still draped over the chair where he'd left it. She spun away from his bathing chamber and called over her shoulder. "Kyli, sorry to interrupt, but I need to borrow my brother. I'll have him back to you shortly."

"I'm not doing this today." Arkaen slammed the door, the impact shaking the room. "You want to talk, let's talk. You *knew*."

Sayli cringed, her eyes straying to the gown again. She didn't need an explanation. He could see it in her eyes.

"You knew, Sayli, and you did nothing."

"I was twelve."

"Not when I came home you weren't. Not when he cast her off."

"I barely knew you by then." Sayli stormed to the window, paused, and sighed. "We've more important matters. Count Skianda is here. He's requested an audience to resolve your differences."

"You think I care about yestermorn's petition?" He crossed to his armoire, yanking the door open. Sayli couldn't be that callous. Not her. Not his sister.

"Aeduhm curse you, Kaen." Sayli spun around, her hair flying behind her. "I know you're angry. We all were. But if you don't talk to Count Skianda this morn it'll be war."

"I'm damned well about to start a war, and it has not a thing to do with Brayden." Arkaen dug in the pile of old gear lurking below his formal clothes, hands itching for blades he hadn't held in years. He couldn't kill Oskari. He knew that. The province needed peace. There. His twin, plain war sabers and the riding boots that had carried him halfway across Serni.

A knock at the door startled Arkaen out of his anger. He snatched his boots and blades, rising to pull the door open. A servant, her plump body shaking under his gaze, scurried in with a tray of oat cakes, fruit, and honey. Breakfast. He'd promised Kyli. He couldn't leave her here alone. She'd been tossed onto the streets too many times already. He waved at the table by his window, the servant darting in to leave her burdens and slip out. Another undeserving witness he'd terrified this morning.

Arkaen turned away, dropping his blades on his bed to pull the boots on. One and the other. His head pounded, hangover nearly forgotten but unwilling to release him yet.

"What are you planning to do?" Sayli again, by his side now, her frustration starting to show in her voice. "Kyli has waited years for justice. She can wait another day. Count Skianda needs your attention now."

"I am not meeting with Skianda." Arkaen crossed to the side of his bed to retrieve his swords, his boots clicking in sharp counterpoint to his still-simmering anger. Much better. And dramatic enough he could make a scene. Disgrace his wayward baron without killing Oskari. "Oskari needs seen to now."

"Gods, why, Kaen?" Sayli caught his arm. "It's been over four years. Nothing you do to Baron Weydert now will help Kyli."

Arkaen pulled free and grabbed his blades. Worn leather wrapped the hilts behind a simple steel cross guard. A decent weapon was like a balm on his hand. A tool he knew he could do something with.

"Do you even know what happened to her?" He spun around, strapping his swords on as he strode to the door. "The pain, the humiliation she suffered. She wasn't just raped, Sayli. He tortured her. For years. And *no one* came to save her, and no one pitied her when she came home. No one even tried to stop him from taking her."

"Eiliin's cursed hounds." Sayli shoved him back, standing between him and the door. "He didn't come for her, Kaen. Emperor Laisia didn't come seeking Kyli."

Arkaen froze, fingers numb, clenched around the belt that held his blades. He'd known, somewhere in his heart. Kyli, even eight years back, would have been too old for the sadist Deyvan's uncle had been. He'd known, but he couldn't admit. Couldn't hear the truth. Didn't need to.

Sayli dropped her eyes, shoulders hunched in guilt. "He came for me. And Kyli volunteered—*sacrificed herself*—so that our home would have an heir. So that our province would be safe. How can you throw her sacrifice away by starting a war now?"

His anger crystallized into a tangible, unbreakable rage. She meant it as a plea to his good sense. That was clear. Sayli genuinely believed that detail would convince him to let this go. Collateral damage. How many innocents had he killed in the name of ending Bloody Emperor Laisia's reign? He'd lost count. So many lives traded for the greater good. But not this one. Not the woman who had endured a torture few even survived for the sake of Arkaen's blood kin. How few had lived to gain the luxury of enduring the nightmares such treatment inspired? Kyli, Lasha… Arkaen.

Lasha's ordeal gifted him the power of the gods, omniscience, and a mission. Arkaen's suffering earned him Lasha and a seat as high lord. Kyli… Blood pounded in his ears. He could tell Sayli was talking. Could hear only the thud of war drums beating in time with his pulse.

"I'm going to kill him."

"Who?" Sayli's voice had broken, the last of her court training gone and her fear leaving a trembling note in his ears. "Emperor Laisia is dead, Kaen. Our *father*, who sent Kyli, is dead. What further blood could help?"

"Oskari's." He stalked past her to the door. "He stole the reward she should have gotten. Her sacrifice should have earned her something, gods damn it, *anything*. And it got her nothing but destitution and mockery. Because of Oskari."

"You can't kill Oskari!"

"Watch me." He yanked the door open. Froze in the casual regard of Lasha, lounging against the far wall.

Lasha's hair and eyes reflected the terrifying darkness of an abyss, as they often did when he was angry, and his fiery veins glowed with an unearthly power. He'd thrown his cloak back to reveal that he also wore his weapons: polished steel bracers that ran halfway up his arms, each guiding three bladed claws that he could extend at need. Those claws had felled nearly as many men during the war as Deyvan's entire army. The deadly metal gleamed in the dim hallway as Lasha gave a slight nod of greeting.

Arkaen's rage burned in his stomach. "Don't talk me down."

"Why would I, kai'shien?" Lasha cocked his head, voice eerily calm in a tone Arkaen recognized too well. Lasha's killing voice. "For what possible purpose would I defend the life of a spineless, witless, heartless, honorless cur who attacks innocent females in the streets of the beloved city of *my* kai'shien?"

Lasha's rage, a match to Arkaen's own, eased something. A pressure to be understood, his fury acknowledged. But the question… He'd seen something. Lasha always chose his words with the precision of a single target assassination ploy, never allowing for extraneous implications. If he was asking, there was an answer, and that meant Lasha had already shared the reason. And there was only one reason, driven by Lasha's impossibly accurate powers.

Arkaen ran a hand through his hair, fury and guilt warring in a clash of old sacrifices made against new injustice to be quelled. How could he let Oskari—all his lower lords, for they'd all contributed to Kyli's shame—go undisciplined? *For what purpose would I defend…* Killing Oskari would start a war, and war would destroy Lasha's carefully orchestrated plans. Arkaen scowled, clinging to the hilt of one blade as though he could disembowel the very corruption that had seeped into so many of his lower lords.

"How many would die?" His hand ached with tension.

"Thousands." Lasha gave the answer like one of the lower lords admitting the gold required to throw a particularly extravagant party. Pride in his knowledge mingled with distaste for the truth of the fact. "Because you could not hold your temper in check."

Arkaen cursed under his breath. But he was right. Damn him, he was always right. "I *won't* let him go unpunished."

Lasha considered a dagger that had appeared in his hand as if by magic. "There are many punishments short of death."

"Sayli—" Arkaen spun around to face her, meeting her wide, terrified eyes. Gods damn it all. Not her, too. "Tell Brayden I'll be late." He crossed to his bathing room door and paused. Glanced back at her. "I don't hurt innocent people, Sayli."

Turning away, he tapped lightly on the door and pitched his voice to as kind a tone as he could manage in his ice cold fury. "Kyli, will you attend me in court this morn?"

Emperor Laisia's grief could not be contained. Both his boys dead on an eve when he had toasted to the health of their murderers, and now barely a nick at the culprit's blood in recompense. When his Serr-Nyen *guests could not point him toward an assassin, he set about slaughtering any who might have conspired toward the deaths of his sons.*

— *from* An Abridged History of the Sernien War

Chapter 12

"If that prissy, cock-loving bastard wants to call on me, he knows where my estate is." Oskari's shout echoed through the enormous, marbled room as Arkaen strode into his great hall, Kyli following his lead and Lasha a half pace behind on the opposite side. A servant by Oskari's side cowered against the far wall, huddling on Arkaen's high lord's dais where Oskari stood in blasphemy against formal tradition.

"No need to yell." Arkaen paused by the door, dropping Kyli's hand and giving the lords closest to him time to notice his presence before he moved.

The great hall fell silent at his words as nearly a hundred courtiers with their attending servants turned toward him. The sea of brightly colored silk and shining gems parted, those closest scrambling back from the doorway with wide, stunned eyes locked on his twin sabers. The lords and ladies further back—the ones who couldn't see him well—stepped back with proper, courtly bows or curtsies. Arkaen smirked at the closer lords. For once it wasn't Lasha they feared.

Arkaen hadn't appeared before his court wearing anything more threatening than a dress sword since he'd taken the throne, but they eyed him as a child would a rabid dog. He paced forward, waiting for each click of his boot heels to echo back before placing the next foot, Lasha stalking a half pace behind. Kyli's soft court shoes sounded in rhythm behind them, a gentle swoosh to his pronounced click. Looking up at his bejeweled high lord's chair, Arkaen plastered a casual smile on his face and met Oskari's angry glare.

"I've had quite enough of your…" Arkaen stopped mid-step, scanning the room as if searching for something. More than half his courtiers fidgeted, shuffled fans to another hand, or glanced at a nearby servant or friend when his gaze swept past. "Mischief, Oskari."

A rustle of cloth and the rising murmur of rumor swept through the gathered crowd as Arkaen stepped forward again. The quiet hiss of Lasha's Drae'gon snarl wound around him and into the room. A gasp to one side, a swish of cloth, clatter of metal, too light a sound to be a sword. Another assassination thwarted by Lasha's power before it began.

Oskari's lips twisted into a sneer. "Can't even walk among your own people without a guard, High Lord?"

"Oh, he's not here for *my* safety." Arkaen drummed his fingers against the hilt of his saber, a counterpoint to the sharp echo of his steps. "As if I couldn't see a trap that plain. Your friend, the new viscount, yes?" He made a point not to look behind him to identify the assassin. His courtiers erupted in mumbled theories again, confirming his guess. "A spineless beggar collecting scraps. I've seen better dagger skill from an untrained child. You've enough wealth to afford better."

"If I wanted you dead, I'd do it myself."

"You might try." Arkaen stepped onto the lower stairs of his high lord's dais. "Though I'm uncertain if you have the balls. What was that you said? Cock lover? I assume you're referring to the rumors about my personal guard." He gave a dismissive wave behind him to indicate Lasha. "Now if I have this right, and please do correct me if I'm wrong, wouldn't that mean I'll *fuck* a man who left you pissing your pants in the fountain square? And did so without even drawing steel."

Arkaen paused on the top step to meet Oskari's eyes. Oskari swiped his tongue across his lips, eyes narrowed in fury. But Arkaen knew he wouldn't dare attack his liege lord for an insult. A pity he wasn't that stupid.

"I'm not entirely sure I should be *insulted* by that accusation," Arkaen said.

"Perversion's illegal by imperial law," Oskari snapped. "Assuming you still serve our emperor."

Arkaen let out a fierce, echoing laugh and stepped onto the dais, forcing Oskari to back away or get shoved. He glanced back at Kyli, pity struggling against the need to prove his point.

"Tell me, Lady Andriole, am I a pervert?"

Several more murmurs erupted from his courtiers at his words. He clenched his jaw tight and forced a casual, bored interest into his posture. Kaen the Promiscuous Bastard flaunting his conquest. This would destroy any dignity Kyli had left.

"My Lord Arkaen," Kyli began, her voice trembling. She stepped forward, head held high. "I can't say as I've heard of a pervert so... enthusiastic with a woman in his bed as my lord was last night."

Arkaen cringed at her brazen boast, unable to stop his quick, worried look at Lasha. Only a special kind of asshole would force the man he loved to listen to the woman he'd just fucked brag about his skill in bed. Lasha wore a partial smirk and watched Arkaen through half-lidded eyes. When he caught Arkaen's glance, his lips twitched into a genuine smile. Thank the gods. Lasha was doing fine. At least one of them was.

"Well, now that we have that settled." Arkaen turned back to Oskari. "You asked if I follow our emperor's law? I don't recall Emperor Corliann making any proclamation on perversion."

Oskari's chest puffed up, condescension spreading across his face. "Perhaps you need a refresher, boy. Imperial law banned perversion near thirty-five years ago when our empire recognized the Laisian pantheon."

"Ah." Arkaen rubbed a finger on the leather wrapping of his blade hilt. "So you don't follow *my* emperor's laws, then, but his uncle's. I believe it's well established that I've never honored Bloody Emperor Laisia's law."

Another round of fearful whispers spread behind him. Deyvan allowed no one to demean his late uncle by using the name the *Serr-Nyen* had whispered at night during the war. A name even the old emperor's most loyal subjects had adopted by the end, when they all feared for their children and their sanity.

"Emperor Corliann has made no retraction of his uncle's laws." Oskari stood with feet wide, shoulders squared and proud. Defensive. "And he's given me no reason to think he intended one. He is a proud patriot of this empire. As am I."

"Gods, how could I have forgotten how close you and Emperor Corliann are?" Arkaen paced to one side of his dais.

Kyli's gaze tracked his steps, the only person in the room not half distracted by Lasha's predatory stalking of Oskari. Waiting for Arkaen's fury to resurface. Her eyes begged him not to. Loyalty or fear. Or, just maybe, an honest concern for Oskari's son. She'd been so defensive of him.

Arkaen turned back to the room, staring Oskari down. "I didn't recall Emperor Corliann visiting your manor home when he came to oversee my trade agreements with his imperial suppliers in Whitfaern last month. Or near half a year back, when he came visiting Sayli. Or after I took my throne, and he came to acknowledge my claim. Did he seek your guidance on that dispute with Mindaine he just resolved? Dirty little trick they tried, claiming a contract with a man over five years dead, wasn't it?"

Oskari's eyes widened at the revelation, the courtiers on the main floor leaning close to catch more details. Deyvan had sworn his circle of advisers to secrecy about that tactic of the Mindanese. But Deyvan would forgive him. Eventually.

"Not your expertise?" Arkaen paced back toward the center of the dais. "I suppose Emperor Corliann has his own value for you. Although, I don't recall your troops fighting by my side in the war. No green and gold defending the lives of innocent *Serr-Nyen* villagers as the old emperor's soldiers sought the extermination of our northern neighbors."

"Sernien!" Oskari's words shook with indignation. "Their province owes allegiance to our empire and they'll use our words. If they can speak them. The Sernien rebels are a bare step above barbarians."

"Hardly *your* empire." Arkaen spun to face him, one hand dropping to a blade. He couldn't kill Oskari. Embarrass, reprimand, and let him go. Anything more would risk revolt. "You didn't shed blood beside Emperor Corliann in the gutters and hills and fields of Serni province. You came to no one's defense."

Arkaen's gaze flickered to Kyli. He couldn't stop the motion, and Oskari's attention turned to the woman whose life he'd destroyed.

"Surely even you can't justify *her* actions." Oskari scoffed at Kyli, turning a mocking smirk at Arkaen. "You're hardly the first she's taken to bed for political gain. Not even the highest rank."

The brazen lie burned through Arkaen's body, every muscle clenched for battle as he struggled to stay poised. Oskari's plan lay exposed, simple and clear to guess. He had to know what she'd suffered, yet there he stood, confident and taunting Arkaen with knowledge he seemed persuaded Arkaen wouldn't dare voice. Deyvan had sworn retribution on any who demeaned his late uncle. A policy Arkaen suggested for smoothing the transition after Deyvan assassinated his own kin.

Arkaen met Oskari's gaze again, a fiery, aching calm stealing over him as his decision formed. Many punishments short of death, Lasha said. He'd intended only a scolding, humiliation, and expulsion from the lord's council. A political castration that wouldn't harm Oskari himself or his family at all. Perhaps such an intent was too kind.

Oskari backed a step away, something in Arkaen's expression turning his confidence into caution, and dropped a hand onto the long sword he wore. A smile crossed Arkaen's face at the movement. He had never refused his lords the right to wear steel in his presence, but none of them had been so foolish as to draw on him. Oskari might be the first. Arkaen turned away, looking across the great hall at the sea of courtiers.

"Let me tell you something about Bloody Emperor Laisia, Oskari," Arkaen suggested. "I learned a lot about the man in his prison."

Several of Arkaen's more loyal lords watched the confrontation with an equal measure of concern and respect. They understood the guts it took to turn your back on a man holding a hand on his blade. For most lords, that mistake might as well be a death sentence. Everyone here knew Arkaen could best Oskari, even with his back turned. A calculated insult in return for the one Oskari had paid him.

"Have you ever watched a woman burned to death?" Arkaen said the words as a statement instead of a question. He knew none of them had. "They always say it's the smell that follows you for years after. I suppose for the first it might be. But after the fourth or fifth, it wasn't the smell that bothered me anymore."

Arkaen swallowed bile at the memory, fighting to keep his expression calm as he paced to one end of the dais again. Several of his lords had gone white at those few words. Kyli, to her credit, stood like a rock at the base of his dais steps, staring at the wall behind him. She knew where he was going before he'd ever started.

"You see, smell is a rather fragile thing," Arkaen said with a glance over his shoulder. "You get used to the rancid stench of burnt flesh rather quickly. The screams, they say, as well. Yes, a few nightmares over those, I'm sure, but again, you get used to it."

The great hall trembled in waves like a true sea. Most of his lower lords and ladies jostled each other for space, trying for a better view of Oskari—a better vantage to hear the dirty little secrets of the Sernien War that Arkaen should have kept hidden—but a few fled the room. Probably those who had secretly supported Deyvan's uncle. Arkaen let them go. He'd made enough of a point to them. He paced back to the center of his dais, his hands trembling on the hilts of his swords, memories flooding his mind. The sour-sweet smoke of roasted flesh lingered in his nose, thickening into a taste that left him gagging. A quick glance at Lasha steadied him. Lasha would fight through hell itself to protect him. He basically had fought through hell to rescue Arkaen from imperial prison.

"But after another dozen or so, when they brought in yet another pretty young woman and chained her to the floor…"

Arkaen let his voice drop to a dangerous whisper and turned back to Oskari. Oskari's face was white, eyes wide, hands clenched on his sword in a grip that couldn't have pulled the blade free if he wanted to. As terrified as the last woman under the torturer's knife had been. Arkaen could still hear her pleas, and the stench of urine old and new replaced lingering, smoky death in his nostrils as they threw another bucket of blood-soaked feces on him. Another glance at Lasha. It was seven years over now.

"They drained as much blood as they could from the girl and then pressed white hot irons against her flesh. She begged for mercy, not from her torturers, but from me. Because they'd told her I was refusing to answer questions I'd answered a hundred times. If I'd just answer, they'd let her go. You think you'll remember those screams and that stench, but that isn't what got to me."

Arkaen paused and watched the gathered courtiers. They leaned forward in excitement. Bloody bastards, delighted by the show and missing the horror of the event itself. Oskari's breath was quick and ragged as Arkaen turned back to face him. Arkaen waited until the silence was almost painful before he spoke again.

"The thing that got to me was after they finished." He took another step closer to Oskari and lowered his voice to an intimate whisper. "When they left her charred body chained to the floor, and I stretched my hand as far as I could and all I could reach were the tips of the fingers on her out-stretched hand. And then, after an hour of watching the charred, stinking body and wondering if there was anything I could have done, she moved. And she looked at me and said, 'please, sir. Mercy.'"

Oskari scrambled back, stumbling over the edge of Arkaen's high lord's chair as he gagged, one hand on his throat as if to prevent himself from puking. Arkaen nodded. He'd puked at the time, and felt like doing so again. The horror of that moment never left him. Except when Lasha lay beside him, stroking his hair. Arkaen cast another glance at Lasha, and the steady presence soothed his nerves. His courtiers, huddled in whispering groups, wouldn't meet his eyes. Even Kyli, alone and abandoned by her peers, looked shaken. Arkaen frowned. He'd pushed this too far, but he couldn't change that now.

"You can imagine my surprise," Arkaen said, returning to a casual, conversational tone. "When I met a charming, beautiful young lady at a formal reception yestereve and then learned this morn that Oskari Weydert had broken her marriage contract because Bloody Emperor Laisia's attentions had ruined her."

Oskari had regained some control of himself, but he only managed an angry glare at the accusation. His claim of indiscretion on Kyli's part was still technically valid. By law, Arkaen could do nothing to punish him for it.

"In my experience, Oskari, things *ruined* by your old emperor don't get up and walk again." Arkaen slid one saber free and leveled the point at a servants' bench on one side of the room. "Have a seat."

Silence hung over the assembled crowd, the quiet swish of a lady's fan adding a hum of tension. Ordering a sitting nobleman to a servant's chair served more than a simple insult. He'd leveled Oskari with a choice.

Challenge Arkaen now or accept removal from the ranks of Arkaen's lower lords. There was no precedent for such a thing, and no clear understanding of who would rule Oskari's estate if Arkaen reclaimed the title granted to the Weydert family line. Arkaen could banish the entire bloodline from Sentar province if he so chose.

Oskari hesitated, scanning the room for any support. Arkaen hadn't looked, but he doubted anyone would be likely to turn on him now. Anyone with the stomach to hear that story and still challenge Arkaen had probably fought in the war. Or at least seen some of the horrors Deyvan's uncle visited upon his people. None of those would support Oskari.

"Do bare steel on your liege lord," Arkaen said. "I'd love to remind you why I rule."

Oskari knew how fast Arkaen was with his sabers, and he wasn't stupid. He walked over to the bench and perched on the edge. Arkaen sheathed his sword and strode to his dais steps, offering Kyli a hand.

"Apologies for the crassness of my former baron, Lady Andriole," he said. "Please, come. I've a seat for you behind the high lord's chair."

The closest lords and ladies to the dais muttered behind their hands, eyes trained on his movements. Formal tradition reserved the chairs set behind his high lord's throne: Left for the heir, right for his consort to be. Or, with less discrete lords of his ancestry, for the high lord's mistress. Kyli couldn't think his offer anything but an empty gesture after their conversation this morning, but his courtiers didn't need to know that.

Kyli considered his hand for an instant, then graced him with a far more reserved smile than he could have managed in her place. "An honor, high lord, but I make my own place." She stepped back among the courtiers that edged further from her, as if her fall from grace might rub off on them.

A genuine smile settled onto his lips. Gods, she had the balls of any five of his *Serr-Nyen* soldiers combined. And enough pride to rule any house. She *would* make a good wife—for someone deserving of her. Her earlier defensiveness of Oskari's son probably meant the marriage had been a love match. He could at least give her that back.

Stepping back, Arkaen scanned the room. No sign of his servants, though he could hardly blame them for avoiding his wrath regardless of direction. He glimpsed brown hair and darker skin among the paler tones that identified his courtiers as true-born blood of the Laisian Empire. Was that her? Arkaen bit off a curse. He'd forgotten about Princess Prillani Kitorn in the mess over Kyli. If the Osuvian princess had caught the spectacle he'd made, there was no telling what she might demand. Asking her to act the lovesick fool for a negotiation was one thing, but asking her to accept his blatant exploitation of Kyli while pretending to adore him may well be a different game entirely.

Arkaen paced across the dais, eyes darting between the various lords and ladies, hunting for the woman he'd seen. There, in a tunic of green and—he sighed in relief. In Oskari's colors. Not the princess. The figure slid through the crowd like an eel through a fisherman's nets, weaving her way as if hunting someone.

"Hail, lass." Arkaen waved the figure forward and froze when she stepped out of the crowd. Narrow, young face belying the wisdom that shone in her eyes. Curly brown hair wound into a braid that ended halfway, leaving the end flowing below her shoulders. The woman Lasha had protected at the fountain. Why was she here, wearing Oskari's colors after he'd nearly killed her?

"M'lo—" She cut herself off, the self-conscious glance she cast behind her as clear as a shout, pleading for the crowd to ignore her slide into gutter speak. "Milord, you need…" She trailed off, staring as if she'd just realized the flaw in her disguise.

Arkaen waved at the servant's bench where Oskari still sat wearing a scowl of pure rage. Time enough to learn what her role was when Lasha could investigate the potential timelines that led to her presence here. He'd said she was important.

"Escort the former baron home, if you will." Arkaen kept his voice level, but his gut twisted with nerves. Lasha'd shown confidence in her role for their plans. But he'd been wrong before, and the last time... Arkaen's long-healed shoulder ached in sympathetic remembrance of Lasha's last mistake. Instinct he'd long ago learned to trust thrummed in his mind. Something was very, very wrong. Arkaen turned away, casting a last order over his shoulder. "And bring word to my new baron, Rikkard Weydert. I've a wife for him."

*Clever keeps ya free. But too clever and ya like to anger some-
one ya ain't got the means to handle proper-like. Know where
yer smarts is put to good use, and never turn on yer crew.*

— Thief's Code

Chapter 13

The high lord's demon loomed over the crowd, his eyes boring into
Niamsha as she spun to face her charge. The Rogue Baron perched on
the edge of a worn stone bench shoved against the wall to hide commoners
from the eyes of the wealthy nobles. Every eye lingered on that bench
now. Except the demon's and High Lord Arkaen's. The Rogue Baron
matched their glares at Niamsha, his fury pouring from him in waves.

High Lord Arkaen turned away, snapping a last order at her. "And
bring word to my new baron, Rikkard Weydert. I've a wife for him."

A scowl stole across her face, quickly smoothed as best she could.
She'd missed most of the exchange, but no one in the palace could have
missed the shouting at the end. And now he'd casually ordered a wedding
as if the betrothed had no stake in the matter. The great, all-knowing High
Lord Arkaen, sure of the right path for everyone. Even some random noble girl he likely barely knew. Stupid, maybe, but the thought comforted
her. His conceit extended to destroying everyone's lives, not just hers.

Niamsha darted forward and grabbed at the Rogue Baron's sleeve with a quick tug before scurrying out of his reach. If she could get him moving, maybe that would give her a chance to slip out of this job before the feud between the high lord and the Rogue Baron got her killed. The Rogue Baron was in no position to help Nijel anyway, now.

But Emrys. If she left, Nijel would have Emrys, and there'd be no easy smoothing over of her family's debts. Holy Aeduhm, this was a mess and no mistake. Nijel'd said present his letter to the baron and act as a servant. Not parade before the high lord in the Rogue Baron's colors while the high lord stripped the baron of his title. And Nijel didn't even know the high lord's demon had saved her from the Rogue Baron only days before. No way any good came of this. Any other job she'd cut and run. But Emrys.

The Rogue Baron rose, movements sharp and eyes burning with fury, and followed her through the room. He shoved his way through the tightly packed, overdressed leeches fawning over the high lord's attention like High Lord Arkaen hadn't just scared them all shitless. She ducked her head, hiding in the crowd of gleaming silk and gems like old table scraps hiding in a pile of new-minted coins. None of her skills worked here. Every step another pair of haughty eyes or upturned nose shunned her presence. Questioned her very existence in a world this far removed from the one she knew.

Niamsha huddled into her tight, ill-fitting tunic and breeches, her single-minded focus on getting out the door. The shoulders of her borrowed uniform, clearly not made for a woman, clung too tight to her chest, and the tunic didn't flare properly for her hips, leaving her constantly smoothing the hem down. Aeduhm's grace. The last thing she needed was to flash her ass at the high lord the morning after he'd screwed another unsuspecting, noble-born damsel. Finally, the door. She slipped out, hurried through the twisting halls of sparkling, polished stone, and escaped into the courtyard.

Fighting to calm her ragged breathing, Niamsha paused in the broad, clean-swept expanse of neat cobblestones that made up the courtyard. The place could fit half the Rendells' house just in this entrance alone. Wasteful. Papa's workshop had served them as common room, kitchen, and studio for his glass work all in one. This space, dozens of times the size of her papa's workshop, served only to separate the high lord from people he claimed he wanted to help.

She needed a plan. Abandon the job and lose her chance to pay off her papa's debts, and now Emrys's debts as well. Run, and hope Nijel didn't take her defection out on Emrys. But she knew he would. Or find another way to aid Nijel from the position he'd chosen for her.

The door slammed shut behind her. Holy Aeduhm. The Rogue Baron. *He* served no purpose anymore. She rushed forward toward the enormous archway that led to the streets beyond.

"Get back here, girl." He caught her shoulder with one rough hand, shoving her toward a gilded carriage to one side. A carriage hung with green and gold cloth. "The high lord gave you an order."

The Rogue Baron stalked behind her as she crossed the courtyard, as if to ensure she followed the order. An elderly man in a green tunic opened the carriage door, eyes fixed on a point somewhere beyond her and far above her head. Valet in front, the Rogue Baron behind. Nowhere else to go. Niamsha climbed onto the cushioned seat, the smooth fabric like a too-fine, too-short fur beneath her fingers. She'd felt nothing like it. Her fingers skimmed the seat, the sensation stealing her focus. What process could make a cloth like this?

"Get your hands off my velvet." The Rogue Baron stepped into the carriage and settled into the space across from her. His eyes narrowed. "What are you doing in my colors?"

She snatched her hand off the seat, fingers fiddling with the hem of the thick, wool tunic. Should have been a simple job. Show up, hand the letter, follow him around.

"I brought a message." The formal tone she'd learned in temple lessons felt thick on her tongue. But the message might be her way to a solution. "For the new baron."

"Lies." The Rogue Baron leaped across the carriage, backhanding her with a sharp smack of knuckles hitting her cheek.

Pain exploded, her vision blurred, and salty liquid caught on her tongue. Niamsha spat, blinking to clear her vision. Red spittle landed on the polished wood floor of the carriage as the Rogue Baron hunched over her.

"I rule my lands," he snarled. "You foreign gutter rat. How dare you set foot in my home and claim ties to *my* family? If you've a message, it's for me."

Niamsha glared up through the strands of hair that had come loose from her braid, a broken lip of skin still seeping blood into her mouth. The pain was worth it. A rift between the Rogue Baron and his son was something she could exploit. Especially if the new baron was anything like his father.

"Then I reckon you'll want this. But I ain't lied. I's sent here with a message for the baron." She dragged the flimsy paper Nijel had given her out of a hidden pouch and shoved it at him. "From Nijel. How you think he's gonna take it, you hittin' his messengers?"

The Rogue Baron froze, eyes going wide. "Nijel?" He collapsed back into his seat, shoving her hand with the note away. "I told him to get rid of your kind, not send them to my door."

They stared at each other for a long moment, locked in a battle of wills Niamsha wasn't sure either really understood. Her lip throbbed with pain. The carriage shook, a grunt from outside and the crack of a whip. They lurched forward, Niamsha catching herself on the side of her seat as the wooden wheels rattled on the cobbled street.

He waved a dismissive hand at her. "Enough time to handle you and your master when I've dealt with this pompous upstart dismantling my province." He leaned back and pulled out a small pouch of fragrant herbs. Removing a pinch of leaves, he placed it in his mouth and chewed judiciously for a moment before spitting the resulting mush into a bit of cloth. A slight cringe proved the taste was foul, but she'd seen Papa do the same before an important meeting. Hygiene, he used to call it. Said the fresh smell made the wealthy respect him. She needed something to make this conceited buffoon think straight.

Niamsha rubbed a finger along the flimsy, too-soft paper Nijel had sent as an introduction. The Rogue Baron thought Nijel wouldn't hold him to their deal. A stupid thought if he'd known Nijel. But he didn't. Another Eiliin-cursed noble bastard, too focused on scheming to understand what they were really dealing with. No one left Nijel's ventures unless Nijel let them go. And he never let them go in one piece.

"You got a problem," Niamsha insisted, waving Nijel's letter at him. "Nijel got plans and you ain't in a place to help him."

"Your master's plans are of no concern to me, girl." The Rogue Baron scowled out the window of his carriage.

Niamsha considered the unopened letter. She didn't know what it said—couldn't have read it if she tried, likely—but Nijel had implied the baron would know her purpose without an explanation. So either the note contained blackmail of the sort the Rogue Baron wouldn't dare stand against, or...

"I s'pect that ain't true." Niamsha offered the letter again. "Nijel's got hands in all sorts a' gutter dregs, but he ain't the type to claim an ally where he ain't got one."

"Don't be obtuse," the Rogue Baron said, snatching the soft paper from her hand. "I had an agreement with your master, but the point is moot now. The work I requested is no longer of use and I no longer have the means to pay his price."

"That ain't how Nijel works."

He glanced at her, frown emphasizing the light wrinkles of his face. "I don't work for your master. If I say the deal is off, then it's off."

Niamsha nodded at the paper. Giving her a quizzical look, the Rogue Baron finally opened Nijel's letter. His eyes flicked across the words, taking in the message as easily as a bar wench collected spare coins from careless patrons. He paused at the end, fingers clenching around the edges of the paper.

"He claims I owe him a debt?" The Rogue Baron's voice trembled, the words sharp as knives. "How dare he lay a claim on *my* resources? I hired *him* for this work, and he was to act at my discretion."

He flung the paper in her face, the flimsy page fluttering in the air. Niamsha snatched at it and shoved the page into the satchel strapped to the inside of the door. She had no intention of being the next tongueless merchant Nijel created. And the only way to pay her debt to Nijel was to succeed at this job. One way or another. The Rogue Baron sneered at her.

"No one would understand the contents, girl. Do you think I'm stupid?"

"Ya ain't real—" Niamsha cut off her retort. He wasn't a baron any longer, but he still had more power than her. And that gave her an idea. Even an unseated baron had connections she could use to sow dissension among Nijel's gang. Maybe get Emrys free. She waved at the paper. "It ain't wise to risk Nijel's plans to the wind."

His hand clenched into a fist, eyes narrowed. Her hasty correction hadn't fooled him. Niamsha rushed to speak before he could strike her again.

"You got a problem, I got an answer."

He hesitated. "What solution could you have to my problems?"

"Revenge." She leaned back, the soft fabric cradling her form. And Emrys now slept in the tattered remains of furniture the Rendells had scavenged. She couldn't help him if the Rogue Baron wouldn't work with her.

"You can't believe I didn't think of *that*." The Rogue Baron turned away with a huff of annoyance. "If it were so simple, I'd do it. The high lord has friends."

"And enemies." Niamsha met his sidelong, critical gaze. "Ain't like he's been so pleasant to the poor. His recruiters taking people from honest work and laws sending too many to the streets."

And the Rogue Baron had been standing in Master Ferndon's home in the middle of the night talking about support if something should happen to High Lord Arkaen. Another useful piece of information.

Niamsha waved out the window toward the old guild district. "Guilds weren't without standing either, and they're done now. I know you've friends there."

"How would you know my personal connections?" His form tensed, one hand sliding to the gilded hilt of his sword.

She'd forgotten. No one could know she was in Master Ferndon's house two nights back. Clumsy mistake. But she could use it. Nijel already had a reputation in the slums for knowing what he shouldn't.

"Nijel's got ways. Ya think he sent me without a plan?"

"I don't like your people spying on me," the Rogue Baron said. "You work for me."

"Nijel ain't real keen on spying on his allies, 'less he has to." The lie sat heavy in the air. Surely he'd see through it. Niamsha continued before he could challenge her words. "But he's had…" What would Nijel say? Not "traitors to handle," but… "Unfortunate misunderstandings to resolve. Can't trust his allies, can't trust his plan. You been talkin' to the master o' the old glasswright's guild 'bout who might take over, something happens to the high lord."

The Rogue Baron crossed his arms, leaning back against the seat as he considered her. Niamsha scraped a fingernail along the hem of her tunic. Nijel might agree with her plan if the baron tried to verify her story. But if he did, she'd surely wish Nijel hadn't supported her claims. Another debt if she was lucky. Or suspicion that she'd turned against the Rendells. The carriage slowed to a halt and shook as the driver climbed down.

"Your master's network is more extensive than I thought. I'll have to handle him swiftly."

The Rogue Baron flipped a latch on the door and it swung open, revealing an enormous stretch of cobbled ground almost as large as High Lord Arkaen's courtyard. Beyond, a house plastered with every bit of delicate glass, gilded decoration, and carved imagery she could imagine sprawled to either side. Niamsha hesitated as he slid off his seat and out of the carriage. Did handling Nijel mean killing her?

"Get out here, girl," the Rogue Baron snapped. "If you've got a plan, let's hear it."

Scrambling out of the carriage, Niamsha dropped to the cobbles, her back prickling with nerves at the open space around her. He could have guards come from anywhere, and she had no allies here. No time to consider her own life now, though.

"I said, ya get revenge," Niamsha said. She needed more detail. Specifics of how to draw out the high lord's contempt for his people. "Ya gotta start with the poor. They ain't got your kinda power, but you don't either. Not nowdays. He made ya look a fool, you do the same. Hit him where he cares. High lord likes when people like him. Make 'em mad at him."

The Rogue Baron cast her a scornful glance and strode toward the wide, decadent steps that led up to the darkened wood of the door into his home. Enormous, sculpted hedge fences lined the outer edges of the yard, taller than Niamsha by a good three, maybe four, hand lengths. No chance of escape. Do this right or die. And Nijel would have Emrys. She hurried after the baron, the thin soles of her boots scuffing against the small, fresh cobbles. Not worn down enough to be smooth, bending her ankles at slight, awkward angles that jarred her balance with every step.

"You haven't told me anything particularly impressive," he said, stepping up onto the smooth stone of the steps.

Niamsha hesitated. It looked so smooth. Almost like glass coating the top of the stone. Stone that smooth underfoot, with that reflective shine… expensive and reckless at the least. The Rogue Baron tapped a booted toe on the top step.

"Have you never seen marble before? Gawk on your own time. I haven't got all day."

"I's just thinking." Niamsha tapped a foot on the stone. That polish. No way to add that after placing the steps. And the Rogue Baron's house was new-built since High Lord Arkaen took over. "Where'd this come from? You ain't got the like to make it, but there's no shops as sell this. Not in no amounts, much less this much."

"I can't say as I recall the specific trader." The Rogue Baron considered the steps intently, running his boot along the surface as if the stone had gained a new meaning to him. "I hadn't considered the availability of marble to the plebeians, but it's hardly rare in a noble's mansion. The high lord's great hall has marbled floors, and any number of the more prominent merchants as well."

"But that's old." The new-built temples didn't have marble, and surely High Lord Arkaen had the gold. Not that he showed much sign of caring for the quality of commoner temples. "What's the high lord built these last years?"

"What are you rambling about? The high lord's castle was fully refurbished under our previous lord. Maybe six, seven years gone by."

"That's as may be," she said. "But that ain't this lord's gold. That's his father's. What's *he* spent coin on? The new temple. That Aeduhm-cursed fountain."

"And a great number of charity programs for the less fortunate among our citizens." The Rogue Baron paced away from her, his expression swirling with ideas like a child's toy spinning on a table. "Education initiatives and training programs to assist those displaced by his banning of guild operations. I suppose I could hire some ruffians to disrupt those."

Niamsha gasped, her stomach plummeting. Those few programs were all the common folk had left. High Lord Arkaen's new laws had torn too many lives apart. She couldn't sacrifice the livelihood of everyone else for her own good. Not even for Emrys. But how to redirect his goals...

"Don't look so shocked," he said, striding to the door. "There's no benefit to me in killing commoners. I just planned to disrupt the events. Maybe pass some regional city ordinances to limit availability. If he can't keep his own systems running, he'll look incompetent."

Thanks the gods he was still thinking too formal.

"Ye'll lead him right to ya."

The Rogue Baron paused, turning back to her. "How so?"

"Formal laws and hired guards ain't real subtle," she pointed out. "Hirelings, they got no loyalty. Serve the pay they's getting, not the man with the coin. And you trust them other noble-born not to turn on ya first sight of a better deal?"

Niamsha considered the stone again. Marble, the baron said. No one in Torsdell had marble to her knowledge. Or at least, few lower born than the baron. Whoever sold this much of the stuff must be desperate for more business. Papa'd always said the only man you could trust was the one relying on your coin to feed his own.

"You find this merchant," she said, kicking the marble step as a reminder. "That's yer first ally. Turn *him* against the high lord. Ain't seen much fine glass headed to the high lord either. Not the decorative kind. I can find ya some of those artists. They'll want a piece o' taking him down. He gets common folk upset in public, making him look bad, high lord'll get upset."

A tiny, wicked smile crept across his face. "Now that I hadn't thought of, girl. I'm more prone to peaceful resolutions, but a little bloodshed could be what this province needs to see the path."

Niamsha's blood ran cold. That hadn't been her suggestion. What was he suggesting, and how had he come to that from her idea to charm the slighted merchants into protesting recent changes? The Rogue Baron chuckled, opening the door and ushering her inside. She didn't dare refuse. Not with him grinning like Marcas had when she'd made her offer. The gleam of his eyes left her shaking. He'd decided on this plan regardless of her intent. Or her cooperation.

He turned down the hall, hurtling them both toward a disaster she had no way to forestall. Muted reflections shone off the carved wood decorating the walls, as if Aeduhm himself had turned His radiant gaze on her blunder. But she'd decided, now. She couldn't avoid the Rogue Baron's plan. She just needed to make sure her debts got paid while she was in this. When Emrys was safe and Nijel satisfied, she could look for a way out. Not that anything satisfied Nijel. But she had to find a way.

The Rogue Baron muttered under his breath as he turned a corner, his musing casual. As if he plotted the murder of untold numbers of innocents every day. "A few neglected guilds and distance traders is all I need. They've enough guards to start a revolt over his trade policies. Minor, of course, but if the commoners join in..." He spun toward her. "Your master, Nijel. He can arrange for some disgruntled citizens to join the revolt, yes?"

Niamsha gulped air, her throat aching with the need to hold back a refusal. Her job was to stay by his side and report to Nijel. No chance for that if she pissed him off now, and if Nijel ever discovered this was her doing...

"He may can." She forced the words out. Her lips quivered, entire body tense. No turning back. Unless she could undermine the plan. "Do your part, Nijel may find something for ya."

"Ha." The Rogue Baron pivoted back toward the hall, striding with new purpose toward the far end.

Niamsha trailed in his invisible wake, her footsteps loud and dire as she walked. Whatever happened, it was her doing. She could have run. The baron's disgrace might have distracted Nijel. She might have gotten away, maybe even freed Emrys. Who knew what the Rendells were teaching him. What lies they were telling to sway him to their cause. But she'd stayed, determined to do the job Nijel had given her. The job he'd never have let go, no matter the added challenge of a deposed baron in place of the ruling nobleman he'd intended to use.

Pushing the guilt aside, she hurried her steps to catch the baron. Nothing to do now but see it through. And save as many as she could.

He will be known by the scars he bears at the hands of the People, yet he will bear them no ill will. Instead, he will offer his life for their protection.

— from the prophecies of the Chosen of the Four Clans

Chapter 14

Kìlashà stalked down the length of Kaen's great hall, following in his kai'shien's steps as the noxious odor of human fear assaulted his tragyna-heightened senses. His Seeker's power seared into his mind, flaring with a dozen possible futures he knew wouldn't—couldn't come to pass. The human female should not have been here. Something had changed. Again. And he hadn't seen it. His vision blurred, distant moments flashing through his mind.

Deyvan collapsed on the ruined stone floor. Blood pouring from three parallel slashes across his chest as he fell from the altar of the Ancient Spirits, used by generations of Kìlashà's people for worship and sacrifice. His vibrant, red hair hung in matted tangles around his pain-paled face and a heavy cough shook his formerly sturdy frame. The jagged edge of the remaining domed ceiling shuddered as a Drae'gon screech sounded from beyond the low doorway. Kìlashà spun toward the sound. No time. If the clan found him here, and Deyvan in this state...

The vision died as soon as it appeared, and there was no telling when it had been. But not past. Deyvan had never been to the temple of the Ancient Spirits north of Sharan Anore and had promised to keep his human subjects from reclaiming the land. A past moment not realized? Deyvan could have no reason to visit the Drae'gon temple he'd sworn to protect from desecration. Not while Kìlashà lived to guard it.

"Kìlashà." Kaen stood between the gilded double doors leading into the bare hallway beyond, half turned to watch Kìlashà's movement. A flash of vision.

"Dammit, Lasha, you should have told me!" Kaen stormed away, feet crunching on the loose stone of the path toward a distant keep. Toward Sharan Anore. "We could have done something!"

Kìlashà laid a hand on the rough, worn stone of the doorway, eyes glued to the blood-smeared altar. A foreign ache clung to his heart, his throat tight with a need to scream, or sob, or plead, burning with a pain that came from no physical injury and could not fade.

"I'm certain you've work to do," Kaen continued. A flick of his eyes and a slight nod of his chin indicated the doors the human female—Niamsha—had left by. She should have been at the temple. Her brother...

Kaen's words cut through his thoughts again. "I'd appreciate your input on the matters Brayden has brought before me, however."

The tone—a slight waver in Kaen's voice and the shaking of his hand—belied the words. Kaen needed Kìlashà's presence for comfort as much as information. But this meeting. This was important.

Kìlashà blinked quickly to focus his vision—and his thoughts. Brayden. Yes, the male noble who had signed the latest petition that had so aggravated Kaen. The strange, unfocused ache of his vision throbbed in his chest. Kìlashà's lips pulled back from his too-human teeth. A snarl slid out of his throat as he fought for the focus his kai'shien needed.

"If other matters are too pressing..." Kaen's voice held a note of tension and his scent altered subtly to include the hint of sweat that signaled concern.

"Naejiin, kai'shien." Kìlashà caught himself before he got further than the denial. Kaen's humans had known the Drae'gon mother tongue once, or their ancestors had. He couldn't risk giving them too many words to seek in their endless histories. The clans hid themselves for a reason.

He raised his chin, meeting Kaen's worried gaze with the calm assurance that so unnerved Kaen's humans. "I will attend your meeting."

Kaen hesitated a moment longer, then turned away with a quick nod, passing into the hallway and striding toward the variety of offices he used for meetings with his humans. Kìlashà sifted through the flames of his Seeker's power as he followed, sorting the ever-changing tongues of possibility as best he could. Kaen's words echoed in his mind. Work to do, if other matters were too pressing. He'd been wrong about Niamsha. Twice, if he counted the discrepancy from the fountain a few days before.

"You didn't warn me she'd be there." Kaen slowed his steps, giving them an instant of privacy between the regular postings of guards along the hall.

No need to clarify. Kìlashà knew well whom Kaen was speaking of. Clearly, Kaen couldn't get her presence out of his mind either.

"I am Seeking."

"Focus on Brayden. I need his support."

"You need the young female."

The words felt right. Definite and immutable. Like the possibilities Kìlashà saw of Niamsha. Except those changed for no purpose. Due to no factors he could ascertain. The fountain... that could have been anything. So minor a change held little meaning. But her presence in the great hall...

Kaen cast him a frustrated scowl, but didn't respond. Turning his focus inward again, Kìlashà scanned the available information. She'd been at the fountain, and she'd been most likely to go to the temple. He pulled a vision to the fore.

The female knocked quickly on the temple door, eyes darting to either side to watch the long, empty alleyway. Something, a shadow or flicker of movement or figure sneaking past, caught her eye and she froze. A scuff of leather from inside and she scrambled through the collection in her worn leather purse, pulling out the coins Kìlashà had given her.

Not entirely accurate. He followed the line for a day, skipping time in minuscule chunks to gather the information as quickly as he thought prudent. False information would be of less use than ignorance. There. He paused the moment, watching. Yes, if she'd not gone inside, she'd have left the city by now. The brother was the key.

Sifting through the visions again, he found the one that led her inside. The younger male was obnoxious, disregarding the sacrifices his sister made for him. But something here led her to Kaen's great hall.

"Don't talk like that out here," the male whispered. "Marc's been trainin' some o' the 'prentices in skills we may need. Just fer the last couple months, but he's got skills, Nia. He can teach ya anythin'."

"Training?" Niamsha pursed her lips in anger.

"I... look, I shoulda said somethin'." He paced away from her, toward the statue. "It's just, you been bent on me getting a trade, and I don't much want one. Marc says I don't got to. He can get me a place as a servant, all I gotta do is wash linens and let him know a bit of info once in a while."

"A servant?" Niamsha frowned, her face flushing. "I don't know, Em." But her voice sounded hesitant.

A clue. She could easily have followed in her brother's footsteps. A safe, comfortable life in contrast to the constant fear in which she lived. No wonder she'd prefer such a path. The importance the Ancient Spirits placed on her life could come to pass later. The full answer would hold more complexity, but he'd found enough to soothe his initial concern. The exact reasons held little weight while Kaen needed him.

Kìlashà turned his focus to the more immediate concerns surrounding the noble-born male Kaen needed to persuade, pulling new moments of possibility forward. Arrived just after daybreak, spoke to Kaen's sister.

Pacing in the third office. The one Kaen used for allies, but the male's posture and muttering spoke of disgust.

They paused by the door and Kìlashà nodded in response to Kaen's quick glance of confirmation. Nothing of value would change by waiting.

Kaen pulled the door open and stepped into the room, waving the male inside to a chair. Kìlashà swept his gaze over Brayden, noting the details that might affect these negotiations. Short hair, square face with hints of the extra fullness common among humans of his stature. Well-fitted clothes that said he'd accepted his loss of fitness with grace.

The creases by his mouth were new. Not the deep, foreboding lines that Kaen said marred human faces when they were too used to displeasure, though. A resting expression of confidence, hope, and joy. For an instant, Kìlashà's heart ached for the pain Kaen endured as his kai'shien. Joy was not a thing well known to the Chosen of the Four Clans, nor to his kai'shien. But regret served no value here.

"High Lord. I'm pleased you found the time to speak with me." Brayden's lips turned down in the frown Kìlashà had so recently dismissed. He didn't take the chair Kaen offered.

"I apologize for the delay, Count Skianda." Kaen paused by his own chair, laying a hand on the back.

That choice held a significance in these negotiations, Kìlashà knew, but he'd never committed the dance of power humans played into memory. Something about sitting first being a sign of comfort, or callousness, or disrespect, or… he pushed the details away. Kaen could play that game without him. Kìlashà's value was in predicting the proper response to Brayden's demands.

"I had some delicate matters to attend to. Please, sit." Kaen gestured to the chair once more. Ignored a second time.

The new creases caught Kìlashà's attention again. He skimmed the timelines, dipping a mental finger into a dozen possible moments. The marriage this male had canceled… a loveless political operation neither had wanted for themselves. But not enough to cause this. A few new ser-vants. Human nobles didn't care for the lives of their hirelings.

Kìlashà crossed the room, disregarding the standoff between the two humans as he perched on the edge of the windowsill. Behind Kaen, a clear view of the room, easy to maneuver as needed should a threat arise. And if something he couldn't handle entered, the window itself served as an escape for Kìlashà and his kai'shien.

"I'd heard of your court this morn already. One could hardly miss the spectacle." Brayden laid a hand on the table before him, leaning forward as if considering whether to sit after all.

Kìlashà snagged the movement, diving into the depths of his power. If he sat…

Brayden sank into the chair with a sigh, all his pomp fading as he fixed Kaen with a disgusted grimace. "Arkie, you knew better than that. Oskari has too many friends to just toss him to the wolves."

No, the colors were too dull for that, Brayden's sapphire tunic closer to a slate blue-gray. A quick sweep of the past identified the error. They'd never been close enough as children for Brayden to utilize the nickname Kaen so hated. New facts, new possibilities.

Brayden sank into the chair, a new, deeper scowl etching into his face. "I've every desire to support my liege lord, but those actions are dangerous. While Baron Weydert is hardly the most powerful of my peer-age, he has allies."

Kaen sighed, nodding in understanding. "And yet, I must deal with insubordination. Even you can't deny that."

No, that was—Kìlashà skimmed further back. Those conditions were too far removed. Ah. If Niamsha had not come, so that Kaen hadn't ques-tioned him and they'd arrived moments earlier to see the messenger leav-ing after alerting Brayden. He corrected the timeline again.

Brayden collapsed into the chair, running a hand through his hair in an unconscious mirror of Kaen's nervous habit. Kaen leaned forward on the chair before him.

"K—My lord, I know you've no love for Oskari." Brayden looked up.

"But chastising him in public will only worsen the unrest in this city."

Spirits curse him. Too slow. He'd missed the moment that mattered. Kilashà shook the vision off and focused on the discussion before him. Brayden still stood, leaning over his chair as Kaen had in the vision. Same words, different actions. Damn these foolish human conventions. A minor flaw, but he *knew* this one held meaning.

"And I assume you're aware of the reasons for his reprimand?" Kaen's voice shook with restrained fury.

"A tragedy," Brayden said. "But what would you have us do? She sacrificed to protect our province. As many of us did while you were off playing hero. What would have happened to *us* if you'd lost in the north, or if your little feud with your father had gone differently?"

Kilashà narrowed his eyes, sliding to one side to examine Brayden more closely. This tirade had no precedent in the possibilities he'd studied prior to this sun's rising. A handful of flares from his Seeker's power, moments of warning flashing before his eyes and blotting the room from his vision.

"It's been five years, Brayden. You're hiding behind excuses." Kaen's voice echoed in his head, far distant from the flickers of time that held him.

Brayden scoffed. "And you're dodging the question. Your ignorance of the girl's troubles is no more our fault than the consequences of any other sacrifice made to counter the damage from a corrupt sycophant *you* left on the throne."

Kaen threw up his hands in frustration. "You know that was complicated."

"Which is why I hate to do this." A dagger flew from Brayden's hand, burying itself into Kaen's chest before Kilashà could free himself from the vision.

Not enough clarity to the actions. False.

"I went to war for my own reasons," Kaen admitted. "I've made no secret of that. But you can't wish I hadn't opposed our old emperor."

"Of course not." Brayden considered the chair beside him, finally taking the seat.

Brayden sank into the chair. "I've every desire to support my liege lord, but this city needs stability. You've proven you can't offer that. I have to support Baron Oskari's claim to the throne."

But Oskari didn't have a claim. Kaen was adamant about that. False.

"Arkaen." Brayden ran a finger along the arm of the chair. "I've believed in your rule. As a child, I wanted to believe in you. But this is bigger than a temper tantrum. If you can't be prudent under pressure—"

"I'll handle Oskari." Arkaen stepped around the desk, perching on the edge. "Give me time. I've already assigned the barony to his son to minimize repercussions. Oskari has friends, but they don't want a war."

Brayden slid a hand to a letter sealed with green and gold wax, a wolf's head in stark relief on the seal. "Maybe we do."

Vague, clear coloring, but not enough detail in the total scene. False. But the pattern was unmistakable. Kìlashà snarled, pushing away from the windowsill.

"Kìlashà, stand down." Arkaen's sharp words were more plea than order.

He stalked forward, tilting his head to meet Brayden's widened eyes at an off angle and let the full, hissing threat of Drae'gon violence flow from his stance.

"Leash your guard, High Lord."

But Kìlashà could hear the fear. Earned, at least. Unlike the terror Kaen's humans had of his very existence.

"Kìlashà!"

Kìlashà tilted his head the other way, cutting off the lingering snarl. "A wise vassal would not threaten his liege."

Brayden's face paled and an instant of silence hung over the room. Then he nodded. "Some rumors are true, then."

"Kìlashà knows many things," Arkaen said, shaky voice screaming his insecurity at Kìlashà. "Tell me he's wrong."

Silence. Brayden dropped his eyes, examining the polished stone floor. Arkaen muttered a curse.

"Dammit, Brayden. You said yourself we've known each other since childhood. Tell me Kìlashà is wrong."

"I won't betray my high lord." Brayden stood, turning away. "But I can't support the volatility you've brought to this province. Give us an heir." He crossed to the door and paused, glancing back. His eyes fell on Kìlashà. "And stop this constant threat of war."

He stepped into the hall, leaving Kìlashà alone with Kaen. The tension that had snaked through Kìlashà's body dissolved and he shook himself, collapsing into the chair Brayden had used with careless grace. His Seeker's power calmed, simmering in his mind once more. Brayden would hold to his word.

"Why?" Kaen stepped beside the chair, arms crossed, frowning down at him.

"I allow no harm to my kai'shien."

"Gods." Kaen threw his hands up. "I could have talked him down. Gained an ally, instead of alienating yet another of my lower lords."

"Brayden would not have followed you. Not at this time."

"You—" Kaen turned away, falling silent as the sentence rang through Kìlashà's mind.

"You don't know that, Lasha. You've never been good at human emotions."

"Fine." Kaen settled into the chair behind his desk. "I'll manage without Brayden. But we need to know what the girl from the fountain means."

Kìlashà nodded. Niamsha held a special place in the power granted him by the Ancient Spirits. Brayden had been predictable. Unknown, but only due to a failure of preparation. Niamsha changed the timelines without aid. Spirits-touched as only two before her had been: Kaen and Kìlashà himself.

The original Serr-Nyen *resistance to imperial rule was led by a woman who called herself Griffon, oft believed to be an estranged noblewoman from old Sernyii. She created a home for those who could not abide Emperor Laisia's rule and sought to negotiate a resolution without bloodshed.*

— *from* An Abridged History of the Sernien War

Chapter 15

Arkaen leaned back in the cushioned high councilor's chair, closing his eyes against the clamor as his fragmented lower lords' council leaned half over the central table to throw accusatory fingers at each other.

"Baron Weydert, the former, overstepped his bounds. It was within our lord's rights to remove him from his seat." His Lord Diplomat, Count Jussi Tenison, by the nasal tone. One of the few who called Oskari a friend without resorting to treason.

"I'm not arguing rights, Jussi." That one… probably his father's Lord Chancellor. Arkaen rarely dealt with the man, though he'd been loyal enough that Arkaen couldn't justify removing him from the post. So far.

Even with eyes closed, the four empty chairs dominated the scene. More than a week of daily meetings—sometime twice or three times before the sun rose again—had etched the room into his mind. Every meeting filled with endless arguments, condemnations, and the looming emptiness of the missing lords. Oskari's seat, halfway to the far door on the right, empty since the scandal in Arkaen's great hall. His son Rikkard had declined to fill the position. Brayden's chair, two seats to his left, had sat empty for as long as Oskari's. Four days ago, the Lord Merchant's vacant seat joined the silent reproach of Arkaen's actions. And this morn, Sayli had begged off, citing other duties that he couldn't help but neglect with so much time spent debating how to soothe the egos of his lower lords.

"What's done is done. Our goal is forming a plan of action."

Arkaen snapped his eyes open to catch the gaze of the new speaker. His Lord Marshal, the final member of his council and ostensibly general of Arkaen's fledgling army. Not that Arkaen had much of a true army serving under the Lord Marshal. Most of the province's seasoned soldiers served more for prestige than a desire to protect their home, and none had seen actual battle. If Arkaen needed an army, he'd be forced to supplement his small reserves with new conscripts. Or, more likely, head north and seek followers among the *Serr-Nyen*.

"My Lord Arkaen." The Lord Marshal leaned forward in his chair. "What thoughts have you? Our lord's council is in shambles and the rumors of Oskari's coming wrath grow. The safety of your people must come before your own pride."

"It is not a matter of pride," Count Tenison insisted. "Lord Arkaen made a statement. To rescind the order now is to abdicate any authority he has. We must placate the Weyderts without reinstating Oskari."

The Lord Marshal scowled, waving Count Tenison's arguments away. "My lord, you've fought battles. You know a losing side when you see one. What would you do if this were a war?"

A patently leading question, phrased as though Arkaen were still an untried boy playing at politics. Tension settled into the room like an impostor stealing one of the empty seats and anger roiled in Arkaen's stomach.

"Lord Marshal, if this were a war we wouldn't be sitting in cushioned chairs around a finely crafted table debating strategy while sipping fine wine." Arkaen's hands tightened on the arms of his chair as he fought to restrain the fury from his voice. "If this were a war, I'd be in the field and I'd target the head—in this case, the head of every noble-born bastard who demeaned my people by mocking and discarding the sacrifices made to stop a tyrant."

From the wide eyes of his few gathered councilors, he'd failed to maintain even a veneer of calm. Arkaen drew in a deep breath, holding the air against the ache in his chest until his thoughts focused only on the need to control his breath, pushing the anger into the recesses of his mind again.

"But," Arkaen continued. "I understand we'd rather I not paint the streets with blood. As such, I am open to suggestions."

A paralyzing stillness descended over the room. The Lord Marshal and the Lord Chancellor fiddled with papers as Count Tenison scanned the room, hunting for an escape. Gods damn it all. He needed Sayli. She always knew how to calm the room after he'd stepped too far from propriety. Arkaen rose. They couldn't offer proposals while frightened of his temper.

"This has been a long debate, and we're all tired." He smiled at them. "I hope you'll excuse my frustration. Let's step aside, take some time to consider our options, perhaps even seek counsel elsewhere. We can reconvene in four days after noontide meal."

"Your pardon, my lord…" Count Tenison fell silent as the attention of the room turned to him. The air seemed to vibrate with suspended anxiety.

Arkaen turned away from the table, drumming a finger in an almost certainly futile attempt to break the mood. "Unless you've a conflict, of course, Jussi. I'm happy to accommodate."

Count Tenison's face eased into a smile. "No, no, my lord. I only wondered where your sister was. She is a voice of—" He broke off, eyebrows shooting up in horror.

"She's a counterpoint to my impatience." Arkaen finished the sentence with a chuckle. "I'm well aware of my shortcomings in that, at least." He cast a long stare at the Lord Marshal. "A symptom of my time at war, where too great a hesitation quickly translates into death."

"But this is not a true war, Lord Arkaen," the Lord Marshal said. "Not yet."

"And I have every intention of preventing one," Arkaen promised. "Which is what Sayli has been doing these past hours. I have set aside too much to resolve this concern, and she felt it was time the other matters of the province be addressed. We've a royal visitor, for one, and at least five requests for my time as arbiter of various matters wait in my study."

"Such affairs must take precedence," Count Tenison said, waving the other two into silence. "Four days, as my lord suggests. We'll discuss what options may be effective."

The statement sounded more like a threat than an expression of understanding, but Arkaen nodded, crossing to the door. None of the others stood. He paused for a moment, door ajar, considering their positions. He'd be facing a united front when they reconvened. But maybe that was better. Their bickering accomplished nothing.

"Good eve, my lords."

Arkaen stepped out of the room and strode down the hall. Sayli should be in her solarium, watching the sun creep behind the hills to the south of Torsdell. A favorite pastime since she'd been a child and the one piece of innocence he'd convinced her to retain. He sighed, one hand reaching for the wall to run a finger along the bare stone.

The careless worries of a mere week past ran through his mind. To face a day where his greatest worry was the mild irritation that drove a handful of his more loyal lords to sign a petition objecting to the tax rate and requesting he sire a child. But those days had passed, as he always knew they would. With the loss of Brayden Skianda's support, his city grew ever more volatile. What reason could Brayden have for refusing to even attend council? The less support Arkaen had, the more unstable his province. If Brayden wanted stability…

Arkaen paused, thinking back over the last meeting with Brayden. He hadn't actually asked for stability. He'd asked for an heir and an end to the threat of war. Not even a whisper of financial concerns. Brayden was a complicated man, but Arkaen had no reason to think he'd refuse to follow *any* legitimate heir. And no law actually stated that a woman couldn't inherit. The Sentarsi high lords had simply never tried.

"And I suppose starting a war is technically an end to the *threat*," he muttered to the empty hall. "Although I doubt that's what Brayden meant."

Getting Sayli confirmed by the lower lords' council as heir might be difficult. But maybe not, given how Count Tenison had reacted. He only needed two of the three remaining lords, anyway. Arkaen chuckled at the idea. The Lord Merchant would be furious, and probably his father's Lord Chancellor as well. No telling what Rikkard Weydert would think. He hurried down the hall, turning the idea over as he passed the last few doors to tap lightly on the entrance to Sayli's solarium.

"Enter."

A clink of dishes and a muffled giggle from the other side. Sayli had a guest. So much for his plans of political scheming. In her solarium, Sayli would only allow a woman to visit. Anything else would start a scandal. But a woman likely meant one of the nobility, which meant he'd have to maintain the pretense of concerned, harried high lord.

Arkaen brushed the loose locks of his hair back from his face, forced a smile, and stepped inside. Sayli half turned from the rose-entwined bench where she sat pouring over a book of some form with her guest, the elegantly gowned Princess Prillani.

"Your Highness." Arkaen's smile softened into a genuine grin. "A pleasure to see you again. I'm delighted you're enjoying my sister's company."

"And why wouldn't she, Kaen?" Sayli waved him toward another bench set to one side, also adorned with carefully groomed roses.

The two seats overlooked a sheltered courtyard set in the midst of an extensive garden of every flower Sayli could make grow here. The expanse never failed to impress him. Some of her collection was local, but others he'd seen in the far north of Serni, and yet more he couldn't place at all.

"Well..." Arkaen cast a sideways glance at Prillani. "Rumor has it my sister is overeager in her negotiations and a bit flighty at times." He stepped around the columns defining the entryway and settled onto the bench, tweaking a loose lock of Sayli's carefully sculpted hair as he passed.

Prillani laughed. "I've found her refreshingly honest. And a great deal more astute at catching a hint than her brother."

"Always a better student at politics than I." Arkaen smiled at Sayli. "What adjustments to my ill-conceived plan have we negotiated?"

"To start, the entire court has learned how close Her Highness and I have become over our shared love of gardening." Sayli gestured at the plants.

"A far better pretext," he agreed. And a comfortable shift for him. A few visits to his sister at opportune times and he could avoid all the scandal of another implied affair without losing the chance to debate trade relations. He couldn't afford more speculation on his bedroom habits after the mess he'd created over Kyli.

"We'd also discussed a few matters of a delicate nature." Prillani considered him over the edge of the book she'd been sharing with Sayli. "My father has a natural-born daughter. In Osuvia, when a ruling family passes the throne out of their direct bloodline, they forfeit all claim to those lands and titles. But my father, naturally loving his true-born child, wants a comfortable life for her. Perhaps a life as wife of an ally's liege."

Arkaen tensed, his hand clutching at the edge of the bench as he turned to consider the two women. Of course Sayli had tried to negotiate a wedding for him. She'd never been prone to relinquishing a cause.

"And I'm sure Sayli has told you that I have no love for using marriage as an exchange of goods."

"Kaen, it's not like that." Sayli reached up a hand to forestall his objections. "She wants a comfortable life in an interesting new land where she maintains her status. You need a willing bride to offer an heir, more so after the scandal you've created. Everyone wins."

Except Arkaen, because Sayli didn't know the sacrifice he'd be forced to make. Lasha might forgive him for fathering a child if needed, but swearing his life to a woman? Choosing loyalty to a wife he didn't even want to soothe the tempers of a handful of human lords who had yet to earn Lasha's respect? Had yet to even try. And he wouldn't—couldn't marry someone without sacrificing his relationship with Lasha. Bad enough he took women to bed. He'd never ask someone to commit to a marriage he had no intention of honoring.

Arkaen sighed, leaning back. "We've talked about this, Sayli. It was not appropriate for you to negotiate behind my back."

"I think perhaps you've misunderstood," Prillani said. "This isn't simply a trade deal. Osuvia desires a closer bond with her southern neighbor. Commerce, yes, but also an exchange of ideals and a mutual defense pact. Wed our true-born princess to the chosen representative of their interests while my father is still young enough to utilize the connection. When our other sister inherits, the relationship will be established. And my father's true-born daughter sounds a good fit for your needs."

"Your Highness." Arkaen met her eyes, voice as firm as he could make it without risking insult. "With respect, you haven't even told me the girl's name. This isn't a marriage proposal or even an offer of alliance.

It's a business deal. I give you trade rights and an opportunity to make political friends and in return you give me a woman to take to bed. I've plenty of those here, and the Sentar ladies come with the benefit of offering a chance to *speak* to them before I commit my life to one."

"And I wouldn't have to arrange a marriage for you if you'd pick a wife," Sayli snapped. "You've lost Count Skianda's support and there's no telling what the Weyderts are up to. The province needs an heir for stability. You can't stall any longer."

He rose, anger simmering at the back of his mind. She only wanted to help. He knew that. But she hadn't seen the aftermath of the Sernien War. She didn't know what could too easily come from the schemes she was pushing back into the lives of his people.

"I will not engage in an arranged marriage." Arkaen paced across the cobbled space to stand in front of Sayli. "That is exactly the kind of heartless intrigue that got us into a civil war to overthrow a malicious despot."

"This is hardly the same thing." Sayli scoffed. "I'm not asking you to ban marriage by affection, I'm only asking you to make the right choice for your province."

"Like Kyli did?" Arkaen crossed his arms, challenging her to contradict him.

Sayli frowned, but after a moment her lips softened into something more like a disgruntled grimace. She sighed. "Kyli was different."

"But she wasn't." Arkaen waved a hand at Prillani. "Our royal guest would have me pledge my hand in marriage to a woman I know nothing of, who knows nothing of me or my lands. What if she's miserable here? There's no chance to send her home. A marriage is more than a contract."

"A pleasant ideal, Lord Arkaen." Prillani smiled, her eyes crinkling in a hint of amusement that changed her compliment into a condescending taunt. "That's never been the way of things. Not in Osuvia, and to my understanding, not here. My sister knows her duty. And if you desire to know her name, it's Milanatrith. Mila for short."

"I'm afraid, Your Highness, that I cannot accept the generous offer—"

"Kaen!"

He held up a hand to silence Sayli. "I spent nearly five years at war to stop this exact kind of political manipulation. I will not trade humans like cattle, and to the best of my ability, I won't let it be done in my home nation. The Laisian Empire does not recognize the validity of arranged marriages. Not anymore."

"My lord, I think—"

"You can't just announce that." Sayli rose from her seat, meeting his gaze with the fierce green fire he'd known from their mother. "Half the marriages in the entire empire were arranged in exactly this manner. Are you going to declare half the Laisian nobility unmarried? That's not how marriage works. It doesn't just end."

He smirked. "My point exactly."

"And I need to clarify once more." Prillani stood, stepping between them as if to end a childhood spat. She cast a kind—and clearly feigned—smile at Arkaen. "Osuvia has no desire to engage in politics with the Laisian Empire. Too bloody a history against too many former allies. We'd rather not be next. My people only desire an alliance, including mutual defense, with Sernyii."

He froze, the implications of her words settling on his shoulders like a strange, poorly balanced pack. He should have realized when she'd used the name at the reception. Not Serni, not the *Serr-Nyen*. With Sernyii. Osuvia didn't recognize Serni as part of the empire. Which meant he'd just spent several minutes bickering with his sister in front of a foreign power determined to support any future Sernien rebellion against his home.

Sayli shook her head. "Serni is part of the empire."

"Our southern neighbors at no point acquiesced to an annexation." Prillani turned her condescending smile on Sayli, voice softening with understanding. "I'm certain your history has taught you differently, but

Sernyii is an independent nation, conquered against its will, deceived into relinquishing its status at the end of a brutal war, and currently discussing a return to independence. My only reason for coming to your home was to discuss an exchange with their chosen representative."

"Then I'm sorry to say—" Arkaen cut off his response, thoughts spinning. Prillani hadn't come on her own initiative. Osuvian nobility believed Serni was planning a second revolt. If the whispered rumors he'd heard from the common-born of Oskari's reception had traveled to Osuvia already... "That my sister's involvement in these negotiations must end."

"What neg—"

"I'm sorry, Sayli." Arkaen stepped past Prillani and grabbed her arm, leading her away from the bench. "If this is not a Sentarsi negotiation, I'm afraid it's not your business."

Sayli fought his grip, her feet scraping the cobbled floor as she tried to force him to stop. Gritting his teeth, Arkaen glared at her and mouthed a warning. She couldn't reveal anything of his loyalties. If he could nurture Prillani's misconception that he valued *Serr-Nyen* lives over those of the rest of the empire, he might find the source of this talk of rebellion. The first time that misunderstanding might benefit him.

"You can't—" Sayli's fervent whisper cut off with a glance behind her. "You aren't a traitor."

He paused at the door, meeting her eyes with a quick prayer no god could have heard. If there were even any gods to hear. Beyond Lasha's Ancient Spirits, who wouldn't care about petty human squabbles.

"Sayli, I need you to trust me."

He pulled the door open, a swift gasp from the other side forcing him a step back to avoid the servant he'd surprised. Orange, red, and gold. One of his, a sealed message in hand bearing the crossed swords of Brayden Skianda's seal. Not the time, but he couldn't ignore Brayden. He forced a smile and offered a hand to take the message.

"Does Count Skianda require a response?" he asked.

The servant's eyes widened. "No, milord. Was left on me table, nothing but yer name."

"Very good. Thank you."

He paused, holding the message in one hand and Sayli's arm in the other, the false smile on his lips. His face ached with the need to break the pretense. One slight frown after receiving a message from Brayden and he'd start a whole new wave of speculation running through the servants and out onto the streets. After an agonizing stretch of uncertain silence, the servant bowed and ran off down the hall.

Arkaen offered the unopened message to Sayli. "To Kìlashà. Only you and him. And tell him I need his insight on Osuvia." He released her arm as she took the paper from him, a final plea for understanding slipping out as she stepped away. "Please."

"Of course." Sayli curtsied as low and proper as any of the lower ladies would, a rift of history and his temper lingering between them. "My Lord Arkaen."

She spun on a heel and strode down the hall without a glance back. Arkaen hesitated, guilt hanging on him like a too-heavy blade at his side. But he needed the information Prillani could provide. Another Sernien rebellion would threaten far more than his province.

"I apologize for the misunderstanding," Arkaen said, turning back to the room and closing the door behind him. "Sayli is rather stubbornly loyal to the land of her birth."

Prillani nodded, tension draining from her posture as she acknowledged his implied treason. As if a man who would turn on his own blood would be a stable ally. But then, Arkaen had betrayed his family more than once already, and Deyvan still trusted him. They'd made those choices together. Prillani had no such history with him.

"I hope we can make an arrangement." Prillani snagged the book she'd been examining earlier, crossing the distance to offer it to him. "I do like your sister. I'd enjoy the chance to be her friend."

Arkaen took the book, recognizing the text immediately. Sayli's newest acquisition for her collection on fashion styles. The pretext of friendship she'd concocted held more than a grain of truth. Another kernel of joy sacrificed to the greater good. Unless he could convince the Osuvians that Deyvan held nothing in common with the old emperor. But foreign diplomacy wouldn't matter if the empire fell apart.

"I'm certain Sayli would love that." Arkaen hesitated, pinned between the intensity of her gaze and the door behind him. "Although my position on marriage stands. More so under these circumstances, as the politics of my position are complex. If I were to wed a foreign power who began negotiations with a land claimed by the empire, but that foreign power refused commerce with the other imperial provinces... I'm sure you understand the optics."

"You play a difficult game, Lord Arkaen." Prillani turned away, pacing through the fragrant lane to run a finger across one of Sayli's prized gardenias. "My father couldn't believe you'd intentionally disrupt your home province to support the Sernien rebellion." She chuckled. "Even I was skeptical, but there's little other explanation. Deposing an already disgruntled vassal and driving away a loyal supporter in the same day?"

She laid a hand on the pillar and smiled at him over her shoulder. Arkaen flipped through Sayli's book, feigning disinterest as he processed the claim. The far northern rumors claimed *he* intended to start the rebellion? Gods, he'd played right into this without knowing. Had Lasha known? He must have. That would explain the sudden violence against Brayden in his study. And now Arkaen had the unexpected chance to find more information from much closer to the source. Lasha always said he needed as many facts as possible for a proper Seeking.

Arkaen smiled up through his down-turned lashes. "Well, Your Highness. The *Serr-Nyen* treated me as family. They've earned whatever respite from tyranny I can grant." He gestured to the benches. "Let's negotiate."

Coin may open doors, but only fear buys loyalty. A man that don't fear ya can be bought fer the right price, and no doubt someone can pay it.

— Thief's Code

Chapter 16

Niamsha stood in the frame of the open window, the cool air brushing the hands she clenched behind her back. The Rogue Baron, seated at a broad table he called his small-build work desk, signed another document and folded the paper into a compact square. He dripped hot green wax on the creased paper before sprinkling a pinch of golden dust and pressing a signet ring into the resulting mess.

"Take this to your master," he said, handing the message to a girl huddled in the enormous chair on the other side of the desk. "I'll send him the coin to begin his trade route once he's completed these tasks."

"Aye, milord."

The girl snatched the paper and ran out the door, her worn leather slippers slapping on the polished stone. Niamsha's own feet ached in the hardened boots the Rogue Baron had given her, unaccustomed to the firm, constant pressure of an unbroken sole. She kicked a foot against the hard stone to ease the pain, but froze as her foot connected. The Rogue Baron hated when she fidgeted. Her cheek still ached from the last time he'd reminded her to stand still.

The Rogue Baron settled back into his seat, not seeming to notice her transgression. "That's two fine-stone masons, a tailoress his sister fired, and near half a dozen far-traders persuaded to spread dissent." He glanced at her. "You've arranged the meeting with the glasswrights?"

"Yes, m—" She cut off the customary honorific, a subtle stab to remind him how much he needed her help. All this was so far beyond her expertise. If he cut her out she'd be dead, whether by Nijel's hand, his, or the high lord's. "Today, after mid-meal."

"Noontide," he corrected, scowling at her. "Have you been going to your language lessons?"

"A course." The slip in pronunciation made her cringe.

"Then work harder. Those mistakes will reveal us both." The Rogue Baron turned back to his papers. "After noontide meal will work well. Bring their leader back if you can. I'll have time to settle the details this eve."

Niamsha nodded. "Yes."

The honorific stuck in her throat again, her omission earning her a glare from the Rogue Baron. Her heart pounded at the look. So far her insolence hadn't earned her anything worse than a sharp reprimand, but she held no illusions that would continue. Better than letting him discard her as a useless servant. She hoped.

A sharp knock at the door pulled her attention away. A young man stepped inside without waiting for a response, his broad frame filling the doorway. At least, the lower portion. He stood over a head shorter than the Rogue Baron himself, though his features held hints of the same jawline and eyes.

"Father, we need to discuss these expenditures." The Rogue Baron's son, Rikkard, froze when he caught sight of Niamsha. "Alone."

The Rogue Baron sighed. "I've told you, Rikkard, she's a valet. You've never hesitated to speak in front of the cook or your sister's maidservants."

"I know where they came from." Baron Rikkard scowled at her. "She appeared out of nowhere, and you won't even tell me who hired her."

Niamsha shrank away from the look. All the power the Rogue Baron lacked hid behind that stare. Thank Aeduhm she had a reason to worm her way out of this discussion. The last thing she needed was the attention of a newly appointed nobleman who already disliked her.

The Rogue Baron rose, his height towering over his son. "This is my house, boy. I'll do as I please within it."

"Father, I don't want to argue, but I don't trust this woman."

Baron Rikkard leveled a finger at Niamsha. His lips pressed tight together, stress wrinkling his face as his hand shook. Niamsha paused in the process of stepping forward. She knew that feeling. Standing before Marcas, body trembling with a fear and desperation she couldn't imagine controlling. But here he stood, challenging the Rogue Baron at a height that made him look still a child, eyes set in determination while his posture spoke of the need to run.

"I want her out of my house," Baron Rikkard said.

Aeduhm's Mercy. Challenging the Rogue Baron over *her*. She couldn't let him throw her out. She needed this chance.

The Rogue Baron laughed, a fierce sound that held no humor. "Your house? I've protected this family for decades. I prevented you from being conscripted into the imperial army and saved your sister from ruin. This house only stands because of the work I did. I won't have you throwing my legacy away to appease a murderous usurper."

"You *lied* to me about Kyli." Baron Rikkard took a single step forward before stopping, closing his eyes in a clear attempt to bring his temper under control. "That's not important. I know you thought you were doing what's right. But it's not your decision anymore. *I* am baron." His voice shook, as if he didn't quite feel the truth of that statement. "I won't stand for you undermining my authority."

Dammit. She needed the Rogue Baron. But his son might be a decent man. Niamsha bit at her lip. If she failed with the Rogue Baron, Emrys was lost. These others, though—Tressa and her not-so-handsome husband and the children she'd played with before High Lord Arkaen stole the security of guild apprenticeships.

"As if you had any—"

"My Lord Baron." The words slipped out of Niamsha's lips before she even knew what she planned to say.

Both men stopped, turning to stare at her. As if they'd forgotten she was there. A power play, not about her at all. And that told her what to do. She raised her eyes, meeting Baron Rikkard's gaze. She reached for her temple training, supplemented by the Rogue Baron's tutor. She had to say this right.

"I apologize for the uncomfortable situation." Niamsha ran a hand down the rough tunic, her sweaty palm sliding with ease. "Your father and I were just talking 'bout my next tasks."

The Rogue Baron's gaze bored into her, but she refused to turn. This point needed emphasized. Too much chance he'd risk their plans by overstepping, assuming his lost title would protect him. Even if it protected him, Niamsha had no such guarantee.

She stepped forward, deliberately turning her back on the Rogue Baron, shoulders trembling. "Your father had a contract with my... master." The word stuck in her throat. She would not claim fealty to anyone, much less Nijel. But there was an image to maintain. "His recent argument with the high lord put at risk his ability to honor his promises. I's—am simply working with him to decide new steps to follow."

"You, girl..."

Niamsha spun around to meet the Rogue Baron's gaze. Eiliin's curse on his stupid pride. She couldn't afford to have this fail. He narrowed his eyes, one hand clenching on the edge of his desk.

"Have a meeting to attend, I believe." The Rogue Baron pointed toward the door, his voice sour. "I'll explain our plans to my son."

Niamsha turned away, sauntering with a tense, forced stride through the room. Niamsha swept a decorative brooch off a side table as she offered a nod to Baron Rikkard. Etiquette demanded she give some further recognition of his status, but she'd never bowed to a nobleman yet and had no plan to start. Her papa raised an independent daughter, and she intended to stay that way. Slipping her prize half up her sleeve, Niamsha stepped into the hall beyond.

The stone expanse still held a comfortable warmth despite the cool temperatures outside, the polished stone somehow holding heat from the fires burning in every room. Niamsha paced down the hall. No reason to go anywhere but the market where she'd planned her meeting with the remnants of the glasswright's guild. Scout the location so they wouldn't surprise her. Mid-meal—noontide, she reminded herself—noontide meal wouldn't be for another two hours and her agreement with the Rogue Baron gave her no other responsibilities here.

She wove her way through the wide, polished halls of the Rogue Baron's home. His son's home, now. Turning a corner, she paused before the first statue, a figure almost half again as tall as she was, towering halfway to the vaulted ceiling. One stone hand held a basket of flowers and the other pushed the carved hair away from the girlish face. Niamsha couldn't place the image. Not a goddess that she knew of, and for all the Rogue Baron's faults, rumor said he revered the true gods of the empire. Could it be some sort of hero from the past? But what could the flowers mean?

Passing footsteps made Niamsha jump, so engrossed in the statue she'd forgotten her goal. A woman half covered in flour in a white-dusted apron and thick, wool skirts paused and smiled.

"Our liege lord's elder sister," she said, nodding at the statue beside Niamsha. "Died at fifteen, poor thing, from a stomach illness."

"But…" Niamsha stared up at the face. He'd had a statue carved of a dead family member? Her mind drifted to the fading face of her mother, round, plump, and smiling. If there'd been a way to save her image so it wouldn't be forgotten... one thing she had in common with the Rogue Baron, then.

"Reckon you're new, yeah?" The woman didn't wait for Niamsha's nod. "Headed to the steward?"

"No, I ain't gotta see the steward." She cursed herself for the faulty speech patterns she couldn't seem to lose. "Been here a week. The Rogue—"

Niamsha cut off at the woman's frown.

"The old baron ain't never been a rogue," the woman said. "He may not like you much, but the high lord gave him reason to be bitter. You stay out of his way and you'll do all right. He got a job for you?"

She nodded, not trusting her speech to avoid another slight. Thank Aeduhm the woman didn't seem truly offended. The last thing she needed was to anger the Rogue Baron further by insulting him in his own home.

"Where you headed, then?"

"The market." Niamsha pointed in what she thought was the right direction, hand flying past the statue's carved dress. "Th—he said meet an old guild master, bring him back. But that ain't for hours, and..."

The woman smiled. "First time you ain't had a job to do? I reckon you've not got your pay, being only a few days in. Here." She dug in the folds of her skirt, pulling out a handful of copper lais and offered it to Niamsha. "Buy yourself a treat. You can pay me back when your own pay come in. End o' the week."

"But—"

The woman shoved the coins into Niamsha's hand and continued on her way, ignoring the protest. Niamsha clenched her hand, feeling with her fingers to decide how much. More than she could count without looking. More coins than she'd ever held in one hand. She opened her palm. Eight, nine... no, she'd missed a few. Twelve copper. Enough to buy a real meal, or maybe a sweetened treat like she'd seen children begging their parents to buy.

The thought of finally tasting such a treat made her mouth water. The Rogue Baron fed her well enough on day-old bread and grain-heavy porridge, but he had no reason to offer her delicacies. Even in good years Papa never had the coin to buy her sweets. A foreign, pleasant smile stole across her face as she hurried down the hall.

The sweet dribble of berry filling on Niamsha's lips left a guilty twinge in her gut. The temple where she'd sent Emrys served nothing like this, and she knew the Rendells wouldn't offer delicacies. He'd be lucky to get food from them. With a swipe of her tongue, she cleaned the last of the treat off and paused by the door to her chosen meeting place.

Shouts of drunk traders and angry serving women mingled behind the door into a comforting racket. Papa had come here once or twice to escape work after a difficult day, though he'd never let her come in and he's always returned home sedate. No sign of the craze she heard from the patrons within.

Steeling herself for the noise, Niamsha pushed the door open and stepped inside. Smoke drifted through the air, scraping at her throat as she crossed the room to a narrow table set against the far wall. A few scowls cast her way set her nerves on edge, emphasizing the poorly concealed mutters of the customers she passed. Niamsha stopped by the far table, tapping a fist on the wood as the tavern keeper argued with a handful of blustery men. The tavern keeper waved the men away, turned toward her, and froze.

"What ya want?" A scowl stole across the man's face. "Yer lord got some muck he needs someone lower'n you to handle?"

Niamsha glanced down, taking in her newly pressed tunic in a deep green trimmed with gold, and immediately realized her mistake. Too fine for a lowborn drink house, no matter that she felt more at home here than in the baron's home. But the Rogue Baron had burned her old clothes, and she hadn't the money to buy something simpler for this meeting.

"Ain't here fer you," Niamsha said. Not true, exactly, but close enough as an answer to his question. She wasn't ready to recruit these men yet. Not until she could prove her old comrades would follow her. "Got a room I can use? Meetin' some old friends."

She could feel the gaze of the nearest drinkers fall on her, and the weave of stillness that swept through the room, silencing the quieter—or more aware—patrons. Nervous sweat trickled down her neck, the stares worming under her skin. Nijel would have taken her head for drawing such attention. But this wasn't for Nijel.

The tavern keeper nodded. "Cost ya three cails, lass. An' I hope ya ain't got many friends."

Money she didn't have. But this she'd prepared for. Niamsha pulled out the brooch she'd stolen from the Rogue Baron, sliding her hand flat on the priceless metal across the table. She left her hand covering the metal, revealing only a sliver of gold. The tavern keeper's eyes locked on the glint of metal. He shoved away from the merchants he'd been serving and crossed to take her offered payment.

"This gonna bring the guards on me head?" His narrowed eyes were threat enough. If she didn't convince him, he'd call the guards himself.

"Baron's gold," Niamsha replied, pointing to the sigil emblazoned on her tunic. "Fer the baron's work. It's good money."

He stared at her, the tension in the air adding to the intensity of his look. After a moment, the tavern keeper flipped the brooch and examined the carved insignia. With a nod, he led her down a back hallway and opened a door for her.

"All I got," he said. "But fer this gold, I'll give ya a pitcher of ale and mugs as well."

"My thanks, goodsir."

She hadn't expected such generosity. The brooch was surely worth more than his price, but the effort to sell it cut that value in half easily. And any of the Rendells would have taken the extra value as payment for putting up with her. The man's honesty left a twinge of guilt in her stomach. She wasn't certain the Rogue Baron *wouldn't* come after him.

Niamsha paced the narrow room, the close walls hovering over her. No windows, one door, and the entire table with its long benches between her and any escape. Not that she should be looking for one, but thieves' habits died hard. Marcas's lessons stuck in her mind—the ones he'd taught and the ones she'd learned to avoid him. Always have an escape. Never claim power beyond what you could prove. Be useful, but not noticeable. Everything she needed to avoid here.

A serving girl slipped in the door, maybe a couple of years younger than Emrys. Her eyes widened at the sight of Niamsha, taking in the finely pressed tunic and leggings. The new, unbroken boots. Hero worship, or as close as poor girls ever got. Niamsha was a shining example of the stable, well-provisioned life this girl would likely never have. The life Emrys thought he was buying by joining the Rendells.

Niamsha took the tray and waved the girl out, pouring herself a mug of ale. The stale, bitter taste of the drink left a grimace on her face and a fire in her throat as a mingled cluster of voices drifted through the door. The first round of meetings to bring more under the sway of her new patron. Niamsha steeled herself, posing behind the far bench and dragging out the formal speech the Rogue Baron had insisted she begin using again. Proper talk demands respect, Papa used to say.

The voices echoed beyond the door, leaving a momentary pause before someone pushed the door open and stepped inside. Janne. Ferndon's boy. All muscle, fawning respect for the rich, and entitled cruelty, mixing into a bull-headed kind of charm that brought all the less savory members of the guild to his defense. Behind him, a handful of apprentices with bowed heads shambled into the room, looking to Janne for direction. Niamsha forced a smile, waving to the benches on either side of the table.

"Go on, sit." Her pleasant tone felt thick in her mouth. A lie, though she'd said nothing to contradict.

A few of the apprentices moved toward seats, but froze when they realized Janne hadn't done the same. Janne smirked, his joy at usurping her meeting written plain on his face, and considered the room.

"This all ya got?" He leveled a steely glare at Niamsha. "Even with yer fancy new place?"

"*Apprentice...*" Niamsha cut the insult off before she voiced it. Janne hadn't got his master's badge yet or he'd be wearing it, but alienating him meant losing the entire group. Maybe the entire guild. "Have a sit, let me tell ya what I got."

Janne scowled, his eyes drifting to the faces of his followers. He might gain some respect by rejecting her out of hand. Niamsha could only hope he wanted the greater sway of leading the group that turned on the old traditions. His pride ought to lead him into that decision, if she'd judged right.

Another form shoved past Janne before he decided. "I wanna know what she has to say." Tressa edged down the length of the table, settling into the bench as close to Niamsha's position as she could.

"Tressa? What'n..." But Niamsha was in no place to turn down an ally. Not even one who should be seeing to her marriage vows rather than sneaking out to talk treason.

Tressa leveled an accusatory finger at Janne Ferndon. "I'm a glass-wright's apprentice, same as him. Not my fault my master took ill. If one of our own has plans to save our trade, I've a right to know."

"She ain't one o' ours." Janne emphasized his point with a shake of his head. "You heard what she been up to? Thievin' for the Rendells, they say. Nia ain't no glasswright. She's a half-breed outcast."

Niamsha's gut churned with anger, her voice aching to defend her mother's blood. But Tressa had pushed back from the table, facing down Janne like she thought he might hit someone.

"Niamsha's father worked the best glass in tha city," Tressa countered. "And her mama was the kindest lady we ever knew. She set yer leg when ya fell, didn't she, *Jainy*. And never told yer father what you was up to to break it so bad."

Janne scowled at the nickname Tressa used, but didn't argue. Not like if Niamsha had said something. None of the guild's old leaders would listen to Niamsha. Not before, when she begged for help to save Papa, and certainly not after Master Ferndon had thrown her out. Better to let Tressa—accepted and loved by the guild—defend her mother's honor. No matter how it twisted Niamsha's insides into a mass of guilt and shame.

The other apprentices milled about in confusion, glancing from Janne to Tressa and back. No one expected two leaders vying for power in this group. And as much as Niamsha loved Tressa, she couldn't allow any leaders here besides herself.

"Past is past." Niamsha dropped down onto the bench, taking another swig of the foul-tasting ale. "Ain't here ta call names. Ya want out, door's behind ya. Want power, maybe some freedom, sit yer ass down."

"What power *you* gonna offer?" All Janne's bluster returned full force when he turned his attention back to Niamsha. A target he thought he could bully. "You been scraping coins from the streets, stealin'—"

"From tha bastards as tore down your guild." Niamsha leaned forward, catching as many eyes as she could. "Don't fool yerselves. Glasswright's guild is dead. Carpenter's guild, artist's guild... Ain't no one coming to save yer coin or yer high an' mighty *patrons*." She spat the last word as an insult, clinging to the memory of Papa turning down overpriced commissions in the name of honor and fair dealing. And the guild's rejection of him as a master when he did. But she needed that arrogance now. "No one, 'cept me."

"Then tell us the plan, Niamsha." Tressa sounded skeptical. Not that Niamsha could blame her. Not yet a fortnight since she'd been begging at Tressa's door.

Niamsha met Tressa's doubtful look. "The Rogue Baron."

The room erupted in exclamations of shock and Tressa shook her head, turning away. Niamsha threw up a hand to get their attention, but no one paid any heed. Janne, of all those gathered, narrowed his eyes as if considering the suggestion.

"I ain't saying…" Her voice died in the muttering of the apprentices. No one here would listen. The Rogue Baron had done too much to alienate the lower merchants for too long.

"What's he thinking?" Janne leaned back against the door, blocking any exit with no apparent effort toward that end. "Baron ain't got the power he used to."

"And why not?" Niamsha seized the opportunity. "High Lord took it from him fer arguing. Fer protecting our local merchants."

"That's insane, Niamsha," Tressa said. "You can't believe that. Foreign trade kept food on the tables. Rogue Baron took that from us. Half the guild's income overnight."

Foreign trade *had* been good for some of the glasswrights. The ones the guild had allowed that honor.

"Aye, Tressa." Niamsha couldn't keep all the bitterness from her voice. Not Tressa's fault, but surely she knew. "Yer papa was on the list. Got all the best o' the local glass stock. Mine… Buying at twice the price from foreign traders and selling barely above cost. Wasn't easy for all of us."

"No trade ain't good either," Janne pointed out. "Now we all fight fer the same few. No one's making anything."

"Exactly." Niamsha leaned forward, catching his eyes. "High Lord ain't buying, means he's setting an example fer his lower lords. They ain't buying, so tha merchants ain't, so on. Baron says the high lord's taking their money fer soldiers. That ain't helping us *or* the nobles."

"And the baron is gonna what?" Tressa demanded. "Conquer the province?"

"He's got a plan," Niamsha said. She could see Janne nodding in the background. Janne's father likely knew something of that plan already, from what she'd overheard in Master Ferndon's home. Niamsha frowned at Tressa. "I ain't saying he's helpin' outta good will. But bringing in good, honest trade, dropping taxes so we's got clients again. As good fer him as fer us. High lord don't care what happens to us, no matter he says he does. Ain't never spent coin buying our goods. Just trying to teach us, change us. Baron wants us to be who we are."

"You're wrong, Niamsha." Tressa shook her head, turning away. "The high lord ain't perfect, but he's doing the best he can. Can't just bring back something that died like that. Never gonna have the trade we used to. And I ain't gonna help you turn on a man as went to war to save the innocent."

She stepped away from the table, walking to the door with slow, reluctant steps. Each footfall tore into Niamsha's heart. Tressa wouldn't help her. No misguided pride between them and no sacrifice to protect Niamsha's innocent friend. A pure, unhindered rejection. And her only ally now was Janne Ferndon. Bull-headed and rude, but on her side.

Tressa stopped in front of the door, staring down Janne as he looked to Niamsha for guidance. Janne Ferndon, who mocked her mother's blood and stole her promised apprenticeship, looking to her for orders. The rush of power almost soothed the loss of Tressa's friendship. Almost.

"Do as you think, Tressa." Niamsha waved Janne aside, her voice too calm for the ache in her throat. "Ain't gonna hold no one against their will."

Tressa slipped out the door, casting a single, saddened look behind her as she disappeared. No time to mourn.

Niamsha turned to the remaining apprentices. "Now here's what the baron needs."

Emboldened by the growing resistance among the Serr-Nyen *people, disgruntled citizens from across the empire flocked to Griffon's side, taking the names of mythical beasts for the protection of their loved ones. Among these were wealthy common-born, minor nobles long overlooked by the empire, and even some sons of higher nobles, well-trained in the art of war and ready to whet their blades in the blood of a tyrant.*

— *from* An Abridged History of the Sernien War

Chapter 17

rkaen paced the confines of his study, the first hints of dawn peeking through his window. He paused by his desk to skim the letter again. The third in as many days, and each one more concerning.

Delivered to the hand of Arkaen Sentarsin—

An insolent opening that could be read as outright rebellion, and a contrast to the earlier messages. But Brayden had promised loyalty. Not acquiescence to Arkaen's demands, but if he'd planned a rebellion Brayden would have said so. They had enough history for that.

"Or I thought we did." Arkaen paused by the fireplace to stare into the cold logs set for the evening fire. No time to worry about what friendships he might have lost. He crossed to the desk once more, retrieving the letter.

*I write as a matter of urgency to bring warning of danger
to yourself and Sentar province. I've taken steps to keep
you apprised of the situation as I hear it beyond your walls.
Recently, I've discovered forces seeking to divide our
province for future occupation by an unexpected enemy. The
methods described for this effort are... concerning. Reports
tell me the work to equalize wealth between common-
born and noble families contributes to the effort, giving
our subjects the opportunity to challenge the demands of
their betters. Your combat-trained reserves are of particular
concern here, led as they are by foreign soldiers of a
former rebellion. As well, the temples offering education
to poor families are rumored to be soliciting peasants into
treasonous actions.*

Rumors the flameguard were corrupting his soldiers made some
sense. Sentarsi nobility didn't trust the common-born, battle-hardened
loyalists who'd followed Arkaen home from war any more than he might
have trusted a personal army from them. But temple lessons recruiting
toward a rebellion? Surely Lasha would have seen it. Arkaen skimmed
the list of Brayden's fresh concerns detailing recent unrest in Torsdell and
focused on the last paragraph again.

*This is a matter that must be seen to immediately. My
sources have revealed information I dare not send in writing
under any guard, and which I am reluctant to reveal even to
you, lest the accusations be true. And yet, I must send this
warning. If you've heard nothing of this, I may yet hope
my information incorrect. I pray you are as shocked by
these dangers as I was to hear the claims. I will hope for a
confirmation of your ignorance.*

—*Count Brayden Skianda*

Dropping the letter again, he returned to the fireplace and settled into
a chair. If Brayden was doubting Arkaen's loyalties, it was time to bridge
that gap. Frustration was one thing, and his reports on growing unrest

had demonstrated his continued loyalty. This talk of treason was another concern entirely. A knock at the door distracted Arkaen from his musings. A servant stepped inside at his call, a heavy tray laden with fruit, bread, and tea on his shoulder.

"Pardon, my lord." The servant offered a half bow despite the weight of the platter. "Her Highness, Princess Kitorn, has arrived and requested to speak with you when you were available. Shall I ask her to wait until you've broken fast?"

"No need, thank you." Arkaen waved to the low table set by his fireplace and rose. "I will need you to take a message to Lady Saylina before you escort our royal guest here."

He pulled the note he'd prepared from his desk and offered it to the servant. With a nod, the servant set the tray down and took the message, backing out the door. Sweeping the various formal requests and invitations into his business drawer, Arkaen pulled a key free. With a twist of the lock, he added Brayden's message to the pile of letters from Deyvan and paused at the top missive, dated three weeks prior on a messenger-bird slip. He pulled it free.

Kaen—

I've heard my cousin made a bit of trouble last month. Again. Try not to start a war this season. The weather's turning cold up there.

—Deyvan

Arkaen's lips twitched in a smile. Deyvan in his most pure form. Flippant, direct, and willing to tear the country apart for his kith and kin. But where *was* Lasha? He hadn't shown up to discuss any of Brayden's messages. Arkaen had been busy, of course, but Lasha could always find a few moments when he had time. Unless the mystery of the common-born woman had Lasha occupied.

"Not unheard of, when his visions take hold." His muttered excuse felt off. Lasha should have known of the messages before they arrived, and certainly this latest warning couldn't be meaningless. Unless Lasha knew Arkaen would respond properly without guidance.

A quick knock from the hall and his door opened to allow Princess Prillani into his study. Arkaen smiled, dropping the note from Deyvan back into the drawer and securing the lock.

"I hope I'm not intruding, High Lord." She nodded at his desk.

"Not at all," Arkaen said. "Simply reviewing the specifics of Serni's arrangement with High Emperor Corliann before our meeting. Please, sit and join me for a morning meal."

"My pleasure."

Prillani stepped over to the tray of food, selecting a slice of apple with the care Sayli might spend on choosing a gown. Watching her with a cautious eye, Arkaen tested the security of his drawer before collecting a folded map and returning to his seat. He waited for her to settle in a chair opposite before pouring himself a cup of the spiced tea.

"So, Your Highness. You'd expressed some concern about our trade plans." He offered the map. "I've outlined the sources of Sernien supply for the stronger metals. You'll see the suppliers we discussed are well positioned for trade with Osuvia, and too far from the rest of the empire for a breach of their contract with our high emperor. They should serve Osuvia's defense preparations quite well."

"I'm sure, High Lord." Prillani took the map, giving only a cursory glance to his indicated locations. "But that wasn't my concern. If Serni is committed to sending half its supply south, the commitment to us you've planned could hinder their options for their own protection."

"And this concerns Osuvia?"

"Well." She cast him a sly smile. "A mutual defense contract does Osuvia little good without the chance for our southern neighbors to defend themselves. How would they come to Osuvia's aid?"

Arkaen took a long sip of his tea, a smile playing at his lips. He'd caught her, hook and all. But Prillani was too smart to have missed the bait in his question. He set the cup down and examined the fireplace, letting the tension hang for a moment longer. The less sure she was of his agreement, the more likely she'd dangle the information he needed in an attempt to goad him into recognition of her suspicions.

"I've mentioned the obligations of High Emperor Corliann toward Serni. Any needs Osuvia had could be addressed to the imperial seat in Whitfaern."

"For external threats that may work." Prillani scowled at him as if he were being particularly dense. "But you surely know—"

She paused, watching him closely. Arkaen made a point of taking another long, slow drink of his tea. This was the moment. Either she would back off, or she'd admit the Osuvian involvement in Serni's unrest. He could only hope he'd sowed enough seeds of potential treason at their last meeting.

"Perhaps we should revisit other provisions of our contract, Lord Arkaen."

He bit back a curse, forcing a disinterested shrug. "If Your Highness wishes. I thought we'd settled any other matters."

"Osuvia prefers a more solid tie, especially when dealing with the native born son of a nation with such…"

Prillani hesitated, hand hovering over the tray of food. She chose a plump strawberry and examined it, as if the end of her sentence hung in the blemishes she might find. Not that Arkaen couldn't read her meaning as clearly as Deyvan's written message. None of the empire's foreign neighbors would trust a true-born noble from the old emperor's reign, and many of the nobility's sons had inherited their fathers' duplicity and corruption, as well.

She met his gaze, holding the strawberry as if to demonstrate her meaning. "Such colorful diplomatic endeavors in your past. Ink is so easily blurred by ambition."

"If I were prone to such responses, a blood tie would hardly aid you. Our late emperor shed plenty of familial ties at the headsman's block."

Arkaen couldn't keep the edge of anger from his voice. A quick breath and he forced a more polite tone. "Although High Emperor Corliann shares little in common with his uncle. To the pleasure of all."

"Surely not all," she replied. "Emperor Laisia reigned for too long to be devoid of allies."

For once, Arkaen could let a genuine smile cross his lips. "The *Serr-Nyen* are quite thorough assassins. With or without their homeland's steel."

"Intriguing."

Prillani popped her strawberry in her mouth and busied herself spreading butter on one of the thick slices of bread. She lifted the piece to her mouth and froze, catching his gaze across the table.

"I do hope that wasn't intended as a threat, High Lord. You've not eaten a bite of your own meal."

With a chuckle, Arkaen reached out to take the bread from her. He took a generous bite, eyes drifting closed at the hint of honey-sweetness in the butter. With a quick swipe of his tongue, he licked the last of the butter from his lips and met her gaze again.

"I was being polite. My cook is exceptional, and I've no reason to wish Your Highness ill."

Settling back in her seat, Prillani chose another slice of bread for herself. "Then I appreciate your generosity."

Arkaen finished the food he'd stolen, offering her the time to consider his statement. For all his denial, nothing could turn his response into anything but a threat to any family she sent to his lands. Not that he wished them any harm, but he wouldn't be blackmailed into a marriage any more than contracted into one.

"Well," Prillani said at last. "If you will not reconsider my proposal for joining houses, we'll need another form of surety. Our efforts to support Sernyii are already in place, waiting only on your word to offer our aid. This trade agreement is the final step."

"I'm afraid I've nothing to offer of such value," Arkaen replied. "I can hardly seek interest in such an alliance among the *Serr-Nyen* nobility. Our former ruler hunted them to near extinction. My sister, beyond her Sentarsi loyalties, has duties here. I'd gladly include a gift of Sentarsi war horses, but I can't think such would satisfy your concerns."

"Certainly not." Prillani scowled.

She'd clearly expected a different response, although he couldn't imagine what. He had no children, bastard-born or otherwise, as any noble in the province would have told her. Did she expect him to commit to some form of genuine treason to prove his intent?

"I will say, Your Highness," Arkaen said, lifting his teacup once more. "I'm rather surprised Osuvia took measures to aid the *Serr-Nyen* before speaking with me." He watched her over the rim of his cup. "If I'd been less inclined to their well-being, that could have been a costly move."

Prillani chuckled, his words shaking her from her frustration. "We're not so rash, High Lord. We have made our connections closer to your home, our resources poised in a more strategic location than the far north. Sernyii could expect our aid quite soon, should they need it."

An ominous statement if he'd ever heard one. Arkaen's nerves tensed, mind racing. If Prillani had people in the province ready to restart the Sernien War… but he had no way of being sure of that. She hadn't actually *said* they were preparing to start a war. Only that her people had made connections to support whatever Serni needed. Gods damn it all, he needed Lasha now more than ever. Even if Lasha were here, though, he couldn't have offered advice on this negotiation. There was no telling what languages Prillani might speak, and she certainly didn't need any *more* leverage over him.

"I have to wonder how your resources could aid the *Serr-Nyen* from within my Sentar lands." Arkaen forced a smile, hoping his fears didn't show. "Pardon my skepticism, but the *Serr-Nyen* have few connections here. Any needs they have are surely better served in their own lands."

"Ah, but we both know they have a very powerful ally here, Lord Arkaen." Prillani collected another apple slice from the plate, her actions once again calm and assured. "One who is working diligently for their interests. My resources are placed to aid that ally as needed. Upon confirmation that Osuvia will have a dedicated ally in Sernyii." She cast him a conspiratorial smile.

"And as I've said, Serni will gladly make a trade agreement, but no marriage will seal this contract."

"Allow me to speak more plainly," she said. "Rumors abound through your nobility. From talk that you plan to abdicate in favor of your sister to rumors you wish to annex the entire province to Sernyii. Osuvia wants no war on their border if it can be helped. Abdicate, allow your sister to rule, and take Sernyii as your land. Repudiation of the Laisian Empire's claims on your birth will serve to seal this deal for the time being."

Arkaen frowned. He'd heard none of those rumors. But then, Sayli had said something about Brayden's worries, and surely no one would bring the concern to him directly. Unless it were in a carefully worded, desperate warning sent under a near-treasonous salutation.

"There are reasons I've not abandoned my rule, Your Highness." Arkaen turned back to her, decision made. "While I appreciate the faith your offer places in me, I must beg time to evaluate the impact. You're welcome to stay as my guest as long as you like, but I may be unable to commit to this agreement without speaking to High Emperor Corliann at our next High Lords' Council in a month's time."

"Osuvia understands." Prillani stood. "I'm certain you'll see the benefit of our offer soon enough. Good day, Lord Arkaen."

Don't matter what ya born to, family's all ya got. Take care o'
family, they take care o' you.

— *Master Trieu*

Chapter 18

Niamsha hurried down the broad lane that led away from the Rogue
Baron's home. Another meeting, another day of half-truths and enticing people who'd scorned her mere days before. Stepping out of the alley,
she paused in the square beyond—one that used to be an empty square.
She plastered herself against a wall to avoid the bustle of merchants hauling goods to and from their stalls.

Food vendors on one wall, cloth and ribbons and flowers sold from a
handful of women a little further down. A new market square developing
at the edge of the Rogue Baron's home. A flash of color on a passing boy
caught her eye, and she noted the thin strip of deep green ribbon wrapped
around his arm. That was new. Niamsha scanned the crowd again, her
heart pounding at the trend. Every merchant sported some piece of green
cloth. Declaring loyalty to the Rogue Baron.

Slipping through the crowd, she paused by a makeshift stall of sweet
buns. One tray held a dozen pastries that oozed reddish goo, the thick
smell of sugar leaving her mouth watering. She'd seen the Rogue Baron's
cook hard at work over a similar tray once and hadn't dared to ask for a

taste. Pulling out a coin, Niamsha bought one and took a careful bite. Tart, flaky warmth filled her mouth. She froze, her tongue swiping the last of the jam from her lips. Amazing. And nobles ate this every day?

Crossing the square, she paused by a group setting up some form of platform. They joked and shoved, good-natured humor leaving no room for grumbling over their work. A new boy stepped around the side, dressed in a disheveled wig and oversized clothes that turned his common garb into a mockery of a noble outfit. And underneath, freckles dotted his face around the wide brown eyes of her brother. Emrys froze at the sight of her, lifting a hand in a hesitant wave.

"Em?" Niamsha glanced behind her, but none of the people nearby showed any interest in them. "I thought..."

He should be with the Rendells. Not that she wanted him in that filth and violence, but Nijel would never let him go. Emrys smiled, running to her with a boisterous grin.

"Nia." He hesitated, but she waved the insolent nickname aside. She needed to know what brought him here in this strange outfit when she'd last seen him apprenticed to Marcas and his slimy crew.

Emrys grinned at her again. "Nijel's got a plan. Got a place for me, a job, an' we can visit!"

"Ya shoulda run." Niamsha scowled. "Torsdell ain't safe no longer. Not with this mess. And Nijel can't be trusted."

"But... He loved yer work." Emrys waved at the crowd filling the market. "An' ya did well. I wouldna thought ta start this if my job'd gone wrong."

"I didn't—" She looked around at the market.

Glasswrights hawking their wares with more enthusiasm than she'd seen since Papa's last market, stonesmiths approaching even the poor to offer trinkets or negotiate sales. The food vendors, flower stalls, and herb sellers that dominated the main market square lined the walls here, as well. More vibrant energy than she'd ever seen. Enough common folk paced the square to keep every seller busy.

Baron Rikkard's complaints to the Rogue Baron came back to her. All those deals with quiet, terrified children. Not just hiring their parents, but turning the children, as well.

"He's been handing out coin to the poor." A bastardization of her own plan. Bribe the poor to hate the high lord. But it couldn't last. When the coin ran out… Niamsha dropped a hand to her belt pouch. Just twelve copper lais, mostly spent by now. But she'd never forget the face of the baker who'd given it to her.

Emrys stared at her, face twisted in confusion. "O' course. Soon as Nijel heard yer plan he put me an' the others to work on it. Near a third the city's talking 'bout the Rogue Baron's generosity. Say he's got plans ta save the province." He chuckled.

Niamsha met his smile with a cautious grin of her own. Emrys was too deep in this. He seemed almost excited by the prospect of the mayhem these plans might bring. Her plans. She couldn't ignore her part in this, and she wasn't sure she wanted to. The Rogue Baron's coin made people happy. But Nijel.

The Rogue Baron just wanted revenge. She could manage him, especially with the extra information on his plan. A few cautious reminders to the right people and the general glee at newfound wealth would be tempered by concern for the debts they might owe to a dangerous noble. But Nijel played a far more complex game than she knew how to counter.

Emrys waved at the group he'd been with. They'd begun some kind of play, hands flying wildly about as they exclaimed rehearsed lines.

"Gotta go. Stay and watch!"

Emrys ran onto the makeshift stage, freezing mid-step to throw one hand up in melodramatic woe.

"What ho, fair lads," he shouted. "Have ye heard of the great plague? The Fearsome Demon of Sernyii has spoken and his curse descends upon us!" He waved a hand toward High Lord Arkaen's palace.

The other players gasped, hands flying to their faces in dramatic unison as though to contain their shock. Niamsha laughed with the other watchers, but her gaze crept to the broad avenue that led to the high lord's palace. Emrys could be in a lot of trouble if High Lord Arkaen disapproved. Besides, she'd met the high lord's demon, and while he'd clearly earned the terrifying reputation he held, there was something about him. Something she couldn't quite place.

"But, Lord Baron," another actor replied. This one wore a finely pressed tunic of yellow trimmed in blue, but a single strip of bright red cloth wrapped around one arm. "If the demon wished us harm, our good and noble high lord would not keep him. Surely there must be a way to counter his evil spell."

"Alas, if only there were a way to send word to our devout emperor." Emrys turned to the south, staring into the distance as if pining for a lost love. "I fear his dear friend, once our true and faithful lord, has been corrupted by dark magic."

Another round of gasps from the cast. Niamsha smiled at the accusation, but she couldn't bring herself to join the laughter of the other watchers. If the burning red lines on the demon's skin weren't magic, what were they? And why did his hair move of its own accord? A thrill of fear shot down her spine at the memory. And his voice. She could still hear the trill as his lyrical voice had twisted a foreign word into a question only he and the high lord understood.

The heavy marching steps of approaching guards interrupted the play, the troop of actors scattering into the crowd. Niamsha stumbled aside as a man brushed past her, tearing her eyes from the interrupted performance. Ten men marched into the square, each armored in chain mail died a flashy red and orange and emblazoned with some symbol of a gold bird with wings spread. They carried short swords and circled the remains of the performance and its viewers. The leader's slow turn stopped as he looked at her. Niamsha's heart pounded. What could they want with her?

"You there." The leader leveled his sword at her. "Boy. Come forward."

Niamsha turned. Emrys stood behind her, face paled to an unnatural white. When she stepped to one side, the leader's sword didn't waver. Emrys stepped hesitantly forward.

"Wait." Niamsha threw herself in front of the guards. Mocking the high lord could earn him a terrible fate. She couldn't let them take Emrys. "Ye've got it wrong. It was me. Ya want me."

"Move, girl." The leader stepped around her to grab Emrys by the arm. "He's dressed for the play. Guard captain keeps the peace, by our high lord's will. He wants none of these common-born scum mocking High Lord Arkaen."

He marched Emrys to the center of the armed men. Niamsha's breath caught in her throat, chest aching with the need to stop them. To protect her brother. She'd promised Papa so many years ago. And they couldn't really hurt Emrys for being in a play, could they?

"Ye can't know I ain't part." She charged after him, stopped by a gauntleted hand. "The play's my idea. I put him up to it."

The leader sighed. "We've our orders, girl. The boy is the architect, and the high lord's demon has vouched for you, besides."

Niamsha froze. The demon had spoken for her? Ghost stories and whispered murmurs from her childhood and the Rendells rang in her head. The demon ate children. But Emrys was full grown near two months by now. The demon's fiery tattoos marked him as cursed by the gods, doomed to wear the lifeblood of his victims as scars on his skin. But why would High Lord Arkaen *or* his demon want her brother dead? Why would the demon send her to Emrys only to kill him?

The leader turned back, his men arranging themselves in a loose circle to contain Emrys. "My captain has spoken. We defend the high lord's honor. I'm sorry, girl. Say goodbye."

Niamsha stared, fists clenched in futile rage, as Emrys met her gaze. Whatever the high lord's plans, she'd see him brought down. She'd get her brother back.

⁕⁕⁕

"They stole Emrys!" Niamsha slammed the door of the tavern, all eyes trained on her. Rage and impotent tears warred for her attention. All her work torn down in one instant. For one man's pride.

"Who, Nia?" The tavern keeper pushed through the room to her side. "Who took yer brother?"

"The high lord's guards." She stormed through the room, vaguely aware that other patrons made room, cleared obstacles. Trailed in her wake like beggars drawn to coins. "He just—" A cough, a choked sob, and she cleared her throat to speak again. "Em was on stage. Just playin', ya know? Like boys do. Not meaning anything."

He'd meant treason against the high lord. She knew that. But this was wrong. Emrys wouldn't have done anything. Not really. He was too kind for the actions Nijel might have demanded. Not ruthless enough. Yet.

"Took me cousin, too," one man said, coming up beside her. "Was selling goods by the fountain, wearing a band for the baron. Next I know they's hauling him off to that new prison. Said too close to the tax table, thought he's stealing."

"That prison out west?" They couldn't have. The giant building that had taken over the old fairgrounds was only used for the worst. No one who went there came back, or so the Rendells always said. "They takin' our kin out to the killing pen they built just fer talkin'?"

But Emrys had done more than talk. He'd incited treason against the reigning high lord, and left alone, Nijel would have him doing more. Inciting true violence, as the Rogue Baron planned. Anyone killed as a result could be laid at her brother's feet.

"High lord's gettin' bolder." The tavern keeper's words drew nods of agreement and mutters of discontent through the room.

Another hardship to endure until the next high lord took the seat. But this lord was new-crowned with no heir. No change in sight. Unless she gave them one.

"Can't just let this go." Niamsha raised her chin, facing the room. Every patron turned to her, waiting for her words. Hanging on her orders.

A dizzying rush swept through her. She could ask them to do anything right now. She was their source of power, and they hers. No need for Nijel or the Rogue Baron to lend credence to her claims. *Niamsha* ruled this crowd.

"The high lord gone too far." She thrust a finger toward his palace. "We ain't gonna let it go. He's—"

"Taken me brother." A harsh voice from the door stole her power, Marcas striding in with his confident swagger. His matted blond hair pulled into a knot at the nape of his neck, he leaned over a table and slammed a fist down for emphasis.

"I saved that lad from temple," Marcas continued, focusing a glare at Niamsha. "Where his own sister left him to do her bidding. But I helped the lad, gave him a home. And the high lord done taken him. You lot gonna let *her* tell ya how to help the lad she abandoned?"

"I sacrificed everything for Em!" Niamsha's voice cracked, her voice taking on the shrill tone of a hysterical mother.

She pushed away from the table. But she'd already lost the crowd. One accusation was all it took. Marcas or Niamsha, and they chose him. No matter she'd been the one making friends in this tavern for days.

Marcas waved her reply away. "Ain't nothing. Did what ya thought was right, I s'pose. Ain't you as got me brother thrown in the traitor's jail."

Except it was her fault. If Niamsha had kept a closer eye on Emrys—checked on him more, or sent him further away, maybe—surely she could have protected him. Prevented him from joining the Rendells and ending in this mess.

"Em ain't no blood to you." Niamsha needed to say the words, knowing how petty it would make her look here. But she couldn't let Marcas claim her as kin. Not after everything he'd done.

"Now, lass," the tavern keeper said, laying a hand on her arm. "Ya know Marc ain't tryin' ta take yer kin. We all hurt when one of us is taken like this."

Marc. The same name Emrys had used in the temple. So Marcas was known here as he had been there. No wonder he'd been able to take their attention without even trying. How much of their loyalty had she ever really had?

Niamsha shrugged the hand away, the phantom pressure leaving a reminder of Nijel's touch in everything she did. Everything she'd seen. Emrys's pay and Marcas's arrival and the loyalty she'd held for a few moments. Even the sympathy her first cry had brought from this very tavern.

"What we doin', Marcas?" She hated to hand her power away, but if Nijel had sent Marcas, then she never had any to begin with. And refusing the help was begging for death.

"As ya said, girl," he replied. "We gotta answer the high lord. Got the baron's support?"

He gestured to her outfit, but Niamsha could feel the scrutiny. Her darker skin stood out in the room like a single light, a contrast to the Rogue Baron's reputation for hating foreigners. If Niamsha had the Rogue Baron's ear, no one could doubt he meant to do whatever the province needed. Except Niamsha, who had sat by his side enduring the insults and backhands when his temper needed an outlet.

"Aye." Niamsha nodded. Emrys needed her now. And the Rogue Baron wasn't any worse than the rest of them anyway. "He's ready."

"There ya have it, then." Marcas made a sweeping gesture to include the entire room. "Me master's got another. Fine lady from up north. Oughta be enough, between them. Take the throne from the basterd, get our city back."

The crowd rumbled approval, heads nodding, some reaching for the sacks they had beside them as if planning to storm the high lord's palace right then. But another noble as an ally? What game was Nijel playing? Niamsha's skin tingled, the hairs on her arms standing on end as a rush of nervous uncertainty filled her.

"Who?" She knew better than to question Nijel's plans. But this held too much risk. An ally no one knew about?

Marcas focused on her again. "Not ta worry, lass. Nijel's got it sorted."

"Ain't Nijel's life on the line," Niamsha said. "He ain't running in front o' the pack. Who's he got us workin' with that I ain't heard 'bout?"

Marcas's eyes narrowed, the anger she'd so feared under the Rendell roof rising to the surface. Here, surrounded by men and women he didn't dare alienate, she felt almost safe. He might hunt her down later—would try, no doubt—but while she stayed among those he needed, he couldn't lay a finger on her.

The door pushed open, allowing another woman to step inside. "Am I late, Marcas?"

The polished voice sounded against the walls like a temple song in a shit house. Niamsha stared at the shadowy figure, her face hidden under the dark folds of her hood. Dark, the shadows of the doorway, no doubt, except—Aeduhm's Mercy. Niamsha jumped from her seat, eyes wide. A full-blooded Yllshanan in Torsdell. She hadn't seen one of her mother's people in the city more than a handful of times, and not at all since joining the Rendells.

Niamsha took a step forward and stopped herself. How stupid was she, to be drawn to a woman just by the golden brown color of her skin? This lady held all the pomp and arrogance of any noble Niamsha had ever seen, despite the lower quality of her garb. Nobles were all alike. Weren't they?

The woman caught sight of Niamsha and smiled. "Is this her? What a beautiful woman, even if sullied by your imperial blood. Nijel did say her Yllshanan roots were strong." She strode forward, offering a hand. "My lady would be pleased to meet you when this unfortunate business is concluded. Your master speaks quite highly of your skills."

Speechless, Niamsha took the woman's hand. Nijel spoke highly of her skills? She hadn't known Nijel knew much about her at all before Marcas recruited Emrys. How long had he been watching her? What plans did he have for Niamsha and this foreign—not lady. Was she just a servant, with manners and speech like any Laisian noble? The woman waited a moment longer for a response, then cast a glance at Marcas.

"Are we prepared? My lady has taken what steps she can to ensure our agreement is honored."

"Aye," Marcas said. "Nijel's ready, soon as the baron makes his first move. An' that's up ta little Nia there."

Niamsha swallowed the lump filling her throat, forcing the thoughts through her mind. Nijel had an Yllshanan noble ready to support this rebellion. And they were waiting on her. No easy, bloodless way out of this now.

Niamsha pulled her hand back from the woman, straightening to as much of a stance of confidence as she could manage. "Baron's ready."

But Niamsha never would be.

As more angry imperials joined the movement, Griffon sought to use her newfound support to draw Emperor Laisia to the negotiating table. But the emperor saw this as a betrayal from all sides and sent assassins to the planned parley. Griffon barely escaped with her life and most of her commanders were killed. Her power transferred to a born imperial as a consequence of her deadly error.

— *from* An Abridged History of the Sernien War

Chapter 19

Arkaen gave a tug on his chestnut mare's cinch, the leather strap biting into his hand as he grunted. Footsteps behind him made him glance back. Sayli strode across the courtyard, dressed in a formal skirt and blouse with her face set in a scowl.

"Where in Eiliin's cursed gaze do you think you're going?" She stopped beside him, arms crossed. "You've matters to attend here."

"I've already told you. I need to speak with Brayden," he said. "That latest message bears an immediate response."

"And I've told you not to demean the seat of the high lord by pandering to lords who've rejected the legitimacy of your rule." Sayli tapped a foot in frustration. "Travel to his estate, even his house in town, is not appropriate. It's like you're challenging your lower lords to call Tribune."

"You can't think that's what Brayden meant." Arkaen pulled the reins of his mare over her head, setting a foot in the stirrup and pausing to meet Sayli's eyes. "He sent a warning. And if he's right… unrest is one thing, but factions in the city talking war? Rumors I'm bewitched by Kìlashà? I can't avoid a response."

"Then make him come here."

"He's made his decisions." Arkaen swung into the saddle. "Demanding he bow to my will is liable to bring more difficulties." He hesitated. He should find Lasha and get an opinion, but… if Lasha thought he needed guidance, he'd have come. Arkaen certainly didn't need to show Lasha a message for him to know what it said.

"I have to go," he said. "Brayden hasn't turned on me, no matter his claims. He's just playing from a different side. I have to work with him if we're going to keep this province in one piece."

"Fine." Sayli stepped to one side. "Just be careful. And take a guard with you."

"I can't. Most hail from father's rule."

Arkaen reached out a hand to tweak her hair with a quick smile. She'd understand his concern. He'd never found a reliable way to screen out the guards loyal to his father, who might choose Oskari in this conflict. Other than loosing Lasha on them, that is. That plan, while effective, would terrify half his province and start a rebellion on its own. But Lasha would have warned him of any danger. Sayli nodded.

"Then be more careful."

Nudging his mare forward, Arkaen rode out of the courtyard. The streets beyond his lord's castle were quiet, only a few wealthier citizens outside. Most backed away at the sight of him, cautious gaze watching him through down-turned lashes. Arkaen kept an eye on the citizens he passed. That hint of fear hadn't been there when he'd ridden out a few weeks before to see to Lasha's vision. He'd deposed a baron since then, bringing the threat of war to the forefront of everyone's mind. This felt more specific, though. Like they feared he might personally harm them.

Another corner and a crowd of young men and women bantering and flirting scattered at the sight of him. Arkaen pulled his mare to a halt. Should have brought his swords. But the image of the high lord riding through his home streets armed as for a battle could only stoke the fires of unrest. Confidence was the best image he could build.

He rode on, the few remaining people he passed seemingly prepared for his arrival now. Anyone on the street had already lined against the walls, eyes firmly stuck to the cobbles by the time he arrived, and he never again came across a group careless of his approach. As if some runner ahead warned every street before he turned on it. As if someone—or something—led him toward a certain goal. His muscles tightened, nerves strung for combat in the peaceful streets.

"I should turn back." He muttered the words under his breath, one hand rubbing at his bare belt loop as he turned the final corner to a broad alley that led to Brayden's home. Four men, barely older than boys, loitered in the middle of the street. Arkaen pulled his mare to a halt again, the scrape of leather on stone clearly audible behind him. "Sayli's going to kill me."

A deep chuckle from behind. "Nay, milor', I ain't think ya gotta worry 'bout that."

Arkaen half turned in his saddle to scout the threat behind him. Only two, though one was a heavy built man with thick mats of blond hair who filled a good chunk of the street by himself. That one would be tough to push past. The other boy with him, similar in build and coloring but much slighter, looked wide-eyed and terrified. One frightened child likely facing an early initiation and the leader. The four in front would be skilled enough to hold their own without direct leadership, then. Arkaen had no weapons but his wits and what he could re-appropriate. And Lasha, who wouldn't miss the fight if Arkaen needed him. He offered a grim smile.

"You gentlemen may want to stand down. I've no desire to take lives today."

Arkaen scanned the leader's figure. Two long knives stuck into his belt. The boy beside him carried one. A chance, maybe, to rush past and head home, but no telling how many of the others he'd passed were part of this ploy. Brayden Skianda's home was the safest destination.

"I'm afraid we don't share yer hesitation." The leader waved a hand at the four men between Arkaen and Count Skianda's home.

Turning his mare to one side, Arkaen watched the slow steps of his attackers as they crept closer. The two behind moved independently. The boy clearly too young for any experience and the leader preserved his safety behind the younger, less important member of the group. The other four, though… they moved as a unit, covering each other's flanks as they stepped forward. Used to fighting together. He'd have to break them up and do it fast.

The boy behind him charged. Dammit. Of course the child first. And the four in front were too far away. He spurred his mare forward, toward Brayden's home at the far end of the street. A sharp cry between them and they split to either side, knives poised to tear into his horse's flanks. Perfect. He could handle two pairs of two.

Arkaen pulled his horse to a stop, shouting a command in Lasha's native Derconian. His mare bucked wildly, as if trying to throw him. A difficult-to-train maneuver that required a well-bred, intelligent mount. Her final kick connected sharply with the boy behind her and Arkaen jumped free as she spun to one side, placing herself between him and the larger leader.

The four in front charged forward, but his momentum carried him to the right. Arkaen connected with one man closest to a wall, spinning to put his back against the stone. He slammed a shoulder into the hard wall, a jolt of pain shooting through his arm. But his opponent screamed, his partner's blade slashing through the thin leather tunic he'd worn. Arkaen wrested the knife from the man's hand and grabbed his throat, raising his eyes to meet the gaze of the man behind.

He slashed the first opponent's throat, shoving the body back.

"I said I'd no desire to take lives. Not that I'd hesitate to do it."

The other three shoved their comrade's body aside, spreading before him. More wary now than when they'd first charged. An unarmed man had just killed an ally. Arkaen would be cautious too.

"Levi!"

A glance to one side. The boy lay on the cobbles, hand reached forward toward the man Arkaen had just killed. Arkaen's mare still blocked the street with snaps of her teeth and swift kicks when the leader got near. She wouldn't hold long if the gang focused on her. But that would let Arkaen get away. He slipped toward Brayden's house, just a couple steps. Testing their goals. Two of the men followed him, blocking easy access. Not a theft.

"Get the high lord." The leader's voice, from beyond the clatter of hooves still.

Both attackers swiped at him, lunging together from opposite sides. Arkaen danced aside, catching one man's arm and dragging him forward to foul the strike of the first.

Combat habits settled into his bones, leading his motions before he evaluated the decisions. One man, the one he held, kicked back. Arkaen slashed his tendons with his blade. A third knife swung in from the side. Dammit. A distraction. Tumble to one side, dropping the moaning attacker he'd just held. Coming to his feet, Arkaen thrust with the short knife. Caught the second man—he'd followed the roll, of course—in the balls. He grabbed the falling body, using it as a shield as he spun to face the final member of the four. Swift kick behind, thick heel of his riding boot connecting with someone's face. Slash the man he held's throat. No time for mercy.

Arkaen did a quick sweep of the field. The leader had slipped past his mare. The boy had run. Three of the four trained fighters lay dead. Decent. But he had no tricks left for these two. No allies to use and the leader's bulk wasn't all indulgence. Arkaen backed away, toward Brayden's home.

"Marc!" The last of the four shouted the name, pointing behind Arkaen.

He didn't turn to look. Either Lasha had come, or Brayden's men, or he was dead already.

The leader froze, face twisted into a scowl. "Another day."

The two remaining attackers fled, dashing under his mare's hooves to disappear down the street. Arkaen spun around and nearly collapsed in relief. Five heavily armored guards in Brayden's blue and silver ran forward, weapons drawn. He backed away, leaning against the wall as they approached, and called a second command to his mare. She settled immediately, trotting to him like an obedient pet.

"My Lord Arkaen." The first guard stopped beside him, eyes wide. "Are you well?"

Arkaen glanced down. His once-fine clothes were splattered with blood, his hand coated nearly to the elbow. The blade fell from his hand, bile rising in his throat. Gods. Another slaughter to his name. And where the hell was Lasha? But these guards looked stunned, paled faces filled with all the terror he'd seen in new recruits on the battlefield. Gritting his teeth, Arkaen pushed away from the wall with a dismissive chuckle.

He shifted his posture into the confident, war-hero swagger he'd used in too many wartime negotiations. "Fine, lad. Whoever owns this city ought to see to the safety of its streets."

The guard stared for an instant before breaking out in a weak laugh at his jest. Arkaen forced a smile, grabbed his mare's reins. The guards were all on foot. A pity. Arkaen's legs were weak enough he'd much rather ride. But that image would be the death of his camaraderie with them.

"Let's head in." Arkaen stepped into the street, turning away from the mayhem. "I've business with your lord."

The guards fell into step around him, two behind, one on either side, and one in front. A shield of innocent flesh between him and any further danger. Arkaen fought to maintain his composure, the swiftly drying, sticky blood leaving his clothes stiff and his hand clenching in disgust. A flash of memory made him smile. Lasha striding through the gates of Sharan Anore, hair and cloak still dripping blood from the carnage he'd sown among the enemies of the *Serr-Nyen*. Deyvan's soldiers had fled. Of course they had. Lasha had looked more demonic in that moment than in any since his transformation.

But only Arkaen had known how the blood clinging to his clothes and skin disgusted Lasha. How long he'd spent scrubbing his own skin raw to remove every trace of the event. Or that Lasha had burned those clothes, save the irreplaceable cloak Lasha had been gifted by his Drae'gon clan-mother. Yes, a nice, cleansing fire would be the perfect place for this outfit as well. Arkaen had no desire to remember the day he'd been forced to murder three citizens in his own streets, regardless of the validity of his actions.

Brayden's gates rose before them, more decorative carvings than true defensive barrier. As any loyal lord would maintain in his liege lord's home city. The courtyard was little more than a wide, open-air hallway where carriages could drop their passengers. Arkaen handed his reins to a stable boy and stepped forward as Brayden burst through the double doors leading into the mansion.

"My Lord Arkaen." He stepped forward, started to bow, and hesitated.

Arkaen smiled, waving the motion away before Brayden could stumble over his public oaths. "Count Skianda. A pleasure. My apologies for failing to offer proper warning, and for the unnecessarily dramatic arrival. I thought it time we resolve our disagreements and hoped you might have an afternoon to discuss. And, perhaps, a bath. In whichever order is convenient for you, of course."

"Yes, please, come in." Brayden stepped aside, holding the door. "I hesitate to even ask you to negotiate in such a state, but—"

"Nonsense." Arkaen stepped into the hallway. "I'm far more concerned for your furniture. Blood doesn't clean well."

Brayden hesitated a moment longer, then led him down the hall. Two corners of tapestry covered walls and they reached a single door that Brayden opened for him, ushering him into a small study mirroring his own. Piles of papers to be addressed on the desk, small fireplace, a handful of chairs. A quick wave from Brayden indicated a bowl of water set under a mirror—designed for long days spent at work, no doubt—as Brayden crossed to his own seat. Arkaen rinsed the worst of the blood from his hands and selected the most plain of Brayden's chairs, hoping the remains of his attire wouldn't ruin the plainer wood, and collapsed into the seat.

Gods, he couldn't imagine having stood a moment longer. If he had to maintain this facade for Brayden, also…

"Kaen, what happened?" Brayden leaned forward in his chair. "Are you all right?"

"It's not my blood." He met Brayden's eyes. Nothing but worry. No shock, no fear. Gods above and below. At least there was that. "Mostly. Someone didn't want me to visit."

"A relief they failed." Brayden leaned back, the slump of relief more genuine than Arkaen had seen from most of his lower lords. "What matters did you want to discuss?"

Arkaen tensed. The message said…

"You don't know why I'm here." Gods damn it all, that actually made sense. Nothing would draw him out like a chance to reconcile with an estranged ally.

Brayden's face paled. "They set you a trap, didn't they?"

"And planned to frame you. It would seem we have a common enemy."

"We've a dozen of those," Brayden said. "But few who would try to murder a reigning province high lord."

A true statement. Oskari, maybe, but he had little reason to frame Brayden for the crime. Certainly not since Brayden had declared his allegiance in flux.

Arkaen nodded, drumming his fingers on the arm of his chair. "Did you send *any* of the messages?"

Brayden frowned. "How many did you get? I sent one, to update you on what I'd learned after the Lord Merchant left council…"

"Three," Arkaen replied. "But it sounds like someone knew what you were doing. You've a traitor, and we need a united front. What does it take to sway your loyalty back?"

"I've told you," Brayden said.

"Broad strokes only. I need specifics. If I name Sayli heir?"

Brayden steepled his hands on the desk, considering. "Not sure it would get past council."

"The lower lords' council is greatly reduced." Arkaen chuckled. "And they're getting rather tired of my temper."

"I believe that was my complaint." Brayden narrowed his eyes across the desk. "I believe that's what's got us in this pseudo-war."

"All the more reason Sayli is the right choice." Arkaen met his gaze, unflinching. This was the moment that would matter. He could feel it. Brayden wanted to relent, and with an unknown enemy trying to bring them both down, they needed to watch each other's backs.

"And the unrest in the city? It needs addressed. Your people rely on you to protect them."

"That answer seems clear to me," Arkaen said. "Locate our common enemy, eliminate him and discredit his schemes, and our province will return to some semblance of stability."

"And that's enough for you? A semblance of stability?"

"Civil war doesn't end when the fighting stops, Brayden. True unity will take more years than I—" Arkaen hesitated. He couldn't admit his intent to step down. "Than either of us have any desire to admit."

Brayden drummed his fingers together, eyes focused on the wall behind Arkaen as his thoughts churned. The sticky blood of Arkaen's clothes slowly stiffened, closer and closer to dried and forgotten. Finally, Brayden sat back with a sigh.

"Name Sayli. And make me a promise you'll scale back the taxes. Too many are wondering what you want all those soldiers for."

A surrender if Arkaen had ever heard one. "I can do that. Anything else you want me to consider?"

"Your d— guard..." Brayden watched him with intense interest.

Arkaen smiled. "Do you know why I didn't consider you a traitor today, when I was ambushed on the way to your keep answering an invitation signed by you in a message sealed with your seal?"

Brayden's eyes widened. The thought hadn't occurred to him, apparently.

"Kìlashà tells me I can trust you, Brayden. He says that despite your frustration, you are loyal to the best interests of this province. And I trust Kìlashà."

"Thank the gods for that," Brayden muttered. "But he's a problem, Kaen. No one's forgotten the trade caravans from Mindaine he drove away a couple years back. If you can't at least keep him under control, he's like to do some real damage one of these days."

"Kìlashà has a reason for everything he does. And he's not a pet." Restating the fact stoked Arkaen's anger. It was long past time his subjects stopped treating Lasha as a plague. Not that the *Serr-Nyen* ever had. But Arkaen's people had never seen Lasha's truly fearsome side.

"I didn't mean..." Brayden's protest died under Arkaen's stare. He glanced down, shuffling papers around his desk with no seeming purpose.

Looked up at Arkaen. "You have to know he's…" Brayden trailed off again.

"Unorthodox?" Arkaen drummed his fingers once, grimacing at the sticky goo between his fingers.

Brayden stared at Arkaen's hand, eyes widening. "*That* needn't be resolved now. Let me offer my hospitality. Please, stay the evening and we'll discuss in the morn."

"My gratitude for the welcome." Arkaen shoved his anger away as he stood. "In the morn, I'd like to know what you've heard about Serni. I need to warn our emperor."

"Then—" Brayden nodded. "In the morn."

Brayden pulled a chord hanging along the wall and moments later a servant stepped in the door, waving Arkaen to follow. His feet dragged as the servant led him through the halls, exhaustion from his brief fight draining the last of his strength. Gods. A bath, a bed, and an evening to forget the politics of ruling. But the latter would be hard to find in Brayden's home. The servant paused beside a door, handing him a key before vanishing further into the manor home. He stepped inside, leaning back against the door with a weary sigh. A scrape of leather from across the room made him jolt upright.

Lasha sat on the windowsill, his cloak waving in the empty air outside and his pale, vein-laced hands planted on the polished wood. Arkaen caught his breath at the alien beauty of the pose. Lasha leaned forward a bit and cocked his head, giving him a sad smile as he looked up through the lock of ebony hair that had come loose and fallen over his temple.

"Gods, Kìlashà. Where—" He bit the criticism off. He couldn't handle a debate over what might have been tonight.

Lasha flinched as if struck. No, Lasha never flinched when struck. Only when Arkaen hit a particularly sensitive topic. His powers had finished Arkaen's question.

"I—"

"You were not in danger, kai'shien." But regret and a hint of fear lingered in Lasha's voice.

"Six men?"

"The leader—" Lasha froze, eyes sharpening into daggers. "Six?"

Arkaen's blood ran cold. "You must have known. Kìlashà, the whole thing was a trap. The message, Brayden's concerns, everything."

Lasha scowled at the floor, his form immovable as though he'd become a part of the window itself. The pose spoke volumes of his concern, his eyes distant but his body tense, ready for action. Arkaen pushed off the door and crossed the room.

"You didn't see it."

"Your sister came to me with a message," Lasha said. "I had not the time to look. She said you had come here to pursue a peace, and I knew the next time you set foot in the city you would face resistance."

"But the message." Arkaen leaned against the wall, studying Lasha's face. Tense, but as closed and confident as ever. Except the flicker of shapes moving in his eyes. A sign his power was slipping from his control. Arkaen hated probing, but he needed to know. "You shouldn't need to read the page to know the message."

"Had I seen it, kai'shien, I would not be surprised by your fate." The bite of Lasha's words cut deeper for the fear hidden beneath.

Silence fell between them, Arkaen's nerves tight. If Lasha couldn't see something—if he was genuinely frightened of an outcome he didn't know—Lasha shrugged, his demeanor shifting between one breath and the next into something more like his usual confidence. A facade, but one intended as much for Lasha himself as for Arkaen.

"I have not spoken of it from a desire to avoid your concern…" Lasha met his eyes, sliding a hand to brush Arkaen's arm. A gesture of comfort Lasha had never needed. "Something taints my visions of late. It is minor, but the female from your fountain acts, on occasion, beyond the scope of my sight. It is in her blood, a call from the Ancient Spirits I have yet to unravel. She must have been involved in this message."

"Is it something that should frighten me?"

He was frightened. Terrified, heart pounding at the revelation. So much depended on Lasha's visions showing them absolute truth. But Lasha would know the severity of the problem. A quick shake of his head and Lasha pushed off the windowsill.

"All I need is additional information."

Arkaen could hear the lie, Lasha deceiving himself as much as anyone. But doubting his words would only make things worse.

"Of course." Arkaen smiled. "You're too good at that damned power to be really wrong."

Lasha's lips twisted into a wry smile and he turned. "Come bathe."

"I don't know." Arkaen leaned his head back against the stone wall, staring at the ceiling. "What if a servant comes by? Gods, Sayli doesn't even know I'm staying. And if anyone catches you…"

He didn't have to finish the threat. Lasha knew the stakes as well as he did. Better, since Lasha could see the potential outcomes through the visions of his gift. Lasha ran a hand along Arkaen's cheek. The touch sent a shock of pleasure through him.

"They will not," Lasha promised. "Brayden's men know not what to make of your arrival. Spend this evening with me."

How he could be so sure after missing the message and ambush… but Brayden's guards would have nothing to do with the woman from the fountain. And Arkaen couldn't have turned the invitation down if it had been made in front of the entire court of his lower lords. Lasha caught his hand in a tight grip, pulling him away from the wall. Arkaen sighed and let Lasha lead him into the other room.

The bathing chamber was dimly lit with a few candles leaving the two levels of elegantly carved stone mostly in shadow. Lasha had already filled the two-person, white marble tub built into the lower floor with steaming water. Of course Lasha had known to fill the tub for him. The scent of roses and soap filled the room. Lasha pulled him forward and stopped at the steps down to the main floor. He moved behind Arkaen and nuzzled Arkaen's neck as he pulled the shirt and tunic off. Arkaen got his own breeches. If Lasha got anywhere near that part of his body... Arkaen shivered in delight at the thought. Lasha nipped at his ear with a fierce hiss and he smiled. That was the fire he'd been missing with Kyli.

"I shouldn't join you," Lasha murmured with regret.

"Another time, love," Arkaen said.

He knew it was a hope more than a promise. They'd rarely had a chance for even this much time together in the years since Arkaen had returned home. Lasha didn't argue. Instead, he led Arkaen to the tub and stretched out on the stone rim. As Arkaen sank into the water, Lasha filled a cup with water and poured it gently over his hair. He let his eyes close again and Lasha ran his hands across Arkaen's scalp to distribute the soap. The gentle touch was more sensual than anything Arkaen had done with Kyli and a great deal more enticing. He'd never really wanted sex the way he wanted this.

"How long?" Arkaen asked.

He didn't want to know when Lasha would have to go, but he couldn't let himself be fooled. This was an oasis of love in a desert of politics and sex. He couldn't stay forever.

"Two hours." Lasha's hand trembled on Arkaen's hair and his voice turned hesitant. "I could come back."

They both knew that was too dangerous. If Lasha slept by Arkaen his power might not warn him fast enough when they were about to be interrupted by a servant.

"Better not, love," he whispered. "I'll miss you."

"And I, you, kai'shien."

Arkaen let himself soak as Lasha's hands finished with his hair and slid down to gently massage his shoulders. Tension drained from him like blood from an open wound, taking his anger, his fear, and his disgust with it. Arkaen felt paralyzed in the cooling water. The calm of this stolen time sapped any desire he had to move. A nagging worry tugged at his thoughts.

"Check on Sayli for me. If they sent assassins against me…"

"I will not allow harm to your sister." Lasha brushed his fingers across Arkaen's cheek and rose. "Be well, kai'shien."

Arkaen sighed, rising from the water as Lasha vanished into the other room. An oasis of love, all too soon stolen by the demands of his subjects. But at least they'd managed an eve together.

Eiliin, bride of Aeduhm and mother of the Divine Children, wept for those lost to Aeduhm's purge. She fled the eternal joy of her husband's table and gathered the lost to her, making a place of their own. Walking among her people, she took their angers, their hates, and their sorrows into herself. And so was Eiliin corrupted by the fury of her people and she ruled over Hell and all its lost souls.

— from the teachings of Holy Aeduhm and His Kin

Chapter 20

Niamsha paced on the lush office carpet, waiting for the Rogue Baron to arrive. He'd said wait, but her patience was running thin. Two days since Marcas had started pushing for action and she could only assume Nijel was getting impatient. No one who understood Nijel wanted to risk his temper. And who knew what the high lord was doing to Emrys while she struggled to get the Rogue Baron moving.

Loud voices echoed down the hall as she paced, and after a long moment, the door swung open. The Rogue Baron escorted Nijel into the room.

"Nisha, dear." Nijel smiled at her, the usual malice in his face tempered. "I'm quite impressed with your work."

"She's a nuisance." The Rogue Baron crossed the room to his chair, taking the seat like a king sitting his throne. "Now what brought you to my home? Our arrangement was to maintain a plausible distance. Avoid implicating each other."

Nijel's smile turned vicious as he shifted his gaze to the Rogue Baron. He took another chair, gesturing Niamsha to one beside him. Hesitant, she glanced from Nijel to the baron and back. But Nijel posed a greater threat than the Rogue Baron. Especially now that the baron held no title. She perched on the edge of the chair.

The Rogue Baron scowled. "I—"

"You, my lord baron, are no such thing any longer." Nijel leaned back, eyes narrowed as he stared the Rogue Baron down. "The only reason you've any power left is because little Nisha here had a brilliant plan."

"I retain my hold on this family, whatever my title," the Rogue Baron said. "And I could have you killed before you got off my lands." His eyes turned to Niamsha, fury lurking in his gaze. "Both of you."

Nijel laughed. "You wouldn't want that, Oskari. We had an agreement, and I've learned to ensure loyalty when needed. Why, all those inconvenient thefts our high lord's allies have suffered could be such a hassle if there were any evidence *you* were involved. Trying to build your standing for a coup, they might think. And I'd hate for the high lord to discover *you* were behind the forged message that just sent him into an ambush."

"I did no such thing. Had nothing to do with any of that!"

"Ah, but who will the high lord trust?" Nijel ran a finger down the arm of his chair. "The evidence and testimony provided by one of his attackers, or the rogue nobleman who has undermined his rule since he arrived, and has already defied him in public?"

The Rogue Baron leaped to his feet, taking two steps around the desk before he froze. His face twisted into a snarl, sending ice creeping down Niamsha's spine. He *could* have them both killed.

"What the hell do you want?"

"A great many things," Nijel said. "From you? An end to your delays. I'm sure Nisha has told you my plan. No proper rebellion starts without bloodshed. Choose a target and rile your followers to object to the high lord's activities."

Niamsha shuddered. He didn't mean a peaceful airing of complaints. She hated to think of the damage the Rogue Baron's stalwart supporters would cause. And the deaths the common people would suffer in an outright brawl between two powerful lords. How many livelihoods would they destroy before they came to some kind of peace?

"I'd have to find a reason," the Rogue Baron insisted. "Can't just send them to burn down some random tavern."

"The jail." Niamsha couldn't believe he'd ignore her suggestions again. She'd heard a dozen or more stories of unjust arrests since Emrys was taken. "I said, m—" She cut off the honorific. What was the name Nijel used? "Oskari. High lord's guards just arrested an innocent boy in the market square. He's got others in that jail, too."

Nijel's gaze settled on her again, leaving her short of breath. Aeduhm grant her strength. Nijel couldn't see her fear or he'd lose all his respect for her.

"And that is why I've let Nisha stay in your dubious care, Oskari." Nijel stood. "Clearly you need the guide."

With a snarl, the Rogue Baron lunged at Nijel. Nijel twisted away, throwing a hand into the Rogue Baron's face. A sickening crunch and blood poured across Nijel's hand. The Rogue Baron stumbled back, catching himself on the desk, one hand clutching at his now-broken nose.

"I expect an assault in three days. I'll mobilize my resources once you've begun." Nijel wiped blood off his hand onto the Rogue Baron's sleeve and turned away. "Do be careful, Nisha, dear. A young lady of your skills is quite extraordinary. I'd hate for anything to happen to you."

He strode from the room, leaving Niamsha alone with the Rogue Baron's burning rage. The Rogue Baron's stare bored into her, her skin itching at the threat. If she let him stew in this anger…

"What'd Master Ferndon say?" She couldn't think of another distraction. No better way to feel the full force of his anger than to leave before he dismissed her.

"That he doesn't trust you to have the best interests of the glass-wright's guild at heart." The Rogue Baron straightened, releasing his quickly swelling nose. "He said I should throw you out."

"My papa was better at glass than him," Niamsha said. Her heart raced. If the Rogue Baron didn't believe her... Nijel wouldn't tolerate failure from her any more than from any other, no matter what he said. "Near put him outta business. He holds a grudge."

The Rogue Baron gave a noncommittal grunt. "You'd better prove yourself able to deliver. You'll be leading this little rebellion."

"Me? I—" She cut off under his glare. Admitting her inexperience with fighting would only put her in a more precarious situation. But how could she get inside the jail to help Emrys from the front of the rebellion?

"You have a problem with that, girl?"

"Course not," Niamsha said, standing to brush imaginary dust from her trousers. With luck, that movement would hide her shaking hands. "I didn't think ye'd want me in charge is all."

He scoffed. "As if you'll do anything worth the time. But if it's your plan, you can face the repercussions." He pointed at the door. "Now get out."

She hurried from the room, closing the door behind her with a sigh. Out of the Rogue Baron's sight, she might have a chance to find a solution. Niamsha started down the halls, biting at her lower lip as she thought. She couldn't leave Emrys. The entire point of a distraction was to save him. Not that Nijel cared about Emrys, and certainly the Rogue Baron didn't, but she'd sworn. First to Papa, then to herself.

What choices did she have? She could ignore the order. She shook her head at the thought. The Rogue Baron would be furious at her refusal. He still had loyal supporters, including some guards. But if she objected to a rebellion, the high lord might protect her. Turn on the baron, swear they'd forced her to the work she'd done. She could prevent bloodshed, free herself from the Rogue Baron's power, and save Emrys. A better solution than any other. Except for Nijel.

Niamsha froze, the brightly lit hallway darkening into a threatening gloom beyond the open doors. Just the shadow of a passing rainstorm, leaving puddles scattered across the cobbled courtyard, but it felt almost as an omen from Aeduhm himself. Having committed herself to the Rendells, she couldn't escape into the safety of some noble house. Nijel showed no fear of noble power. And…

The realization hit like a slap in the face. If Nijel knew of an attempt to kill the high lord and the Rogue Baron hadn't done it, there was only one answer. She couldn't shelter in the palace of High Lord Arkaen while Nijel was working to have him killed. At best, she'd get dragged into the plot. More likely, she'd end up dead beside him. Nijel could offer her another choice, though.

Forcing her feet to move, she paced into the cool afternoon air. The Rendells had plenty of thieves. She'd never seen it as an asset before, but now she needed that expertise. She just had to find one of the Rendells she could stand to work with.

She paced down the lane away from the Rogue Baron's estate. Where could she even go? She couldn't just walk back into the Rendells house even if she'd known who to ask. And she didn't know. Most of the men she'd dealt with had more in common with Marcas than any of the more subtle thieves they told tales about. Eli might fit the job, but after his cowardice at her last job had left her to Marcas's mercies she couldn't bring herself to ask him. And any contact with the Rendell house risked an encounter with Marcas. Nijel could only protect her so far, as his parting comment implied. Though Niamsha had never understood why he took such an interest in her and Emrys.

The long, bare stone wall beside her made her pause again. Where *had* she gone? A glance behind. A door marked with a carved relief of two lovers identified the temple to Thirena, Goddess of Love, youngest of the children born to Holy Aeduhm and his cursed bride, Eiliin. She'd found her way to the endless street High Lord Arkaen's redesign of the temples had created. A perfect place to think. She smiled, striding with more confidence toward the far end. First the wheat stalks depicting Marpaessa's temple, followed by the temple to Her holy twin, Edros of the Day. Beyond those doors, the temple to Istvan looked far too serene for a place where Emrys had been corrupted. She hurried past the war-like uncle to the Divine Children, Satar of War and Justice, to knock on the final door. Aeduhm's holy temple.

An acolyte in pale yellow robes opened the door, and after a brief discussion he led her inside. The halls here felt nothing like those of Istvan's temple, paneled in light wood with light cloth runners on the floors as if trying to reflect all the glory of Aeduhm's Eternal Feast where the worthy sat in His gaze for all time. The acolyte led her to a small alcove set off from the main hallway by a privacy screen. Just large enough for the altar draped with a tapestry depicting Aeduhm's Feast and a kneeling bench set before it. Niamsha thanked him, stepping inside to kneel.

She stared for a long time at the tapestry, searching for words. How to explain all she'd done? Aeduhm demanded loyalty to His Word, and nothing in the holy scripture approved theft or cheating others.

"Holy one, I failed my charge." The words felt right. She had failed. Failed to protect Emrys, failed to live a proper life, and failed even to attend holy sermons with any regularity.

"All would fail such a strenuous demand." That voice. Soft, musical rhythm that haunted her for days after her encounter at the Lord's Fountain.

Niamsha spun in a clumsy fall, catching herself on the altar. The high lord's demon stepped around the edge of the privacy screen, considering her posture.

"I did not intend to frighten you." He cocked his head to one side in curiosity, but his hand traced patterns on the wall, revealing his agitation. "Nor to interrupt your false prayers. I am in need of your aid."

"I ain't got no plans to help those cursed by the gods, demon." Her heart pounded at her own insolence. But she couldn't agree to help the high lord's demon while sitting at the feet of Aeduhm's holy temple. Perhaps this would be her test. Her chance to prove herself worthy of Aeduhm's Table.

The demon's lips twitched into a nearly invisible smile. "Kìlashà."

"I ain't got time fer yer games." Niamsha pushed herself upright, turning away to straighten the tapestry. "I got prayin' to do."

"Your prayers will grant you no boons. And I have no time for human foolishness. I need your knowledge, and you need my skills."

Her hands trembled, upsetting the cloth again. She didn't need a demon, but a thief. Someone who could sneak into the jail and release Emrys while she created a distraction. He couldn't mean…

"Indeed, I do."

Niamsha turned again, meeting his eyes. The inky blackness seemed to eat away at her soul. Aeduhm couldn't possibly approve of this partnership. This demon had taken uncounted lives to support the high lord's ambition, and rumor said he delighted in seducing innocent folk into forswearing their values. And yet, something about him—his gaze or his posture—spoke of a desperation too familiar to her.

"You do what?"

The demon stared into her, his eyes an eternal hole from which she couldn't seem to climb free. The air came too quick, too light, leaving her near fainting.

"I do intend to assist in the release of your brother." He leaned against the wall. "Provided you offer the information I need in return. I will require your answers in advance."

Aeduhm's Mercy. He'd read her mind. Her palms slid on the cloth, sweaty with nerves at the thought. But… absurd. Mind readers were con artists, tricking their victims into giving away information and fleecing the target for a fortune once they'd established a connection. And the demon had all the information he needed on her desires. He'd known about Emrys at the fountain, and he'd spoken for her to the guards who arrested Emrys. Though how he'd known to do so…

Of course he'd assume she wanted Emrys freed. Soothed by her deductions, Niamsha leaned back against the altar. Sacrilege, maybe, but she had little chance at Aeduhm's Eternal Feast in her current state. She swallowed the lump of fear and wet her lips.

"What questions ya got?"

"Nijel."

Her hands clenched at the cloth behind her. Of course he wanted Nijel. The high lord must be going crazy trying to find him. No thieves' guild showed the discipline Nijel demanded for their safety, and she'd lost count how many times Nijel had warned them to clear out only hours before a guard sweep came by the Rendell house.

"You are familiar with this male." The demon's voice left no room for a denial. "You will give me information on him. Where does he come from, what does he do, and how does he threaten the stability of these human lands?"

Niamsha drew a deep breath. What could she say? What might he already know? Anything Nijel wanted kept secret would bring a death sentence, but if she could argue he'd already known, she'd have a chance. Nijel had spies in the temples, though. Marcas had nearly taken over Istvan's temple, and however holy the gods themselves, their priests were only men.

"Nijel ain't nobody." Better to say nothing. Nijel couldn't punish her for staying silent. But the high lord might, or his demon might take her blood for a snack.

The demon's eyes narrowed, his fingers resuming their agitated tracing of the wall. "While your statement is ironically accurate, I have said already that I have no time for human foolishness. Nijel holds sway over your actions, at least insofar as having involvement in sending you to the cur of a former baron you now serve. Who is he?"

"I…" Niamsha trembled under his gaze. "He… Nijel's a friend o' my papa's. Asked a favor."

"That is a lie."

She clenched her lips shut, afraid to say more. He knew something, but he wouldn't say what and she couldn't risk guessing. The merchant from Nijel's study swam before her eyes. Nothing could be worth facing Nijel's wrath.

"For what purpose would you lie to me?" He muttered the words under his breath, showing no interest in her potential response. "Not loyalty. And They would not have sent me to her if she knew nothing."

His focus snapped back to Niamsha, head cocking the other direction. Like a dog trying to understand a strange creature. An angry, confused dog with a reputation for violence.

"Your fear is quite strong. But you have no need to fear me, Niamsha Pereyra."

He pronounced her full name perfectly, even adding the slight pause before the final syllable of her last name so it sounded almost like he was reciting verse. Just like Papa used to. Fear clawed at her throat, skin icy as her breath froze. He couldn't know that pronunciation. No one knew. Only Papa had ever said her name that way. The demon knew everything.

Except Nijel. For some reason, he needed her information about Nijel.

"I ain't scared o' you."

"Another lie. I have not lied to you."

She dropped her eyes, shame flushing her cheeks. "That ain't… I mean, I can't talk 'bout Nijel. And it ain't about you."

He nodded. "At last, a truth. And yet you must speak to me, or your brother will not be freed."

"Emrys is innocent, and your bastard of a master took him for a show. Just to stir up the common folk." She glared up at him, anger flaring. How dare he hold her brother hostage against her actions?

"Fascinating." The demon showed no concern for her accusations. "False, but not a lie."

"What—"

"Your brother, Niamsha, has not the childish purity you would attribute to him." The demon's inflection, so matter-of-fact and almost kind when he said her name, gave her yet another set of chills. "He has engaged in any number of duplicitous and unsavory exploits, many of which have placed lives at risk. That he did not risk them by design is hardly complimentary to his intelligence."

"Yer wrong. Em's a sweet boy. Just needs a better hand."

The demon frowned. "I have not the…" He paused, eyes deepening to an eerie, near-sentience for an instant. "Ah. You intend to say a proper model of appropriate behavior would restore his good will." The demon shrugged, a strangely normal gesture that almost hinted at something human underneath. "You have confused your brother's temperament for the one you wish he had formed. But it matters not. Believe as you will. I have no objection to setting him free, if only you will offer the aid I desire."

Her anger simmered in her thoughts. He was wrong. Had to be wrong. Emrys was a good person. But, as the demon said, it didn't matter. She could free Emrys if she just convinced this monster to believe her. And she could use this creature to her advantage. He knew a lie, but she could tell him something close enough to the truth.

"Nijel…" What facts would be innocent enough? "Met him through the Rendells. He protects me. And Em."

"And his involvement in the ongoing hostilities in these lands?"

What *was* Nijel up to? She'd thought he just planned on carving out a little empire of thieves to rule from the shadows, but now… Alliance with a northern noblewoman? Planning to kill the high lord himself? How could that help the Rendells?

"Dunno. Not really."

The demon's eyes narrowed again. Niamsha rushed to add more before he called her lie again.

"He likes nice things. Ain't got many. I reckon he plans on gettin' more."

"You are skirting the edge of our agreement," the demon said.

Niamsha's heart thudded in her ears. So many things could go wrong. If he guessed what she was hiding… Nijel would kill her. Or worse, start the job and not bother to finish her off.

"But you have not lied. And I can hardly fault one so weak for her fear."

Relief flooded through her. "So ye'll help?"

"One final question." He stepped closer, his hair twining around his face in its first show of the terrifying power she'd seen in the fountain square. "Tell me the exact details of the moment you met Nijel. The smells, the time of day, who you were with, the location. Everything."

The meeting came back to her with the force of a vision from the gods. Crouching in the rain under a barely passable awning from a long empty shop, the stench of water-logged dung heavy in her nose. Her stomach aching, hunger crawling its way up her throat as if to eat her own bones in order to fuel her body for another day. And footsteps. Firm, confident, as a boy barely older than her waved his entourage to a stop before her. Blond hair pulled into a neat tail and pale gray eyes filled with concern. The words spilled out of her with a freedom she'd never felt. As if this demon offered an understanding none of her own kind could.

"And you were alone?"

His musical tones soothed the probe into a gentle prompt. But… none of this could matter, except the demon thought it did. If her meeting with Nijel could teach him whatever he needed to know, she couldn't risk letting him know the truth. Who knew what powers Eiliin had granted this creature. For clearly he spoke with Eiliin's divine speech, coercing her into a trust she could never have felt otherwise.

Niamsha looked up, forcing all her conviction into one last lie. "Aye. Em was at temple."

A flicker of something in his eyes. Almost a picture, shadows against the blackness where no shadows could be. The demon nodded, as if she'd confirmed something he had long suspected.

"Then we have an agreement."

"Ye'll set him free?" It seemed impossible that earning his help had been so easy. "Ye'll get the high lord to let Em go an' we can—"

The demon shook his head. "I said I would assist in his release. I made no promise to speak to my kai'shien on the matter. He has other matters to resolve, and the resulting conflict would cause too much un-intended strife. Lead your little uprising, he will focus on resolving that, and I will free your brother." He turned away, but paused by the door to cast a last glance at her. "Be certain you have a plan for your brother's safe haven or he will not survive the release. And see to your weapons' training. You have too much potential to fall victim to a spineless churl like Marcas Rendell."

The name cracked the last of her confidence. He knew. He'd always known about the Rendells. But then why ask about Nijel? Aeduhm's mercy save her. What was this thing?

A proper lady respects all her guests. A wise one sets spies upon them.

— High Lady Katrivianne Istalli Sentarsin

Chapter 21

Saylina swept through her receiving room, tweaking the table drape here, a cushion angle there, shifting the location of the tea and sweet cakes closer to the guest's seat. A perfect display of power and respect. She needed everything perfect.

A gentle rap on the door broke through her preparations. Saylina crossed the room to stand by the host's seat. Caela muttered a greeting and gave a deep curtsy, her skirts pooling on the floor.

"Please come in, Your Highness." Caela stepped outside, offering the illusion of privacy Saylina has requested.

Princess Kitorn swept into the room, her steps as precise and measured as if she were being presented to the entire court. Her gaze noted Saylina's preparations, pausing on the elegant tea setting, shifting to the immaculate couches, and settling on Saylina's hand-carved oak serving table.

A gift from Arkaen, and one of a dozen presents he'd showered on Saylina since he returned from war. Almost as if he couldn't stop himself from buying her fine, decorative items to hide—who knew, really?

Something about the Sernien War still ate at him, even now, and Saylina would bet anything that was the reason he'd demanded she leave during his negotiations with Princess Kitorn.

"What a beautiful sitting room, Lady Saylina." Prillani gathered her skirts to take one of the seats. "I'm so pleased you sent me an invitation. I'd hate for our little misunderstanding over your brother's negotiations to harm our friendship."

"Of course not," Saylina said. As if inciting treason from a loyal son of the empire was an insignificant action. Saylina forced a smile and took her own seat. "I must offer my own apologies, though. If I'd realized what you intended, I could have told you Kaen's response. I'm so sorry you couldn't come to an agreement."

Princess Kitorn hesitated, her focus suddenly turned sharp at the words. Perfect. Something Saylina had said must have hit a note of truth, which meant Arkaen hadn't agreed to everything Princess Kitorn had wanted. She'd known Arkaen wasn't truly the traitor his words had implied.

"No," Princess Kitorn said. "I respect your boldness, Lady Saylina. But if your brother had spoken to you on the matter, then you'd know that isn't precisely true. We only lack a few details to have an arrangement that suits us both."

Princess Kitorn's calm sent shivers down her arms. Or maybe it was her words.

"I never said that he'd spoken with me, Your Highness." A carefully phrased truth, given they both knew Saylina had intended Princess Kitorn to make exactly that assumption. "I only meant that I'm confident my brother won't engage in any treasonous negotiations."

Princess Kitorn laughed. "Well, negotiations we've certainly had."

But Saylina didn't miss the omission. Arkaen would be quite likely to discuss an alliance that didn't break Serni's allegiance to Emperor Corliann.

"But I'm afraid I can't give you specifics. Your brother had made quite clear that such matters are beyond the scope of your involvement."

A taunt if she'd ever heard one. So much for friendship built on mutual respect. But Saylina could hardly blame her. Arkaen had said exactly that in her solarium.

"Well, he's right I've no connection to Serni."

Saylina busied herself pouring tea, the anger of Arkaen's condescending dismissal rising in her throat. But his final plea clung to her memory. *Trust me.* Arkaen might not be the best trained politician, but he wasn't stupid. And somehow, fighting a northern war against his homeland, he'd become personal friends with Emperor Corliann. He wouldn't reject that friendship on a whim for a woman he'd shown no genuine interest in.

"What I wanted to discuss was actually quite different," Saylina continued. "I was curious about your gown at the reception. That's a style I hadn't seen before, with that deeply cut back and the narrow skirts. The Laisian Empire has such provincial mindsets after our recent unrest, we never get anything new."

"I see!" Princess Kitorn's eyes lit up, her posture relaxing. "Wasn't that dress beautiful? A gift from my father's new trade vizier. I hadn't been able to wear it before."

A symbol of trade. Saylina had suspected as much. Osuvian styles tended to shift with the seasons, and this late in the year the north would be too cold. But that meant the Osuvian king was trading far to the south of his realm, which would explain his concerns over the Laisian Empire's territory. Emperor Corliann had inherited several unpleasant policies regarding foreign trade.

Saylina matched Princess Kitorn's smile. "I'm delighted you chose this reception to share it. Is the style common in Osuvia, then? My ladies were quite scandalized by the riding slit and the cut of the bodice. No Laisian lady would wear such to a formal ball."

"No one seemed offended, Lady Saylina." A note of defensive pride clung to Princess Kitorn's voice.

"Of course not! You looked exquisite and entirely proper for your position. I'm so sorry if I sounded critical." But if Princess Kitorn was proud of that dress, it meant Saylina could likely get her to brag about its origins. "You and I had discussed how similar fashion is between Osuvia and Sentar, so I was commenting on how unusual such a difference is."

"Ah." Princess Kitorn settled into the couch, a smile stealing across her face. "Forgive my too-hasty defensiveness. I've become used to criticism." She hesitated a moment. "The style isn't native to Osuvia, actually."

"Well, that explains my confusion. Where do I send Kaen to get me such a dress?" Saylina took another sip of tea, cultivating disinterest. If Princess Kitorn knew how much she was revealing by sharing the origins of that gown... but the secret wouldn't be kept long, anyway. "Is it Mindanese? Surely Osuvia hasn't begun regular trade with Yllshana after the difficulties your nations have shared."

"No, no." Princess Kitorn gestured to the west. "There's a small island nation out in the western seas. They've the most intriguing cultures, actually."

"And Osuvia has trade with them? That's exciting."

Terrifying, actually. The western islands hadn't united under one ruler for generations. If they'd found one—and if that ruler had allied with Osuvia—the political shift of power should have reached her long before Princess Kitorn wore one of their dress styles to a local reception.

"The solitary nature of the western isles is legendary. I'm jealous you've been able to visit."

"Well, they weren't always forced to guard their borders so tightly," Princess Kitorn replied. "I apologize if it's an unpleasant topic, but you must know how your emperor's predecessor left everyone cautious."

Sayli dismissed the insult with a shake of her head. "Of course. Emperor Corliann's uncle put everyone a bit on edge." Saylina smiled again, leaning on the air of innocence that served her so well in Arkaen's court. "I didn't mean to veer into politics, though. With our trade routes so disrupted, I couldn't guess who has maintained access with the more distant kingdoms. Still, I didn't know anyone kept access to those lands."

"Recently re-established," Princess Kitorn admitted. "My father is seeking new allies of late. The Northern Conquest gave him pause, though—" Princess Kitorn broke off, clearly realizing her mistake.

Saylina picked through the fruit. "Everyone is seeking allies these days, Your Highness. I'm sure your father is simply looking out for the well-being of his realm. Why, even Kaen has been at it, talking to Mindaine for Emperor Corliann. Peace is so much busier work than war. But I imagine you know of Kaen's talks. He'd hardly represent Serni well by ignoring the imperial ally between them and the coast."

Princess Kitorn couldn't possibly miss the hint. Except, Saylina realized, Osuvia had an ally in the sea. If Mindaine found themselves facing the seafaring warriors Arkaen's tutors used to tell tales about, they may well be too busy. With Mindaine fighting the bestial fighters of the western isles and Serni allied with Osuvia, a challenge to Emperor Corliann's rule could be more severe than she'd considered.

"I'm certain your brother's oversight means nothing." Princess Kitorn sounded as determined to convince herself as to inform Saylina. "We were discussing trade, after all. Hardly a reason to bring another foreign power into the mix."

"As you say."

Saylina hid a smirk in the rim of her teacup. They both knew Arkaen's omission meant more than that. Now to lead Princess Kitorn into an admission of her long-term plans for Arkaen.

Reaching for a honeyed oat cake, Saylina froze at the sound of shouting from the hall. And, a moment later, voices outside the door. And Caela's cry of fear. Saylina leaped to her feet as the door burst open. A flurry of swords and rough men filled the room and she backed away from the carnage with eyes wide and heart pounding. What...

"Ah, My Lady Sentarsin." A blond man, a year or two younger than Saylina herself and far too young to command the surrounding chaos, strode into the room. "Exactly where you're supposed to be. I do so love when matters go according to plan."

"What are you doing?" Princess Kitorn rose, arms crossed in fury as she glared at the blond man. "This is not the plan. I've spoken to your lapdog and your errand girl. You're not supposed to be here."

The denial settled in Saylina's heart, a grim revelation. She gripped the windowsill behind her, staring at Princess Kitorn. "You wouldn't."

"I understand your anger, Lady Saylina," Princess Kitorn said, holding up a hand as if to beg her indulgence. "This is a misunderstanding. Your brother—"

"Is as good as dead already." The blond man smirked at her. "Or soon will be. There's been no misunderstanding, my lady, but don't be too angry at your new friend. She's a tool misled by pawns. Albeit a useful one."

With a wave of one hand, he sent his men forward to grab Saylina. Nowhere to run, and no use trying to scream. If they'd gotten this far into the palace, they'd either bought the guards already or lured them out.

"I am not a *tool*." Princess Kitorn stepped toward the man, intercepted by rough men and knives as she got close. "I am a princess of Osuvia and an avowed ally to your cause. How dare you disrespect me?"

The first group grabbed Saylina's arms, pulling her away from the wall and wrapping her wrists with a coarse rope that rubbed her skin raw in moments. Her instincts told her to fight, muscles aching to pull against the bonds she knew would hold. Saylina fought the urge back. Until she knew what this assault meant, her best course lay in waiting.

The blond man smiled at Princess Kitorn. "Well, dear, I did say you were useful. But you're beginning to grate on my nerves."

Another pair of broad-shouldered, hooded men grabbed Princess Kitorn, forcing a gag into her mouth as they secured another set of ropes on her wrists. She fought as Saylina hadn't, kicking and screaming into the cloth they'd shoved into her mouth. One man cursed, shaking a hand trailing the slightest amount of blood. Either Princess Kitorn didn't have the discipline Saylina did, or she knew something about what this meant. The latter was a chilling thought.

The leader stepped around Princess Kitorn's struggling body to examine Saylina. "You, however, are quite a prize. A pleasure to finally meet you, my lady."

"Hardly a proper meeting." Saylina forced a level of calm into her voice that her pounding heart and aching breaths denied. "I don't even know your name."

"And you shall not. I'm hardly such a fool that I would reveal that valuable commodity to someone who is still an enemy. Perhaps if we ever become friends…"

"You're making an exceptional first impression for that." Her sarcasm felt strange, a levity she didn't feel hanging in the words.

The leader chuckled. "And yet, friends are made in the strangest of places. Take these, for instance." He waved at the men holding her. "Once, in my childhood, the thought of mingling with such common-born, brutish thugs would have been laughable. But I've found few truer companions. And no one is quite so loyal to their benefactors as a man who's had everything taken away." His eyes narrowed. "Or a woman who has no alternatives."

"Then you've misjudged your target," Saylina said. "I have the power of the entire province behind me."

"Do you?" He glanced around the room, noting the empty side rooms and the cooling cups of tea. "I don't even see your maid. No guards rushing to your rescue. Your dear brother is busy handling the baron he sent into open revolt. When the Sentarsi nobility learn that your beloved high lord has been in open negotiations against his homeland with a foreign neighbor…" He smiled at the still-struggling form of Princess Kitorn.

"And here you are having tea with the very same foreign diplomat. Why, in your position I might be concerned the nobility would think *me* a traitor as well. They'll certainly lose any questions about *his* loyalties."

"You'll never convince the province my brother is a traitor." But she knew he would. Arkaen's loyalties had been a source of contention for years before he took the high lord's seat. That damned war left a bad taste in everyone's mouth, justified or not.

"Well, on that point we'll have to disagree. I've found your countrymen quite simple to maneuver." With a confident swagger, he crossed the room to stand by the window, staring out as if admiring the view. "A shame, really, to send such a pleasant city into chaos." Glee flavored his words, revealing the lie. "More so that you won't be here to see your brother's handiwork. You think him so noble. If only you'd seen what he has truly done."

Dread settled into Saylina's stomach at his musing. Arkaen had faults. Everyone in the province knew that, and she knew too well how dirty the war had gotten before the end. Even without open battle in the city, Torsdell's streets had mirrored the unrest beyond the province. Riots in the streets between the emperor's loyalists and those who supported the rebellion. Her father leading the guards out to put down unrest in a bloody slaughter that had left the people fearful for months. Oh, gods… Arkaen was leading his men against the former Baron Weydert's open revolt, the leader had said.

"You can't think this will work." Saylina tugged at the bindings on her wrists, the rope tearing at her skin as fear tore at her thoughts. "Kaen is not who you think he is. And there is nowhere in this province where he won't find me."

The leader smiled at her, his grin equal parts malice and charm. "Of course, dear. You'll be found. That's the point. Without a chance to find you, he won't have enough incentive to act. The question is whether you'll be alive when they find you. My associate can be so impatient, and your spirit is likely to infuriate him. Do be careful with that tongue."

Saylina stared at the handful of men surrounding her. "But why?" None of them were familiar. None that she'd seen in any audience or petition or even in the recent unrest in the city. "What are you hoping to accomplish? Killing me just makes Kaen's claim more solid."

"Possibly," the leader said with a shrug. "I don't actually care about the rulership of *these* lands. But your brother took something from me that he can't give back. In return, I intend to take everything he cares about."

He snapped his fingers, striding from the room as his men grabbed her, one hand under each shoulder to hoist her off the floor. Saylina gave a sharp kick, her delicate shoes connecting with all the force of a wet rag. The men laughed at her struggles and dragged her from the room.

Under new leadership, the Serr-Nyen *began to attack imperial soldiers, appointing a general known as Lord Phoenix. As the tide of each battle turned, this general came forth and spoke to the captured soldiers, perverting their minds into treason. So it was that from each defeat the empire's foes grew as though the* Serr-Nyen *formed a magical beast reborn over and over in the fires of war.*

— *from* An Abridged History of the Sernien War

Chapter 22

The rumble of angry voices floated in the window of Arkaen's private study, setting his nerves on edge. Too close to the sounds of indignant *Serr-Nyen* villagers chased from their homes by Bloody Emperor Laisia's men. Like the morn he'd been taken prisoner in a small village far north of Sharan Anore, when the emperor's interrogators finally caught up to him after weeks of—Arkaen shook the memories away. Those interrogators were long dead now. Lasha's fury hadn't spared a single one. His eyes drifted to the belt carrying his double sabers, propped against the wall in easy reach, and Arkaen sighed. No time for daydreams this morn with the constant threat of fighting hanging over the city.

He picked up another report from the desk and flipped a page. More factions sprouting up throughout the city, claiming allegiance to whatever noble title sounded impressive enough to them. One even claimed loyalty to his mother's Istalli duchy, as if the bloodline hadn't ended when his uncle died a mere two years after reaching majority. The duchy's land had been symbolically gifted to Sayli as a babe in preparation for her eventual dowry, but she held no claim on the title.

Another page. No violence yet, but his guards reported rapidly escalating arguments and a few shoving matches they'd been forced to resolve. A missive from the captain of the guard fell from the pages.

My Lord Arkaen—

While your guard remains ever loyal to the ideals of Sentar province, let it be known that our training does not lend itself to resolving domestic disputes. Matters should be resolved in as efficient a way as possible—

A sharp knock at the door broke his focus and a servant ushered in his three remaining councilors. The Lord Marshal crossed immediately to stand before Arkaen's desk, feet spread and arms tucked behind him in a mimicry of formal attention, while Count Tenison stepped to one side. His father's Lord Chancellor stayed by the door, likely ready to bolt the instant this meeting turned against them.

Arkaen gestured to the chairs scattered through his study. "Please, sit, my lords." They could only be here to accost him over the council meeting he'd planned and missed, and he'd rather face them on an equal level.

"We'll stand, thank you, Lord Arkaen." The Lord Marshal, with just enough huff to sound like a parent scolding an unruly child.

Count Tenison stepped forward. "Your pardon for the interruption, but we've a concern that cannot wait for your convenience. A meeting was set for several days past, just after noontide meal, and you did not arrive. The province cannot be brought to peace if you will not discuss solutions with us."

"You'll have to excuse my distraction, gentleman." Arkaen rose, turning away from them to stare out his window at the city beyond. "I've just survived an attempt on my life and I'm a bit busy trying to keep the city from deteriorating into civil war now that the guard captain is wavering in his allegiances."

Count Tenison scoffed. "I'd hardly call a single message asking to resolve the unrest a threat of treason." He paced to the fireplace, leaning against the stone.

"Snooping through my missives, my Lord Count?" Arkaen raised an eyebrow, meeting Count Tenison's gaze over his shoulder.

Count Tenison turned a bright red. Not really a surprise that he'd sent spies to Arkaen's palace. More so that he'd reveal them, even by accident. He must be more worried than he wanted to admit.

"My lord, I only—"

"I'm not angry," Arkaen said. "I might have done the same in your place. But you've misread the message." Arkaen turned back, taking the note from his desk. "Take a second look."

He offered the paper to Count Tenison. After a moment of hesitation, Count Tenison stepped forward and took the page, scanning the contents. He frowned, glanced at Arkaen, and scanned the page again.

"Can you not see it?" Arkaen drummed a hand on the top of his desk.

"Even if he can, the rest of us can't," the Lord Marshal snapped. "What do you mean? I've heard nothing of rebellion in the ranks."

"Indeed, Lord Marshal, I doubt you would." Arkaen shrugged, cultivating a posture of indifference. He couldn't afford to look worried when they thought they had a solution. And probably one he'd hate. "My army is a separate unit from my guards, but even among them you have a certain... distance from the common soldier. Quite normal, really, but it means they're unlikely to confide in you."

He took the paper back from Count Tenison, dropping it on the pile of other business as they watched, waiting for him to explain. The tension grated on his calm, the rules of this damned game leaving him aching for a straightforward battle. At least with a blade in his hand, he knew how to handle an enemy.

The Lord Marshal fidgeted, finally breaking posture to lean over the desk. "If I've missed something as a result of holding my rank in high regard, then tell me what."

And there was the breaking point. A forced reminder that Arkaen held knowledge and resources they didn't. That his rule served a purpose they had no desire to resolve on their own.

Arkaen settled into his chair again. "The captain makes a point of saying he's loyal to the ideals of Sentar. Do the three of you consider me a proper representation of Sentar province's ideals?"

None of them spoke. He waited a full count of ten as the three of them found every corner to examine that might hold an answer. And not a one looked at Arkaen. An answer he'd expected, if not relished confirming.

"More to the point, my lords," he said. "How confident are you that the captain of the guard considers me a proper representation of Sentar province's ideals?"

"All the more reason to come to a resolution." The Lord Chancellor crept froward. Far enough to avoid an appearance of hiding behind the Lord Marshal, but no further. "We've discussed the situation. The lower lords' council will choose you a bride to give stability to the realm, and in return for our efforts, you'll give the council power over the treasury. As such, we can—"

The door burst open, two guards marching in as a servant scurried past. Arkaen had barely a moment for a flood of relief at the interruption. This plan of the lower lords' council was worse than he'd anticipated...

"Milord Arkaen!" The servant rushed forward. "The town—"

One of the guards, an older man with graying hair, shoved the servant behind him. "We've been assigned as a personal detail for your protection. I'm afraid blood was shed in defense of your province."

Arkaen snatched his sword belt from the wall. "Where?"

"I must insist you come with us to a safe location, high lord." The guard stepped between him and the door, barely an arm's length from the edge of the desk. Blocking the direct path outside.

"Like hell." Arkaen strapped his swords on, the familiar weight a comfort to his racing pulse. "What caused the situation?"

He strode around the desk, stopped barely five steps into his motion by the first guard's hand on his shoulder. Arkaen froze, temper sharp as he turned to meet the guard's determined look. One hand settled onto the hilt of his saber. The man was just doing his job.

"I'm going out, soldier." Arkaen narrowed his eyes, voice sinking into a deadly calm. "You can guide me, and in the process protect the man you were ordered to guard, or I can take your hand off for the trouble of pushing past you."

The guard snatched his hand back, face white.

"My Lord Arkaen, I must object." Count Tenison, nasally voice stuttering over his fear. "If anything happens to you, our province has no heir."

Arkaen spun to face him. They didn't have time for this nonsense. No choice but to force a decision he'd intended to coax from his lower lords.

"High Lady Saylina Sentarsin is my heir until such time as another legitimate child of the Sentarsin line is available to claim the title. If you've a problem with my choice, I encourage you to file a formal complaint naming a suitable replacement. In the meantime, I've a kingdom to rule and a rebellion to halt."

Arkaen stormed past the guard and the Lord Chancellor, yanking the door open.

"My Lord Arkaen."

"Gods damn it all." Arkaen whirled around, pulling a sword free on instinct. He glared at the Lord Marshal. "What?"

The Lord Marshal stood once again at attention, holding the arm of the terrified servant. "Battle is at the jail, apparently. How many soldiers would you like me to bring?"

Arkaen slid his saber back into the sheath, running quick calculations. The local branch of his reserve army would put down almost any fighting in short order, but would take forever to raise. Not to mention the resentment it would build. The worst—and best—rebellions hid in the shadows until they had the power to win an all-out battle and then still found ways to pick at the edges. He needed this fight in the open. But too few men and he could risk losing dozens of his guards. He didn't even know if this was a true battle or just a scuffle between commoners that had gotten out of hand.

"Send your second to raise the reserves and leave them on alert." The decision hung heavy on his heart. If he was wrong, he was going to pay a steep price in blood. "And speak to Jarod. I need my *Serr-Nyen* flameguard."

"But…" The Lord Marshal hesitated. "My lord, the Serniens are of concern. If the local guard is uncomfortable already, you can only exacerbate the situation. Surely—"

"And what choice is there?" Arkaen scowled. "Wait to raise the army? The battle will be over and the province may well be at war. I'd rather not start one just yet."

He spun on a heel and left before yet another servant, guard, or lord could find a reason to make him stay, the two guards a step behind him. Strange, to walk into battle without Lasha by his side. But with any luck, this was no battle at all. And Lasha—after his visit to Brayden, Lasha had been too quiet. But no. The gods of the Drae'gon wouldn't abandon their Chosen, and Arkaen couldn't stand to doubt him either.

The guards in the foyer flung the doors open, Arkaen's expression— or possibly the escort behind him—warning against any delay. He paused on the steps and cast a glance upward, taking stock of the weather. White fluff scattered through the sky in a thin cover, but no sign of storms. Thank the gods. Nothing worse than fighting in rain, where the leather on his sword hilts just felt like soggy mush and his feet were constantly in danger of slipping. No matter if he fought on grassy fields, dirt turned to mud, or the worn-smooth cobbles of his city streets, rain was ever the enemy of a solid stance. But this couldn't be a true battle. He'd have heard something before now. Lasha couldn't have missed that. Surely he couldn't.

He rushed down the steps, crossing the courtyard with quick strides.

"Milord, I'll get horses." The younger of his guards turned toward the stables.

Horses would take several minutes to saddle, and he couldn't run them through the city without risking harm to innocent citizens. And the jail wasn't far.

Arkaen shook his head. "No time. Faster to walk."

"But…"

He broke into a jog at the gates to the city, plotting the route as he ran. Behind him, two sets of heavy tread proved the guards followed his lead.

A series of streets and a pattern emerged. Empty streets near his palace gave way to frightened groups huddled near corner shops. Huddled groups turned into larger crowds, moving down the street toward a growing rumble of anger.

Something was causing a spectacle, and Arkaen had a sinking feeling his city guards would be in the middle of it.

He'd placed the newly built jail on the outskirts of town as a place to house the accused until a determination could be made. The field holding the sprawling complex overflowed now, smoke rising from the far right side where the jail stored various supplies in a small shed. Arkaen ran past the last line of onlookers, stumbling to a halt at the chaos beyond.

Two flurries of activity. Directly in front, arrayed in ragged battle lines, a motley collection of commoners faced his noble-born guard units. The fire-red uniformed guards thrust short, narrow blades at a crowd of men and women armed with everything from branches to daggers to bare hands. To his right, guards flocked around a central figure. The guard captain, standing before the jail shouting orders at the men in the middle.

"Captain!" Arkaen charged into the slaughter. "Call them off."

"Milord!" The captain's voice rang over the sound of angry shouts. "Ye cain't—"

Arkaen's sabers slid free with the ease of well-practiced dancers in a formal show, the grips solid and comforting against his palms. He slid between one of his guards and a young woman clutching a heavy branch. Batted the guard's clumsy stab aside—twisted away from the swing of the branch.

"Stand down, soldier." Arkaen took a single step forward, blade held in guard.

The guard stumbled back, eyes wide with shock. Arkaen spun around, batting a dagger away in time to take only a light brush with the blade. The sting of sweat in a fresh cut throbbed on his side.

A shout rose from behind the crowd of commoners, largely unintelligible in the clamor of battle. Something about high lord's blood, though he couldn't tell if they were calling to shed it or avoid it.

Another slash and Arkaen swatted a second blade away from an innocent neck. His guards backed away, every step he took a shield between their orders and the crowd.

Arkaen raised his voice, shouting over the sounds of fighting. "Stand down. Fall back."

The guards closest froze, a handful backing away. Further toward the distant trees, they either didn't hear or didn't care. Arkaen shoved through the crowd. They had to stop. This conflict… they'd tear the damned city apart.

"Milord, stop."

He spun around. A brawl behind him. Several of the guards who'd stepped back struggling against a woman and two children. Children holding knives, stabbing at the exposed legs of the men. Gods damn it all.

Scrambling to get between them, Arkaen shoved his guards back again. A scuffle of hands, boots sliding on crushed grass. A sharp sting from his calf.

"Shethka-se." Arkaen muttered the Derconian curse Lasha favored as he spun away from the pain and glanced down. Just a scratch on his leg, blood pouring into his boot. Damn thing hurt like the venom of Eiliin's hell hounds, but no real damage.

Shoving another man back, Arkaen found the attacker. One of the boys he'd seen earlier. Innocent child, hand clutching a kitchen knife, sprawled on the ground, his mother collapsed beside him. Bawling, screaming, tears streaming down her face. A Sentar guardsman pulled his blade free. The crowd around them stumbled over each other to get away. Shouting, somewhere by his ear, as the earth drank a child's blood. His vision blurred, just an instant, but the parallels…

Unmistakable. Unforgettable.

A Serr-Nyen *boy lying face down in his own puke, blood mingling with the slop, his mother's body barely two paces beyond, beaten, torn, and bloody. Days old, because the imperial bastards couldn't be bothered to give a burial. And they'd left none of the town to do it properly.*

"Milord, we have to retreat. It's too dangerous for you here."

Arkaen flipped his sabers into guard positions, angled the hilts slightly to either side to guard flanks as well as front. Stalking forward across the carnage—three, four, five steps. The guard looked up, eyes wide with shock and horror, blade covered in innocent blood.

"I—he—I…" The man's stuttered words rang empty. "He was gonna…" The guard pointed at the body. "He was—"

"A child." Arkaen thrust his blade through the guard's chest, thick leather uniform offering little resistance. "You murdered a *child* for giving me a *scratch*."

The metallic tang of blood permeated the air. The guard's face floated before him, eyes wide and mouth hanging open. Arkaen yanked his saber free, slashing his throat with the other blade. Even a murderer deserved a quick death. He scanned the field.

The city folk broke, fleeing his guards and their blades without even pausing long enough to grab injured, dead, or trampled. Maybe half the group rallied around a smaller figure near the woods. A problem for later.

Arkaen turned toward his guards. They backed away, blades held forward. Too many blades covered with an ominous red shine in the morning light. The field, once peaceful but for the sprawling complex of the jail he'd built against the edge of the trees, now in ruins. Grass torn, crushed, and far too much of it blood-spattered, while bodies lay strewn across the space like the discarded waste of a fleeing army. Only half the figures moved at all, groaning in pain or crawling toward something, and most wore common cloth instead of the brightly colored leather uniform of his guards.

Gods. There was no stopping war now. How many had his men killed?

The crunch of boots and shouts of frightened citizens echoed through the field. He couldn't afford an escalation now. What could he do? Arkaen stepped forward, toward his guards. Forced his voice as calm as he could manage.

"I said stand down. Treason is met with death."

Anger spread through the sea of faces. He'd driven a wedge that would haunt him the rest of his reign. But if the citizens trusted him to protect them, maybe he could hold the province together long enough. Just enough to get someone else in charge for the war Lasha saw coming.

A line of soldiers emerged from the crowd and marched between him and the guards, brown leather jerkins plain but for the small insignia of a bird leaping free of flames stitched onto each shoulder. Each man and woman held a short spear in one hand and a long, narrow shield in the other, forming a wall between him and the guards that wore his colors as another group did the same behind. Safe among soldiers more loyal to him than any born under imperial rule.

Jarod stepped forward with a deep bow. "Milord Phoenix. How may the *Serr-Nyen* serve?"

Arkaen frowned at the man. "Jarod…"

He'd just made a vicious claim about treasonous actions. The Lord Marshal stormed to the edge of the soldiers encircling Arkaen.

"Let me through," the Lord Marshal snapped, shoving against the crossed spears of two soldiers before him. "I've business with the high lord."

"When Milord Phoenix is prepared for your opinion, he will ask for it," Jarod said, his full attention still focused on Arkaen.

Arkaen gritted his teeth. "Jarod, when your people followed me to Sentar you agreed to abide by my laws." He grabbed a corner of his own delicate silk tunic, wiping the blood from his blades. "My law recognizes High Emperor Corliann as ruler over all these lands, which I hold in trust for his glory. The *Serr-Nyen* answer to imperial law or face penalties for treason."

"As you say, milord." Jarod didn't bat an eye at his threat, though he dropped the treasonous title. "Where's milord's dragon?"

Arkaen bit back a curse. Not entirely devoid of treasonous titles despite Arkaen's words. But no one here would know the context of that one.

"Kìlashà has his own matters to resolve."

Arkaen tried not to think about what could have distracted Lasha so completely that he'd missed saving an innocent child from a guardsman's sword. But Lasha never traded lives without good reason. If Lasha knew. At Arkaen's feet, the cooling body of the boy lay limp and forgotten. Arkaen gestured down.

"See he gets a proper burial." He scanned the ruined field again. "See they all get a proper burial. Even the traitors."

Jarod nodded. "As milord wishes."

A few sharp commands from Jarod and the *Serr-Nyen* broke into teams, groups of three sorting bodies and aiding injured. Two men stepped beside him, lifting the body of the boy with all the reverence of priests carrying a holy artifact. Another two soldiers, women this time, stepped behind him, spears in guard position.

"My Lord Arkaen," the Lord Marshal snapped, stepping forward. "What in all the gods' names happened?"

"A tragedy, Lord Marshal." Arkaen slid his swords in their sheaths and waved at the crowd still clogging the street end. "See what you can do to calm the people. I need to speak to the leader of this group."

The remains of the fighters, mostly just poor citizens with whatever they could hold, milled at the edge of the clearing, numbers dwindling as individuals slipped into the trees. Arkaen crossed the space, his flameguard pacing behind him and the two men carrying the boy's body in front. Arkaen stopped a good distance away, gesturing to his men to set the boy down. He couldn't find the mother who'd collapsed over her son's body. Maybe gone, frightened of his wrath, or maybe just too lost in the crowd for him to see.

"I've brought your child back," Arkaen called. "I could not save him, but I've done what I can."

He stepped back, waiting for several long moments for someone to step forward. Finally, a man crept forward, eyes darting to either side as if he thought someone would charge from a hidden vantage to attack, and picked the boy up. Arkaen nodded. At least someone would see to the body.

"This violence serves no one," Arkaen said. "Let me speak to someone who leads you. Someone who can voice your concerns. Let's find a peace."

The group milled about, bodies shifting as if an ocean wave, flowing in and out and away and back. After a few muttering breaths, a pair of men shoved a young woman forward. A young woman with flowing, silky brown hair and deeply tanned skin, staring at him with wide brown eyes he'd started to recognize on sight. The woman from the fountain. So this was his wayward baron's doing after all. And with her present, there was no telling how much Lasha had seen.

"Well," Arkaen said. "How is Oskari doing these days?"

Yer smart enough, lass. Work hard, they'll be askin' you what ta do next. Best know what helps the most folk 'fore they come askin'.

— *Master Trieu*

Chapter 23

Niamsha stared at High Lord Arkaen, hands trembling. Eiliin's Cursed Breath. What was she supposed to say? She didn't have demands, just Nijel's orders to distract the high lord and force his hand. The body of the guardsman he'd killed drew her eye. Gods, she'd certainly done that. No placing that death on any hands but the ones that started this violence.

"How is Oskari doing these days?" High Lord Arkaen's voice held an edge of fury still, the anger that had driven him to kill his own guard lingering in his gaze.

But what made a man murder his own subjects for protecting him? Maybe the boy's strike had been off—she'd been too far to see perfectly—but even a missed strike could have cut deep. Without that guard's intervention, they may well have faced a massacre from enraged guards as the high lord bled out on the ground.

She swallowed the lump of fear choking her breath, grief for the dead lingering in her thoughts. Janne Ferndon had run, but she'd seen the mangled hand he clutched to his chest. No more glasswork for him.

The tavern keeper cradled his nephew to one side, hidden behind the crowd. But his sobs rang in her ears, as much created by her own sorrow as heard over the fields. How many others had she killed in this effort? One that hadn't even freed Emrys. Or at least, not yet.

"Don't be shy, girl." High Lord Arkaen smirked. "I'm sure he's sent you for a reason, and Oskari never does anything without a purpose. What message would he like me to glean from this carnage?"

"I…" Niamsha stared past him, at the efficient men and women cleaning blood from blades, carrying bodies back and forth. How many battlefields had these strange, new guards swept clean after High Lord Arkaen's bloody legacy? "The Rogue Baron got no use fer any lessons writ in blood."

"He's taken a title, then?" High Lord Arkaen asked. "A bit dramatic, don't you think?"

Dammit. She'd forgotten. But then, a strong enough myth held sway long after the power itself waned. Nijel used the tactic every time he vanished into the north for weeks on end. No way he could know what the Rendells did while he was away, but no one ever dared thwart the rules he'd left behind. Not even Marcas.

Niamsha pulled herself to the most intimidating height she could manage, almost as tall as High Lord Arkaen. "Ain't been his choice. Barony sits with the family head. *You* made him a rogue."

"A barony sits on the head of whoever a province high lord deems fit." High Lord Arkaen drummed his finger on the end of his sword, eyes narrowing in anger. "As personal confidante to High Emperor Corliann, who *personally* approved my ascension to the seat of high lord, I could name my gods-damned horse baron of Oskari's family estate if I so chose. In my leniency, I've allowed Oskari's eldest son to take the title."

"Not sure a horse'd make it through all the groveling without shittin' on the floor."

Should have kept her mouth shut. She knew it the moment the words left her lips. But High Lord Arkaen's expression softened. His lips twitched. Almost a smile.

"Perhaps. But I've yet to see Rikkard present himself for formal confirmation. At least I know where the horse is."

The ridiculousness of the moment hit like a shock of cold rain. Arguing with the high lord over his right to name an animal as a nobleman while corpses rotted on the ground around them. No one could be so callous. But here they stood.

What message did the Rogue Baron want to send? The Rogue Baron just wanted High Lord Arkaen off the throne, and Nijel wanted him dead. But so much could be done if she could usurp their power. The high lord hadn't asked the Rogue Baron what he wanted. He'd asked Niamsha.

"The Rogue Baron ain't gonna let you take honest work from folk like these." She gestured at the group behind her. Most of those still present were the Rogue Baron's servants, hireling guards from traders, or Nijel's additions. But he didn't need to know that. "Ye wander home an' start tearing down guilds as gave security to crafters. Undo years o' contracts, sending folks to the gutters. And ain't a thing your schooling does to help 'em find more work. The Rogue Baron plans ta bring their chances back."

High Lord Arkaen smiled, a bitter twist of his lips that spoke volumes as to his belief in her words. Failure.

He stepped closer, leaning forward for an intimate whisper. "Nice try. Oskari's opposed every measure for support of common workers that I've fought to pass. He's the reason so many are starving on the streets." Turning away, he gave a dismissive wave and strode away.

"If your lord has any suggestions, have him send them my way," he called over his shoulder. "The province well knows I've a soft spot for the poor my measures have displaced."

Niamsha cursed, letting her feet carry her back to the group. The Rogue Baron would have her head if he heard what she'd asked for. And he likely would. Too many had heard High Lord Arkaen's parting comment. How could she turn this to look like she'd supported his goals when all he wanted was the high lord dethroned?

A flash of black caught her attention. The demon paused at the edge of the woods, watching her with head tilted in his too-common, bird-like stance. Time for the next steps. If he'd done the job he promised, Emrys should be free of the prison. She just needed to get the guards moved away so she could sneak him out. And the bloody field gave her a chance.

Niamsha strode forward, shouting her demands. "You want demands? Let your people stay to bury their dead. And get the butchers out of here, so we can work in peace."

High Lord Arkaen paused, turning slowly to consider her. "I'd every intention of offering myself and my men as spare hands to dig the graves."

Niamsha choked on her shock. Nobles didn't dig graves, and even their servants and guards were above the task. Most merchants found the coin to pay a gravedigger even, barring a string of unusually bad luck. How was she going to get Emrys free with the high lord standing right there?

"Are you sure you'd prefer them buried here?" He glanced toward the town. "Surely they've family their souls would rather be near."

As if the poor on his streets would have crypts set aside, or even plots of land where the dead could lay near each other. As if any living in this city had the chance to think so far ahead as to know where their body would rest after death. Gods, these nobles had no idea.

"We ain't got land like you." She could hear the bitter edge to her voice, but nothing kept it from her words. She didn't even know where her mother's body lay, and her papa had been left in a triad-grave somewhere beyond the borders of town. She'd never had the chance to visit. "Not enough room in the garden for the whole family, an' makes the cabbage taste off."

High Lord Arkaen's entire form tensed, the poise clear even from a distance, one hand clenched on the end of his blade again. "I certainly wouldn't want funny tasting cabbage."

Something frightening emanated from his focus despite the absurdity of his words, his eyes fixed on a point behind her and to the right. On the edge of the forest. Aeduhm's grace. On the demon, no doubt, who shouldn't have been here at all. Niamsha scrambled for something to say. Anything to distract from what the demon might have been doing. To protect Emrys long enough for her to sneak him free.

"Kìlashà." His voice carried over the field. "You'll find a suitable site? And the remains of those better rehomed?"

The demon strode past Niamsha, barely sparing her a glance. "Of course, kai'shien. Most are in a mass grave far north. A project, perhaps, for those of your people seeking work. You may desire to leave these here, however. Humans mourn as my people do not. A day, at most."

High Lord Arkaen nodded. "Lord Marshall." He walked toward the cluster of guardsmen. "Set up a perimeter. The girl tells you who may pass. This is a shrine to the fallen."

The second noble, all polished buckles and fancy weapons, blustered at the order. His hands up in protest, the Lord Marshall paced by High Lord Arkaen's side, their argument fading into the general rumble of voices across the field. Niamsha stared at the demon. He'd done her work for her. Distract the guards, send the nobles away, establish a solid location for planning. What did he expect her to do?

The demon turned to meet her gaze, pausing mid-step almost as if he'd known she was watching him. He must have suspected she would. Like his guesses in the temple. Predicting her reactions like a fortune teller guessing the vague prophecies that would draw the biggest crowds. She'd need to throw him off if she planned to ever win a conflict with him. And eventually there would be a conflict.

Niamsha drew in a deep breath, gathering her courage as she marched across the field to the demon. "You do what we agreed?"

He considered her for a long moment in silence, seemingly ignorant of the eyes of her fellow townsfolk and the guards alike. All attention focused on them, Niamsha's gaze wandering despite her resolve to keep his attention. Every eye gleamed with a need to learn what a simple girl like her had to discuss with the high lord's demon.

"Intriguing." The demon stepped to one side, cocking his head and narrowing his eyes as if examining a strange bug found in his gruel. "Time bends around you as a rock in a stream, and yet when you try to change it you fail. Their plan for you must be complex."

"I ain't following no one's plan."

"Ironically accurate, as before." The demon smiled at her. "Your brother waits, as discussed. See to his transition, lest he fall prey to the very fate you hoped to preserve him from."

Niamsha scowled as he followed in High Lord Arkaen's forgotten wake. The guards scattered before him, hands raised in warding gestures she recognized from her days at temple. He was—she shook her head to clear the musings. Whatever purpose Aeduhm may have for such a creature, she had enough troubles without meddling in the plans of the gods.

She headed back toward the milling group she'd assembled on the edge of the field. A swirling mass of confused merchants, beggars, and thieves mixed with bitter soldiers. Aeduhm grant her strength. They needed to focus on one goal now, and she'd barely managed to get them in one place for the beginning of this. The idea had been riot, maybe rough up a few guards. Not start killing with whatever knives and clubs they could find. But that was false. Nijel had demanded blood.

"Ya got a pretty speech fer us?" One of Nijel's supporters, smirking through broken teeth.

"People died here!" Niamsha thrust a finger behind her at the carnage. "Our people, not some high an' mighty noble bastards. How you gonna mock them?"

Her pain, fear, and anger poured out of her with the words. Gods. If the demon had brought Emrys out as she'd expected, he'd be dead. She'd have gotten Emrys killed.

Have a plan for his safe haven, the demon said. She knew where Emrys was going, but how to get him from here to there? Niamsha spun around, the loose end of her hair flying with the speed of the turn. Some heated debate across the field between the guards and that other noble. High Lord Arkaen had already gone. Too busy to deal with the aftermath of his own brutality.

"Whatcha thinkin'? He said…" The rough voice still held the ache of sorrow. A stranger, but one who'd lost blood on this field. A pain Niamsha knew without needing to know the speaker.

Niamsha waved at the bodies, laid out in pairs, groups or singles depending on what the high lord's soldiers had decided. No organization she could see, except the guards in their vibrant uniforms. Those bodies were covered with a single sheet each, a flurry of people tending to the preparations need to remove the still forms.

"See who's there." Niamsha stared at the argument, an idea forming. "I'll get someone to see about them guards. They may well give us a buffer."

"They tried ta kill us."

Another voice she didn't recognize. Niamsha turned back, a bitter smile creeping onto her face.

"Aye. And the high lord killed one o' them for it." She glanced back. "Eli!"

She'd seen the coward whose incompetence had left her at Marcas's mercy a week past, skulking in the back of the fight to avoid any real danger. Nijel'd probably sent the little bastard to force her to prove she could work with anyone. She'd damned well work with whoever she had to if it meant Emrys was free and safe.

"I ain't gotta listen to ya." Eli skulked forward, arms crossed in defiance across his narrow frame. Marcas's sullen glare and broad shoulders mixed with Nijel's athleticism and hygiene. He should have been formidable. If he'd had any balls. "Marcas said."

"Take it ta Nijel," she snapped.

Their eyes met, his hazel to her brown. A count of five terrified thuds of her heart. She couldn't lose control of this crowd. Not if she wanted Nijel to keep protecting her from Marcas. And control meant not waiting for agreement. Like Nijel with the Rogue Baron. He'd never waited for the baron's agreement before giving orders.

"Tell that noble we're askin' the guard for help with our dead." She pointed at the argument in the distance. "An' when you got the captain alone, tell 'im his men deserve better. It ain't right, yer lord killing yer men for doin' their jobs. Even if that job is killing our kids. He come to us, we ain't gotta try and kill him, he can put the high lord in 'is place."

Eli frowned. "Why ain't you doing it? You got such great plans, you do 'em."

"I gotta report to the baron." Niamsha straightened, presenting the task like an armor, the authority she'd weaseled from the Rogue Baron's hands the only shield against his suggestion. Her only chance to get Emrys free and safe.

"Ya heard her, boy." The first man from before, his voice grimmer than when he'd mocked her leadership. "Girl's got a solid plan. Get to it."

Eli scowled, glaring between her and the man behind her for several long breaths. Finally, cursing under his breath, he stormed away to follow her orders. Niamsha bit back a sigh of relief. Nijel would never reveal a fear that someone might refuse his instructions. If he ever felt such. And if she planned to mimic Nijel...

"Gotta see ta somethin'," Niamsha announced, pointing at the carnage they'd made of the field. "Get started on them."

She walked away from the crowd, head high and refusing to look at the death she'd caused as a dozen pairs of eyes watched. A strong leader didn't ask their followers to obey orders, they expected it, and punished if it didn't happen. Crossing the field, crushed grass slipping under her boots, Niamsha couldn't stop a nervous glance back as she paused by the door to the prison. The group had drifted apart, some following her order and others heading home. No one looked her direction. She slipped into the prison. Two torches lit the stretch of hallway, a series of metal doors built along the length, and the dank, heavy smell of old straw lingered like a foul soup in the back of her mouth.

"Em?" Her whisper seemed to echo off the empty walls.

A shuffle of feet in the straw, a couple of coughs, and a door creaked open only a few feet down. Emrys poked his head out, hesitant, until he saw Niamsha. A bright grin crossed his face and he hurried out. The blue and silver uniform he'd worn when she saw him last was smeared with mud and other grime, but she couldn't find any sign of true injury.

"I thought…" She ran forward, throwing her arms around him. Safe. Emrys was safe, and the demon had kept his side of the bargain. Even if she'd broken hers. A tickle of guilt. But Nijel would have killed her, and she'd had no other way to free Emrys.

"Sorry." Emrys's breath stirring the loose strands of her hair were a balm to her soul. Holy Aeduhm couldn't curse her for protecting such an innocent boy. Her brother.

Emrys gave her a final squeeze and pulled away. "Better get gone. Nijel'll be waitin' for me."

Ice ran down her spine at the words. He couldn't want to go back. Not after they'd got him arrested for treason. He headed toward the door, missing—or maybe ignoring—the shock on her face.

"Em, ya ain't goin' back to the Rendells."

"I gotta," he replied. "Nijel needed ta know the inside o' the jail. I don't tell him and don't show on the headsman's block, he'll be lookin' for me."

"You didn't." Niamsha froze, staring at him. "You *didn't* go get caught a'purpose…"

Emrys shrugged. "Nah, but someone was gonna." He looked back, frowning at her. "Nia it ain't that big. Nijel knew we's gonna get into it, he had plans fer getting us out. I thought you was it."

She couldn't breathe, air burning in her lungs as she struggled to comprehend. He'd known. Nijel had known Emrys was in jail. And Emrys had known he'd go to jail. And Nijel had known, when she suggested the riot, that she'd be trying to get Emrys free. But Nijel hadn't suggested it. What if she'd thought to burn the new temples to restore the old ways? Would he have corrected her?

She knew that answer. Her heart ached for her misguided brother. But there was nothing more to do. Just get him out of this mess, as she'd meant to do so many times.

"Tell me what Nijel needs," she said. "I'll get him word. You ain't goin' near the Rendell house."

Emrys slammed a hand into the wall. "Dammit, Nia. I'm grown. You ain't got no part o' my choices."

"You been grown a whole month." The scorn felt foreign on her lips, especially directed at Emrys. But he couldn't know what he was dealing with. He'd never really dealt with the streets. "I been raising you fer near six years now. Almost think Nijel picked you up outta that tree when you was eight an' fell. Or fed you on the streets after Papa died. You stay clear o' the Rendell house. Let me handle it."

"My sister ain't ruling my life." He paused, hand tapping at the wall. Turned away. "I'm goin'. I ain't living under yer rules no more. You ain't thinking o' me, just yerself."

"Em!"

He stormed out, leaving her alone in the thick stench of the prison. His accusation, an echo of Marcas from the tavern, weighed on her shoulders like a heavy load of scrap glass. She'd never betrayed him. Never had, never would. Never could. No way he thought that. Emrys knew she loved him.

Niamsha hurried out, blinking in the light of the sun as she scanned the broad space. The demon's warning haunted her. If she didn't get him somewhere safe, Emrys would end up back in jail. Or worse. There. Dammit. Emrys, by the spread of dead bodies, bantering without a care as he and Eli lifted a body together. How did anyone—how could they joke about anything while hauling the bloody corpses of innocent lives?

She took a step forward. Paused. A handful of people were watching. Nothing she could do here without proving her earlier excuse a lie. Niamsha crossed the field, an empty pang in her gut. Emrys was one of them now. A Rendell.

The noble that High Lord Arkaen had left in charge let her pass with barely a glance. Beyond the carnage, the streets were too quiet. This corner of town was barely more than a slum, always full of shouts of the latest goods someone had dug out of a noble's rubbish pile. No chance to take a day for respite. Even Papa used to find that time, though it kept them poor. Said no coin was worth losing family. But she'd lost Emrys, and to something far less valuable than coin. To his own Eiliin-cursed pride.

A couple corners and a wagon blocked her path. Unguarded, which didn't feel quite right, but Niamsha had no time for that. She backtracked, about to pass the street, when voices made her pause.

"I've done what you asked. As best I can, with the hobble you've given me in that girl." The Rogue Baron, voice sharp and boots heavy on the street behind her.

Niamsha ducked behind a water barrel set in the street, peering out to see who he might be talking to. Not that she had much doubt. Nijel stepped out of a doorway, his clothes as pristine as if he'd been to a bathhouse and not a hovel in the slums.

"I think she's been a refreshing aide," Nijel said. He crossed to the cart, checking something in the back covered in a thick cloth.

"I don't trust her." The Rogue Baron stopped in the doorway, glaring down the street. "Her dedication to these plans is... lacking."

Nijel chuckled. "A dreamer, Oskari. She believes in saving this city from its own corruption. She'll learn, and in the meantime, she's never even considered betraying me. Not in any way that mattered."

"Not good enough. I'll trust her as long as I can see her and no more." The Rogue Baron stepped out of the doorway, his voice carrying out. "Now get those women off the streets before someone catches you with them and we're both hung."

"Very well." Nijel's voice carried down the street with a confidence that proved no one here would dare reveal his crime. "I'll take my prize and have yours delivered to your study. Treat her well. I'll not get you another."

Niamsha clapped a hand over her mouth. Nijel had *stolen* someone for the Rogue Baron?

Lord Phoenix was known among the Serr-Nyen *for his lightning-fast blades, his silver tongue, and for the man who always followed at his side: a fierce killer known as the Dragon.*

— *from* An Abridged History of the Sernien War

Chapter 24

Arkaen stalked down the empty streets, shoulders shaking and his few cuts burning with residual pain. The steps of the *Serr-Nyen* guards behind him echoed off the stone walls. He couldn't even walk the streets of his home city alone after this afternoon's deaths. And he should have stopped it. Somehow, there had to be a way. Instead, nearly two dozen citizens lay dead in the jail's open field. And Lasha had done nothing to warn him. Or prevent it.

He glanced to the side, Lasha's slender form matching his steps with eyes near-glowing an obsidian black. The fiery veins marring Lasha's skin seemed to flow with fresh blood—no doubt the source of the rumors about their origin. Every shift of his weight, twitch of his eyebrows, or wave of his hair in the breeze held a deadly beauty. A walking statue of power incarnate. Power incarnate that had allowed a child to die under his very nose.

"What happened?" Arkaen's voice held a reproach he could only wish he'd hid better. But Lasha would have known. Lasha knew everything.

246

"Battle is always complex, kai'shien." Lasha frowned, voice distant and mind clearly focused on his visions more than Arkaen's question.

"Why didn't—"

"For the reason I have not told you many things." Lasha spun to face him, eyes narrowed in fury. "Too much knowledge breaks the needed timelines. A fact you well know." Lasha stormed forward several steps, throwing another glare back at Arkaen. "You think I do not mourn? You think I would not trade near anything to save those lives?"

Arkaen thrust a finger back toward the field. "You could have been there. You *were* there. What pursuit could be more important than saving an innocent child?"

"Were any on that field innocent, I would have saved them." His melodic voice was raw with anguish.

The words shook Arkaen to the core, and even more so, the raw emotion Lasha so rarely showed. Something had not gone according to plan, and Lasha was more concerned than he wanted to admit. But his words rang in Arkaen's ears. If any on the field were innocent. The guardsman, eyes wide in horror. *He was gonna...* He was going to kill Arkaen. But no. Lasha said if *any* were innocent.

Arkaen forced calm into his voice. "This is going to start a war, Kìlashà. You know that."

Lasha scowled, crossing his arms as his gaze focused on the cobbled street. "War has been inevitable. If these deaths bring those potentialities into being, so be it." Lasha met Arkaen's eyes, his pupils shrunk to an overlarge blob that left nearly all of the whites of his eyes visible. "You will not agree, as you never have. But I cannot value the life of one who desires my kai'shien's death higher than the life of one marked by the Ancient Spirits. No matter the youth of the former."

"He missed," Arkaen said.

"Did he?"

A stupid question. Of course the boy missed or Arkaen would be far more injured. The angle of the dagger, with that tightly clenched a fist, the attack would never have connected. Not unless he'd fallen before he'd struck, maybe, and the angle…

Lasha shrugged. "Perhaps so. But a lack of competence hardly improves my opinion."

Arkaen sighed. They could argue this point all day without coming to a finish. And Lasha's argument held merit. If his gods had directed him to protect the woman from the fountain and her life had been at risk, then he'd had no choice.

"A tragic death," Arkaen said. His heart ached, guilt fighting against his next words. "But a life traded for the greater good."

With a nod, Lasha turned back to the street. He stood for another moment, then shook himself as if waking from a vision. A twitch of his lips signaled his change of tone.

"Your sister has a present for you, kai'shien. You should learn what she has brought."

"Still protecting me from too much knowledge?"

"I would hate to ruin the surprise."

Arkaen smiled, starting toward his keep with lighter spirits. If Lasha warned him but wouldn't tell him details, then Sayli had done something kind. Not rare, precisely, but he'd upset her over the mess with Prillani. A present Lasha approved of meant she'd probably forgiven him.

The sprawled buildings on either side lost some of the condemnation as he walked, Lasha's presence suddenly a pleasant companionship rather than a warning against future defeat. He examined Lasha's pace. The fiery veins that traced his perfect structure and build highlighted the mask of lean grace and distant confidence that he rarely dropped. Never, to Arkaen's knowledge, before the Sernien War had brought them together. The Drae'gon allowed no weakness in their Chosen. No sorrow over lives traded to fulfill the plans of their gods. And certainly not over the loss of feeble humans to a senseless massacre. That Lasha still sought to preserve human life was a testament to his Drae'gon clan's failure to mold him into the creature they'd desired.

"You know I don't…" Arkaen didn't know how to finish the sentence. Lasha needed no reminding of the tragedies he hadn't prevented.

"I am aware, kai'shien." Lasha watched the sky in pensive contemplation. "Only you have ever granted me the generosity of assuming I might care for lives lost. But it does not make them cruel. It is natural to fear what is not understood."

Arkaen chuckled. "You're perhaps too considerate."

"I did not say they were not cruel." Lasha glanced behind them. "Only that their fear is not what makes them so. See your *Serr-Nyen* guards. They fear more than any, and with greater reason. But the worst they have visited upon others is bit of light treason."

"I need to talk to Jarod about that."

"Do not."

Arkaen hesitated. Lasha never gave advice on interpersonal relationships. The reasons behind human reactions were so rarely clear from Lasha's visions that he'd never been entirely comfortable predicting human opinions.

"It is a matter of pride, kai'shien."

Lasha turned the final corner leading to Arkaen's keep and froze. Another gods-damned vision taking over his thoughts. Arkaen paused beside him. The street was empty. Unusual, but given where'd he'd come from Arkaen couldn't blame his people for caution. He hadn't been lord long enough to fully eradicate the fears his father had bred among the citizens.

In the distance he could see a small group of soldiers and servants gathered in his courtyard. A second glance. A small group dressed in imperial purple.

"Deyvan's here?" Arkaen frowned. "Why didn't he send word?"

But the answer was obvious. Deyvan was Sayli's surprise. A visit from an old friend who just happened to wield the power to silence any objections Arkaen might face in his rule. So thoughtful of his dear sister. And yet, if Sayli had invited him—

"Why has he not entered your home?" Lasha's whispered question chilled his blood to ice.

If anyone knew why Deyvan chose to loiter in the courtyard it would be Lasha. Arkaen turned, feet leaden, to face Lasha. But whatever power lived in his body at that moment, it bore little resemblance to the man Arkaen loved. The inky hair had deepened, turning into a living, breathing abyss that writhed like a mass of snakes, and all color had drained from Lasha's skin to leave a shimmering veil more ephemeral than spider-silk. As if the wind itself had coalesced to hold the organs inside Lasha's body now that his skin had faded. The last time Lasha had gone so deep into his power he nearly hadn't returned.

"La—"

Arkaen cut the nickname off before he could voice it, eyes darting as the forbidden word hung on his tongue like honey. He couldn't risk revealing their relationship to prying ears. Not even here, where the only visible onlookers were *Serr-Nyen* soldiers, many of whom must remember the carefree intimacy he and Lasha had shared in the Sernien fortress of Sharan Anore.

"It's been raining to the south," Arkaen suggested. "Perhaps Deyvan arrived late, delayed by weather."

A flimsy excuse. Lasha would have seen that in his visions.

"Deyvan was not late."

Lasha strode past him, focused entirely on the keep ahead with an intensity that made Arkaen's skin crawl. Arkaen hurried his steps to keep pace, fighting for measured breaths. No reason to alarm anyone. Or at least, no more than Lasha's fearsome appearance already would.

As they approached, Arkaen could tell Deyvan's entourage wasn't loitering in the courtyard for fun. Servants in three different noble's colors ran on dozens of errands and Count Tenison stood on the far side, just at the base of the stairs, hands waving as he tried to calm a figure hidden behind soldiers, horses, and at least one carriage. No small feat, hiding Deyvan from view. He'd led armies as much by being the easiest to find as by any great strength of leadership, though Deyvan always had a dozen or more contingencies in mind. This fiasco must have his worst fears running rampant.

Arkaen ran forward, passing Lasha to push his way through the crowd. Only a few steps and a scream rang out behind him. They'd seen Lasha, then. The servants in front of him scattered, most of the crowd parting to let them through. But the soldiers pulled blades. Gods damn it all.

"If any one of you kills my cousin"—Deyvan's thunderous baritone carried over the group—"I will personally remove every one of your fingers with a dull blade. Now stand aside and let me speak to my high lord. I assume he's there somewhere."

Arkaen breathed a sigh of relief as the soldiers hesitated, milling about for a moment before stepping to either side. The hall that opened between the still-jumpy soldiers bristled with bare steel. But Lasha need fear nothing from these men. As soon as they saw Deyvan's welcome they'd stand down.

Deyvan almost looked short under the sweeping arches of Arkaen's high lord's palace, his broad shoulders and usually unruly red hair tucked neatly into plain traveling leathers and a single tail held by a leather band. The hilt of his broadsword poked over his shoulder where he always strapped the blade for travel. Not a diplomatic visit after all. Deyvan was riding to war.

"Kaen." Deyvan's voice warmed at the name, a smile stretching the edges of his thick beard. "Why are you covered in blood?"

"My Lord Emperor." Arkaen swept a deep bow. The last thing he wanted was anyone claiming he didn't show proper respect to his liege. Too many complaints against him already.

Arkaen waved at his ruined clothes, taking in the smeared blood of his guardsman and his own. "I'd hardly call one smear and two scrapes *covered* in blood. You should have seen me after the assassination attempt."

"Lady Saylina's concerns have merit, then?" Deyvan crossed the courtyard to tower over Arkaen.

"She's not one to embellish."

Lasha paused by Arkaen's side, scanning the crowd as if seeking something. Deyvan's grin broadened and he clapped Lasha on the shoulder.

"You look pale, cousin. Should spend more time in the sun, less on your books."

Lasha gave a half-hearted snarl in response.

"He's had a difficult day, my Lord Emperor." Arkaen explained, hoping to distract from Lasha's distress with little chance of success. Deyvan had never been as cautious with their secrets as Lasha preferred.

"All the more reason he should find a pretty face to take to bed." Deyvan shot Arkaen a sideways glance, grin slipping into a conspiratorial smile.

Arkaen fought to keep a straight face. Deyvan's cheer, feigned or not, was infectious.

"I understand things have been a bit hectic."

Lasha stepped forward, ignoring their banter, his gaze sweeping the soldiers, then the windows of Arkaen's keep. Dammit. If Lasha was still worried, they'd better get somewhere private where Arkaen could determine what was wrong.

With a casual wave, Arkaen strode past the remaining lines of soldiers and into his keep. Deyvan's heavy steps behind him sounded as the strike of a hammer sealing a tomb door after interring the last of the dead. Fighting to keep his walk casual, Arkaen led them to his great hall—empty, with all the commotion outside, and the closest location he could find to escape prying eyes. He'd barely closed the door behind himself when Lasha paced to the far end, topping the dais with a single leap and running a hand along Arkaen's high lord's seat.

Lasha spun around to fix his eyes on Deyvan. "Where?"

"Pardon, cousin?" Deyvan raised an eyebrow. "I've recently arrived. I'm not certain who or what you're searching for."

"Lady Saylina Anneline Sentarsin, daughter of one Katrivianne Istalli by Johannus Sentarsin, sister of my kai'shien, Arkaen Kalwren Sentarsin." Lasha's eyes focused, the ebony in them sharpening into daggers. "Where is she, Deyvan? She should have been present to greet your arrival, but I saw her not in those gathered nor in the rooms above."

The precision of Lasha's words shredded the last of Arkaen's comfort, his nerves shattering on the perfectly enunciated honor names Arkaen's mother had gifted to her two children at their births. Names that Lasha had never before heard and yet knew now with certainty. He'd never have bothered to dive that deeply into Arkaen's past if he held sufficient information to find Sayli. The room was too hot, the air too close, the door's metal latch too cool under his hand. How could *Lasha*, of all people, not know where she was?

"I'm sorry to disappoint." Deyvan's voice turned sober. "But I've not seen Lady Saylina in near a year now. I'd hoped she was simply detained by her duties."

Arkaen's heart pounded in his chest. "I hope, Kìlashà, that you aren't saying you've lost my sister."

No wonder Lasha had stopped dead on seeing Deyvan and his retinue in the courtyard. He'd known their presence meant Sayli was missing. But where in all the gods' names could she be? No noble-born lady could simply disappear without someone noticing she'd gone, and if anyone knew where she was then Deyvan would have been told the instant he'd asked. Or Sayli would have been notified by now, and would have sent a message.

Lasha's gaze transferred to Arkaen, his posture a monument to his immeasurable power. But his eyes... the black abyss faded as Arkaen watched, the pupil shrinking beyond the edge of the whites, and smaller still to reveal more and more of the white ring. And finally, for the first time since his transformation more than six years past, shrank below the outer edge of his natural irises, revealing the gray eyes Lasha'd been born with.

"Cousin, are you well?"

Deyvan's fear seemed to shake Lasha like a physical blow, his skin flushing suddenly with the natural coloring that matched his skin almost perfectly to Deyvan's lightly tanned complexion, his normally vibrant hair falling slack and lifeless to his shoulders.

"I—" Lasha choked off the reply, uncertainty thick in his voice as Arkaen had never heard it. "I'm sorry. I can't find her."

Gods above and below. The vulnerability in those words tore at everything Arkaen held true. Lasha couldn't have failed—truly *failed*—to find Sayli. Too many options for her location? Commonplace. Sayli could be flighty, and Lasha rarely bothered to track every spare thought anyone chased, much less someone as routinely predictable as Sayli. But couldn't find her at all? It wasn't possible.

Arkaen swallowed a lump of fear, pushing down the furious demand that rose in his throat. Lasha would do everything in his considerable power to locate Sayli. If Arkaen and Deyvan could keep him from collapsing under the guilt of his failure. He glanced toward the far door, at the empty chair a half step behind Arkaen's high lord's chair and far to the left where Sayli sat when she attended court. Where she had sat.

"She's not just gone." The words tore free from Arkaen's lips. A denial that brought sense with it. If Sayli had left on her own, there would be people who knew where, and if someone had taken her there would be clues. "I've resources of my own. I'll find her."

"And you know you have my entire army at your back," Deyvan added. "She's likely just out for a walk, anyway. Abducting a high lord's sister from her own home with the emperor on the way has to be the stupidest plan I've ever heard. Few criminals are truly stupid."

They all knew Sayli wasn't taking a walk. Or if she was, something even worse was wrong and they didn't know of it. If Lasha could be this wrong—could find no trace of a woman he knew personally and had seen mere days before—Lasha could have miscalculated any number of dangerous gambles they'd staked their lives and the stability of Sentar province on. He pushed the thought away. Borrowed problems for another time. Now he needed Lasha focused and effective.

Arkaen jogged across the room to catch Lasha's hand, the skin too warm under his grip. "I'm sure she's fine."

Lasha snatched his hand away, spinning in a circle to search the room. Looking for witnesses, because he didn't trust his power to warn him of spies. But he'd checked this room two dozen times at least. They *knew* it was secure. At least, if Lasha's power had been reliable at any point in the last five years. Arkaen's heart skipped another beat.

"Kai'shien, I—" Lasha had never sounded so unsteady. So frightened and so… human. "I'll see to this power. Find what falsehoods might have twisted the timelines. But…" He stared at Arkaen, tongue sliding across his lips. "Find her, kai'shien. I made you a promise, and I do not know if she's safe."

Turning away, Lasha fled the room before Arkaen could object. Arkaen stared at the door, hands shaking.

"What happened to my cousin, Kaen?"

He shook his head, trying to focus. "I don't know. He's—I've never seen him like that."

Deyvan crossed to the dais, collapsing on the steps that led to Arkaen's high lord's chair with a careless poise. His eyes narrowed as he frowned at an invisible speck on his sleeve.

"I've not either. Not since Serni."

Arkaen scoffed in disbelief. "When did you see him that shaken in Serni? I can't have been there for that."

"You were there." Deyvan's gaze held the intense focus Lasha so often mimicked. "You were damned near dead, unconscious and bleeding out on the floor of that bathing chamber he built. And for an instant before that thing that lives in him took over, I thought he'd throw himself from the gods-damned rafters. He looked like he'd genuinely forgotten how to breathe."

The old wound in Arkaen's shoulder ached, just enough to remember the searing pain of the strike. Memory, not true pain.

"He's always blamed himself for that." Arkaen scowled. "But it wasn't his fault, and neither is this."

"I'd hardly be one to blame my cousin for failing to be prescient." Deyvan shrugged. "But he listens to me about as much as I listen to the chairs in my study. My point was that he pulled himself together then, and he'll do it again now."

Arkaen ran a hand through his hair. "I hope so."

"He will, Kaen. Why wouldn't he?"

"Because this isn't a mistake." Arkaen sank into his high lord's chair, leaning his head back against the hard oak. "He made a mistake, but that's not what's shaken him. He said he can't find her. Not that he doesn't know where she is."

Deyvan laughed, a sharp bark that broke the tension for barely an instant. "I don't see the difference. You've always been so caught in the exact words, but that means the same thing."

"No, it—" Gods damn this worthless power. Arkaen barely understood how it worked. "He doesn't see a future, but what might be the future. So, if Sayli goes shopping, he can see every shop she might visit at any moment, but that's a dozen or more. Too many options and nothing but her whims to decide between them. He'd be able to tell me she was shopping, but not where she was."

"But here, he can't find her." Deyvan nodded. "Not too many choices, but none. Still—" Deyvan pushed himself upright. "Does that mean she's dead?"

The question clawed at his throat. It might. Lasha never failed to find someone he could confirm existed. If he couldn't find her at all, it might well mean Sayli no longer existed. But...

"I don't think so." Arkaen shook his head, the motion as much to remind himself as for Deyvan. "He would find the body. If she were—" He couldn't say it. Not aloud, where the word might become real. "He'd find where they left her."

"Then we've work to do," Deyvan said. "He can't fail to find her if she's standing in front of him. Where do we start?"

The matter-of-fact tone shook Arkaen free of his fear. Sayli needed his help. Time for wallowing in self-doubt when she was home safe.

"Her maid." Arkaen rose and led the way to the side door, gesturing Deyvan to follow. "Sayli's been negotiating with Camira Weydert for me to smooth over the status of my lower lords, and that's led to daily tea at a high-end tavern. Sayli's maid will have gotten her ready, so she'll know the last time Sayli was home."

Arkaen hurried his steps through the halls, pausing for just a moment at a turn that would lead to Lasha's door. But he had too many other matters to handle now. He could check on Lasha later. When he had news that might help. The stone walls shifted from bare to tapestried as he approached his sister's rooms. Turned a corner.

The door was open. Halfway down the hall, but he could tell from the corner that her door was open, a pile of silks pouring out of the room. He ran, only to catch himself short of the carnage. The silks held a woman, pale hair and skin stark against the stone floor, blood pooling under her head. Sayli's maid.

"Eiliin's cursed breath." Deyvan muttered from behind Arkaen. "She *was* taken."

The lords will never think you a power until you've a man on your arm. Use their ignorance.

— High Lady Katrivianne Istalli Sentarsin

Chapter 25

"**W**here is she?" Saylina lunged from the silk couch, swiping at Baron Weydert—Oskari. He wasn't a baron any longer by Arkaen's decree. Her hand jerked her back, the chain and cuff around her wrist leashing her to a heavy blackwood statue. "Where did you take Princess Kitorn?"

Oskari shook his head. "Please calm down, Lady Saylina. You'll hurt yourself. I can't have you bruised at our wedding."

"I will never wed you." The very idea brought bile to the back of her throat. "And if you think threatening my life or that of our visiting princess will change that then you've been terribly misinformed."

She tugged at the statue, her feet sliding on the rug set beneath her couch. This wood was heavier than stone and more expensive than any five other decorations in the room combined. If she dragged the thing down, she'd set his finances back years. And likely still be chained to it.

"No one's going to hurt the princess," Oskari said. "What a disaster that would be. My ally simply needs her contained for a short time to direct his plans. She'll be returned home when he's done."

"As if that makes any of this acceptable? You've abducted a member of the Osuvian royal family."

Oskari slammed a hand into the wall, setting one of his shelves rattling with the vibration of the delicate trinkets displayed there. He muttered a string of curses under his breath.

"Do you think I wanted it this way? My homeland is facing war, now. I've sacrificed my daughter to further this cause. If your brother had given me any choice..."

He stormed away, staring out the window as Saylina processed his words. Aeduhm's mercy. Sacrificed Camira? She'd been a dedicated servant to the province despite Arkaen's rejection, working with Saylina to resolve the recent disputes and trying to manage her father. What had Oskari done with her? Saylina's anger chilled into a shaky fear, hands clammy and a nervous sweat rising to her skin. If he'd hurt his own daughter, what might he do to her?

"You can't really blame Arkaen for your choice, though." Saylina could hear the doubt in her own voice. Even Oskari couldn't be so deluded, could he?

"You don't understand." Oskari scoffed at her. "Women's wisdom. Your father thought so highly of your political reasoning, but he deluded himself. Seeing his beloved Katri, I imagine."

"What—" Her father had rarely spoken a kind word to her. That he might have praised her to a close friend went against all her understanding of the man who had raised her. And Arkaen had killed him.

"And that's why." Saylina plopped down on the couch, the realization clear. She looked up to catch Oskari's gaze. "You blame Arkaen because he killed Father. But he had no choice. We all knew what Father planned. He'd lost his loyalty to the Laisian Empire."

"The empire is dead." Oskari shrugged, leaning against the tightly shuttered window. "It died over four decades ago when the High Lord's

Council shoved a barely weaned boy onto the imperial throne and put a grown woman with ambition in his bed."

"Don't be absurd. You can't excuse our late emperor because he had a troubled childhood." Saylina scowled. "He terrorized our empire. Raped women." Her hands shook as she recalled Arkaen's story. "Tortured my brother."

"He was a bloody, malicious bastard and everyone knew it," he admitted. "But your gods-damned brother would have been fine if he'd stayed home and done his duty. Instead, he ran off and left us weakened. Without an heir or a proper general for our armies." Oskari shook his head. "Doesn't matter anymore. Done is done. But if we're going to bend knee to an emperor, it ought to be one born to the bloodline. Not the nephew of a woman married into the family in hopes of controlling a malleable child."

Gods protect her, he made sense. Emperor Corliann seemed a decent man, but he didn't have any true imperial blood. He represented a desperate compromise by the high lords to keep the empire together after the Serniens had assassinated the old emperor and his children. Saylina pushed a strand of hair out of her face. Or tried to. Her hand tugged on the chain again, nearly forgotten in the revelations from Oskari. Her wrist throbbed as the metal cuff rubbed against the skin where her abductors had bound her hands.

"I'd almost believe you," she said. "Except the Laisian bloodline is dead. And even if it wasn't, how could abducting noblewomen and killing Arkaen help you supplant Emperor Corliann?"

Oskari laughed. "You greatly underestimate your brother's influence, Lady Saylina. The entirety of the northern provinces follow Deyvan only because he does. Without him—"

"Without him we return to civil war, then. How many do you plan to kill for this plan of yours?"

"Dammit, I understand, girl. He's your kin and you care for him. You don't want him hurt. But think of the larger picture. We've already had one Bloody Emperor Laisia. How long until the next?" He threw a hand forward in entreaty. "Wed me, I'll take the throne and stand a buffer between the northern barbarians and the rest of the empire."

"And murder countless innocents in a war designed to prevent something that may never come to pass." Saylina turned away. As far as she was able, chained to a couch facing toward his window. "Am I supposed to think you noble for that?"

"I honestly don't give a damn what you think." He dismissed her indignation with a snort of derision. "I'm just offering a chance to do some good. It'll be easier on everyone if you help me. Sentar gets a proper-wed heir to take your brother's place. I've a son soon to be wed who can follow me, and though I've no love for the woman, she does what's needed."

He crossed the room, grabbing her chin and forcing her to look up into his eyes. They blazed with fury, his blue irises almost alight. Like Arkaen's fury when someone insulted Kìlashà.

"But if your pride is too precious to you, my lady—" He bit the title off into an insult. "If your delicate honor matters more than the lives of your people, know this. I will take this throne, by force if needed. And if you won't aid me, those deaths are on your head."

Her cheeks ached under the grip of his fingers, his intensity boring into her. After several breaths, he thrust her back against the couch and stormed to the door.

"Think on it." Oskari slammed the door behind him, the sound of his cursing carrying through the door as he left her alone.

Rubbing at her face with her shoulder, Saylina yanked against the chain. Nothing to do but wait like a meek prisoner. Arkaen would come find her, but if Oskari and his blackguard of an ally were to be believed, they'd planned for that. Her indignation faded as she struggled, the truth of her situation sinking in. If Oskari meant what he said—if marrying her was nothing but a convenient shortcut to his plans—but no. He wouldn't have worked so hard to convince her if that were true. And besides, Oskari had been trying to blend his family with the Sentarsin line for as long as he'd had any power to try.

Rumor said Oskari had tried to arrange a marriage between his sister and Saylina's father when they were both new to their seats. A failure as much to chance as her father's choice, given Oskari's sister died before coming of age. Oskari had followed that by planning a match between his daughter and Arkaen while the girl was barely free of her mother's belly. His claims of concern for the province were nothing more than an excuse for treason. Without Saylina, Oskari would be fighting a war just to take the province, and Emperor Corliann would hardly overlook the murder of his close friend. Oskari would lose any greater plans he might have.

Saylina examined the cuff holding her captive. Tight enough to scrape at her skin, but maybe… she squeezed her hand as narrow as she could, folding her thumb under the rest of her hand. The rough metal bit into her skin, but the base of her hand slipped further into the cuff. A thrill of triumph rushed through her. As she'd thought. Built for male hands. Her own were just delicate enough to slip free. Gritting her teeth against the pain, she worked her hand back and forth, scraping at her own skin as she inched her hand slowly free. If she could get the cuff down her fingers, she could—

A sharp pain stabbed into her hand as her thumb jammed too far. Saylina bit her lip to hold the scream in, whimpering against the pain. Tears built in her eyes, blurring her vision. So gods-damned close. She twisted her hand again, giving a grunt as the movement jarred her injured hand. Another fingernail of movement. Almost there. Another twist, and another. The metal tore into her, blood slicking the surface. Easing the passage of the cuff over her hand. She swallowed bile again, the feel of her own mangled hand rubbing back and forth across the metal turning her stomach. Finally, with a final tug, she pulled her hand free. The pain burned through her hand. But she was free.

Saylina jumped from the couch, running to the door, and froze. He must have set guards, right? She hadn't heard anything, but Oskari couldn't be so overconfident as to think she didn't need guarding. She looked around, eyes settling on the window. No telling how difficult it might be to escape, but that was a better route. She crossed, peeking out through the shutter slats to assess her chances.

Oskari wandered the gardens, the blond man from her abduction following beside with a smug grin. Their conversation was barely more than a murmur, but their path took them closer to her window. Hesitant, Saylina considered her choices. The window would certainly get her caught, but what could she use to get past the guards Oskari must have at her door? As she pondered, the conversation below drifted up to her.

"You can't keep her *here*, of course," the younger thief said. "Our arrangement requires you maintain an appearance of innocence for the time being."

"That's hardly a choice now," Oskari replied. "The boy isn't stupid. He'll know I was involved. Especially since your girl overplayed her hand at the prison."

Their voices faded a bit as they paced through the garden. Saylina edged closer to the window, her hand throbbing at every shift. But this was something Arkaen needed to hear.

"Likely. But without proof, he cannot act. He's bound by his need to appear loyal to these lands."

"If I try to move her, he'll have that proof. He's got the resources to have spies in my house."

The blond man shrugged. "We can do something about that. I have the means to identify any spies and the proper associates to exact revenge for their betrayal."

"I want a clean death for them." Oskari's disgust was plain in his stance. At least he seemed to have some morals. "They've been loyal to their vows, they simply swore to someone other than me."

The other man scoffed. "You're getting soft. But no matter. My people will identify your problems, gather any information they may have, and kill them swiftly. You, however, must find a secondary location. I have a few suggestions, but you'll know best where your people can hold their ground."

Oskari started to complain, but the man threw a hand up to forestall the response, leading him a few steps further. With a glance behind her, Saylina cracked the shutters a tiny bit, leaning out to listen.

"We've no time to debate, Oskari. The emperor arrived today. We can't allow *him* to learn of these plans."

"Emperor Corliann?" Fear shook Oskari's voice. "You were supposed to manage that. What happened to your distraction?"

"You're a fool if you thought that would keep him away forever," the other man said. "As with your high lord, he isn't dull-witted. I've a location you can utilize until you find a proper haven for your prize."

They turned around, striding back toward the keep. Toward her window. Saylina scrambled back into the room, slamming the shutters closed with a quick snap. The clack of wood echoed through the room. The end of her escape attempt, no doubt. But the emperor had taken her message to heart. He'd never have come if he'd thought she'd misread the situation. With imperial resources, Arkaen should be able to track her down no matter where they took her. None of Oskari's supporters would dare deny the will of Emperor Corliann.

The door flew open, a pair of guards scanning the room in distress. They focused on her and their postures relaxed. One came forward to return her to her chain. Just a little longer and she'd be free. As she followed her guard back to the couch, the younger man's words echoed in her ears. *You'll be found. That's the point. The question is whether you'll be alive when they find you.*

Most well-guarded among the Serr-Nyen *was the identity of their new leader—Griffon's replacement and the man from whom Lord Phoenix took orders. He answered to the name of a foreign beast previously unheard of in the empire: the fox demon Kumiho.*

— *from* An Abridged History of the Sernien War

Chapter 26

Arkaen paced the receiving room of Sayli's chambers, scanning the space. Receiving couch along one wall with accent pillows laid at precise angles. The formal tea setting spread across Sayli's oak serving table—a gorgeous, hand-crafted masterpiece that Arkaen had gifted her when he first returned. Something beautiful for his beautiful sister. Grief tore at his throat, the ache of strangled sobs threatening to break through. But she wasn't gone. No one could just disappear from the high lord's palace.

Forcing his focus on the details again, Arkaen examined the scene. Nothing out of place. Except her maid's body, dead at least several hours by the tightness of the muscles, skin still warm enough to have died this morn. But that meant they had taken Sayli while he still lounged in his study. Impossible, but an incontrovertible fact. Dead bodies never lied, and he'd seen enough in the war to know how to read the signs.

A clatter of boots in the hall outside heralded Deyvan's return with several of his guards. The soldiers stopped at the door, noting the scene and whispering among themselves.

"Anything of note?" Deyvan stepped over the maid to pause a few steps into the room.

"Nothing." Arkaen waved at the tea. "She'd been entertaining some-one, though I didn't know Camira ever came here. But this wasn't about blackmailing me. Either they have plans for her alive, or they plan to kill her. And if they want her—" He choked on the word again. Cleared his throat. "They'd have done it already."

Deyvan nodded. "So we investigate. Who sent those assassins you mentioned? That'd be my first guess."

"Too many options." Arkaen leaned back against Sayli's windowsill. "Could have been Oskari, or a band of adventurous thieves, or…"

He trailed off, reluctant to admit his reservations over his father's old guards. So far none had acted against him. Unless he counted the battle earlier that day.

Deyvan smirked at him. "Back to making friends, I see."

"It's complicated," Arkaen said. "Too many of the lower lords know exactly what I thought of my father's rule and why I left. And I ask for their loyalty now? I almost don't blame them for being wary."

Deyvan gave a careless shrug, dismissing his explanation as easily as a hunting dog abandoned a false trail when it found the prey. The analogy gave him pause. False trails and misdirection. He'd met someone recently who dealt heavily in both.

"They lured me."

"Surely you didn't *just* realize that." Deyvan scoffed.

Arkaen shook his head. "Not what I meant. Of course I was lured out of my palace. It's the only way this works. I mean—" It seemed so obvious when he thought the timing through. Everything started the night he met her. "The instability. It's been simmering for years. But in the past week, since Kìlashà sent me to the reception. Why would she choose Oskari's estate? I should have seen it."

"Maybe you'd better explain, Kaen. Who chose your rebellious baron's estate for what?"

"The princess." Arkaen pushed off from the window. "I've someone you should meet, Deyvan. I may start a war bringing you to her door, but I'd bet anything she has Sayli."

"Perhaps—"

Deyvan cut off at Arkaen's glare. The air congealed into a palpable battle of wills, Deyvan's ice-blue eyes boring into Arkaen. War. Revealing Prillani in all her animosity to the Laisian emperor *would* be war, especially if it came with an accusation of abduction. Arkaen ground his lips together into a scowl. She was the only unknown force. Any other would have taken Sayli before. When Arkaen had no ability to protect her.

"It's her, Deyvan." Arkaen's hand slid across the hilt of his saber. It had to be her.

"If we're going to accost a *princess*." Deyvan's voice took on a sharp note at the final word. "Perhaps you should put on something clean. No point starting a war over poor manners."

Arkaen glanced at his tunic, torn and blood smeared, and muttered a curse. The stiff fabric hadn't seemed to matter with Sayli's life on the line. But Prillani's interest in her hadn't been feigned. She wouldn't hurt Sayli. The abduction likely served as a demonstration of power, or possibly a bargaining piece to get him to agree to her marriage plans. Sayli might not even realize everything Prillani had done.

Gods, he hoped she didn't. Sayli deserved a genuine friend.

Running a hand through his already unruly hair, Arkaen crossed the room. "I'll be out in five minutes. Gather your guards. I don't trust mine."

He ran from the room before Deyvan could question him, tugging at the laces that held his tunic and undershirt secure. By the time he reached his door, the remnants were hanging free from his shoulders. A few moments to scrounge through his armoire and into fresh clothes before he slipped out the door again. He darted through the halls, slowing just a moment to pause by the turn to his guest quarters. Lasha had never looked so shaken.

Gods, what was he going to do? Lasha held every answer, knew every choice they needed to make. If he'd lost that…

Arkaen shook himself out of his worry, turning back to his path. He could restore Lasha's confidence once he'd found Sayli. Once his sister was safe. His footsteps pounded in time with his heart, aching with fear. What if he was wrong? What if someone else had taken her for ransom or just to hurt Arkaen? What if Lasha never recovered?

The doors to his courtyard stood open when he turned the corner. He stepped into the sun where Deyvan held sway over Arkaen's still-congested courtyard. A swirling mass of servants and angry guardsmen circled a stable center waiting in the middle of the courtyard. Six horses, two of Deyvan's guards, Deyvan, and two guards in Arkaen's customized *Serr-Nyen* uniforms—stoic amid the chaos as Deyvan lifted a hand in greeting. Arkaen jogged down the steps.

"My lord, I must object." Count Tenison fell into step beside him. "Our emperor says you plan to leave again. Some concern for Lady Saylina's safety? You can't possibly put yourself in harm's way again."

"I'll explain when I return." Arkaen pushed through the crowd to Deyvan's side.

Deyvan nodded at the *Serr-Nyen* guards. "Your Sernien flameguard insisted. I figured they'd suffice."

Arkaen nodded, taking the reins of his mare from a young woman he vaguely recalled from a raid on an imperial storage facility six years before. Gods, what was her name? She'd taken that nasty wound to her thigh, leaving her unfit for standard combat the rest of the war.

"My lord." Count Tenison grabbed his arm. "I insist. After the ruinous events at your new jail, we simply cannot—"

Arkaen spun away, pulling one blade free and catching himself just before the pommel connected with Count Tenison's throat. Nothing would bring war faster than assaulting a member of the lower lords' council. But he didn't have time for this.

Arkaen slammed the sword back into its sheath. "My sister is missing, Jussi. I don't give a *damn* about anything else right now."

Count Tenison stared at him, eyes wide in terror, his hand on Arkaen's arm grabbing at the fabric as a lifeline. Arkaen cursed. He should have known better. Brayden had said it after the mess with Oskari. The situation was far too grand for a temper tantrum.

"Lord Arkaen." Deyvan's voice held the sharp bite of reprimand. "If you plan to start a war, announce it so we can be on our way."

A murmur rippled through the crowd. Arkaen cast around and found a servant, grabbing the tunic before the man could back away.

He pointed at Count Tenison. "Take Count Tenison to my study and see he gets whatever he needs from my palace." Arkaen stepped back, turning to his horse. "I'm the one she wants, Jussi. If I send someone else they'll be dismissed, maybe even killed. I *have* to go."

Grabbing a handful of his mare's mane, Arkaen leaped into the saddle and rode out the gate, Deyvan and the guards following close behind. The empty streets echoed back the clack of the horses' hooves on hard cobbles as he navigated once more through the city. Right and through the fountain square, still and silent as he'd never seen it. Only the gentle ringing of water broke the eerie quiet. No guards. Where were the guardsmen he'd assigned to watch the square?

Arkaen slowed his mare to a walk, scanning the area. Nothing. The aftermath of the fight had spread this far already. War was inevitable, Lasha said, and Arkaen couldn't help but believe him. Nothing would stop this short of bloodshed.

"Gods damn it all," he muttered, urging his mare into a trot.

Deyvan rode up beside him. "From what Sayli said, I doubt there was much choice, Kaen. Baron Weydert has been pushing you since you returned. You were going to come to blows, eventually."

Arkaen nodded, lips pressed into a frown as he wove his way through the town. A turn here, through another deserted square, around a long, arcing lane. Finally, the broad street that led to his extensive visitor's estate came into view, the two-story manor home easily large enough to house any foreign dignitary and host a small reception. Not that choosing to hold the royal Osuvian reception at Baron Weydert's estate meant anything per se. Sentar tradition allowed any noble to host the formal reception of a foreign dignitary. But considering recent events, Oskari's apparent fascination with the Osuvian princess held an ominous undertone.

Pulling his mare to a halt in the entry of the small courtyard, Arkaen frowned at the flurry of activity. The stables bustled with servants polishing tack, saddling mounts, and harnessing a finely matched pair of dress stallions to a carriage. Several more scurried from the guest's lodge to the stables and back, ferrying boxes and other accoutrements to the carriage or pack horses. Deyvan cast Arkaen a sidelong glance.

"It would seem your princess is leaving, Kaen."

"Indeed." Arkaen nudged his horse forward, raising a hand to catch the attention of one of the servants.

The young woman ducked past him, arms loaded with a bundle of furs. She dropped into the barest of curtsies, proving she knew enough to recognize his status regardless of whether she knew who he was. All the motion swirled around him, a drifting center of calm in the frenzied work.

"I've come to request a visit with Princess Kitorn," Arkaen called, scanning the windows of the manor house for any sign of a response.

Shuttered tight, most of the rooms beyond dark and to all appearances empty. His words drew the attention of several servants, though. For half a breath the entire courtyard froze, all attention focused on him. As if they hadn't even noticed he was there before. And then they ran.

Some servants fled into the stables or the manor home, seeking what protection they might find behind Arkaen's own walls. Others hurried away down the lanes that led to the guest house's gardens—fallow this season, as he'd been too concerned with Oskari's growing protests to import the seeds he'd need for a proper winter garden. Clearly he should have been concerned with foreigners sowing rebellion, as well.

Deyvan rode forward, his chestnut stallion pushing through the crowd to draw some focus away from Arkaen. Two to avoid instead of one, sowing additional confusion. Deyvan stood to his full height in the stirrups and shouted over the crowd.

"No need to flee, goodsirs and madams! We've only come to talk."

Arkaen grabbed one of the servants who came close, backing away from Deyvan without noticing Arkaen immediately behind.

"Why are they frightened?" Arkaen demanded. "I've never hurt your people. You're my guests."

The man's wide eyes latched onto Arkaen's face and he shook his head. "Not you, milord. She's gonna—"

"Where do you all think you're going?" The woman's voice, precise but thickly accented, echoed from the doorway and across the courtyard. "You've orders to prepare our lady's belongings for her journey. Why—"

Stepping onto the top of the stairs, she froze and stared at Deyvan. The deep brown of her Yllshanan skin drew Deyvan's eyes like a moth to a flame. Prillani's maid and head of her entourage. Her eyes locked onto Deyvan, each sizing up the other. Arkaen released the servant he held and rode toward her, the few remaining servants parting before him.

"I've come hunting your princess," Arkaen said. "I hadn't heard she'd decided to return home."

"High Lord Arkaen." The maid curtsied, bowing her head in respect.

An excuse to break eye contact with Deyvan, probably. He could be intense.

"I thought my lady informed you," she continued. "We have business with a northern trade partner. I'm certain she simply forgot to mention the schedule."

Even if he hadn't known better, Arkaen could hear the lie in her words. A hasty excuse to cover for a visit she hadn't expected. And the servant's words came back to him. *She's gonna…* Either fear of Prillani herself or of this poised maid, clearly their leader, and used to being obeyed despite being born of common blood. Arkaen feigned a polite smile, his guts twisting into a nervous ball of terror. If Prillani was preparing a hasty departure, where had they taken Sayli?

"Your princess implied to me she intended further discussions," Arkaen said. He waved a hand at the manor house. "Let's step inside so I can speak with your princess to discuss this miscommunication."

She hesitated. "Not possible, I'm afraid. My lady has already left the city. I must join her."

Arkaen swung down from his horse, snapping a command as he strode forward. His mare followed at a sedate pace, but one ear kept flicking forward. Toward a boy crouched near the stairs. The twitch of his mare's ear served as a warning, perhaps, as she guarded his back. Deyvan glanced at him.

"A war-trained mare, Kaen? Seems a bit unnecessary." Deyvan smiled at the maid. "Osuvia is our ally."

"She saved my life several days back."

The boy drew Arkaen's attention again, slipping along the edge of the manor home. Something about him nagged at Arkaen's memories. The shaggy blond hair. Not uncommon by any stretch, but why did it bother him so? His mare's ear twitched again, one hoof pawing as she paused for half a step.

"If you've such an interest in my lady's servants, you can visit her home when our business is done, High Lord." The maid turned away, ignoring the protocol even Osuvia must have. Commoners didn't dismiss noblemen. Certainly not an emperor while a guest in his lands.

Another glance at the boy. He'd ducked his head, one hand resting on the knife at his side. A knife too long for a servant's eating blade. The child's gaze latched onto him. No, onto his mare. And that was the final reminder.

"I must protest," Arkaen said. "You'll find time to speak with me or I'll haul you to the imperial court to answer for your attempted assassination of a Laisian imperial high lord."

"Assassination?" She sounded genuinely stunned, turning back to stare at him.

Arkaen leveled a finger at the boy. "That child stood beside their leader as he ordered his fighters to take my life. By my official title. If you harbor the boy knowing his crime, you're as complicit as he."

"My lady would never—" The maid gestured to another of the servants, who ran forward to grab the lad. "The boy isn't one of ours. He brought a message, sealed by our lady's seal. I assumed he was one of your messengers."

"You've already lied to me once," Arkaen said. "Claiming Princess Kitorn's departure was planned when we both know she intended to stay longer. You'll forgive me if I demand your time anyway."

She scowled. "That's hardly a proper way to treat your guests, High Lord."

He paused at the foot of the stairs, his guards joining him on either side and Deyvan riding up behind. The boy's struggles as her servant turned him over to Arkaen's guards drew her attention.

"Fine." She sighed. "Follow me."

She led them into the manor home, most of the preparations here already complete. The foyer was bare of any additions from Princess Kitorn's visit, the side table covered by a dust cloth to protect the finish. Servants had swept the hall beyond clean, and as they topped the stairs, he could see both of the twin studies stood empty and darkened. The maid chose a small sitting room with couches still uncovered, taking a seat in the one chair. As if she ruled the house and not Arkaen. Presumptuous, but not worthy of a fight in this moment.

Arkaen crossed to the window, but Deyvan spoke before he could find the right words.

"Well, goodwoman, I think you've a predicament," Deyvan said. "My high lord accuses you of involvement in an attempted assassination."

The maid looked at Arkaen. "A bit tasteless to bring the emperor to my lady's door after your recent discussions, isn't it, Lord Arkaen?"

"And why would that be?" Arkaen smiled. "I never once denied my loyalty to my imperial home. If your princess misunderstood, well…"

"You made the implications. You know what they were."

"As do I," Deyvan said. "Lord Arkaen and I have no secrets. But I'm not here to debate your nation's political decisions. My high lord's sister has been abducted and evidence points toward your princess's involvement."

"Impossible!" The maid leaned forward, seeming to hold herself in the chair by simple force of will. "Her Highness has always shown kindness to Lady Saylina. To accuse her of harm… Insulting. What do you think you have?"

"I'd every desire to believe in your princess's sincerity," Arkaen replied. "But Sayli is missing, and Her Highness is the only new player. Where was she this afternoon?"

"Answering your sister's invitation, Lord Arkaen." She crossed her arms, fixing Arkaen with a stern glare. "How dare you claim evidence when you don't even know what Lady Saylina was doing?"

"Princess Kitorn has been colluding with my former baron."

But she did have a point. He hadn't spoken with Prillani since the ambush, and Sayli had her hands in a dozen negotiations. He'd found nothing to directly tie Prillani to any of the problems he'd experienced. Only the eerie coincidence of her arrival right as everything began. And the boy who'd tried to kill him, that Prillani's maid claimed was just a messenger.

"Your princess spoke to me of an ally to *Serr-Nyen* autonomy in my province. What did she mean?"

Arkaen had assumed Prillani meant him. But what if she knew something he didn't? What if she'd been hinting at an alliance she intended him to investigate?

"I can't guess." The maid shrugged. "If Her Highness wished your family harm, she wouldn't have spent so much time seeking to ingratiate herself with you. Seek your traitor elsewhere. I have a journey to prepare for."

"Where?" Arkaen considered the messenger boy. Too tense. As if he expected something to happen.

"My lord, you can't think—"

"Answer the question." Deyvan came to Arkaen's side, watching the messenger as well. "Where are you going, and why did your princess leave without her entourage?"

She followed their looks, frowning. The child cowered under the combined scrutiny.

"Her Highness said she traveled to an ally with her local contact. I thought it was you, Lord Arkaen."

"As I'm sure you were meant to," Deyvan said.

Arkaen pushed away from the wall, stalking to the boy's side. He grabbed the narrow face, tilting up until the messenger had no choice but to look into the fury of Arkaen's eyes.

"Where are they?"

"They?" The maid's voice shook with her realization.

Arkaen ignored her, holding the boy's gaze with barely restrained temper, his muscles aching for release. This little bastard had tried to murder him, had aided in the abduction of his sister. Fear filled the boy's face, his complexion paling. Arkaen could feel the skin beneath his fingers tremble. Could hear the boy's mouthed prayer. *Aeduhm guard me from evil.* As though Arkaen were the one who had slaughtered an innocent servant and abducted two noblewomen. But innocence shied from Arkaen as surely as from this boy. His own guardsmen's blood clung to his fingers, beyond the ability of any water to wash it clean, and Lasha's question hung in his ears. *Did he?*

"Answer Milord Phoenix." One of Arkaen's flameguard. Treasonous, but Deyvan would understand.

Shaking his head as much as he could while held in Arkaen's grasp, the messenger glanced at the guard. Back to Arkaen. Mumbled another prayer.

"Speak, lad." Arkaen pitched his voice to a coaxing plea, prying his fingers away. The anger and fear left him shaking inside, but that emotion could only hurt his case. "I'll forgive your crimes. You didn't choose this life. Why suffer for it?"

The messenger shook his head again. "Can't. He'll—"

Prillani's maid rushed across the room, her hand smacking into the boy's face. All chance of diplomacy lost, no doubt. But Arkaen couldn't blame her.

"Tell—where—princess is!" Her voice broke in her anger, her thick accent leaving the words almost unintelligible.

Arkaen grabbed her arm. "Let the boy be, goodwoman. He's a child, not a mastermind."

She snatched her hand away, drawing herself up to a prideful sneer. "In my lands, Lord Arkaen, children are responsible for their actions."

"And he'll be punished," Deyvan promised. "But we don't beat children. Lord Arkaen, you have a place for the boy?"

Arkaen scowled. He had a prison, but he'd just fought a battle there and named it off-limits as a memorial to the fallen. He could leave the boy in a servant's room in his own keep and put a guard on the door.

But someone had abducted Sayli from that very keep. Arkaen turned to Deyvan, shaking his head.

"Perhaps you should take charge of him. My guards are suffering a loss of loyalty."

A tug at his waist, shouts of warning from Deyvan and Prillani's maid. Arkaen ducked under the boy's clumsy strike, his own dagger flashing past his nose. The boy choked, a gurgling grunt as one of Arkaen's flameguard shoved a spear through his back. Arkaen scrambled out from beneath the falling body.

"Eiliin's tits." Deyvan grabbed him, pulling him to his feet. "Are you all right, Kaen?"

"Uninjured." He muttered a curse. "But that was our only source of information."

And what in all the gods' names had possessed the boy to try to kill him here? He must have known he wouldn't succeed. That it would cost his life.

"Allow me to offer another potential contact," Prillani's maid said, brushing at her dress as if to wipe away the spectacle of violence before her. "When Her Highness thought *you* sincere, Lord Arkaen, she sent me to meet with a woman aligned to Sernyii's cause. I don't know her name, but she was of Yllshanan blood mixed with imperial, and she wore the uniform of a nobleman's servant. Green and—"

"Gold." Arkaen sighed. "Niamsha. Of course she's mixed in this. She's at Oskari's estate, if she's made it back yet. But I can hardly go pounding on his door demanding he return my sister."

Deyvan's perverse laughter broke the tension. "No need. Your high emperor has just arrived to reports of unrest in his northern province. Surely a visit to hear the concerns of a recently disgraced nobleman is warranted."

"I don't like it, Deyvan," Arkaen said. "Too much has gone wrong, and—" He glanced at the maid. No reason to reveal more information than she needed. "My chief adviser struggles to understand Niamsha's actions."

Deyvan's eyebrows shot up. "All the more reason, Kaen. We need direct information."

"Then be careful." Arkaen retrieved his dagger from the dead boy's hand. "And if you see her, don't trust the girl."

With a nod, Deyvan strode from the room. Arkaen sighed, turning to Prillani's maid.

"What are we doing while we wait, Lord Arkaen?"

"Come with me." He strode to the door, his flameguard falling in beside him. "I'd like your thoughts on the scene where they were taken. Maybe you'll see something I didn't."

A proper tool knows not only what to tell and what to hide, but also what not to hear. You hear something you shouldn't, there's only two options: buy forgiveness with leverage of your own or wait for the headsman's block.

— Thief's Code

Chapter 27

Niamsha cursed, staring at the plain wood chairs she'd pushed against the far wall of her room in the Rogue Baron's home. What, in Aeduhm's Holy Name, had Nijel done? A prize for the Rogue Baron? Nothing good could come of those words, especially not when he'd referred to the prize as *she*.

Pacing the room, her booted feet trod silently on the thick rug the Rogue Baron's cook had given her. To keep the room warm, the woman said. But this room, a luxury of open space filled with two chairs, a window, and a proper bed with a straw-filled mattress, needed no more charms. More privacy than she'd ever had, even under her papa's roof. And the cook said this room was evidence the Rogue Baron disliked her.

Niamsha ran a hand over the rough fabric of her bed. Scanned the room again. All this—comfort and safety beyond any she'd known—if she just kept quiet. If she waited, let the nobles figure out this mess of a conflict and kept her head down.

Papa wouldn't know his little girl now.

Her shoulders hunched in shame, hand trembling against the fabric. She couldn't keep this quiet. No one decent would keep this quiet. No matter the cost she might pay, Nijel's work needed told. Needed stopped, before someone got hurt. Honor before hunger, Papa used to say. And thief or not, her papa hadn't raised the sort of wretch that would let an innocent woman be sold like common street goods.

Niamsha grabbed the door handle and pushed out into the hall before she could change her mind. Nijel'd said the Rogue Baron's study. She threaded her way through the polished stone halls toward the public study. A walk she knew far too well after the last weeks. And one she didn't dare finish without a story to tell. If the Rogue Baron was already inside, he'd have no qualms hitting her for interrupting without good reason. But she hadn't yet reported on the events at the jail, and he'd certainly want to know how High Lord Arkaen had acted.

The study door sat open, just enough to prove someone waited within. Taking a deep breath to slow her frantic heart, Niamsha stepped inside. A large, red-haired man in plain brown clothes turned to look, examining her as she froze. A quick glance around. No one else in the room. And a heavy sword with a wide blade and long handle leaning against the desk beside the man.

"Well, you're certainly not Oskari," the man said. "Is he running late? Later yet, I should say?"

"I—"

Aeduhm's Mercy. If Nijel hadn't meant *this* study, then where—but maybe she was too late. Maybe the Rogue Baron had already moved whoever he'd taken somewhere else. The red-haired man's ice-blue eyes held her attention. She needed an answer.

"Sorry, ser, I's just…" No gutter speak in a fine lord's home. Dammit. But she couldn't fix her speech now. "Just lookin' fer me brother."

She backed away, glancing down the hall. Still empty. But if this man expected the Rogue Baron to arrive, she'd better get out of here before her blunder got her in trouble.

"I doubt Oskari has more than one foreign-born servant." The man's voice was loud. Too loud. Anyone might hear him. "I'm honestly surprised he has one, given how hard he fought Kaen's laws on foreign trade."

Ice trickled up her spine, the implicit threat in his words eating at her nerves. The Rogue Baron knew about her, of course, but the threat of revealing her blunder held as much weight as this man obviously hoped it might. Another glance down the hall. If the Rogue Baron was coming, she'd better stay. Claim she'd been entertaining the guest. One hint that she'd seen this man and run could goad the baron into acting on the suspicion he'd voiced to Nijel. Niamsha slipped back into the room, closing the door behind her.

"He knows I'm here." She crossed her arms, leaning against the door so she'd have a warning if someone tried to enter.

"In this manor home, I'm sure," the man said. "But here, in this study? I think not, or you wouldn't have looked so terrified on seeing me."

"Wrong door. Ain't nothin'."

He smirked. "We both know it is. Who were you looking for?"

Niamsha's heart pounded against her ribs. He'd already refused to believe her story. But if he was one of the Rogue Baron's allies, she'd regret ever pausing in this room. He certainly had the look of nobility. Hair polished and slicked into a neat tail at the nape of his neck, fingers clean and pale as only those that had never seen a day's hard work could be. But his palms were thick with callouses. Her gaze slid to the sword. Not someone she wanted to challenge, no matter the circumstances.

He followed her look. "That blade's not really suited for a noble's study. More of a war blade, best when I've got a reliable shield mate to cover my flank." He looked back at her. "And I'd hate to scar such beautiful skin."

A rush of heat to her cheeks. Was he flirting with her? Impossible. Imperial nobles didn't care for foreign half-breeds. She knew that far too well.

"I ain't looking fer no one." Niamsha shook her head to emphasize the denial. "Just got lost."

"I see."

His eyes bored into her, her palms sweating against the sides of her tunic as she fought to remain calm. No telling what he might say. Or to who. What if Nijel had sent him? No one got the sort of power Nijel held without friends able to make problems disappear.

The man shrugged, suddenly careless and dismissive. "Very well." He turned away, leaning back in his chair. "I only asked because I am also looking for someone. A young lady with exquisite green eyes. I thought perhaps you'd seen her."

Niamsha let out a sigh, grabbing the door handle and turning it a half turn. Paused. He was looking for a woman and had come to the Rogue Baron's estate. She should leave. Whoever this man sought, he'd either find her or she was long gone. Unless Nijel had made a present of her.

"Why ya think she's here?"

He turned his head, just enough to give her a sidelong stare through his blue eyes. "Why has this detail piqued your interest?"

Aeduhm curse his maddening caution. But she felt the same. If he revealed her… but he may well be in the same place. One of them would have to trust the other. And she couldn't afford to trust first.

"Can't just say." Niamsha glanced behind her, the door a flimsy guard against the risk of interruption. Released the door handle to cross her arms again. "Who are ya?"

He let out a boisterous laugh, shattering the tension long enough for her to worry about drawing attention from beyond. Before she could react, he rose, turning to lean against the Rogue Baron's desk with a casual disregard that would have gotten her backhanded and possibly banished.

"I suppose a little humility never hurt." He flashed her a grin. "You must be quite new among the noble houses."

Niamsha bit at her lip. She'd missed something, and by his smile it would be important. But no hiding her inexperience now.

"Couple weeks. Barely."

He nodded, watching her for several long moments. "Call me…" He hesitated, glancing at the door. "Kumiho."

A false name. She shouldn't trust him with her name at all. But she had nothing else, and she couldn't remain a mystery girl to him if she planned on getting any information. No risk, no reward. "Nia."

Kumiho raised an eyebrow at her. "Is that all? That's a bastardization of a noble heritage if I'm any judge."

The rush of heat to her cheeks again. How many Laisian imperials would bother to even wonder if that was her true name? Or maybe he planned on rooting as much information from her as he could, to use at a later date against the Rogue Baron. Or against Nijel. Or against her.

"If that's what you prefer, though, no shame in it. I only thought—"

"Niamsha." She couldn't hold the name back. Even to a stranger, couldn't discredit her mother's pride in her homeland. She straightened, lifting her chin in what she hoped looked like defiance. "Niamsha Pereyra, but Imperials ain't never get it right."

Kumiho smiled again. "Niamsha Pereyra." Only a hint of mangling the 'yr' that tripped up so many tongues. "Now that is a proper, and beautiful, Yllshanan name. Thank you for sharing it."

The intensity of his gaze ate at her, finally forcing her to drop her eyes. What did he want from her? His gaze bored into her like fragments of Eiliin's cursed soul formed into azure needles, extracting some knowledge she couldn't fathom from her posture or movements or who knew what else.

"Have you seen my missing lady, Niamsha?" Gentle, coaxing voice. "She'd be about your age. Brown hair, pale skin. Rather slight in figure, and a bit taller than you."

She cast a glance up at him, hands clenching in the fabric of her tunic. He had to be looking for the woman Nijel had taken. Too much coincidence. It couldn't be another. Unless he was testing her, working for Nijel as a spy. That soothing tone was identical to Nijel's most placating—and most dangerous—pretense.

"I ain't see no one." She shook her head, shoulders trembling. What if he really was trying to help? "She ain't come here that I know. They ain't—"

She watched his expression as she cut off, hunting for any sign of predatory joy. Focus, immediate and fierce as she spoke the words, but no triumph. Maybe his claims weren't all lies.

"They?" Kumiho dropped his gaze, examining something on a piece of paper beside him. But his free hand gripped the edge of the desk hard enough to turn his knuckles pure white. "Anything you can share is valuable. If someone you know saw her, they may be able to direct me to her next destination. I've a friend rather frantic over her well-being."

Too calm. She knew that voice, cultivated for the moments when everything fell apart and you didn't dare show your fears. When her papa had died and she'd realized the former guild masters had no intention of honoring their duty to his children despite the 'prentice fees Papa'd paid for them. When she'd looked into Master Ferndon's eyes and been sure that any word of reproach would land her in the new-built jail.

Her heart ached for this stranger—Kumiho—who would hunt a woman across the city for the sake of a friend. And he had power. Some, at least, to walk into the Rogue Baron's study with a sword meant for war and casually usurp the baron's desk as a stool. Maybe her best plan for stopping Nijel lay with Kumiho.

"Niamsha?" He watched her out of the corner of his eye, frozen in an inquisitive pose.

"I ain't able to speak to it all." The words rushed out, as fast as she could to make sense. If the Rogue Baron—or, Aeduhm save her, Nijel—discovered her talking to a noble about the little she'd seen... No telling where she'd end up. "Out west, past the fine houses where the old market was before the gods-damned high lord took our fair field for a prison."

She paused. Kumiho narrowed his eyes, muttering under his breath as if marking her betrayals as she spoke. Her hands shook, arms tingling with raised hairs. Already she'd said enough to damn her. From either side of this conflict.

He waved a dismissive hand. "Go on. I'm simply marking your landmarks. It's been many years since I roamed the city with any freedom."

Niamsha's heart pounded in fear. But it was done now. No turning back.

"I ain't seen the girl. But I's coming back from the fight by the prison an' one o' the houses as used ta be a fine ale house. He said she was a nice prize—"

Her breath clogged in her throat. To betray Nijel, here in a house where he'd sent her to do his bidding. What if he found out? Nijel didn't need to kill to make a point. The merchant's whimpers as Nijel's guards dragged him away echoed in her ears.

"Who, Niamsha?" Kumiho demanded. "I can't act without a name."

She licked her lips. Kumiho needed to know. If Nijel ever learned she'd revealed him, he'd kill her. But Papa hadn't raised a coward or a liar. Or a slaver. She wouldn't let Nijel do this. *Couldn't.* Not and face her mother and Papa when she passed. Which wouldn't be long when Nijel found out.

"He runs the thieves. The Rendells. They answer to Nijel." The name fouled her tongue like rotten meat. "He and the Rogue Baron got plans. Reckon, the girl ain't here, she gotta be down south in the Rendell house."

Kumiho snatched the blade from beside the desk, pushing off to cross the room. "That's enough. Come with me. If they find out you've told me—"

"Can't." Her fear hung in her throat like a gag. But Nijel would know if she left. And he had Emrys. "Gotta find me brother."

"You're actually looking for your brother?" He sounded stunned, like it had never occurred to him that she'd told the truth.

"Not like… it ain't—" Niamsha scowled, rubbing her arms as a chill shook her body. "He's one o' them. But not true. Not like the ones born to it. He's young, and he don't know. I gotta—"

What would she even say if she found Emrys? He'd rejected her—abandoned her twice already. Kumiho set a gentle hand on her shoulder.

"I understand." His hand laid a heavy weight on her. A warning a part of her knew better than to ignore. "Please, don't risk yourself. Some are already too far gone, and they can't be saved. No matter how dearly we love them."

Niamsha shook her head. "I gotta try."

He closed his eyes, a momentary flash of grief crossing his face. "Then be safe. Should you need my aid, come to the high lord's palace, seek the guards in plain clothes, and tell them Kumiho expects you."

With that he slipped out the door with a deftness she'd never have guessed a man that broad could manage. Niamsha shuddered, glancing around the empty room. No guards, no reason for Nijel to protect her. Except he couldn't know what she'd done. Yet. But she'd better find Emrys before he did. Before *anyone* did.

Niamsha scurried through the halls of the Rogue Baron's home, the circuitous route steering her clear of the few servants and guards she'd become friendly with. No time for a chat. The Rendell house was close—enough that she had a chance of getting to Emrys before Kumiho could make it back to his own noble house and bring forces to bear. His parting words echoed in her ears. But no. *Emrys* could be saved. He was barely more than a child. He couldn't be lost completely.

The sharp murmur of raised voices floated down the hall, escaping from a heavy wood door halfway down. The Rogue Baron's private study. He never entertained guests there. Niamsha slowed, straining to overhear what little she could. Anything could help, and for better or worse, she was bound to Kumiho's fate now.

"I asked for a well-veiled plot to remove the high lord from power," the Rogue Baron snapped. Niamsha could hear the fury even through the thick wood. "You've given me the beginnings of a war. And now the emperor is traipsing around town like a guard dog. I can't take the province with him sticking his nose in."

"Calm yourself, Oskari."

The second voice sent shivers down her spine. Nijel. She'd betrayed Nijel while he was in this very house. Niamsha crept along the hall toward the far end where a side door would let into the courtyard. But Kumiho would want this information. Especially if the emperor was here. The Rogue Baron didn't sound happy, but Nijel always had a plan.

"Your feud with our high lord is of relatively little importance," Nijel continued. "But I'll get you what you want, nonetheless. I *am* a man of my word."

"Little importance? The high lord is the only reason I'm working with you at all."

"Of course." The sneer in Nijel's voice carried clearly through the door. "And I'm the only reason you have a shred of power left. But you're still useful, and so you've nothing to fear. I have plans for His Imperial Majesty."

A moment of silence hung in the hall, setting Niamsha's nerves tingling. If they were done—she couldn't afford to be in the hall when either of them came out. But Nijel's plans for the emperor would be too important to miss. She crept further from the door, close enough to the corner to slip around it if someone stepped out.

"What plans?" The Rogue Baron's voice held all the caution Niamsha felt. "High Emperor Corliann is a good ruler."

"But a false one," Nijel replied. "He usurped the throne from its rightful owner."

"The Sernien rebels—"

"Oh, yes, the *Serr-Nyen!*" Sarcasm dripped from the words. "Ever the villains of this empire. They stole into the palace decades ago and murdered the young princes, poisoned Emperor Laisia's five subsequent wives, and then slew Emperor Laisia in his own bed with tamed warig pups. My, but the *Serr-Nyen* spend a great deal of time in the imperial palace. One might think they've a summer home there."

"Of course the stories are exaggerated," the Rogue Baron said. "But Emperor Laisia died in the war. Not from a kinsman's blade."

"Don't be daft." Nijel's tone was turning sour. A sure sign he was losing patience with the Rogue Baron. "Your good Emperor Corliann is as much a kin-killer as your high lord. That he didn't hold the blade himself is simply a testament to his cowardice. But no matter. Delude yourself as you wish. I've matters to attend to in my own house. You've my lieutenant to aid you with matters here, and I'll contact you when we're ready to move forward to our next steps."

Niamsha darted around the corner. Marcas was here? She should have known better. Nijel wouldn't be here without a reason, and the Rogue Baron already had a prisoner. He'd need help keeping the lady under control. Time to get out and decide who to help later. She'd have no chance to do anything if Marcas—

"Well, lookie here."

Niamsha looked up, eyes going wide at the sight of Marcas lounging against the wall. Of all the worst luck she could have. And backing away would only put her in sight of Nijel and the Rogue Baron. One chance, maybe, to get free.

"Got a job fer the baron." She pointed down the hall behind him. "Needs the merchant hirelings to cause a ruckus."

"Reckon I'd have heard that, lass."

Marcas grinned at her, tapping a hand on a long dagger shoved into his belt. A blade too long for throwing and too wide for sliding between windowpanes. Marcas wasn't here for guard duty. Nijel planned on him killing someone. *I have plans for His Imperial Majesty*, Nijel'd said. No need for guessing what those plans might be.

Niamsha raised her chin, looking down at Marcas as best she could. Mimicking Nijel's haughty air.

"I got places to be. You need something?"

"Nijel said ain't no one can hear his talk." Marcas pushed away from the wall, striding toward her. "And as I heard, you ain't s'posed to be back just yet."

Her heart pounded in her ears. But Marcas couldn't touch her. He'd promised Nijel, and Nijel would never let that slide. Even if he learned Niamsha had turned on him, Nijel wouldn't pass her off to a flunky like Marcas. He'd see to her punishment himself.

But if Marcas had guessed why she was loitering in the hall outside that door—he could tell Nijel whatever he wanted, and there'd be no proof to contradict it. Marcas paused only a step from her, eyes traveling up and down her body as if Nijel'd never interrupted their meeting weeks before.

"Can't lay a hand on me." Niamsha shuddered under the stench of his breath, too close to ignore. "Nijel said. And nothing you say gonna make him let go his tools afore he's ready."

"Might be so." Marcas shrugged. "But word is baron ain't got such a high liking to ya. How 'bout we visit his guest, let Nijel see ta his business. Check with the baron when he's done?"

"Ye can't—"

Marcas grabbed her by the throat, cutting her protest short as she gasped for air. But he didn't dare hurt her. He couldn't. For the first time, Niamsha wondered how far Nijel's protection would really stretch. She clawed at Marcas's hands, stealing tiny breaths through her mouth as he leered at her. One hand left her throat and Marcas let out a harsh chuckle. He rubbed at his crotch, the bulge there leaving no doubt what he planned to do if the Rogue Baron allowed. Her skin crawled at the thought.

Just as Niamsha's strength started to fade, Marcas dropped her, grabbing one shoulder to drag her through the halls toward an unknown destination. Her feet stumbled on the floor, eyes blurry with tears of pain as her neck throbbed. Marcas opened a door and shoved her inside. Blinking her eyes clear, Niamsha focused on the figure directly in front of her.

A young woman rose from a padded silk couch, turning a scalding glare on the door. Brown hair twisted into elaborate designs that framed the delicate lines of her pale face. A deep set of emerald eyes scanned Niamsha and Marcas, hunting a weakness. The woman trailed one hand along the couch, the other tightly bandaged and held at an awkward angle beside her. Pulled away from the woman by a gilded chain.

"Aeduhm's blessed arsehole."

Niamsha backed away. Slammed into someone behind her. A heavy hand fell on her shoulder. Hot, foul breath in her ear. She rushed forward, away from Marcas, gaze flicking around the room for an escape. Painted and paneled walls, priceless sculptures and paintings, a solid shelf built into the wall holding trinkets and enough books to purchase half the slums if they sold well. And Marcas, between her and the only door, with a mocking grin creasing his face.

The woman grabbed Niamsha, pulling her back. "You'll have to go through me for the girl, and I don't think Baron Weydert would care for that very much."

Marcas sneered. "Keep her. That's the plan. Contain the bitch till baron's ready to handle her."

Turning away, Marcas stepped out of the room and as his footsteps paused, his muffled voice drifted through the door. Letting the guards know not to let Niamsha out. A few hours and everyone would know. No help from outside. Which left only one option.

She turned to the woman and offered a hand. "I'm Niamsha."

The woman smiled. "Saylina. A pleasure." She took Niamsha's hand in her delicate grip and gave it one quick shake. "Now that we're introduced, shall we see to getting free?"

*This trio—Kumiho, Lord Phoenix, and the Dragon—formed
the three pillars of the Sernien rebellion, transforming a disor-
ganized collection of followers into an efficient tactical force.
They struck only where they could win and won more frequently
as their ranks grew under Lord Phoenix's recruitment.*

— *from* An Abridged History of the Sernien War

Chapter 28

Arkaen stood by the window of his study, hands resting on the wooden sill. The lazy spiral of fat snowflakes drifted past, landing in the courtyard below. An early snow and one that wouldn't stick beyond the night. But enough to remind him of frozen nights in Serni hiding from the emperor's soldiers. The same deadly chill clung to him now, Sayli's absence hanging over the keep like a specter.

A knock at the door turned him away. He settled into the chair behind his desk and called a greeting, his temper already simmering. If this wasn't news of Sayli...

Count Tenison stepped inside, a servant following behind with an armful of papers. Shivering in the chill of Arkaen's study, Count Tenison cast a glance at the cold fireplace. Logs set for a fire Arkaen hadn't bothered to start.

"Pardon the interruption, my lord," Count Tenison said. "I've some matters from council that require your personal attention."

"It can wait."

Lasha still hadn't come out of his room. Not since the crushing weight of his failure had left him devoid of the power his Ancient Spirits granted. Two and a half days without Arkaen's closest adviser. Spent in agony, turned away every time he'd gone to check on his beloved. Two and a half days since she'd been taken.

"I'm sorry, my lord." Count Tenison's voice broke into his thoughts. "These cannot wait."

Arkaen rose, anger boiling up from his gut and lodging in his throat. "Are you implying that the squabbles of my lower lords are more critical than the life of my sister? Of your province's heir and of my bloodline?"

"I meant nothing of the sort, of course." Count Tenison's face paled, and he threw a defensive hand up as if to ward off an attack. "We all sorrow over Lady Saylina's loss. But it has been three days. We've searched every noble home, sent runners across the province, hired the best trackers and assigned guards to every street. She's not here, my lord, and there's no sign where she might be."

"I don't believe you." Arkaen slammed a hand onto his desk, impotent anger bursting out in what Brayden Skianda would have called another temper tantrum. "The Weydert house only allowed *your* guards in. What was in there? You've been in Oskari's confidence for years, Jussi. You've heard his plans."

"I heard nothing of this," Count Tenison insisted. "I would never sanction—"

"Where would he go?" Arkaen stalked around the desk, chasing Count Tenison further from the door. "What allies does he have? Where might he find a safe haven?"

"I don't know!" Count Tenison slipped away toward the door. Another potential ally driven away. Assuming Count Tenison wasn't a traitor already.

Arkaen stormed back to his window, letting Count Tenison go. If he'd known anything, he'd have long since caved. If any of Lasha's predictions over their years here had been true. And Lasha was right about Brayden.

Count Tenison sighed. "I pray to Aeduhm and His holy children every day for our lady's safe return. But I cannot do more than I have, my lord." He straightened, lifting his chin with pride. "You must do the same. Honor your duty to your province and see to these issues from council."

Arkaen's anger warred with the pull of his duty. He couldn't listen to the petty demands of his lower lords while Sayli sat in captivity. But he'd returned for this, not for her. He'd sacrificed the joys of a simple life among Lasha's Drae'gon clans to argue with pompous braggarts over these trivialities. If he threw that sacrifice away now, he'd disrespect everything Lasha had done as well.

Arkaen collapsed back into his chair, dropping his head into his hands. "What do you have for me?"

Crossing the room, Count Tenison swept a page from the collection his servant had brought and placed it on Arkaen's desk.

"On the matter of your succession—"

"Settled." Arkaen glared at Count Tenison through his hands.

"Lady Saylina is missing. We cannot move toward stability without a secure succession, and there's no certainty she—"

"Jussi." Arkaen straightened in his chair. "The succession of this province is resolved. If you'd prefer a second option, bring your concerns to Deyvan."

"I…" Count Tenison glanced behind him. "Of course, my lord. I'll speak to High Emperor Corliann on the matter."

"What else?" Arkaen's temper simmered in his voice. He was going to regret letting Count Tenison corner him like this.

"Your household guards." Count Tenison laid another page before him. "There's been some concern over increased theft, primarily from your loyal followers among the lower lords. A minor issue until recently. The Sentarsin House Guard seems to have been inactive of late."

"Since when?" Dread added itself to the brew of tension roiling in his stomach. He'd never forget the glares from his household guard when he'd preferred his *Serr-Nyen* flameguard for escort after the riot at his jail.

"Since the unrest several days ago," Count Tenison replied, confirming his suspicions.

"Dammit." Arkaen scowled. "Seek Jarod of my flameguard. He can see to the safety of my streets."

"With respect, my lord." Count Tenison paused as if expecting a reprimand. When none came, he continued. "The lower lords' council fears the image of foreign-born guards patrolling the streets."

"Then I presume you have an alternative?"

"We do." He tapped the document he'd placed on Arkaen's desk. "Count Skianda and I will offer members of our personal household to reduce the burden. Between us, we believe we've enough men to ensure the safety of Torsdell."

Arkaen tapped a finger on his desk, considering. "That's expensive, Jussi."

Count Tenison swept a deep bow. "A minor inconvenience for the security of my home."

"Then you have my gratitude." Arkaen's recent accusations gnawed at his conscience. "And my apologies for doubting your loyalty."

"I could hardly blame you for fearing the worst, my lord. These are difficult days." But the relief was plain in Count Tenison's voice. "We'll need your signature here."

Arkaen skimmed the page. Mostly what Count Tenison had said. A few lines awarded a temporary transfer of power over peace-keeping and added tax easements. Reasonable, considering the service they were providing. Arkaen grabbed a pen, dipped it, and signed. A few drips of red and yellow wax and he pressed his signet ring in, sealing the order. Count

Tenison took the paper as soon as he was done and placed another on his desk.

"As Rikkard Weydert has not come forward to swear his oaths of loyalty, the disposition of his father's barony must be resolved." Count Tenison tapped the name at the bottom of the paper. "Viscount Kaeys has been a loyal servant of the empire for nearly a decade."

"Elevated under Deyvan's uncle?" Arkaen recognized the viscount distantly, though he couldn't put a face to the name. Hadn't he befriended Oskari once?

"I understand your hesitation, my lord," Count Tenison said. "He did swear oaths under Emperor Laisia, but given your questionable reputation among the older nobility, that is a boon. It shows you hold no grudge so long as your lords remain loyal now."

Except Arkaen did hold a grudge against those lords who had accepted titles under Bloody Emperor Laisia. Anyone who'd earned fame under a man determined to perpetrate a genocide had no place in Deyvan's empire. But he couldn't tell Count Tenison that.

"I gave Rikkard more than a barony," Arkaen said. "Has he agreed to take Lady Kyli Andriole to wife?"

Count Tenison frowned. "He has, my lord, but—"

"Then I'll give him a bit longer." Arkaen leaned back in his chair. "I bestowed the honor as much on her as him, and I won't take it from her until I'm certain they intend to reject my position. And planning a wedding can consume a couple. Perhaps it's slipped their minds."

They both knew that wasn't the case, but it was a reasonable enough falsehood to let him delay. Count Tenison nodded, taking the page back.

"Of course, my lord." His disapproval tainted the words. "The other matters…" Count Tenison glanced at his servant. "They can wait until a more opportune time."

"Thank you for your service to our province." Arkaen forced a smile, the twist of his lips foreign after so long consumed by his fear and anger.

Count Tenison bowed again, backing away. He turned at the door and paused, whispering something with his servant. The servant waved a paper from the pile he carried, his eyes darting to Arkaen.

"Jussi."

"Yes, my lord?" Count Tenison looked at him, ignoring the continued complaint of his servant.

"Where's Deyvan? He isn't one to sit idle."

"No, my lord," Count Tenison said. "Our high emperor has been in conference with the maidservant to Princess Kitorn. I believe they left to investigate another home where she thought—" His eyes widened, concern spreading across his face. "I'm sorry I didn't mention it, my lord. I believe High Emperor Corliann wished to learn what might be there before he brought it to you. He feared raising your hopes for no gain."

Arkaen nodded. "He means well."

And Deyvan had been searching for something in the town. Arkaen wasn't entirely certain Sayli was the only thing he hoped to find. The servant muttered something at Count Tenison again.

"I'm sorry, my lord." Count Tenison took the paper, returning to Arkaen's desk. "High Emperor Corliann did send a message for you. He requested you see to the well-being of his cousin, Lord Kìlashà. I gather he feared his cousin had taken ill. I didn't want to trouble you with something so trivial. I'll send—" He stared at the paper and swallowed visibly. "I'll pay the visit myself."

"He requested this before the entire council?" An excuse tailor-made to suit Arkaen's needs. If he could help Lasha regain some level of confidence, they might get a hint to follow.

"He did," Count Tenison admitted. "But your lower lords will understand. Now is not the time to trouble you with social graces."

"Thank you for the offer, my Lord Count." Arkaen forced another smile. "I won't ask you to take this task as well. Lord Kìlashà has not ingratiated himself among my nobility. I'll see to the emperor's request."

"As you say."

The blatant relief would have angered him any other day. But today Arkaen had plenty of other targets for his fury. Besides, Count Tenison had done his best to be useful.

"Good day." Arkaen rose and followed Count Tenison into the hall.

Arkaen strode into through his keep, turning toward Lasha's rooms. His footsteps clicked quickly on the stone floor. Too fast for an appropriate, dutiful visit. But gods, he needed *something* fixed. This cursed day.

Forcing himself to slow his stride, Arkaen's heart pounded against his chest. He needed Lasha whole. For his power, yes, but also… Lasha. How could anything break Lasha's confidence as badly as he'd seen? Even Deyvan's story of Sharan Anore wasn't the same. There, Lasha's power had taken over. Here, it had simply vanished. From his skin, his speech. Everything.

Arkaen turned the final corner and glanced down the hall. Empty, thank the gods. He tried the door. Locked, as he'd feared. Leaning back against it, he gave two slow knocks on the wood. A long pause. Three quick taps in return from the other side. Lasha didn't want to see him.

Arkaen sighed, his eyes drifting closed. He repeated the signal, two slow knocks and wait for a response. Tap-tap-tap. *Go away.* Arkaen repeated his pattern. *No.* A long silence from Lasha. Tap-tap-tap, pause, tap. *Go away, please.* Arkaen hesitated, scanning the hallway for any sign or sound of someone approaching. Nothing.

"Let me in, love," Arkaen whispered.

A frantic scrape of cloth against stone came from the other side of the door, followed by the click of the lock. Lasha yanked the door open and Arkaen slipped into the room. Lasha slammed the door and glared at him. His eyes were narrowed in anger, but his hair and midnight pupils were tame and his shoulders trembled. He'd yet to reclaim his power.

"Are you insane?" Lasha's voice was harsh, and he refused to meet Arkaen's eyes.

"I'd rather die beside you than leave you in pain."

"So yes."

Arkaen stepped toward him, reaching out a hand to brush his cheek. Lasha turned away. Arkaen fought a wave of fear as Lasha stepped away and collapsed into his plush chair, reaching onto his table without looking to grab a book.

"I said go away."

"When I know you're okay," Arkaen replied. He crossed the room to lounge on the bed beside Lasha's chair, one hand twisting the covers into a knot of pure tension as he peered at the book. "And currently you are not."

The book trembled as Lasha's hands shook. Arkaen reached a hand out again, but Lasha twisted away. With a sigh, Arkaen dropped his hand.

"It is not safe for you to be here," Lasha scolded, swapping to Derconian with a scowl at the door.

Arkaen followed Lasha's example and swapped languages. "I come at the express request of my emperor, who made the request before the entire lower lords' council."

"So you've got a quarter hour before you're expected?"

"Gods, I don't care. I need to—" He cut off, rolling onto his back. "How can I help?"

"You cannot, kai'shien." A soft whisper, filled with sorrow and the slightest hint of Lasha's inhuman power and confidence.

Arkaen turned his head, watching Lasha with an ache in his heart. The fiery veins had faded to thin pink lines now, and his skin still mirrored Deyvan's far more than the ghostly pale pallor he usually wore. Lasha looked up. The dark abyss of his eyes still hid under slightly large pupils ringed by his natural, gray irises.

The transformation, more defined now than even in Arkaen's great hall, revealed the sharp lines of his face and the broad-set eyes that marked him as a true-born son of the late Emperor Laisia. Something about Lasha's power hid the features when his connection to the timelines was strong enough to mark his skin. For all that power, Lasha looked so vulnerable without the certainty of his visions filling his eyes. Arkaen smiled at him.

"There's my prince."

"I haven't been a prince in nearly thirty years, kai'shien," Lasha said, his lips twitching into his momentary smile.

He cast a narrow-eyed glare at the door, as if afraid someone might overhear the admission of his heritage, but Arkaen shrugged. No one would understand their words anyway. Derconian was a dead language as far as anyone in the Laisian Empire was concerned.

"Your Emperor Laisia made clear when I was still a small child that he had no desire for a son such as I," Lasha added. "Jaylen Laisia is dead."

"Only so long as you wish him to be," Arkaen said. "I happen to think you're rather handsome as a human."

"I have not been human for as long. Humans do not have kai'shien."

"Nonsense," Arkaen replied. "Your *dragon* clan doesn't get to claim all love in the world just because they have a poetic name for it."

"Drae'gon." Lasha's scowl faded at the old taunt despite the sharpness of his words. He knew Arkaen was teasing. "My people are not pets for your humans to tame and ride. You know that."

"And *you* know that I have never loved you for your clan or your power or your skill with a blade."

"Why?" Lasha's strained voice sent daggers through Arkaen's heart.

"They say Jaylen Laisia was a sweet child, known for his gentle heart and love of all things," Arkaen said. "My people think you so terribly fierce, but the Kìlashà I have always known is as gentle and kind now as he was then."

"You feared me, once."

"You were an ass," Arkaen reminded him. "And I was very young."

"As was I." Lasha smiled. "I hope I'm less of an ass now that we're older."

"Not really," Arkaen said. "But I've adjusted."

Lasha laughed, a soft, carefree sound that soothed Arkaen's fear more than their conversation could. Lasha rarely laughed at the best of times. Arkaen ran a hand through Lasha's hair and the strands twisted of their own volition to twine around his wrist in a sensuous caress that let his hand slide free with ease. The color had deepened again. In the blink of an eye, Lasha's skin paled back to the paper-thin, near transparent white that he'd gained after saving Arkaen in the bathhouse of Sharan Anore. The natural, pinker color of his skin drained like blood pouring from a wound and pooled into his fiery veins. An always terrifying change that revealed Lasha's power and hid his heritage. Lasha frowned at the glowing red of the veins that crossed the back of his hand again.

"Sorry, kai'shien."

"Don't apologize for being more handsome than I." Arkaen leaned closer to speak in his ear. "Keeps my vanity in check."

Lasha laughed again, rising to push him gently back onto the bed. Arkaen's eyelids drifted closed as Lasha leaned over him, his breath brushing along Arkaen's cheek. The kiss still took him by surprise, pouring liquid fire through his body as he let out a quiet moan of pleasure. He reached a hand up to run through Lasha's hair, but Lasha pulled away, tearing the breath from his throat.

"Do we have time?" Arkaen whispered.

Arkaen cracked his eyes open to watch Lasha consider the question, his head cocked and his skin glowing with power. The abyss of Lasha's pupils expanded further to snuff out the last of the white in his eyes as he scanned time for the likely possibilities. Lasha's lips parted and his breath caught. A statue of power and desperation. The answer was no.

"We'll find it," Lasha said.

"There's my kai'shien," Arkaen murmured. He pushed himself up and grabbed Lasha's shirt with his free hand, pulling him down onto the bed.

By the Ancient Spirits he will be called to the aid of the clans, weak when the People find him, and yet he will command the strongest Seeker's power known to the whims of time.

— from the prophecies of the Chosen of the Four Clans

Chapter 29

Kilashà crossed the stone floor of his chambers, one hand trailing on the back of a chair as his thoughts swirled. His hair fell heavy over his brows as it hadn't since the Ancient Spirits had marked his skin with Their power years before, the ever-taxing simmer of his Seeker's power quiet. Silence, as deafening as the din of a thousand futures thrust upon him at once, deep enough to drag all the breath from his lungs if he allowed it to do so.

But no. He was not some weak, mindless human child. He was Kilashà san Draego de Mìtaran, Chosen of the Four Clans. The Seeker's power bent to his will, not he to it. He reached for the power, weaving through time to pull a known vision to the fore. First, the throne room in Whitfaern where Deyvan ruled.

"Raeky, where we goin'?"

Kilashà shook his head. Not the vision he'd planned. But it wouldn't release his thoughts.

Jaylen, barely four and still slightly pudgy with baby fat, his jet black hair cut close to his scalp, looked up at young Prince Raekeen.

Raekeen smiled through golden locks of hair, pushed his cloak back, and revealed a pair of wooden practice swords that hung by his side. "Father doesn't know. Let's play, Jayl."

Jaylen—

Kìlashà. His name was Kìlashà, son of the Drae'gon clanmother Mìtara, who'd raised him as her own. Jaylen Laisia was dead.

—squealed in childish delight. Raekeen led the way through the orchard Father's cook loved so dearly, ending in a small clearing. Jaylen rushed to the center, spinning in circles in the fresh afternoon sun. Father never allowed them to play. A crack of a nearby branch and his joy died. A small girl fell from a tree, far away, but near, yet her scream was empty and her tears silent. In an instant, he knew what would happen. What Father would do.

Kìlashà thrust the vision away, pulling himself free of his power once more. He stumbled forward, sight still fogged with the strength of the vision as he caught himself on the windowsill. It couldn't matter. Decades before, when Kìlashà was too young to know what power he held. The loss of one human girl couldn't mean anything. He'd already followed the line when his Seeker's power had been under control and predictable. The voice of the gods granting him knowledge of all time, objective and pure. If his power had ever been pure.

The door flew open and he spun to face it, heart pounding as he'd never felt it. Kaen, followed by Deyvan, Kaen's face haggard and eyes bloodshot. Deyvan paced in an agitation Kìlashà had never seen from him.

"You have to find her," Deyvan snapped, rounding on Kaen as if he intended harm. "She should be somewhere and she's vanished as surely as Sayli did."

But Deyvan would never harm Kaen. They were as close as brothers. As close as Jaylen and Raeky, before Raeky's blood had spilled across the floor in a monument to the treatment Caildenn planned for his younger son.

Kìlashà gave a sharp shake of his head, focusing on the current moment. Prince Raekeen's death was a tragedy long past, and Kìlashà had no father.

"Of course we'll look, Deyvan." Kaen pulled the door close behind him, his gaze flicking to either side in a quick search for observers before he latched it and turned away. "But I told you not to trust the girl. She's had her hand in too much. She's probably playing you like she did me."

"Don't be obtuse. The girl trusted me and I left her there. Now she's vanished." Deyvan crossed to the chair beside Kìlashà. "Cousin, I need you to find someone."

A flash before his eyes of trees, bright sunlight filtering down through the myriad leaves. "I am uncertain if I can, Deyvan."

"Kìlashà, are you well?" Kaen was at his side in an instant, one hand hovering barely a breath from Kìlashà's shoulder.

No. The answer echoed through his body as a foreign, crippling, *human* need. Kaen's body, close enough to smell his rose-scented soap even without the aid of Kìlashà's tragyna brews, radiated concern. Death to them both if anyone stepped through that door. And he couldn't tell how likely such a future was. But Deyvan had come. No human of these lands would interrupt their emperor in confidence with his high lord. Or so Kaen told him.

"I will be well, kai'shien." The lie sat heavy in his gut, a falsehood spoken without need. Drae'gon did not lie. A vision flashed before his eyes.

Kaen stood poised by his desk, one hand still lingering on the papers his human subjects had delivered as he regarded Kìlashà through a mask of regret and the slightest of smiles. "Your Drae'gon understand love. They mate for life. It's hardly true to say you didn't expect this."

"But it is not the same." Kìlashà *cocked his head, searching for the words to clarify the distinction to his kai'shien. "The Drae'gon have not the fragility of human hearts."*

Kìlashà pulled himself free. Nothing to be gained from that moment. He'd long known his human blood tainted his Drae'gon training. That it perverted his Seeker's power as well as his nature was only one more reason the Chosen should not have been born human.

"I'm sorry, cousin." Deyvan collapsed into the chair beside Kìlashà's bed. "I shouldn't pressure you. As if you haven't enough problems. It's just—"

"Whom do you seek?" Kìlashà raised his gaze, forcing his eyes to focus on the cousin of his human blood. "I am uncertain if my powers may be of assistance, but I will attempt to find what information I can."

Deyvan looked up, the blue of his eyes dark with fear. "A young woman in Oskari's home. Gods, she was just like me when I was younger. Terrified and trying to save her family. Dark hair, Yllshanan bloodline, but not full. She called herself—"

"Niamsha Pereyra." Kìlashà felt the name in his blood before it could escape Deyvan's lips. "You have met Niamsha, and she has come into difficulty once more."

"How did… Of course." Deyvan scowled. "Whatever that thing is, I wish it would offer more valuable information. I know the girl's name. What we need is her location and how to protect her."

Kìlashà dipped a finger cautiously into his power, splitting his attention between the control he needed and the words he must say. "The Seeker's power granted by the Ancient Spirits is not a being in itself." The power flowed to his will, visions of time long past hidden behind the present tongues and flares of time. As they should be. "I have known

Niamsha, and she has been touched by Their power as well. I believe I can find her."

Kaen relaxed, settling against the window beside Kìlashà. "Find her quickly. I don't trust the girl and Deyvan's smitten with her."

"I am not *smitten*. I'm concerned for the well-being of a girl who helped us."

Kìlashà pushed their banter to the back of his mind, weaving into the simmering depths of his Seeker's power. Niamsha. He knew of true moments of her life. He need only find one. The Seeker's power resisted his pull, sluggish with his own fear. But these moments held value beyond his own success or failure. The Ancient Spirits had shown Niamsha to him for a reason. To allow her to suffer simply because he could not master the human weakness of his bloodline would be the greatest of blasphemies.

His eyes drifted closed and he focused, sinking deeper into the power that sang in his blood. The fires burned as brightly as ever, hidden behind the shield of his own uncertainty, burned into ash by the confidence grant- ed by the Ancient Spirits. His hair shifted back from his face, as if blown by a breeze, the dragging weight lifted from his shoulders. Kìlashà slid a thought into the inferno—through the inferno—to dip into the river of time beyond. An instant of confusion—

Niamsha walked down the corridor, an echo of her running in the same direction, as a third, vague image danced in the empty hall beside the young male he'd seen at the temple. Each image paused at the same moment, turning to stare into Kìlashà as though she, somehow, had been granted his power.

"The answer is not in this present." Her voice echoed with all the power of a goddess, the images spinning in unison as if she'd never paused.

Kìlashà pulled his thoughts further from the scene, examining the parallel timelines to find the similarities. There. Each vision sang with an echo of her true self, a fragment of time that might have been and might still be combining into a truth deeper than fact. What she had done influenced by everything she might have done and might still do.

Confident in the truth of the young female, he pulled the triple image into the moment when he'd first met her and followed her through the days since. Not at Oskari's home by choice. But he couldn't find the force that had sent her. Kìlashà paused at the moment, desperate to investigate. But if he lost this truth he might not find it again. The river of time was a fickle tool, never revealing what he'd intended to find.

He pushed forward, through her arrival in the throne room and return with Oskari. There. A moment that mattered. That shifted the path of his visions in ways he hadn't predicted. Kìlashà reached for the vision. Faltered in his grip on Niamsha. Blinked eyes open to stare at the stone floor beneath him.

"Gods, Kaen! Is he all right?" Deyvan's hand under his arm, holding him upright.

"Let him be, Deyvan." Kaen, followed by the scrape of a chair. His kai'shien's gentle grip, guiding him into the seat. "If you want to find her, he needs to focus."

Kìlashà launched back into the vision, freezing the progress of his hunt to immerse himself in the fading instant that still held a glimmer of Niamsha's true nature.

"I's just thinking." Niamsha tapped a foot on the stone, noting the polish of the stairs. The triplicate image ran down the steps as Oskari chased and crumpled at the top of the stairs under a harsh blow. "Where'd this come from? You ain't got the like to make it, but there's no shops as sell this. Not in no amounts, much less this much."

"I can't say as I recall the specific trader," Oskari said. "I hadn't considered the availability of marble to the plebeians, but it's hardly rare in a noble's mansion. You saw the same in the high lord's great hall."

"But that's old. What's he built these last years?"

Secure in his grip on Niamsha, Kìlashà skimmed forward. Another hole in his vision—Niamsha stood in a study, but outside, storming off under orders to lead a rebellion. Nothing of the moments inside. He should be able to see—but he skipped over it, pushing the desire to seek further aside. And there. Deyvan and Niamsha in Oskari's study, the conflict, the chase. And Niamsha dashing into a room with another young female. Saylina. Oskari had taken Saylina.

But no, he would have seen that. Something—the hole in Oskari's study, the hole before Niamsha arrived at Arkaen's home.

Kìlashà blinked, eyes dry from hours of Seeking, muscles sore and mouth dry. Deyvan paced by the window, red hair disheveled as though he'd run through a windstorm. Kaen pushed a pungent brew into his hand. With a grimace, Kìlashà took a long swallow of the tragyna, the foul, lingering taste softened by the generous honey Kaen had included.

"My gratitude, kai'shien."

"Did you find anything?" Deyvan's voice, harsh with an emotion Kìlashà couldn't place, sounded as a gong, awakening the revelations of his visions.

"I found them." Kìlashà pushed himself to his feet, swaying ever so slightly as he regained a sense of the physical world. Another swallow of the tragyna. He would need that strength. "And I can retrieve them. Niamsha is at a thieves' safe house beyond your city walls. With Saylina."

The gods ain't left much to mortal men. But what They gave, ya don't squander.

— *Master Trieu*

Chapter 30

Niamsha stumbled back, the Rogue Baron stalking around the worn couch after her as the woman—Saylina, she'd said—snatched at his sleeve. Niamsha slammed into a rickety bookcase, shaking the neat lines of priceless books above.

"What did you hear, girl?" The Rogue Baron froze, barely beyond the reach of her hand. Easily close enough to kick her if she lied. "Don't tell me nothing again. Your master's servant says you were spying in that hall for half the conversation."

"I ain't one ta listen on Nijel's business." Niamsha gestured at Saylina, the movement hopefully too quick in the safe house gloom to reveal her trembling hands. "Whatcha even doing with yer prisoner? Not real safe, keeping a noble lady captive in yer own home."

Nijel would have seen through the distraction, but the Rogue Baron frowned as if considering her words. Not as conniving, or less smart, or maybe just unsure of her personality. Any would serve her purpose if he accepted the claim.

"Let her be, Lord Weydert," Saylina stretched one hand out, pulling against the chain that held her close by the side table. Far too fine for the surroundings. The damned thing had taken five men to move it from the baron's home. "My brother won't take kindly to you harassing his people. And you'll get nothing from me if you hurt her."

The threat drew the Rogue Baron's glare, and Niamsha stared at the woman in confusion. Who were these nobles she'd met today? The earlier one, Kumiho, who'd offered protection without her asking. Now this girl, chained to an Eiliin-cursed table and threatening her captor for Niamsha's sake. What did she expect Niamsha to do for her?

"I ain't needing yer help." Niamsha pushed herself upright, drawing the baron's attention again. She met the Rogue Baron's gaze, holding her head high with a silent prayer to Aeduhm for what little protection He might choose to grant. "You ain't gonna hurt me. Nijel wouldn't let ya see the end of it."

Unless Nijel believed Marcas. But Nijel'd spoken for her only a few days past now. He might not have even heard from Marcas yet, and even if he had, Nijel didn't trust one man's word.

"I don't need permission to punish a servant." The Rogue Baron swept his hand at her face, the blow a loud crack in the silent study.

Pain exploded from the old bruise he'd given her a week past in his carriage. Niamsha coughed, eyes blurring from sudden tears. She blinked the water free, her cheek throbbing, and straightened. He wanted her to cower, and she refused to give him the pleasure of seeing her fear. Niamsha's heart pounded against her chest. She met his gaze again.

Her voice wavered. "Nijel may feel different."

Or he might not. Especially after the treachery Marcas planned to report. Though how he'd verify what Marcas said… Her gut gnawed at her, remembering Emrys's words. *You ain't thinking o' me, just yerself.* But surely his anger wouldn't push him to real betrayal. He wouldn't back Marcas just to spite her.

The Rogue Baron took one step forward and froze at a light tap on the door behind him. The door cracked open, just enough for an elderly man in a servant's tunic and hose to offer a message.

"What is it?" The Rogue Baron glared over his shoulder at the servant.

"Our high lord has requested your presence." The man held out the missive. "Sent to the estate, my lord. I've informed him you are out on business, but he will expect you shortly."

Not a true reprieve. Niamsha's breath huffed out in fear. His servants had given him the perfect excuse to ignore the high lord's summons as long as he liked. The Rogue Baron's gaze slid back to her, a nasty smile creeping onto his face.

"I'll see to it when I'm done."

The man bowed and left, his eyes studiously averted from the scene inside the room. Loyal to a fault, no matter the horrors that loyalty excused. Dread settled in Niamsha's stomach. The Rogue Baron stalked forward.

The first blow knocked her to her knees, pain overwhelming her focus. A kick, her back slammed against the sharp edges of Nijel's bookcase. Several tomes fell, light as feathers in comparison. Niamsha coughed, pain sharp in her chest. Another blow. Her lip split under the force of his foot. She coughed again, blood from her lip mixed with the spit that dripped from her mouth.

She lost track of the blows as a high-pitched shrill wove through the room, mixing with her ringing ears. Saylina. The woman who had argued for her. Niamsha pushed herself away from the baron, her body weak from spasms in every muscle and injury. Another sharp kick to her gut.

"You don't give me orders, girl." The Rogue Baron stalked away. "Your master works for me."

Niamsha gasped for air, her lungs aching and temper seething. He'd be nothing if not for her. Nijel would have taken him apart. She forced herself to her feet, glared at the Rogue Baron as he pulled the door open.

"Ain't you glad I saved yer ass?" Her voice rasped, and she licked her lips, the salty, metallic taste of blood mixed with her sweat sharp on her tongue. "Nijel woulda had yer head."

The Rogue Baron smirked back at her. "I highly doubt that, girl. Not if you're his best."

He slammed the door behind him, his voice carrying through the door as a muffled snap to Nijel's guards beyond. Niamsha grabbed the bookshelf, holding herself upright out of sheer pride, and let her eyes drift closed. Everything hurt, her knees trembled, and her stomach twisted with nausea.

A scrape of something heavy on the stone floor. Niamsha dragged her eyes open, fixing her gaze on the source. Saylina threw her slight form back, her full weight pulling against the heavy chunk of sculpted wood at the far end of her chain. Another scrape as the piece moved barely a pace in response to her efforts.

"Aeduhm's grace." Niamsha spat blood on the floor, pushing off the bookcase. "Ain't gotta hurt yerself."

"You're one to talk." Saylina leaned back against the statue, fixing Niamsha with a stern glare. "You should have just told him. What's he going to do that he wouldn't already?"

"Baron's got power." Niamsha crossed the room, setting each foot with care to minimize each jolt of pain through her body. "He hears I know something, he may start hunting witnesses. Like that lord as was looking for ya. I ain't got no desire ta get him in trouble."

Saylina frowned at her. "Looking for me? Who was it? Lord Weydert isn't without allies, but few among the established nobility need fear his wrath."

"Didn't say." Niamsha met Saylina's emerald eyes and shrugged. "Not a real name. Just said—" Niamsha struggled to pronounce the strange, foreign name he'd given. "Kumiho."

Saylina's eyes widened. "Kumiho? Gods above and below. He was *here*?" She paced back and forth on her chain. "Kumiho. I've only heard the name in passing, but he's a friend of Kaen's. In hiding since the war, so he must have resources. Still, if he's here…"

She trailed off, green eyes turning thoughtful. Just like a noble girl. Waiting on some lord to swoop in and save her. Niamsha shook her head, the swift movement leaving her momentarily dizzy, and sighed.

"Look, I ain't got much time," Niamsha said. "We doing this?"

"You don't… What do you mean?" Saylina spun to face her. "I'd intended to prepare further. You told Baron—Oskari that your mutual ally would protect you."

"I lied."

Niamsha scanned the room again. One wall held a delicate, dust-covered portrait of colored glass. Each pane of glass was a different shade that blended to build a true masterpiece filled with razor-sharp tools. Setting her feet with care, Niamsha headed toward the portrait, one hand on the wall for balance as she neared the decoration.

"What are you doing?" Saylina's demand echoed in her ringing ears. "We need to delay the guards. Kaen's on his way to Oskari's manor already, I'd bet. That summons was a distraction. He'll find us."

The name rattled in her thoughts. An echo of Kumiho's words the evening before. Two different nobles relying on the same person could only mean…

"Kaen." Niamsha stared back at Saylina. "Ya mean High Lord *Ar*kaen? Yer that Saylina?"

Saylina's lips twisted into a wry smile. "Yes. My brother, Lord Arkaen, will not leave his sister in captivity. Not if you've told his old war friend that Oskari was involved in my disappearance."

Dread settled back into her gut, deeper than when the Rogue Baron had raised his fist, and her shoulders shook. Aeduhm grant her the Mercy of His Table. She'd be dead long before she saw the streets again if Nijel found out she'd revealed this plot. Even as little as she'd known when she spoke.

"You may be the dumbest bitch ever born noble." Niamsha pushed her ragged hair back from her face. "Ain't no one knows where here is.

Even s'posing they did, think fer a minute. Rogue Baron had you taken… from where? Yer bed?"

Saylina scowled. "I was hosting tea. Negotiating with our visiting royalty. Watch your tone, girl. I protected you."

"Shit lotta good you did tied ta that thing." Niamsha waved a hand at the statue, anger burning. Even snatched and bound the woman wanted her submissive to power. Niamsha shook her head, the room spinning for several breaths after she stopped. "Just sayin'. Rogue Baron had you taken from a place you oughta been safe, and you all born high and mighty. You really think he ain't planned fer yer brother ta play hero?"

Silence hung between them. Saylina's tongue swiped across her lips, her eyes narrowed. But after a moment, Saylina sighed.

"I'm sure he's planned for Kaen," she admitted, voice tight as though the very admission caused her pain. "But Oskari has never faced my brother. Not really. Kaen's been pandering since he got home, but he'll stop at nothing to protect me."

"Pardon if I ain't prone ta waiting." Niamsha grabbed the portrait from the wall and froze, caught by the beauty of the glasswork. Gods, she hated to break it. Must have taken a guild master weeks of work. "Nijel ain't gonna take kind to me getting cozy with the nobles. 'Specially not you."

With a twinge of guilt, Niamsha covered her face with one hand and threw the frame to the floor, angling so it hit as close to flat as possible. The glass shattered with a light clink of glass breaking, the frame holding the larger chunks in place. Niamsha picked through the remains, selecting a large shard with the remains of the portrait's eye and a swath of hair.

"If you insist, then come here." Saylina tore a strip of her dress free with a sharp jerk. "You'll cut your hand to bits with that."

"I ain't collecting a keepsake."

"Give me that."

Niamsha stumbled across the room to her side as she tore a series of additional strips and pulled a narrow length of something too smooth and white to be wood from her hair. Saylina gestured for the shard of glass and Niamsha handed it over. In a few quick twists of her ruined dress, she fashioned the hair pin and glass into a makeshift dagger, the slim handle held tightly against the glass with a web of silky cloth.

Saylina handed the result back. "I wouldn't trust it to hold long in a fight, but should let you get one, maybe two good strikes in."

"Where ya learn that?" The question slipped from Niamsha's lips as she examined the blade. Not solid, as Saylina had said, but should last long enough. Better than cutting her hand open.

"I was a young noblewoman during the reign of Bloody Emperor Laisia," Saylina said. "We all learned unusual arts back then."

Niamsha considered Saylina with new respect. Her papa had rarely spoken to her of Old Emperor Laisia, but she'd overheard the whispers when she was young. Before Emrys was born when her mother had worried late into the night. She'd never understood what her mother feared—certainly didn't now any more than then—but Saylina clearly did.

"So we getting free?" Niamsha turned the makeshift weapon in her hand. She couldn't afford to run into more than one or two guards. But how many knew she'd lost her position with the Rogue Baron? It'd only been a day.

"You are. My escape would remove Kaen's evidence of Oskari's treason." Saylina paced beside the statue that held her captive. "Careful with those boots. You'll want to be quiet for this. I'll can call someone in and you can take the chance to run while I have them distracted."

"You stayin'?" Niamsha asked, turning to stare. "I ain't just gonna…"

Abandon this noble girl, like she'd ignored Emrys for the chance to turn on Nijel? Nothing she could do for Emrys, though. And who knew what torment he might be suffering for her sake. Saylina met her eyes, a fierce determination hiding the fear she must hope Niamsha couldn't see.

"Lord Weydert won't risk harm to me," she said. "I'm his only chance for a legitimate claim to the high lord's seat."

The same fear had lived in the merchant's eyes over a week past when Nijel had questioned him about rumors he should have kept quiet. But the Rogue Baron wasn't Nijel. This woman didn't know real fear.

Niamsha headed toward the door, her steps finally stable. Or enough to walk easily, at least. She glanced back at Saylina.

"When yer ready."

Saylina nodded, took a deep breath, and screamed at the top of her lungs. The sound ripped through the room, shrill as a banshee wail. Gods, this woman must have practiced that. Another defense mechanism? How many did she expect to need?

A scramble of sound outside the door and the handle jiggled. The door flew inward, stopping just short of Niamsha as two guards in the Rogue Baron's green and gold stormed in to search the room. Now. Saylina's eyes flickered toward Niamsha as she backed away.

Niamsha's resolve shuddered, the bulk of two fully armed men breaking her confidence. She'd never taken a life before. Never drawn blood, not even when the high lord's guards surrounded her little rebellion in the field by his new jail. Bodies pressing on either side, her breath sharp and fast in her throat. The ache of her lungs, stomach, and face tore her from the moment of panic. This wasn't some minor gamble. Saylina's life hung on the success of this ploy.

Her feet moved of their own accord, the sharp clunk of her boots a reminder of Saylina's warning. But no time now. The first guard spun toward her. Niamsha thrust with the shard of glass, cutting the side of his face. He fell back with a shout. Niamsha fell hard, her strength failing at the wrong moment. Or the right. The second guard's sword flew over her head. Right where she'd been a moment before.

Her heart pounded. That strike. Death just waiting for her moments away. Niamsha stabbed, careless of her aim. Hit something hard and shoved. The glass broke free from its binding and cut deep into her hand. A sharp grunt, shift of weight. She fell forward onto her elbows, the second guard collapsing beside her. Her shard of glass protruded from a thick leather pouch at his belt, a swiftly reddening bruise on his temple.

"Get up!" Saylina shouted. "You were supposed to run. Find my brother and tell him what you can."

Aeduhm's mercy. Niamsha scrambled to her feet. Hesitated a moment longer. Saylina swung the leg of a broken table at the second guard. Even if she knocked them out, those chains weren't coming loose without a key. And no chance they could get that damned statue moved with any speed.

Cursing again, Niamsha ran down the hall. Another ally abandoned for her own safety. And this one hadn't even betrayed her. Her vision blurred, tears coming to her eyes as a sob choked her throat. Emrys... Gods, she should have done something for him. But wherever he was, she couldn't do anything for him now. This noble, though—Saylina. She could still help Saylina. If the bastard high lord would listen long enough for her to get the message out.

Niamsha stumbled through the next room, the layout vaguely familiar from her earlier days in the Rendells. Nijel would have any decent entrance guarded, but somewhere... Niamsha found the narrow door that led out a side garden. Small enough, if her memory held true, that Nijel'd only leave one guard. She collapsed against the door, dragging air into her straining lungs, and fumbled at the door. Slick blood ran from her fingers down the handle. Pain shot up her arm. She pushed the door open, stepping out and slamming the door behind her. A distant figure glanced back, but she crawled into a nearby bush to catch her breath.

Ragged breathing consumed her, the world nothing but pain, scratchy branches, and her heavy rasp for air. But she was safe. For a moment. Just enough to catch her breath, get her bearings, and run again. As her breathing smoothed, she became aware of other sounds. Shouting by a distant door. The loud, rhythmic clopping of horse hooves on cobbles. The nearby guard running toward the commotion as a single, female voice raised above the rest.

"Where are you taking me? I am a princess, formal guest of your high lord. You cannot do this."

Not Saylina. Thank Aeduhm she wasn't out here... though surely someone had heard. What if she'd been wrong? What if the Rogue Baron didn't value her as highly as she thought? Niamsha pushed the thought away. Nothing to be done now except keep her promise and seek out the high lord. But her rebellion had served as the distraction for Nijel to abduct Saylina. The high lord would kill her.

Niamsha pushed herself onto her hands and knees, crawling through the thick bushes until she could peer out to the broad lane beyond. The old merchant's house to her right swarmed with activity, a carriage and horses drawn to the front door and a figure inside struggling against someone. The woman, no doubt. Nijel's lackeys ran to and from the door laden with everything from pillows to weapons, too erratic for Niamsha to guess their purpose.

With a grimace, she inched out of the bushes and hurried away from the activity as quickly as she dared. As fast as her aching body could carry her. Her steps echoed back with every jarring stride, neck prickling with nerves. Any moment someone might turn and see her. Might realize the danger she posed to the Rogue Baron's plans.

It felt like an eternity before she found a street she knew. A slum alley than ran past Nijel's warehouse. Who knew what goods he had inside? How many of his wares breathed, screamed? Bled. She'd never considered what Nijel might sell before, but if he'd steal the high lord's sister to please the Rogue Baron...

"Where ya goin'?" The voice, too high a pitch to be Marcas, though the same malice lurked under the words.

Pulling free, Niamsha spun around. Dark hair, cruel tilt to his smile. Newly come to the Rendells when Nijel had sent her away. The man drew a long-bladed knife, and she dashed down a narrow alley across the street. The heavy tread of boots behind her. Niamsha stumbled into a jutting corner. Caught herself and blinked her eyes clear.

A shadow detached itself from the alley ahead, resolving into the smooth grace of the high lord's demon. With a muffled scream, Niamsha turned back. The Rendell boys and their new companion, barely paces behind her. Her mouth went dry, aching body shaking like a loose bit of cloth in a high wind.

The demon's cloak brushed past her shoulder. The older man threw a dagger, but the demon knocked it aside carelessly. His form seemed to blur, the speed of his movement beyond anything human. A sickening squelch of metal entering flesh. Her stomach turned. And the older thief coughed, blood tinting his lips as he collapsed in the alley, throat punctured in three places. The Rendell boys fled.

Backing away, unable to pull her eyes from the dead face of her pursuer, Niamsha jumped when a hand caught her chin.

"You are injured." The demon frowned, as if the beating she'd suffered were no more than an inconvenience to be managed. "That was not seen."

"What the—" Niamsha's words died. What, exactly, would she ask? Why did he save her?

Considering her cheek, he shrugged and released her face. "Come with me, Niamsha. My kai'shien has need of you."

She backed away. "I ain't gonna follow you."

The demon turned, ignoring her protest. "Unless you would prefer to die in the streets."

The threat set her trembling again. But he was right. He didn't even need to do it. Any one of Nijel's boys would take her life. Except maybe Emrys. If he had any of the boy she'd known left at all.

"Can ya help Em?" she called.

The demon froze. Cast a look back at her. "I will care for your brother to the best of my ability, though such may not bring the results you desire."

The poise of his stance comforted her. No good reason, but damned if she could distrust him. He meant what he said, at least, and she'd rarely found that. And the demon always seemed willing to help her. Niamsha nodded, pushing herself to a half jog to catch him. No other choices. As if she'd ever had any.

Imperial generals knew if they could but cut one of these legs from beneath the rebellion it would crumble. But Kumiho was impossible to find, often away from the rebel fortress and invisible to imperial spies. The Dragon was death incarnate with his blades. And Lord Phoenix managed to evade every trap as though blessed with the gods' own favor.

— *from* An Abridged History of the Sernien War

Chapter 31

Arkaen strode into his great hall, the formal clothes he'd donned for the occasion clinging to him and hampering every move. But he shouldn't need the freedom of his more casual wear in his own hall. Unless Oskari's reach had grown longer than he thought.

Only a few of his lower lords stood in the room, muttering amongst themselves. Arkaen's arrival drew everyone's attention and silence descended over the room. Taking half a breath to evaluate the attendance, Arkaen walked toward the dais at the far end.

"Thank you for joining me, my lords." Arkaen forced a smile, his stomach roiling at the hesitant stares of the lords. As withdrawn as he'd been, they could have plotted anything. How many had crossed the boundary into proper treason?

"I hope you'll forgive my recent distraction," Arkaen said. "There've been a few matters more serious than expected."

Arkaen reached the end of the hall, stepping onto the dais and turning to consider them. No one present that he hadn't summoned. Not that anyone else had a reason to know he was holding court today at all, much less at an hour before the eve's meal. But the three barons Oskari had swayed to his side stood by one wall, and Arkaen's two rebellious counts waited in their standard places. Near enough to the dais to hear everything, far enough to avoid being obsequious. The careful positioning was far more deliberate in a mostly empty room.

A handful of other lords, all former allies of Oskari, milled about the room, but one of the counts stepped forward.

"I'm sure you've brought us here for a purpose, High Lord. How can we aid our province?"

Arkaen nodded, sweeping his gaze over the man. Lean, clothes perfectly tailored with a precisely trimmed beard. A stark contrast to the several days of stubble that left Arkaen's face itchy. That Lasha teased him about.

"Of course, my Lord Count," Arkaen said. "You may aid your province and your empire both in one gesture. Renounce any lingering ties to the former baron of House Weydert, Oskari. You may also relinquish any and all wealth you've gained through continued contact with this traitor to the realm as a tribute to your loyalty, so that I may use it to rectify the damage he has caused to my people."

"My lord, you can't be serious." The count glanced around him, noting the shock on every other nobleman's face. They'd assumed he'd gathered them with an offer of peace, not a demand for atonement.

The count reached out a hand in entreaty. "This demand would destroy my family. It would damage the stability of many of your lower lords' houses. Surely—"

"Should I value your prosperity over the lives of my people?" Arkaen sank into his chair, looking down his nose at his lower lords. "How many families were destroyed when Oskari incited a violent riot in my streets?

Should I beg for your forgiveness after you've funded the workings of a man who murdered dozens of innocents? How much should their lives be worth, my Lord Count?"

"But…"

They stared at him, the utter confusion igniting his anger. The fools genuinely thought they had nothing to do with it. As if Oskari had gathered his funds and his followers entirely devoid of connections and their continued trade with him was a separate matter.

"You can't penalize us for the violence," the count insisted finally. "None of us sent any men. We tried to dissuade him—"

Arkaen gave a bitter chuckle. "So you're telling me you knew he intended open rebellion and did not report such treasonous plans? You're hardly helping your case."

"It was just talk, my lord. Oskari wouldn't—" The count's argument died under Arkaen's furious glare.

The other lords fidgeted, the rustle of silk as loud as a shout of fear. Even these men, for all their promises they weren't planning a revolt, knew that Oskari *would* lead one if he thought it profitable.

"He wasn't there," the count said, trying his defense again. "And if it were his, he'd have stood at the head. I don't believe Oskari had anything to do with the difficulties at your jail."

"Difficulties?" Arkaen pushed himself up from the chair with ponderous care, his whole body tight with the need to lash out. "Difficulties, my Lord Count? Oh, no. The province guards shed innocent blood with a truly horrifying ease—"

"As did you, High Lord." Righteous indignation shone in the words.

"And I would again," Arkaen replied. But the guard's last words hung over him. *He was gonna…* "Perhaps I'll start with the blood of those lords who maintained trade agreements with the baron I deposed, undermining Baron Rikkard's efforts to stabilize his holdings. I'd thought to show mercy for the good of this empire. Bring together those who had betrayed me and offer a path to reconciliation. But if you'd rather sling arrows, my Lord Count, I've an army and experience on the field."

The count's face paled, and Arkaen didn't blame him. An internal conflict in a province so divided would be messy. One poor judgment or unlucky strike and Arkaen could find himself in grave danger. But Deyvan had arrived. No one held any illusions as to Deyvan's support, and by extension, that of Deyvan's armies. Not that Arkaen could allow this to devolve into true conflict—Lasha's plans required the Sentarsi nobility intact—but the threat left a satisfying hint of fear in their expressions. They'd attacked his family, after all. Aided, even unknowingly, in the abduction of Sayli.

The far door swung open, breaking into the rising tension to reveal Count Tenison, followed by a handful of servants. The knot of new arrivals hurried through the chamber toward Arkaen.

"My apologies, High Lord," Count Tenison said. "I'd only just heard you chose to hold court this eve. I hope this means you've received positive—"

Count Tenison fell silent, noting the terror on the faces of the others present. He turned in a circle, nodding as he caught sight of each lord as if taking a tally. Impossible for him to miss the intent of this meeting.

"Count Tenison." Arkaen sat, letting his voice take on the pleasant tone he'd started with. "A pleasure to see you. I apologize for omitting your name from these invitations. I had some very specific matters to discuss, but I think your fellow count and I have come to an agreement, yes?"

"My lord." Count Tenison stepped forward. "You can't hold your lower lords accountable for actions that aren't theirs. You have only rumors to connect any of the recent events to Oskari, much less your other lords, and thus far no one has found the girl who made the claims."

"You doubt the word of High Emperor Corliann?" Arkaen smiled, the bitterness of his deception hanging on his tongue. Arkaen would gladly doubt the girl who'd told Deyvan. But Lasha agreed with her.

"I am certain our high emperor was told exactly what he relayed," Count Tenison said. "But none of these lords was named in that accusation. Even had they been, would you take the word of an avowed thief over that of your lower lords?"

"I would trust the judgment of my emperor over the empty promises of men who have already betrayed me once." Arkaen drummed his fingers on the arm of his chair. "And any loyal son of the Laisian Empire would do the same."

"Why would you trust him?" The other count leveled a finger at Count Tenison. "He's been closer to Oskari than any of us."

"Perhaps because Jussi came to the lower lords' council and argued to uphold my order while *you* snuck around behind my back and maintained a trade relationship with Oskari."

Count Tenison frowned. "But my lord—"

The door opened again, this time to the gasps and scrambling forms of those few nobles standing near. Enough to tell him Lasha had finally returned. And Lasha should have brought Sayli home.

"Kìlashà." Arkaen called over the heads of his nobility, fighting the urge to leap to his feet and run forward. "Come tell me what you've found."

Kìlashà stepped through the door, his skin full-colored and his fiery veins muted. Too clearly hovering on the edge of his humanity rather than consumed by his power as he had been when he'd left. Arkaen's heart skipped a beat. Gods above and below. What could have happened?

The gathered lords did their best to avoid any acknowledgment of Lasha's presence at all as he strode through the room. A strange blessing, for if any had looked too closely, they might have seen the distinctly Laisian blood beginning to show in his features. Another day of safety for the secrets Lasha and Deyvan kept.

"Kai'shien." Lasha's voice held as much poise as ever despite how shaken he looked. Not as bad as before, then. "I have retrieved the female Deyvan desired me to locate."

"My sister?" But Arkaen knew the answer. If Lasha had found Sayli, he'd have said so.

"There were alterations."

"Where is she?" Arkaen could hear the fury in his own voice, his hands clenching against his will.

Lasha flinched. Not a proper cower, as Arkaen's lords might have done faced with his wrath. Just enough of a reaction to remind Arkaen how fragile Lasha truly was in this moment, standing before Arkaen's lords with the revelation of his failure plain for all to see. The Chosen of the Four Clans of the Drae'gon people did not fail.

Arkaen swallowed the bulk of his anger, shaking with the effort to bring himself back under control. "The young woman may have some information. High Emperor Corliann said she helped him. Perhaps she can help us now. And I know our emperor will want to know she's been returned safely."

Frowning, Count Tenison raised a hand as if to protest. Lasha beat him to it.

"I said I had retrieved her, kai'shien. Not that she is safe. Deyvan may visit the female when your physic has done what little he can to ease her pain."

Guilt fell on Arkaen like the heavy blow of a war hammer. His anger might have injured the woman more, and clearly she'd already suffered. For what, only Lasha's Ancient Spirits knew.

"Will she live?"

Lasha cocked his head, the flow of his power returning to drain the edge of humanity from his features. Arkaen's lords murmured in fear and Arkaen tensed. They'd never seen Lasha's power behave like this. Had never really believed Lasha had any power beyond that of swift reflexes and fierce skill with his blades. What might they try to research in Arkaen's older histories after seeing this demonstration?

After several agonizing moments of searching, Lasha shrugged. "Her injuries will not be permanent, although they are quite severe at this time. I encourage you to distract Deyvan from her presence that she might recover."

"Of course," Arkaen said. "When will it be safe for me to speak with her?"

"If you have need you could now. But such a discussion would waste your time and hers. She knows nothing."

Arkaen hesitated only a moment. "Count Tenison. Since you so strenuously deny Oskari's involvement in these matters, perhaps you'd care to join me in speaking—"

"Nothing, kai'shien." Lasha's sharp interruption caught him off guard. "She does not have the knowledge you seek."

"I see."

Arkaen paused, tension thick in the air as he met Lasha's eyes. Pure black, no iris or white, the ebony drawing against Arkaen's resolve. The absolute depth of Lasha's powers, as confident as his knowledge ever got. The same certainty he'd shown when he said he knew where Sayli was.

"I hope you'll forgive me, Kìlashà," Arkaen said.

Lasha's eyes snapped closed, a flash of hurt crossing his face. His power revealing Arkaen's decision before Arkaen could speak. The words lodged in Arkaen's throat. To deny the truth of Lasha's visions… But Sayli hadn't been where he'd seen her.

"I'll speak to the young woman and hear her story." Arkaen turned to Count Tenison. "Will you join me, my Lord Count? Her words may surprise you."

"I will await you in your courtyard, kai'shien." Lasha's voice shook, not with fear or pain but with barely restrained frustration. "When you speak to the female and she tells you of the smuggler's den beyond the southern end of your town—" He caught Arkaen's gaze again, his determination driving home the point. "You will wish to visit. As I have already located it, I shall accompany you, that you may see for yourself that there is nothing of value there and nothing to lead to your goal."

Arkaen's heart ached at his decision. But he had to know. "And I will be delighted to discover that you were right."

Lasha stormed from the room, his anger somehow more comforting than it had any right to be. If Lasha was that certain, he had a reason to trust his power.

"Perhaps, my lord, we ought to ask your guard to take us to this smuggler's den first," Count Tenison suggested. "If the girl is injured, she should rest, and we hardly need her to tell us something he already knows."

"Very well." Arkaen preferred that choice anyway. He'd still need to talk to Niamsha when he returned, but for the moment he could allow Lasha to demonstrate that his power was working. That might let Arkaen find the information Lasha needed to locate Sayli once again.

"After you, my Lord Count."

Arkaen stepped into the courtyard to meet Lasha's accusing gaze. Transformed in an instant into pity. Of course Lasha would understand his desperation. The stable hands hadn't finished saddling Arkaen's mare, standing beside Count Tenison's horse, but Lasha already sat astride his feisty white stallion. The stable hands finished with Arkaen's mare, scurrying back as he approached.

"I will show you, kai'shien."

Setting a foot to his stirrup, Arkaen nodded and swung onto his horse. The ride through the city felt endless, Sayli's danger heavy on Arkaen's shoulders, all three silent in their own thoughts. If Sayli were truly gone and Niamsha injured, they could no longer be certain that Sayli lived. Not that Arkaen had ever been sure. Lasha could always find someone he knew existed.

Lasha led them out to the southern edge of town, the ramshackle buildings an accusation of the indignities Arkaen had yet to solve. But he couldn't do anything while Oskari threatened war. Beyond, a riot of trees spread in the distance where the farmers had yet to clear and a wooded hillside showed signs of a stonecutter's trade. Such a riot of foliage—all shades of orange and gold in the chill air—compared to the grasslands of Serni. The road narrowed quickly to a lane only wide enough for one horse at a time. Lasha turned them off, around a bend in an overgrown path, and pulled his horse to a halt before a mass of scattered huts.

One there, likely the privy. A small garden behind an overgrown hedge. A larger building with few windows and one main door, falling off the hinges but repaired. The entryway was deserted except for a brightly colored scarf hanging from the bush it had clearly blown into. Count Tenison pulled his horse to a halt, staring at the buildings.

"Oskari would never stay in such a place."

"I would have said the same." Arkaen dropped to the ground, grabbing his mare's reins and leading her forward. "But he hasn't many options, Jussi."

Striding to the doors, Lasha tied his horse to a post set beside the door for that purpose. There he paused, casting a glance at Count Tenison.

"I am certain your lord will find plenty to examine, kai'shien," Lasha said. "But the valuable information is in the parlor."

"A place to start, then." Arkaen followed Lasha's example, tying his mare's reins beside Lasha's. He turned back to Count Tenison. "Coming?"

"My lord, this is not a place Oskari would be. There is no point—"

Lasha stepped over to a bush and lifted the lost scarf, holding it out. Only then did Arkaen recognize the patterning. Yellow, with blue edging, and a new green and gold emblem sown in. Kyli Andriole's house colors mixed with Rikkard Weydert's. Count Tenison made the connection almost as fast.

"If we think the lady was here..." With a disgruntled sigh, Count Tenison tied his horse as well and joined them.

Dropping the scarf, Lasha turned to lead them into the maze of interconnected rooms. More than Arkaen would have guessed from the size and poorly laid out for any practical use. Except, perhaps, hiding illegal goods. He stopped by a door pushed open just enough to reveal carnage within.

Books scattered across one corner, a priceless statue carved of finely polished blackwood lay on its side, the detail battered so the piece was unrecognizable and smeared with a thick liquid. Blood. He could smell it as they stepped inside, smears on the worn rug behind the tattered sofa, spattered across the books, bookcase, and rough floor. And a thick, congealed mess to one side where someone had been injured more seriously. Lasha paced through the room, pausing by each spot.

"A guard." He pointed to the first smear, little more than a minor cut, likely. He crossed to another smear. "Second guard." To the statue, tapping a foot against a shard of glass bound loosely to a long hairpin. "Young Rikkard."

Lasha paused, his head cocked to one side as Arkaen's stomach plummeted. He'd forgotten about Kyli in the days since their tryst. What had he doomed her to in forcing her marriage to Rikkard Weydert? Lasha cast Arkaen a glance, lips twisted into a wry smile.

"He is not involved, kai'shien. It appears he discovered his father's actions and attempted to intervene."

"That's nonsense." Count Tenison's denial felt weak as he stepped into the room, surveying the damage. "Oskari wouldn't..."

"We've proof his household was here, Jussi," Arkaen said. "Either Oskari sanctioned some form of fight here, or Oskari was murdered here. There's too much blood for another conclusion."

"Time offers many conclusions." Lasha paced to the bookshelf, his hands clenching in fury as his hair swirled in agitated tangles. "Niamsha."

Arkaen crossed the room to stand beside the larger tangle of blood, bits of torn rug, and hair. Light brown hair, one group of strands held together by a chip of something green that sparkled. Lasha joined him, staring at the spot.

"Shall I order a funeral, Kìlashà?"

"Several." Lasha paced around the edge of the spot. "But not Saylina's." He knelt, pulling something from the spot and offering it to Arkaen.

A delicate twist of colored glass with a hook on one end, the metal of the hook smeared with blood. Arkaen's hand shook as he took the earring. Fear twisted into rage at the befouled metal, soaked in his sister's own blood.

"My lord, this looks dire, but we cannot draw conclusions without proof." Count Tenison paced across the room. "You've proof the Andriole girl was here, not Oskari. Once we've spoken to him—"

"Can you find him for me, Jussi?" Arkaen bit off the words, struggling against the burning anger as he stared at the delicate glass. "I've summoned him to court and he never arrived. Instead, we come here and find this." He held up the earring, eyes narrowed into a furious glare. "Do you know what this is?"

Count Tenison frowned. "A woman's earring, my lord."

"My sister's earring," he corrected. "One I gave her for a birthing day present not three months past. Tell me, Jussi. Why is it here?"

"I think—"

He leveled a hand at another mess, a pile of broken glass beneath an empty hook. "I recognize that, as well. That is a picture in colored glass of Oskari's late sister. Why would *that* be here if he was not?"

"Perhaps it was stolen," Jussi replied. "We've had an increase in theft."

"Stolen, and hung on the wall where prisoners had access to it? I think that unlikely." Arkaen paced closer, temper flaring as the words boiled out of him. "If your dear friend Oskari has nothing to do with my sister's disappearance, then why was his son here? Why was his sister's image and his daughter-in-law's scarf here? And why did I just pluck my sister's prized earrings out of a mess of blood in a room that reeks of his presence? Whose blood do you think that is, Jussi?"

"I have told you, kai'shien." Lasha stepped between him and Count Tenison. "She was here, and Oskari has plans of which you will not approve. But he did not hurt Saylina. She has too much value."

"I'd love to believe you." The challenge hung on the tip of Arkaen's tongue, demanding an explanation, though he couldn't bear to shake Lasha's confidence any further.

"Your sister lost her earring attempting to save them." Lasha stared at the blood streaking the carpet. "And failing. But this was not Oskari's hand. Even he has more virtue than such actions."

Arkaen stormed past Lasha to grab Count Tenison's tunic. "Where do I look next? You've networks. What have you heard of his actions, Jussi?"

"I—" Count Tenison pulled away, spinning in a quick circle as if looking for a clue in the destroyed room. He ended staring at Arkaen, eyes wide with shock. "I don't know. He's vanished as far as my sources can tell."

Vanished. None of the nobility could simply vanish. But every resource had found them nothing, as if someone knew their plans and how to avoid them. Arkaen turned back to Lasha. But if Lasha had any other information, he would have shared it before. Arkaen's heart sank. Sayli in the hands of someone who could do something Lasha didn't even want to speak of. And he had no way to find her.

"Emperor Corliann has troops, and the *Serr-Nyen* are loyal." Arkaen cringed at his own words, the plan a truly horrifying thought. Soldiers were poor investigators en masse. Little patience with the slow progress too common to a systematic search.

"My lord, you can't intend that." Count Tenison took a half step forward and froze. "Martial law on such a scale hasn't existed since Sentar accepted Laisian rule."

"I'll tear this entire province apart if that is what it takes to find her." Arkaen strode out the door, one hand tightly clenched on his sister's earring. Something beautiful for his beautiful sister. Beauty she might never truly know again.

Eiliin and Her Husband now battle eternally over the souls of mortal men, always the perverted goddess seeking more to fill her demonic kingdom. Seek the glory of Aeduhm's Eternal Feast in His Three Teachings: First, to know the wisdom of humility, and seek aid where needed.

— from the teachings of Holy Aeduhm and His Kin

Chapter 32

A sharp knock on the door sent Niamsha scurrying across her sparse room to huddle on the bed. Everything hurt—more than the day the baron had hit her—but two days of physic's care and a comfortable place to rest had taught her how to live with the pains. The physical ones, at least. No one would tell her what the high lord found when he and his demon returned to Nijel's safe house. And she'd heard nothing of Emrys.

The knock came again, gentler this time. She climbed off the soft wool cover and crossed the room. Niamsha paused by the door, frowning at the polished handle. High Lord Arkaen's physic never left her alone. But at least she had a physic checking on her. Still, hadn't he been by barely two hours past?

A third knock and she sighed, yanking the door open with a scowl. Kumiho—no, Emperor Corliann, as she'd learned after her arrival. Gods, she'd talked to *the emperor* and not even known it.

Emperor Corliann dropped his hand, a bright smile flashing onto his face, his vibrant red beard unruly. His gaze swept over her injuries. The anger that lit his blue eyes never reached that smile, but Niamsha backed away. Papa'd warned her about a noble's anger.

"Niamsha, how good to see you again." Emperor Corliann gestured to the plain wood chair she'd been given. "May I come in?"

She nodded, watching in nervous vigilance as he crossed the room and settled his broad frame into a chair far too small. Niamsha cringed. The emperor in her room and Niamsha couldn't even offer him a decent seat.

"Whatcha come for?"

Harsher than she intended. But everyone came for something. The high lord for information on the Rogue Baron's plans. The demon for facts about her time with Nijel. The physic for proof she'd followed his orders. And now Emperor Corliann, down from his throne in the imperial palace to gossip with the common folk. The whole reason she'd got herself into this mess in the first place.

But no. Papa hadn't raised a slaver, and from what little she'd heard, the Rogue Baron had every thought to enslave Lady Saylina under an unwanted marriage contract.

Emperor Corliann leaned back in the flimsy chair. "I came to check on you. You were injured for aiding me, and I was worried."

"You ain't got means to learn without coming on down here?"

"I do, of course." Emperor Corliann examined her closely. Seeking something she didn't know how to answer. "But that seemed callous. I can't prefer to visit?"

Niamsha hesitated. "Ain't like I know ya."

He chuckled, staring up at the narrow slit that served the room for a window. His silence ate at her, charged with some purpose he didn't choose to share. After a moment, he shrugged.

"I suppose that's true." He dropped his gaze to meet hers once again. "But few do, these days. And my two primary confidantes are involved elsewhere of late. I find myself a tad lonely. You seemed, perhaps, similarly forlorn."

Niamsha broke the intense stare, sweeping the room for something to look at. Something to discuss or ask about, or even just comment on. Her life held no value to any noble. Certainly not him. Everything she had, he must have a dozen better made. Nothing to share between them.

Emperor Corliann sighed, rising. "Apologies if I'm intruding. You've had a difficult several days. I'm sure you'd prefer some privacy."

"That ain't—" Niamsha muttered a curse under her breath as he paused. "I ain't meant to send you off. Kind of you to come. Only…" She scanned the room again. "Noble-born ain't got much in common with the gutters. All I know is dirt and pain."

"I've spent my fair share in dirt and pain." Emperor Corliann leaned back against a wall, his smile creeping onto his face again. "Not everyone is defined by the things you see now. Surely you had something beyond serving Oskari, yes? You said you'd only been there a short time."

Her chest throbbed with the pain of grief. "Em. I had Em, and now I ain't even got a hint whether he's out livin' or in someone's hole."

"Your brother?" Emperor Corliann nodded without waiting for her response. "I asked Kìlashà to hunt for him, but he and Kaen haven't found anything yet. And I've got nothing to do beyond offer my men. I hate being impotent."

Niamsha stared. The *emperor* was complaining about not having power? "Ain't stayin' home an' waiting fer news part a being noble?"

"I've never been terribly patient." Emperor Corliann smirked, staring into the wall and clearly seeing something not truly there. "Some have even said I'm too reckless. Dangerous."

His focus had passed beyond the current discussion into a history Niamsha couldn't fathom. No point in telling her, anyway. Niamsha couldn't do anything under the high lord's thumb. Unless she had help. And everyone knew Emperor Corliann was a friend to High Lord Arkaen.

"I ain't thought *you* had much need to sit still." She watched his face intently, hunting for any sign he saw through her probing. "Ya wanna do something, what is it? An' who's stopping ya?"

Emperor Corliann turned his eyes back to her. "Young men and women like you, dear. I've too many depending on me to risk being foolish now."

"So ya need someone as got nothing? That others ain't gotta rely on?"

He stared, eyes slowly narrowing as he evaluated her words. Niamsha's heart pounded, her hands shook. She wasn't even sure she had the strength to take on a project, much less the nerve to see it through. Not after last time. The fierce pain of the Rogue Baron's foot in her gut— shoulder, face—shuddered through her body. Worse for the memory than the moment, because nothing could save her from it again. Unless she refused to leave.

"No," Emperor Corliann said at last. "I have not come to recruit a new tool for my efforts. I was concerned about your well-being. Sending you back onto the streets would defeat the very purpose of my visit, regardless of the benefit."

"But Em!" The plea burst from her lips. "Ya ain't found him, and if the high lord can't… Em ain't got a purpose like the lady. What's to keep him safe?"

"You are not well," Emperor Corliann insisted. "I'll not risk your safety for his."

"Ain't yer choice."

Except it was Emperor Corliann's choice and they both knew it. He held all the power and all the resources.

Niamsha spat on the floor in disgust. "Or shouldn't be."

"I'm trying to help you."

"Yer getting my last family killed."

She met his eyes again, gritting her teeth. Time to ask, and maybe he'd actually tell her the truth.

"Ya found Nijel yet?"

"We haven't." Emperor Corliann scowled, turning his glare on the door. As if he thought the very idea of him being angry might harm her. "None of Kaen's sources have heard of the man, Kìlashà can't find a hint of him, and anyone connected to the ever-growing thievery ends up dead before we can get answers from them."

Niamsha nodded. "Sounds like Nijel."

Her chest ached. Real pain and remembered terror both. But Emrys had waited long enough, and Lady Saylina had been kind. If she could help either—or even both—didn't she have to? Papa would be proud of a daughter who helped innocents. Of a daughter who kept her promise and cared for her brother.

"I can find him."

Emperor Corliann spun toward her, taking a step forward. "What?"

"He ain't gonna be at a Rendell safe house." She shook her head, rejecting her own falsehood. "Not now. But some o' the boys might. They ain't gotta know I been here, helping. I can find Nijel. You just gotta send enough o' yer men ta get me out."

"I will not risk your life for this foolhardy quest," Emperor Corliann said. "We don't even know if this Nijel can lead us to Oskari to begin with. Only that Oskari hired Nijel to assist with his rebellion against Kaen. They could easily have parted ways by now."

Niamsha pushed herself to her feet. The ache of her chest and face throbbed in protest. But she'd made a promise. To Papa. To Emrys and Lady Saylina. To herself.

"Nijel ain't no one's hired hand." She crossed the room, ignoring his muttered protest to pull the door open. "They made a trade, an' Nijel don't let a trade go south. Ya don't skip out on a Rendell deal."

Emperor Corliann grabbed her shoulder. "Wait, Niamsha."

"You gonna stop me, gonna have to do more'n talk." She pulled free, stepping out the door. "I ain't leaving Em in Rendell hands. An' that lady, she wanted ta help, no matter she couldn't."

"Let me at least make some plans. You'll get yourself killed alone."

Niamsha scowled. But damn if he wasn't right. First among Aeduhm's Teachings was the wisdom to seek aid when needed, and nothing she did would get her free of Nijel's clutches without help. She nodded.

"Just rest." He waved at the bed. "I'll talk to Kaen, come back with a plan in a couple of days."

"Ain't gonna twiddle my thumbs." Niamsha leaned back against the far wall, the support more needed than she wanted to admit. "You making plans, I'm part of 'em."

He shot a frustrated glare down the hall but nodded. With another careless wave, he led her away from the room and down the bare corridor. She struggled to match his pace, the pain in her body sharp, as if protesting her foolish plans. Finally, he paused at a door with a light rap on the wood. Movement inside, a long pause, and the door opened. A woman's face poked out, eyes going wide as she saw Emperor Corliann, a light dusting of flour still lingering around several strands of hair.

Niamsha yelped in surprise, backing around the corner. The Rogue Baron's cook. What was she doing here, in the high lord's palace? Emperor Corliann darted around the corner.

"What's wrong?"

Her finger shot toward the corner. "She ain't safe. One o' the Rogue Baron's."

Emperor Corliann smiled. "No. One of Kaen's. He had her planted in Oskari's manor for information. I understand why you're surprised." He stepped back, gesturing her forward.

The reminder shook her nerves. High Lord Arkaen had a cook in the Rogue Baron's house. Nijel had planned Niamsha as a spy for the Rogue Baron. Anyone could be one of Nijel's. Niamsha shook her head.

"That one ya may know," Niamsha said. "But how many ya don't?"

He nodded, glancing back down the hall. "A fair point, and one I should have considered. If we're to rely on your anonymity, we'll need to protect your identity. Kaen trusts his informants, but I don't know them." He took a few more steps toward the door and peeked around the corner. "Wait here for just a moment."

Niamsha shuddered as he vanished. Protect her identity? She'd betrayed Nijel in public already. Little chance Nijel trusted her now. But maybe he'd left some of the newer boys behind. The ones who wouldn't know her anyway, even if they knew that "Nisha" was a traitor.

Another moment and muttering emerged from around the corner, fading down the hall. She crossed her arms, fingernails digging into the skin of her arm. If just one decided to turn back. Leave the other direction. But when someone stepped around the corner it was Emperor Corliann, a sharp jerk indicating she should follow. Niamsha followed, hurrying into the room to stare at the few that remained.

High Lord Arkaen looked like he'd run the length of the city three dozen times since she'd seen him last, his slouch as improper as any she'd seen and his usually clean-shaven face now sporting days of neglected stubble. His demon hardly looked any better. Pale as a ghost, the fire of his demonic scars nearly blinding in their glow.

Niamsha glanced behind her, at the still-pristine grooming of Emperor Corliann. He hadn't exaggerated the high lord's efforts, despite everything she'd heard. High Lord Arkaen was a far cry from the lax ruler indulging his time in women and wine she'd heard him described as on the streets.

High Lord Arkaen caught her astonished stare and grimaced, his eyes drifting closed. "I'm aware. Gods, what I wouldn't give for a bath and a decent night's sleep." He nodded at Emperor Corliann without opening his eyes. "Deyvan says you have a plan, Niamsha?"

"I ain't real sure—" She scanned the room, pausing at the two other doors on either side. Anyone could be listening there. No telling who Nijel had already bought. But not the high lord or his demon, and Emperor Corliann… she couldn't believe it of him either.

"The doors are not watched, Niamsha." The demon raised his gaze to meet hers, head cocked to one side. "Though it is wise of you to be concerned. And whoever your Nijel is, he has not spoken to the three of us at any point in any of our timelines."

"They do say the paranoid are the ones to survive," High Lord Arkaen said, cracking his eyes to give her a smile. "Any ideas you have will have to be better than what I've got. I'm down to sending soldiers to traipse through stranger's homes looking for hints with no knowledge what they're seeking. For all I know, they already walked through Nijel's house and everything seemed in order."

Aeduhm's Mercy. With the high lord's soldiers searching every home in the city, she had no chance of finding the Rendells without finding Nijel. Unless they hadn't found all the houses yet. Too much to hope. But she had to ask.

"Where they start?"

"Pardon?" High Lord Arkaen regarded her with increased focus.

"Yer guards. They been on down south?" She waved a hand in the general direction of the Rendell house. "Couple shacks down by an old noble's mansion, run-down but fer a couple rooms."

"And a wing in the mansion with two dozen narrow beds clearly used for whoring," he added. "They found it, and the nearby hideouts. What should we have looked for?"

Niamsha bit at her lip, frustration ready to tear free. No chance to hunt whatever stragglers Nijel might have left. No clues as to where to look next. And Nijel wouldn't be anywhere in sight. Not with the high lord's guards everywhere.

"Rendells run outta there," she said. "Was hopin'—" Niamsha slammed against a wall, eyes burning with fresh tears. No way to find Emrys now.

"Ah." High Lord Arkaen's single word held a world of understanding. "I'm sorry. The guards searched there yestermorn and the entire area was already empty. By a few days, at least. But it was a noble plan."

"I can't say I'm disappointed," Emperor Corliann added. "I didn't like sending you into danger, anyway."

"Her choice, Deyvan," High Lord Arkaen said. "You'd walk into any danger for your family, as would I. I'd never deny her the right to try."

"If you are certain of that belief, kai'shien." The demon pushed off the wall, eyes focused on a distant spot as he navigated to her side without a single foot set wrong. "I have found a second such opportunity."

"What?" Niamsha leaned forward, hope pounding against her chest in time with her pulse. "How ya gonna find 'em?"

"I will not, or I would not send you." The demon dropped his gaze to stare into her soul with his pure black eyes. "You have encouraged Oskari to make alliance with a trader of marble. The trader himself has little connection, but there are watchers. Should he turn to my kai'shien for aid in repairing his reputation, he would meet one of several possible ends. However—"

"You want her to pretend to be in Oskari's employ?" Emperor Corliann asked. "To a tradesman who knows nothing of this plot, and we'll just hope the assassins watching that tradesman decide to bring her to Nijel rather than kill her? What if those assassins know she's been here?"

"Of course they know." The demon shrugged, turning away. "No effort was made to conceal her presence until this day. But that can be used to our advantage."

"That doesn't sound particularly safe, Kìlashà." High Lord Arkaen ran a hand through his hair, scowling at the resulting tangle of loose hairs in his grip. "There's risking danger to aid family, and then there's throwing yourself in front of a knife for no gods-damned reason. This is leaning toward the latter."

The idea made sense. Risky, of course, but no better way to get Nijel's attention than show up at an ally only she ought to know about. Except the demon did, so no telling who else might have heard.

"All plans bring hazards, and I can see no certainty in the outcome," the demon said. "But there is a chance, here, that her risk may be rewarded."

Emperor Corliann's objection mirrored High Lord Arkaen's first, another damned noble trying to decide her fate without her input. Niamsha ignored their argument, thinking through the plan. If the Rogue Baron had kept in touch after fleeing his home, heading to the fine-stone trader wouldn't get her anything. But the baron was like all nobles. Like these, arguing over her fate so hard they seemed to have forgotten she was still in the room.

Niamsha glanced toward the door and the demon caught her gaze. Ignoring the debate as she was, watching Niamsha as if nothing else mattered in the entire palace. She shuddered and looked away. Not the one she wanted paying attention to her.

"Dammit, Kìlashà, say something." Emperor Corliann's face had turned a red that nearly matched his hair, arms crossed in obvious fury.

"It is not your decision." The demon kept his gaze trained on Niamsha as if to emphasize his point. "Nor is it the choice of my kai'shien. This decision resides with Niamsha alone."

"You can't ask that of her." High Lord Arkaen pushed up from his chair, hands set on the table. "She doesn't understand—"

"I'll do it." Niamsha stepped forward, meeting High Lord Arkaen's eyes before he could protest. "You think I ain't got a clue what this is? 'Course I know. Ya'll ain't been in the Rendell house. Ain't seen Nijel. I know better'n you. But I made a promise."

High Lord Arkaen narrowed his eyes. "I didn't mean Nijel." He gritted his teeth and dropped his eyes, waving at the demon. "He's using you as bait. It's a tactic I've seen before."

Niamsha nodded. Of course. No better purpose for an untrained woman in a battle zone. And it wouldn't be the first time she'd played the role. Niamsha shuddered at the memory of the man's face when Marcas and the gang had stepped from the alley. Years past now, and nothing to be done but use the skills she'd earned.

"Ain't the first to see that use," she replied.

"I don't like it." High Lord Arkaen studied her as if seeking a weakness.

The demon shrugged. "And when you have an alternate suggestion, I will gladly seek those consequences."

"But we've another problem." Emperor Corliann paced beside the table, scanning some paper before him. "Whoever this is, we aren't dealing with mindless thugs. She can't just walk in and ask where they are."

"If we're doing this, I don't see a choice. What else can we do?"

Emperor Corliann offered the paper to High Lord Arkaen. "This. The rumors say you're headed back to Serni." He rubbed a hand through his beard, a scowl marring his face. "We have her hint that might be true and any proper imperial loyalist won't have a choice but to come forward. You'll get your Successor's Tribune and have a chance to put Oskari in his place."

"But why would she even know?" High Lord Arkaen asked. "It's not like I have a reputation for confiding in common thieves."

"Talked to him on my own." Niamsha nodded at the emperor, avoiding the intense gaze of the demon as he examined her like a strange toy he had yet to understand. "Use that fer a source."

Emperor Corliann smiled at her. "Precisely. And I recall telling you my name was Kumiho. Drop that name to Oskari's eyes, we'll have them out of hiding."

"No!" High Lord Arkaen slammed the paper down on the table. "Deyvan, that is too dangerous. You'll reignite the hunt for the *Serr-Nyen* leader and it'll cost lives. I'll have to plan a scapegoat to take your place. I won't spend innocent lives. Not even for Sayli."

"There won't be a man-hunt," Emperor Corliann said. "It's an admitted thief spreading rumors to a treasonous baron who abducted the last remaining family of a reigning high lord. They won't dare champion the cause."

"I'm not worried about Oskari." High Lord Arkaen shoved the paper again. "That's sealed under Brayden's hand, and I believed it because it sounds like him. If my loyal lords hear that the traitor who assassinated our last emperor is taking refuge in my lands…"

"So lie." Niamsha scowled at him. The answer was too obvious. "Ain't like I got plans to spread the news. Reckon you ain't planning on the Rogue Baron having a tongue to speak with. Who's gonna say?"

"Exactly." Emperor Corliann shrugged. "You don't have to like it, Kaen, but it's hardly the first lie you've lived with."

High Lord Arkaen sank into his chair, glaring at the emperor. Finally, he looked away with a reluctant nod.

"If we are decided, then, I will retire to prepare." The demon crossed to the door in a show of insolence that would have drawn a prison sentence for anyone else. "At sun's rise, Niamsha. I will follow to see you safely through."

"Wait, that ain't what—"

The demon slipped out the door.

"I know you're impatient, but we need to prepare." Emperor Corliann stepped forward, gesturing her toward the door with one hand. "Let me see you safely to your room."

"Em might die," she snapped. "You give a damn 'bout that?"

"I understand your fear," High Lord Arkaen said. "But we haven't a choice. This only matters if we act quickly when Oskari is found. At this moment, I'm not sure I've enough energy to lift a blade, much less duel with one."

"But…"

"Get some rest. I'll get my bath and a few hours of sleep." He ran another hand through his hair and grimaced. "If I can get Kìlashà to agree to leave this afternoon instead of morning, I will. I value your brother no less than my sister."

Not likely. But he clearly believed it, and she couldn't argue with his reasoning. She'd seen men half dead with more spunk. If her life relied on High Lord Arkaen, she had little faith in returning. Not that she had anything to return to, if she lost Emrys.

With a sigh, Niamsha nodded, turning away. A sudden thought made her pause at the door.

"You got some noble foreign lady staying here?"

"No," High Lord Arkaen said. The sudden, intense focus had returned to his face. "All foreign dignitaries reside at the guest house on the edge of town. But we are missing a princess, if you've found one."

She fiddled with the hem of her shirt, considering. Aeduhm's curse on Nijel. But the woman's scream from the Rogue Baron's home wouldn't leave her.

"Was a lady," Niamsha said. "Didn't see her or nothing. Said she's a guest o' yers. Reckon she's lying."

"You met Princess Kitorn?" Emperor Corliann appeared before her, eyebrows raised in surprise as one hand grabbed at her arm. "Where did you see her? Was she—" He glanced at High Lord Arkaen.

"I ain't seen her, like I said." A chill ran down her back. "She a princess? Fer true?"

"She is." High Lord Arkaen's voice held an insidious note. "What do you know of her?"

"They's putting her in a carriage," Niamsha said. "Don' know where they's going. She's pretty mad at 'em fer it."

Emperor Corliann cast a grim look at High Lord Arkaen. "Not held captive with Sayli, then. That's going to be more complicated."

"So it would seem." He scowled. "Get your rest, Niamsha. We'll leave this afternoon."

Nothing worse'n a man or woman as hurts those that aid 'em.
Some'un gives you a hand, you repay with yer own.

— *Master Trieu*

Chapter 33

Niamsha crept through the late afternoon gloom, hairs on her neck and arms tingling. She yelped as loose stones skittered down a hill to her right, scanning the trees stretching to either side of her narrow trail. Squinting to make out any detail in the dim shadows. Nothing. No mysterious blobs of darker shapes, no bits of foliage that failed to move properly in the wind. Or at least, nothing she could identify as one of the watchers the high lord's demon had warned her about. She pushed the nerves to the back of her mind, inching forward again.

A shallow curve in the trail revealed the dim glow of lights ahead. The fine-stone merchant's house. For an instant she froze, feet stuck to the dirt of the path as she stared at the home. If Nijel had even an inkling that she'd betrayed him, this was nothing but suicide. But how could he not know? Marcas would have told him, and maybe even… No, Emrys wouldn't have turned on her. Not like that.

Forcing herself to keep going, Niamsha focused on the impact of her boots on the hard-packed dirt. The light brightened as she came closer, revealing a squat cottage larger than her papa had owned, but only a little.

Except the fine-stone mason likely didn't have a workshop inside. Maybe even a room each for his children. If he had any. Her steps crunched on gravel as she stepped into the light, crossing the small entryway to knock on the door. Several breaths of silence. A muttered curse from inside. The door flew open.

"Who are you?" A young man glared at her over a wavering candle flame.

"Came fer a message," Niamsha said.

The plan ran through her mind, stupid in its simplicity. Ignore the merchant, talk as if Nijel himself stood before her. The Rendell watchers would know she wasn't visiting the merchant and would decide from there.

"A message?" The man scowled. "I don't got no message for you. Or you saying you got one for me?"

"High lord wants his sister," she said, fighting for a calm tone. Fear would only alarm the merchant and maybe alert Nijel to her deception. "Ya want him… handled. I got things ya may wanna know."

"What?" The man stumbled back from the door. "His Lordship can't possibly imagine that his sister is here. In what way would I want to *handle* my liege?"

Niamsha kept her face as impassive as she could manage, focusing on a point on the far wall. Smooth rubbed wood, not rough finished like her papa's home. A tiny detail, but enough. This merchant was well enough off to feed his family. Set money aside to care for his children, as Papa hadn't been able to. And she was about to ruin his life, using him in this ploy.

"Get out." The merchant thrust a finger at her. "Whatever you're planning, I want nothing of it."

She held her ground, the finger hovering almost under her chin. He could force her out, but it wouldn't matter now. Nijel would get her message. Better if she stayed, though, to drive home the importance of her information. At least they hadn't killed her yet. A good sign.

"I said—"

"Send the lass in."

Aeduhm's Mercy. That wasn't Nijel. She'd know the rough cadence of Marcas's voice anywhere. But Marcas didn't work observation jobs.

"I ain't given you permission to use my house," the merchant protested. "I—"

Whatever Marcas flashed at him sent the merchant's face white. He backed into a side hall, staring at Niamsha, and waved her inside. Mouth dry with fear, Niamsha stepped into the house. The demon better keep his word.

Marcas slouched in a chair and leered at her, a tightly bound figure by his feet. Forcing steady footsteps, Niamsha walked into the room, counting to three on each breath while her heart pounded against her chest. No fear. She paused by a window, the shutters latched and a thick, stinking hide covering the window to prevent any spying. Maybe the demon would be able to hear, though he couldn't possibly see inside.

"Nia." Marcas's sneer carried into his words as he spun a mug of ale on the table beside him. "How ya been, lass? Nijel said ya'd come, but I ain't thought you this dumb."

She swiped her tongue across her dry lips. "Ain't got much choice."

Marcas's gaze bored into her, the threat of his fury demanding that she drop her gaze in submission. A move that would sign her death warrant as sure as any. Niamsha met his eyes and straightened.

"How's Em?"

His lips twisted into a cruel smile. "Yer brother? Nijel's got him all settled. Ready ta pay his sister's price when she don't come home."

Her blood froze into ice, trudging through her body with an aching pace that left her light-headed. Nijel wouldn't—couldn't hurt Emrys. He hadn't done anything. But then, she knew how Rendell debts worked.

"Said you had something?" Marcas downed a quick gulp of ale.

"Ain't thought…" But she'd better have an excuse. And she did, given by the emperor himself.

Niamsha crossed her arms, hoping for a defiant stance. "Trying ta get Nijel's attention."

"Ya got it." Marcas waved at her. The figure by his feet shifted, moaning. But she had no time to guess who it might be. "Ya want somethin', out with it. Nijel ain't real patient, and I ain't got time to play with ya."

His gaze roamed over her body, making clear what type of play he had in mind. But even without Nijel's protection, the demon would stop him. Wouldn't he?

"Em." She threw the name out like an accusation. "Whatever plans Nijel has, he got a system. Pay fer what ya get, and ain't strange ta pay in blood. I want Em safe."

"And what you got fer us?"

"The lord's plans." She forced a deep, slow breath through her lips. "Something 'bout a traitor from up north, name o' Kumiho. Heard he's s'posed ta be gone, but he ain't. High lord's keeping him."

"Heh." Marcas reached beside his chair and pulled a tiny, cloth-wrapped bundle from the floor, setting it on the table. "Nijel don't need you fer that. He got spies, girl. But you got yerself some new connections, and Nijel has a mind ta use 'em. Here's a plan fer ya."

He unwrapped the first layer, tossing the cloth into the fire in a plume of acrid smoke. The second layer of cloth revealed the shape. Some form of bottle. The final layer joined the other two in the fire, and Marcas set a vial of clear fluid on the table. Niamsha scowled. Nothing good came in that small a vial.

"Nijel sent it." Marcas waved at it, like he thought she'd want to check it out just for fun. "Wants you ta give it ta the high lord's little pet."

"I ain't a killer." But could she really afford morals when Em's life hung in the balance? Could she refuse to poison a demon to save her brother?

"Ain't gonna kill him," Marcas said. "Least, not if ya do it right. Nijel says it'll stop him from following, is all. Reckon it's some sort o' sleeping pill."

Niamsha stepped away from the wall, her feet dragging as she walked toward him. Only a fool would believe that was a sedative.

"And Em'll be safe?" She stared at the vial. A viper hidden in clear liquid. "High lord ain't gonna be real happy. Nijel ain't gonna take it out on him 'fore I got a chance to get back?"

"Said ta bring the high lord on up when yer done." Marcas chuckled. "Reckon that won't be hard, less he kills ya right there."

What kind of thankless wretch would take this deal? Poison the creature that had saved her life in return for the life of a brother who had abandoned her. But she'd promised. Promised Papa, promised herself. How long could she defend her choices with that promise? But this wasn't just protecting her brother. Nijel intended to kill Emrys because of what *she'd* done.

Reaching out a shaky hand, Niamsha took the vial. "I ain't sure what the demon drinks."

"Some sorta tea. S'posed ta hide the stench," Marcas said. "When the job's done, Nijel'll wait on the outskirts o' town. Out by the old noble's road, he got a house as belonged to the high lord's mama. Said he ain't gonna wait long."

A location for the high lord. That was all he'd asked for, and Marcas had given her a reason to run. If she didn't care about Nijel's other plans. But her papa would want her to ask. At least get what bits she could.

"Where you headed?" She jerked her head in the approximate direction of north. "He got trades up north?"

Marcas narrowed his eyes, watching her with malicious greed. "Aye." He kicked the bundle at his feet and it moaned. Distinctly female. "Takin' this'n up north. An' he ain't dumb, neither, so don't go thinking he don't want ya to know. S'posed ta tell the high lord his princess'll be long gone. Now get on it. 'Less you thinking you might want a piece of *our* deal."

Niamsha headed toward the door. "I'm goin'."

Another task. Aeduhm help her if she didn't deliver that message. Nijel and High Lord Arkaen would both have her head, no matter it was clearly some form of trap.

Marcas scoffed. "Shame. Coulda been fun. Don't forget that drink, Nia. Emrys'll be countin' on ya."

She froze, feet leaden. Nijel wouldn't hurt Emrys. Not without reason. But if she failed at his tasks... and she already knew Nijel had spies in the high lord's palace. Forcing herself into motion again, Niamsha fled the house with as much poise as she could manage, sliding the vial into her belt pouch.

Her feet carried her down the path at twice the pace they'd carried her up. Around a bend, the rest of Torsdell stretched before her with lights dotting a few of the houses in the street ahead. Niamsha broke into a jog, darting through the first few streets to pause by a tiny hovel smashed between two larger shops. She paused, glanced to either side, and tapped on the door. Three quick raps, followed by two.

The door swung open to reveal High Lord Arkaen, dressed in ratty brown leather pants and a loose shirt, his two swords belted around his hips. He ushered her in with a jerk of his head, scanning the street beyond. Niamsha slipped inside, gaze sweeping the room. Emperor Corliann scowled into a mug of something steaming, slouched in a chair by a small fire, barely a spark in the fireplace. By the window, the high lord's demon paced in obvious agitation.

"Tell me he wasn't there." High Lord Arkaen stormed past her, spinning to level a glare at her.

"What?" Niamsha's eyes darted between the three men again. What did they think... had they heard the job after all? But then why didn't they kill her?

"Kìlashà says he couldn't see anything," the high lord said. "We didn't know if we should come in or not. Tell me Oskari wasn't there."

Niamsha shook her head. "What ya s'pect? They ain't dumb. Ain't no one gonna leave the windows wide fer spies. 'Sides, was just Marcas."

High Lord Arkaen leaned against the wall with a heavy sigh.

"Kìlashà doesn't see in the way you or I would, Niamsha," Emperor Corliann explained, his voice calm despite the fury in the set of his lips.

Not her they were mad at, which could only mean they didn't know what she'd agreed to. Or thought she wouldn't do it. But she didn't have a choice.

"Told me where," Niamsha said. "Reckon he knew I'd tell ya, though. I ain't got no clue where it is."

High Lord Arkaen nodded. "I'm certain he has a trap set. He'd be a fool not to, and he certainly sounds no fool. Where?"

"He said…" The words caught in her throat. These people had helped her. She couldn't send them into the heart of Nijel's plot without a warning.

"Gods above and below. My apologies." High Lord Arkaen turned away, his voice thick with sympathy as he crossed to the fireplace. "You've just faced your greatest fear and here I am interrogating you like a traitor." He dished a ladle of steaming liquid into a mug and offered it to her. "Tea?"

Niamsha stared, her words still frozen behind her lips, and stepped forward to take the mug. Warmth and a spicy scent of pine and cinnamon. She took a sip, the honey-sweet liquid burning down her throat and easing the tension without any conscious effort on her part. Her eyes burned with tears. She couldn't betray them. Except she had to.

"Have a seat." High Lord Arkaen swept a pile of equipment off a chair and pulled it toward her. "Take a moment. This eve won't likely change anything."

"No." Niamsha shook her head. "Nijel got plans. Faster you act, less chance he might be ready. 'Cept he is now."

"Then no need to rush." Emperor Corliann took a long sip of his own tea. "And honestly, Kaen, he's probably prepared for you. Maybe thinks he's prepared for Kìlashà. He can't have any idea I'd be here."

"Nijel got spies," Niamsha protested. "And he heard 'bout you being here. He'll know—"

"That I arrived and poked around." Emperor Corliann smiled at her. "I've barely been among the Sentarsi nobility since arriving, and I've made a rather large deal about province matters being beneath me. I'm supposed to ride out tomorrow morning. He'll have no reason to think I'd get involved."

"I'd believe it of Oskari," High Lord Arkaen said. "But I'm not so sure about this Nijel. Something feels wrong there."

"Nijel knows." Niamsha took another sip, reconsidering her opinion of High Lord Arkaen once more. Not as naive as he liked to appear either. "Said ta tell ya the princess is gone. An' Marcas is heading north."

"They sent the princess to Serni?"

She met Emperor Corliann's wide eyes and nodded. "I reckon, if that's north."

"Gods damn it all." High Lord Arkaen's eyes drifted closed.

"We have to go after her." Emperor Corliann rose, his height absurd in the tiny room. "Kaen, we can't leave a foreign dignitary in the hands of bandits. She'll... Aeduhm's Mercy. What if he kills her? What if he convinces her people *you* sold her to him? Our empire doesn't have a great record with foreign visitors. Though admittedly selling one to bandits would be a first."

"I can't." High Lord Arkaen opened his eyes, anguish turning the deep brown almost black. "You can't ask that of me. He'll kill my sister."

"Ain't ya got soldiers?" Niamsha's voice felt small, snaking through the tension between them. But the answer seemed so obvious. "Send one set north, keep th'others here."

"Soldiers need a leader," Emperor Corliann replied.

"But there is no reason for such a leader to be my kai'shien." The demon's musical tones startled her. So quiet she'd forgotten he was there.

"I need my general." Emperor Corliann shook his head. "I don't want to go north without Kaen. He holds too much sway there."

Niamsha clamped her mouth shut on an objection. Anywhere Nijel was headed wouldn't care a rat's arse for the high lord. But they knew something she didn't. Or thought they did.

"What you desire and what you need are far from identical." The demon paced across the floor to a smaller pot with a lid.

Not the one High Lord Arkaen had used for her tea. Niamsha's hand twitched, and she rubbed the solid form of the vial in her pouch. That was the substance Nijel wanted her to poison. No risk to anyone else, and surely Aeduhm had cursed this demon already. But he'd helped her.

The demon looked up, the obsidian of his eyes focused on some distant point. "My kai'shien must stay to preserve the peace in these lands. Once that is stable, he may join you."

"A fair compromise, Deyvan," High Lord Arkaen said.

Emperor Corliann paced to the door and back, his steps heavy in the ramshackle home, shaking the flimsy walls with his anger. Finally, he stopped by the door.

"Fine." Emperor Corliann set a hand on the door handle. "I'll take what soldiers you can spare north, Kaen. Join me with the rest when you can."

"Take them all." The demon stirred the pot beside him, a foul stench permeating the room as he mixed the liquid. "The claim here will not be won by strength of arms."

"The *Serr-Nyen* will object." High Lord Arkaen swept a pinch of ash onto a slip of paper and dripped several drops of his tea on top, making a smeared black paste. He pressed his signet ring into the result and handed the paper to Emperor Corliann. "Tell them Lord Phoenix requests they split their efforts. Fifteen to my aid, the rest to support Lord Kumiho's efforts."

Emperor Corliann nodded. "I feel better with your flameguard at your back, anyway."

The demon rose in a sharp jerk, turning to stare blankly at the door. "Deyvan. Do not, under any circumstances, return to Sharan Anore."

"I can't swear to that, cousin."

Niamsha spun to face Emperor Corliann at the term. *Cousin*? Surely he couldn't claim actual blood tie to this monster. Emperor Corliann showed no recognition of her surprise, frowning at the demon's expression. But no. The demon was slender and pale, where Emperor Corliann was broad shouldered and flushed with the ruddy coloring of native imperials. From build to coloring to even the angles of their faces, no two could be more different. But the passion was real. Emperor Corliann felt drawn to this demon by some force beyond his control.

"You know I can't promise." Emperor Corliann glanced at the high lord, as if seeking an answer. "I must follow where the trail leads or this will be war."

"Do not, under *any* circumstances, return to Sharan Anore." The demon's eyes blazed with the heat of a hell-borne threat. A servant of Eiliin. He had to be.

High Lord Arkaen stepped between them. "We'll be done with this before it matters, Kìlashà." He fixed the demon with a firm stare for several breaths, then turned to Emperor Corliann. "A moment alone before you go? I've an idea. Perhaps we can minimize the need for combat allies with a message to my lower lords."

Emperor Corliann nodded, leading the high lord outside. Leaving Niamsha alone with the demon. She stared at him, the fiery trails of gods-cursed skin burning in the dim light.

"What else did the mindless oaf ask of you, Niamsha?" The demon fixed his eyes on her.

"Said…"

The abyss of his eyes caught at her soul. Demon, cursed by Aeduhm to wander the dark places where only Eiliin held sway. The pulsing lines of red flowed with the burning blood of innocents. But he was kind. He'd helped her. Saved her from the Rendells after the baron's beating. He'd promised to protect Emrys, and the only way to protect Emrys was to slip the liquid into his drink. Nijel didn't bluff. Not even through a messenger. Her heart ached, palms sweaty and hairs on her neck standing on end.

"Nothing." Niamsha shook her head in denial.

"A lie." The demon's eyes narrowed. "I tire of your deceptions."

"Threatened Em," she said.

He couldn't call that a lie. After a moment, the demon nodded.

"A truth, but not the entirety." He considered her for several more breaths, then rose with a careless shrug. "The Spirits have sent you, but They have not yet taught you to trust Their will. Humans are difficult students."

He crossed the room, slipping out the door and joining the soft murmur of voices beyond. A chance. Her only chance. Niamsha stared at the door, frozen. But she couldn't risk staying put. Emrys needed her. And the demon was cursed at best, a hell-borne corrupter at worst.

Dashing across the room, Niamsha fumbled the vial from her pocket and yanked the stopper free. A few drops. How many in a pot this large, though? Aeduhm bless her, she couldn't risk it not working. Niamsha dumped the vial into the mixture, giving a couple swift sweeps of the spoon he'd left behind before returning to her chair. Now to wait. And pray. Gods, if she was wrong. Aeduhm's blessing on the high lord's demon. He'd been kind, whatever his past. If she'd given too high a dose, the death of a decent person fell on her hands. If he could die at all. If he was anything close to human.

High Lord Arkaen stepped back inside, followed by his demon. They muttered under their breath in conversation, ignoring her for a moment. Then the demon crossed to the pot of tea, took a quick sniff of the pot, and nodded. Dished a ladle into a cup.

And handed the cup to High Lord Arkaen.

This one shall be as the Chosen's Right Hand, called to the defense of the People for love of their savior.

— from the prophecies of the Chosen of the Four Clans

Chapter 34

Kìlashà stirred the tragyna brew, the simmering of his power a dull ache against his own pride. Failed. Kaen's sister should be safe already. Should be home. But his Seeking had led him astray time and again. He ladled another mug of the tea into his own cup, turning to face the filthy room his kai'shien had demanded they use. Niamsha perched on the edge of her seat, lips parted in some human emotion, her breaths swift and nervous. Something he should be able to see. He reached a hesitant thought toward the flames of possibility.

"Dammit, Jayls, run!"

Shoving the vision away, Kìlashà wavered at the force of his power's warning. But one decades too late. A Drae'gon Seeker's power didn't bother consuming the Seeker with useless warnings. Unless, apparently, that Drae'gon had the shame of being born to human blood. Kìlashà brought the tragyna brew to his lips, blinking back the confusing double image of the debris-strewn room and the blood-smeared bed where Raekeen had died, and tossed his head back in a long gulp.

His Seeker's power consumed him the instant the liquid touched his lips.

Pain shot through Kìlashà's body as he collapsed on the floor, his limbs unresponsive to his own needs. Gasping for air, Kaen's shout of rage echoed like a drumbeat.

Kìlashà thrust the vision away, spitting the remaining tragyna tea from his mouth. Too late. A dull ache seeped into his limbs, his throat tight and struggling for breath. Seconds, maybe, to find an antidote. His gaze swept across the room, seeking aid. Kaen. With cup in hand, raised for a sip.

"No!" Niamsha threw herself across the room before Kìlashà could speak, knocking the cup from Kaen's hand.

His body froze, sluggish to his commands, like dragging a hand through melted stone.

"Lasha!"

Kaen was by his side, clinging to his arm as Kìlashà fell to his knees. But no. The Ancient Spirits would not let him die like this. He must find an answer. They would provide it.

Only one possible chance. Kìlashà fell heavily against Kaen as he flung himself back into his power.

Pain. Aching, terrible tightness in his stomach, limbs burning so they jerked of their own accord. Kìlashà lay on his side, curled around the ball of agony tearing through his center. Distant scuffs of boots on stone and crying, sobs heart-wrenching.

"Didn't know!"

Not helpful. Likely, but uninformative. The bright, solid colors and factual precision of his vision sent a shock of pure fear through him. Kìlashà pushed the feeling away. No time for human weakness.

Kìlashà pushed through the inferno blazing in his mind. Burning in his limbs and starting in his stomach. Touched the river behind the wall of flame.

Pain was a distant memory. A thing known but no longer felt. And with the loss of pain came the loss of touch, of smell, of all things beyond the ever-changing flow. Ever-twisting, all things mixed with all they might have been.

A sharp bite, sting of metal digging into his cheek.

"Dammit, Lasha, talk to me!"

The body was gone, the physical thing that his kai'shien desired long dead.

No.

The will of the Ancient Spirits undeniable. His failure the tool with which an unknown enemy had murdered Their Chosen.

He could not die. *Would* not die. Not while his kai'shien needed him. Kìlashà forced his mind out of the river, focusing on the grainy, rough wood beneath him. Shoved against it to slump against a wall. Kaen's desperate brown eyes bored into his.

"Featherfew." Kìlashà's voice was barely a whisper.

Kaen vanished from his narrowing sight, the rustle as Kaen hunted for the herb loud as a scream. Kìlashà took the moment to dip into the timelines again. A painkiller would do nothing but ease his passing, and he needed to live.

Kaen pulled a sealed vellum pouch free, dumping it into the tasteless brew he called tea. A quick stir and he added a handful of dark green leaves with bright white veins.

Kìlashà held the image for an instant, pulling himself free to speak.

"Bilebeirn." The words burned his aching throat, but a glance from Kaen convinced him the message was heard.

Kaen tore the leaves into shreds, steeping them whole, though they should have been dried. No time. But it should work. The final piece he had dried already. Kaen pulled out another sealed vellum pouch. Added three carefully measured pinches of the blood red powder inside.

"Bloodseal."

Kaen spun from the hearth where he'd been brewing the mixture. "That's a poison all its own."

A wave of dizziness stole his breath, and Kìlashà collapsed on the floor. His gut burned with the fire of death and his limbs trembled. A sharp jolt of pain. His arms jerked of their own accord. Kìlashà lay on his side, curled around the ball of agony tearing through his center.

No. Not now. Kaen needed—

"I'll manage."

"Do not—" Another jolt of pain. He whimpered at the ache. Forced the words out. "The female. Do not kill—"

"Like bloody hell." Kaen's steps faded as he shifted away. "Rest."

Agony poured through every inch of his body, lungs straining to draw air against the inexorable slowing of his blood, his heart. His spasms worsened, every twitch a new torment. And death loomed ever closer. A release. Escape from the plague that had been his life. His power flared.

"Raeky?"

"It's all right, Jayls." Prince Raekeen smiled at his younger brother, patting his head. *"Father's mad, but he'll get over it. You just frightened the cook is all."*

Father wouldn't, though. They both knew that, and Kìlashà could feel the lie as his younger, human child had not. Prince Raekeen had always known... Would be waiting for his little brother.

Kìlashà pulled himself free, the agony soaring through him again. Too much comfort in those moments. He couldn't afford the risk that his body would fail while he indulged in childhood fantasies. Human fantasies. But the Spirits cared about those childhood dreams. They had used those moments in speaking Their will.

He pushed from the floor, tried to sit. And failed. Until a dim figure settled beside him, coaxing him into leaning on a foreign, familiar shoulder. Spoon-fed a burning, bitter liquid into his lips. Kaen.

Clinging to the truth of his kai'shien, Kìlashà fought through the fog. Dragged a hand up and took the cup to drink the second half in a single gulp.

Featherfew and bilebeirn would take time, but the bloodseal went straight to work, fresh fire through numb veins, forcing his organs to push faster, harder. In a healthy man, a death sentence. The warring poisons sapped the last of his strength and Kìlashà faded completely.

At last, Emperor Laisia found the ally he needed to break the Serr-Nyen *rebellion: Griffon. She feared what the three foreigners might do to her homeland and in her desperation, she revealed the identity of Kumiho to her few trusted allies. No sooner had she done so than Lord Phoenix and the Dragon located her, killing her and any remaining supporters she had. And then they set their sights on Emperor Laisia.*

— *from* An Abridged History of the Sernien War

Chapter 35

Arkaen slumped against the rickety wall of the shanty he'd chosen, Lasha's body collapsed over his lap, and stared at the ceiling. He traced the flow of Lasha's hair with one hand, the frantic energy that had taken him drained with the loss of direction from Lasha's orders. Nothing to do but wait. And deal with the bitch who'd poisoned him. Arkaen's eyes settled on Niamsha, huddled in the hasty restraints he'd fashioned from his sword belt.

Her lips gaped open, shock written on her face like a hand-drawn map. She knew. Gods, how could she not, after watching his panicked response. But it added another complication to dealing with her.

"You." He couldn't keep the fury from his voice and wasn't sure he wanted to. "Have one chance. He said not to kill you. Convince me he was right."

Arkaen's own words sent ice through his body. *Was* right, like he thought Lasha was already dead. But no. Lasha's breath had steadied since his collapse after downing the last of his antidote and his seizures had stilled. Unconscious, but stable. He hoped.

"I—" Niamsha's gaze dropped to stare at Lasha's slack form, her shoulders trembling. "Didn't think it'd do that. He said…"

"You are *not* helping your case."

She flashed him a glare. "What ya want me ta say? Want me ta lie? Say it weren't me? He's got me brother. Said he'd kill him. When Nijel kills…"

She dropped her eyes, trailing off as another shudder shook her body. Not fear of him. Arkaen had seen that look—that fear—in the eyes of too many *Serr-Nyen* villagers describing what Bloody Emperor Laisia did to their families. Just the right twist to win his compassion, and for a moment he wondered if she'd planned it. But Lasha defended her. No human guile could tug at Lasha's heart as it so often tugged at Arkaen's.

He ran one hand through Lasha's hair again, his other hand finding the spot just under Lasha's chin where the beat of his heart throbbed against his skin. Weak. It took several tries before Arkaen was sure he'd found the rhythm, and more than once his own pulse raced in renewed fear. Finally, he found the beat, slow and steady against his fingers. A flood of relief as he tracked the pace. Slow and weak, but Lasha would live.

Focusing on Niamsha again, Arkaen feigned the anger her terror had so quickly extinguished.

"He lives." Arkaen's sharp tone rang false even to his own ears, but Niamsha seemed too frightened to notice. "If he dies, so do you."

Deyvan would never let him make good on the threat, but he needed to say it. To protect Lasha in what small ways he still could.

But empty threats aside, Arkaen had no time to wallow in his anger. Sayli still suffered under Oskari's restraints and whoever this Nijel was, he needed dealt with now. No time to wait for Lasha to recover, which was no doubt the plan.

"You told Deyvan that Nijel wouldn't leave Oskari when he could still use him?"

Niamsha nodded, eyes still downcast. "Ain't like ta waste a tool."

"Then you can lead me to both," Arkaen said. "Assuming you weren't lying about knowing where."

"I ain't lied…" Her gaze shifted to Lasha. "Least, not 'bout that. Said the lady's at yer mother's home. From when she was little."

"Predictable, I suppose, to choose a place of meaning to me."

Arkaen shifted under Lasha's weight, straining to one side to reach a heavy oilcloth cloak he'd thrown over a chair on his arrival. Tugging it free, he folded a bulky pillow out of the result and substituted that for his own lap, freeing himself from Lasha's unconscious body.

Arkaen rose, running a hand through his grimy hair. "Can't say *I* would have chosen a stronghold where my enemy played as a child, though. If I set you free, you won't run, right?"

Niamsha glanced up at him. "Run?"

"Flee from the wrath of your terrifying high lord? Apparently I've a reputation for a bad temper."

"Seems right true ta me." She regarded him through cautiously narrowed eyes, body tense. "Ain't never seen folk so feared over harm to a demon before. Nor so spittin' mad."

"Kìlashà is not a demon."

It was too much to hope she hadn't made the connection. Cunning of her to pretend to have missed it, though. A chance to save her neck were he a less scrupulous man and setting the bait for blackmail when she revealed what she'd learned. A plan he'd have to nip in the bud as soon as he'd returned Sayli home and dealt with Oskari and his thief. But for now, she could play her games and think he didn't know.

Arkaen crossed to her chair, releasing her hands with a few quick twists of his sword belt. He swung the belt around his waist and added his twin sabers to the mix. Rearmed and far more comfortable for the fact, Arkaen scanned the room for anything of value. An old bed frame. Likely solid enough for his needs.

"Come here." Arkaen nodded at the frame, placing a foot to break a long stretch of wood loose. "Help me break this down. I need to build something to carry him."

"Ya can't…" Her eyes darted to Lasha and back. "He's no help."

"Obviously," Arkaen replied. "But I can't exactly leave him here. Not if I want him alive at the end of this. I'll send him to the palace with my guards when they arrive."

Niamsha slunk a few steps closer, watching him work with a puzzled look. The first board he'd scavenged snapped in the middle at the first sign of pressure. He pulled another free and tested it. Stable enough, with proper weight distribution. A few more boards and he had three solid enough to hold Lasha's weight. He cast around for some form of cloth, eyes falling on the cloak he'd used as a pillow. With a grimace, he crossed and slid it out from under Lasha's still form.

"Sorry, love," he whispered, laying a hand on Lasha's cheek. Cool to the touch. Lasha's body returning to its normal state.

Three sharp knocks at the door, pause, two knocks. Arkaen gestured at Niamsha.

"Grab the door."

Arkaen rummaged through Lasha's herb pouch as she opened the door. The racket of his soldiers piling inside halted abruptly. Someone stepped close.

"Lord Phoenix." Genuine fear hung in Jarod's words. "Is your dragon all right?"

"He should be." Arkaen tossed the cloak to Jarod. "I've several boards chosen. Make a carry litter."

"Yes, milord."

Pulling out a handful of Lasha's tragyna leaves, Arkaen turned to the pot of spiced tea he'd been drinking. And froze. Turned his gaze on Niamsha.

"You didn't poison the other tea, did you?"

She backed away, eyes widening at his tone as several of the *Serr-Nyen* soldiers reached for weapons. Arkaen raised a hand to stop them. Niamsha glanced back and forth, scanning the new arrivals.

"I ain't touched it." Her voice shook and her eyes never left the closest soldier.

Gods, if only he could be sure. But if Nijel had convinced her to poison Lasha, who knew what else she might do. Arkaen bit his lip, muttered a quick prayer, and dipped a cup from the pot of tea. Jarod crossed the room, reaching a hand toward the cup.

"Your pardon, Lord Phoenix," he said. "We haven't come this far to watch you die in a run-down hovel."

Arkaen hesitated. But damn if he wasn't right. If she *had* poisoned both, there'd be no one to make an antidote for Arkaen. He handed the cup to Jarod, who downed half the liquid in one quick swallow. They stared at each other for a long moment, both tense, breaths coming in shortened bursts.

Finally, Jarod shrugged, finishing the cup. "Little over-brewed, milord."

With a sigh of relief, he crumbled a few of Lasha's dried tragyna leaves into the pot, stirring the mixture as the pungent smell wafted through the room. Niamsha came to stand beside him, arms wrapped tightly around herself.

"What's that?" She nodded at the brew.

Arkaen watched her movements from the corner of his eye. But no sign she had any more of whatever she added to the first set of tragyna tea.

"A tea unique to Kìlashà's people." He took a cautious sniff of the concoction and fought back a wave of nausea. "Smells like Eiliin's foulest hell hounds and tastes about as bad. But it has uses."

She nodded, scuffing a foot on the wood floor. "I ain't…"

Her uncertainty lingered after her words faded. A regret all too familiar to Arkaen. So many lives lost under his blade, and damage done in the name of protecting those he cared for. How could he condemn her for doing the same?

"You're hardly the first."

"First?" She peered over his shoulder, cringing at the stench of the tragyna.

"To reject him," Arkaen said. "Dismiss his intent and even try to kill him. All for a lack of knowing who he is."

Niamsha's eyes bored into him. "He? That one's demon spawn. Who *you* think he is?"

"Milord." Jarod stepped up behind him, standing with arms crossed behind his back. "We're ready."

Arkaen dished a cup out of the brew, pinched his nose, and swallowed the drink in one quick gulp. His throat burned, stomach roiling at the foul taste as bile rose in his throat to combat the stench. One breath, deep through his nose despite the smell. A second. And the effects kicked in. Sound sharpened, his eyes focused more precisely on the exact colors of the room around him, and the remaining weariness lifted from his limbs.

He turned to Niamsha. "Kìlashà is someone far more important than you, or I, or any of us."

Rising, he slipped Lasha's packet of herbs into his belt pouch and swept Lasha into his arms, cradling the limp figure as close as he dared. No need to give additional fuel to Niamsha's blackmail opportunity. Crossing the room, he settled Lasha in the makeshift carry litter, shifting him to as comfortable a position as he could manage.

"Get him home, and keep an eye on him." Arkaen straightened, pointing out four of the *Serr-Nyen* guards for the task. "At least two of you on guard at all times until I return. And tell Lord Kumiho not to delay his efforts. His task is too important."

His chosen flameguard nodded, stepping forward to arrange themselves around Lasha. Arkaen watched with a heavy heart, aching to follow beside and watch over him. But he had no time for fear. Not now, with his strongest ally incapacitated. Arkaen swept the door aside, forcing himself to stand stoic as they carried Lasha away.

"All right." The calm determination of his own voice surprised him. But Deyvan would have laughed. Typical Phoenix battle nerves. Always steadiest when the plan had gone all to hell. At least the challenge he'd planned with Deyvan should still work. If Oskari held to the rules.

Arkaen turned to Niamsha and the remaining guards. "We've a baron to kill."

꧁⋆⋅☆⋅⋆꧂

Niamsha stared at the soldiers—eleven men in the plain brown of High Lord Arkaen's personal guard milling about the room as their companions carried a fallen demon with the care she might show to a dear friend. A hand fell heavy on her shoulder.

"I got half a mind to clear my lord's conscience, girl." The one who'd asked Lord Arkaen about the demon, his eyes narrowed and angry. "He ain't one to take revenge and I honor his commands. But fer you…"

Niamsha trembled, her skin crawling with the memory of what she'd done. That potion did something more than she understood, and these men cared more for the life of that demon than she'd known. Her shaking took over, a poor mimicry to the desperate, convulsing pain of her victim as he gasped orders to High Lord Arkaen.

"Don't scare the girl, Jarod." High Lord Arkaen dumped the last of the tea over his small fire, sending a burst of steam into the air. "She's a traitor, but only out of necessity. Keep watch on her and keep her alive."

"Beggin' pardon, Milord Phoenix, but she ain't just a pawn. I seen her running that riot." The guard, Jarod, tightened his hand on Niamsha's shoulder.

"I'm right here." She pulled her shoulder out of the grip, the pain of his fingers lingering on her skin. A reminder that even a supposedly kind man had cruel servants. Niamsha stared High Lord Arkaen in the eyes, his anger still simmering behind the sympathy he claimed to feel. "You ain't gonna send me to the cells, may as well use me."

He chuckled. "Use you for what, girl? You expect me to trust that you'll fight by my side less than an hour after you poisoned my—" He hesitated, eyes boring into her, and smiled. "Poisoned Kìlashà."

Something in that pause and that smile tugged at her guilt. Marcas, or Nijel, or whoever's plan this was, knew something she didn't. Something High Lord Arkaen thought she'd learned. His desperation when the demon fell, and his anger… like Papa when her mother fell sick with Emrys. But this was a demon, and a male one at that, not the high lord's wife.

High Lord Arkaen stalked closer. "Why would I trust you?"

"What choice ya got?" Niamsha waved at the guards surrounding them. "You need a distraction. A way in. Ain't no one gonna think these are anything but soldiers, and not enough of them. You plannin' on strolling in the front door?"

A smirk spread across his face. "Yes, actually. But you do have a use. I need a few men to head in separately for a different task." He tapped a finger on the door frame beside him. "You'd be more liability with me, anyway. Three or four men should keep you in line…"

"Nah, Milord Phoenix." Jarod shook his head. "We ain't letting you wander into a viper's nest without yer full guard."

"It won't matter, Jarod," High Lord Arkaen said. "You're more a show of force than anything. If Oskari decides to kill me without honoring the

Successor's Tribune then I'm already dead. All fifteen of you and Kìlashà combined would be hard pressed to win that fight. Without him…"

"Begging your pardon, milord." Jarod stepped forward, arms crossed in defiance. "But I don't give a damn."

High Lord Arkaen stared Jarod down with an intensity that made Niamsha's skin itch. She hugged her arms to herself, shoulders tight as the air seemed to thicken into something tangible holding the scene still.

"Someone has to find my sister." High Lord Arkaen broke the silence with a slow and deliberate voice. "I'm hardly sending the girl in alone. She's proven she can be bought."

"Ain't like I wanted to." The words escaped Niamsha's lips before she thought about them, the accusation hitting harder than she'd thought it would. And how could she blame him? She *had* turned on him barely a day after promising to help. She'd agreed to help him, then heard Nijel's demands, and she'd poisoned the demon's drink. Shame ached in her throat, but she forced herself to continue. "Didn't have a choice. Nijel got me brother. I oughta let him die fer someone I don't even know?"

"I didn't say the price was cheap," High Lord Arkaen replied. "But bought is bought, whatever the cost. Could you really promise that you'd stay loyal to me if this Nijel held a blade to your brother's throat?"

Niamsha swallowed, dropped her eyes, and shook her head.

"As I thought." He turned back to Jarod. "And that settles it. I need my flameguard."

Every remaining guard in the room straightened, feet sliding apart in perfect unison as they all slammed a fist to their chests. Eerily stoic and more coordinated that anything she'd ever seen Nijel, or Marcas, or even the Rogue Baron achieve from their followers.

"Your flameguard serve, Milord Phoenix." Jarod dropped his fist to his side once more. "But we won't watch you throw your life away."

High Lord Arkaen nodded. "A compromise, then." He waved a hand at the rest of the guards and they relaxed back into whatever tasks they'd been occupied with before. "The bulk of the guard go with me. Jarod, you escort the girl. She says she wants to help, give her a chance, but don't let her out of your sight. You have two jobs. Free my sister and find Nijel."

"I gotta find Em," Niamsha insisted. "Can't leave him, not if Nijel's men may think I turned again. He's just…"

But he wasn't a boy. Not any longer. The boy she'd known was long gone and likely beyond redeeming.

"I understand your desire, Niamsha." High Lord Arkaen cast her a sympathetic look. "But there's too much at stake. If the nobility kill my sister the entire succession of the province is thrown into flux. And I hate to be the one to tell you, but you can't be sure he isn't one of them already."

Niamsha scowled. Emrys *was* one of the Rendell boys now, but that didn't mean she should abandon him. Not like he'd abandoned her after the riot. But she wouldn't do that. Wouldn't be the one who left family to die because they'd made a mistake.

"He's still my brother."

"And if we can save him, we will." High Lord Arkaen whispered the promise, an agreement they both knew he wouldn't honor. He stepped forward, close enough to Jarod that she almost thought he intended harm. "But you find Nijel, and do *not* let him escape. At any cost, Jarod. I can't let him keep this up, no matter what it means."

Jarod nodded. "Aye, milord. Any cost."

High Lord Arkaen turned away, throwing a quick gesture at the rest of the guards. "Fall in."

Arkaen stalked up the overgrown path that led to the Istalli manor home, Niamsha pacing nervously at his side and the *Serr-Nyen* flameguard arrayed in formation behind him. The untrimmed hedge fence that trailed each side of the lane held too many shadows and not enough light to know what might lurk there. A nervous tremble swept through his body. Lasha would know what hid there. What danger to prepare for. But Niamsha had taken that knowledge from him.

He pushed the still-simmering anger away. No use alienating her when he needed her to draw this Nijel out where he could deal with the traitor. Pausing by a slight thinning of the hedges, Arkaen ran a hand along his sword hilt as if to check the grip.

"Niamsha, you'll want to double back here," he muttered, keeping his eyes focused away from her face. His neck prickled with tension. "Through those bushes, follow the path around to the keep. Grate by the water outlet is loose."

With a satisfied nod, he strode forward again. Niamsha's steps faltered as she turned, but Jarod clapped a hand on her shoulder from the other side and guided her forward. Arkaen fought back a bitter smile. Nothing worse than forcing her to face a dangerous enemy alone to further his goals, but she'd given him no other choice.

A turn in the path ahead made Arkaen slow his pace. No point rushing into more ambushes than he had to. Arkaen gave Jarod a quick wave, and he nodded in return.

"Come on, lass." He steered Niamsha toward the brush. "Let's find that brother o' yers."

Arkaen's heightened hearing tracked the rustle of branches as they crept away. No sign of conflict. One step complete.

Two other guards stepped up beside him, filling the hole in the loose formation as he turned the corner to face the guards at the door to his mother's estate. Former estate, though he'd always treasured the location—home of his childhood adventures. Two vaguely familiar men in plain clothes flanked the door, each with a patch of green and gold cloth pinned to the shoulder of their shirts. New recruits to Oskari's cause. Arkaen dropped his hands to his sword hilts and strode forward, pasting on a determined smirk.

"Good eve," he called, pausing several steps away.

The Serr-Nyen formed a ring behind him, protecting him from ambush as much by placing their own bodies between him and arrows as by show of arms. The men on either side of the door glanced at each other, brows furrowed in confusion. For good reason. Oskari had more guards than Arkaen's current retinue in his usual employ. Now that he'd added these—and who knew how many more—the soldiers Arkaen had brought were laughable. If he'd intended a proper assault.

"I've come to speak with Oskari Weydert." Arkaen fixed his gaze on the upper curve of the door between them. Above their heads and sure to offend. "I understand he's challenged my order, claiming to retain his title as baron. An honorable man would challenge my authority before a Successor's Tribune. Thought I'd make the journey simple. I'm sure Oskari *claims* he's honorable."

Both guards dropped hands to sword hilts, and the right guard started forward, eyes narrowed. He paused at a wave from his companion.

"Strong words from a murderer." The left guard sneered, rapping on the door with his free hand. "Let the captain deal with you."

Captain? Arkaen barely had time to register the title when the door opened to reveal his former captain of the guard. Less than a fortnight and he'd already aligned himself elsewhere. With that loyalty, his service was hardly a loss. Still…

"I'm disappointed, captain." Arkaen dropped his gaze to scowl at the captain. "I'd thought your integrity cost more."

"As if you've a right to condemn." The captain crossed his arms, frowning at the trees behind Arkaen.

Archers there, as he'd suspected then. No surprise Oskari had bows trained on his own front doors. Clearly his new recruits weren't the most reliable.

"I'm certain the baron will answer your challenge," the captain said. "But I won't allow your foreign army inside."

Arkaen scoffed. "You don't think I'm stupid enough to set foot in enemy territory without guards." He waved back at the flameguard. "And ten men is hardly an army. Though perhaps *you* have never had the balls to face a true army."

The captain's face set in a scowl of anger, but he kept any retort behind his clenched teeth. After a few breaths staring into Arkaen's feigned confidence, the captain sighed. He scanned the group behind Arkaen and pointed out three men.

"They can accompany you, high lord." The captain leveled a challenging look. "If you need more, you're hardly the swordsman you claim to be."

Perfect. Arkaen let a smile of triumph play at his lips. Seven flameguard left outside would give them a decent shot at clearing his path out after Oskari's inevitable betrayal.

"If you insist."

Arkaen gestured behind him and three of the Serr-Nyen soldiers stepped up beside him. The rest scattered around the entryway. A passable mimicry of settling in to wait, though they were almost certainly scouting the area for defensible positions. Arkaen strode forward, crossing the dozen steps to the stairs and paused, waiting for the captain to move.

"You'll take the oath before you step inside," the captain said.

"That's not how it works." Arkaen's skin prickled at the demand. "The Successor's Oath is mutual and taken together."

"By tradition, not law." The captain shifted into a wide-legged stance, hands on hips—and therefore on the hilt of a heavy blade. "You've murdered your own guards in cold blood. You'll take the oath."

He could feel the wrongness in his very blood, like a warning from Lasha's previously disinterested gods. With Their messenger incapacitated, perhaps They *had* decided to send a message to Their remaining pawn. But there was no way to know what, exactly, he should do to resolve the problem. And if he refused, the entire plan would collapse. Niamsha left alone in a den of traitors she intended to betray, his flameguard cut down by arrows from an unknown number of archers. Sayli, abandoned. No, if Lasha's gods wanted to help, They'd have to give him more than a bad feeling.

Arkaen shrugged. "Very well. Not like I'd any intent to avoid it." He pulled a knife from his belt and made a small incision at the side of his hand, squeezing through the sting of pain to release a sluggish drip of blood onto the stairs. "I swear, by the blood of my kith and kin, to hold the laws."

Two drops of blood on the stones as he finished the ceremonial opening. Tradition said he should drop ten, but he doubted the wound would bleed long enough. Arkaen met the captain's eyes as he continued. "Hand combat, to death, between House Sentarsin and House Weydert."

Five drops, and the drip of blood had slowed further, a sixth wavering on the edge of his hand. By tradition—not law—an oath over less than seven drops of blood was invalid. But a deeper cut would hinder the use of his hand. Arkaen squeezed harder, forcing another tiny drip of blood free. The sixth drop of blood fell.

"Champions to be the heads of house, seconds the heirs, and so until one house stands no more." Arkaen squeezed his fist again. The slide of blood on his skin, pooling in a final drop, hovering over the steps. "The victor to rule all lands held by the vanquished." The blood fell. "Forfeit holding the weight of a defeat."

The captain scowled at the stairs. "Stingy, but sufficient." He gestured to the doorway behind him, sending one of the other guards to bring the message as he stepped aside. "I'm sure you'll recall the way."

Arkaen strode forward and paused on the threshold. Something... The rustle of brush, heavy huff of breath released for focus. He spun around, movements sluggish in comparison to the heightened senses from Lasha's tragyna tea. There. A glint off a metal tip as the arrow flew. Arkaen dashed inside. Feet slid on the blood-slicked stone as more bowstrings released.

Pain burst through his side, fresh, warm blood blossoming. He slammed into the wall, wedged into the corner by the door's frame. Twisted to check his injury. A long gash, deep enough to coat his shirt with blood. Thank the gods the arrow hadn't stuck. He had no time for an extraction.

A groan from the doorway drew his attention. Two of his flameguard collapsed with arrows deep in their flesh. Gods damn it all. But he couldn't help. Not even if he'd had the time. Those would be death wounds.

Arkaen tore a strip of cloth free from one sleeve, wadded it into a tight bundle, and pressed the result into his wound. Shouting and the clash of swords rang from outside.

"Flameguard, fall back!" Arkaen yelled the command, praying they heard over their fury. No use getting them *all* killed for this mess.

A scuffle of movement and three flameguard filled the doorway. Two held small bucklers held to deflect what arrows they could as the third ran forward. The two guards slammed the doors shut as soon as they were clear.

"Lord Phoenix." The third man gaped at his wound. "We gotta get you—"

Arkaen waved the suggestion away. "I've a duel to fight. Get this bound."

"You can't…"

Arkaen stared the man down. "*Forfeit holding the weight of a defeat,* I said." Not that victory was likely with this wound. Oskari didn't have Arkaen's skill, but he wasn't a complete fool with a sword. And gods save him if Rikkard joined the duel.

"But milord—" The man looked away.

"I fight, or I abdicate." Arkaen grimaced as his wound throbbed. Lasha would kill him for not finding a cleaner stop for the blood, but infection wouldn't matter if he died in the duel. Arkaen nodded down the hall. "We've a battle brother in there, and I've a blood sister taken captive. You fought in Serni. Do I leave men behind?"

The man shook his head with a scowl. "But your dragon's ill and your army's scattered. This fight..." He held up a hand to forestall Arkaen's words, biting at his lip. "I'll help you fight, Lord Phoenix. But I ain't gotta like it."

Arkaen gave a humorless chuckle. "Neither do I."

The man set to work, tearing fresh strips of cloth free to patch at the edges and over the top of Arkaen's blood-soaked plug. The sounds of fighting outside died, though Arkaen couldn't tell if his flameguard had fled or been killed. Nothing he could do either way. Finally, the guard fashioned a makeshift tie out of his sword belt, the thick leather digging into the wound painfully. But it held the cloth in place. Enough, Arkaen hoped, to keep him from tearing the bandage free mid-fight.

"Best I can do, milord."

Arkaen nodded. "Best we can all do."

He pushed off from the wall, testing his movement. The bulky cloth at his side threw his balance off, but only slightly. The pain throbbed throughout his body, but Lasha's tragyna brew helped. The thought reminded him of Lasha's herb pouch. Arkaen dug out one of the fresh tragyna leaves, grimaced, and tore off a chunk to chew. Less potent than the tea, and by extension less foul, the pulpy mixture still sent a renewed wave of strength through him. Enough for the coming battle, he hoped.

Storing the herbs again, Arkaen glanced at the drawn faces of his flameguard. Frightened as they hadn't been since the war. He couldn't blame them. Pain shooting through his body, Arkaen assumed the cocky swagger he'd used as a *Serr-Nyen* general.

"Let's go kill us a traitor, gentlemen."

Second, to refuse all desires for personal glory, for all wonder belongs to Him.

— Second of Aeduhm's Teachings

Chapter 36

Niamsha stepped out of the narrow tunnel, feet soaked and smelling like noble's soap, into the laundry chamber. A fresh vat of clothes sat over an enormous fire, the warmth filling the room with a faint hint of flowers. At least it hadn't been a sewer. *The water outlet* had certainly seemed more ominous when High Lord Arkaen told her to use it. She crossed the room, the comforts of a clean-swept, cozy room at odds with the guilt that hung over her.

She'd killed the demon.

Slipping something into his drink hadn't seemed so terrible. Just a sedative. Nijel wouldn't have wasted her use on a sedative and she'd known it. But there was knowing, and then there was watching the creature writhe in pain, gasping out instructions to a frantic... What even *was* the relationship between that demon and the high lord? Not master to servant, that was certain.

Jarod stepped out of the tunnel, scanning the room for any movement. "Reckon Lord Phoenix knows his way around."

He crossed the room to the door without any further attention to the comforts inside. Accustomed to luxury, no doubt. Niamsha pushed the jealousy away and followed. What luxury could a murderer expect, anyway? Though it *was* just a demon. Any proper servant of Aeduhm would celebrate her triumph over a cursed hell beast from Eiliin's dominion.

Did hell beasts gasp for air like he had? Did they plead with their masters to spare the woman who'd poisoned them?

"No time fer ruminating, girl," he said, peering out the door.

Niamsha hurried to follow. If she had been wrong, the only thing to do now was keep her word going forward. If she could help save the lady—and if Emrys could be brought back to a decent life—maybe she'd find some way to atone. If she had anything to atone for.

Jarod led her out of the room, through a series of corridors. Either he knew the place himself, or High Lord Arkaen had entrusted his guard with far more information than her. Not surprising, given what she'd done. They stopped at a split, their hall heading in two different directions.

"All right, girl." The guard turned to her. "Yer Nijel. How bad's he?"

"Ya mean…" Niamsha frowned. How bad was Nijel? Bad at what?

"Milord Phoenix," the guard said. "He ain't coming out o' that fight unharmed, and he plans on taking this leader o' yers after? How good's yer Nijel in a fight?"

Niamsha shrugged. "Never seen him fight. He never needed to."

The guard cursed under his breath. "Reckon he's damned good then."

"No, can't say that." Niamsha shook her head. "Could be—" She fell silent at the guard's smirk.

"In a den o' thieves, you ain't never seen him fight." He met her eyes with a confident stare. "You seen them others fight?"

She nodded. All the Rendells fought, half the time against each other. A constant pecking order of who fell third, fourth, fifth in command. And the occasional blood bath where someone challenged Marcas for second.

"There's yer answer," Jarod said, seeming to read her mind. "Leader that ain't gotta defend his place among scum is a leader can take 'em all at once."

"But—" Niamsha glanced back. "How we gonna handle him? High lord can't think…" His words echoed in her memory. Find Nijel at any cost.

"I s'pect he wants us to draw the bastard out. Keep him busy." Jarod shrugged. "Not exactly a great plan, though his dragon was better at those."

Niamsha could feel the threat in his glare. The high lord's demon would have been with them but for her. A shiver ran through her at the thought. Whatever happened, if they failed, it was her fault.

"High lord said find his sister," Niamsha said.

Jarod nodded. "Aye. And I reckon the lady may know something of the layout." He gestured for Niamsha to follow. "Lord Phoenix said there oughta be a parlor this way. Place ta start."

She followed him down the hall, moving as quickly as they dared. No telling what the Rogue Baron might have here. After a short while, a scream from ahead sent them both running toward an open door ahead. The struggle within paused as they approached, but Niamsha could immediately see it had nothing to do with them. A guard—one of the baron's—struggled with someone else inside the room. Niamsha froze, looking around for any others, but Jarod rushed forward.

With a strange shout in some foreign language, Jarod crashed into the guard. Gods-damned noble-trained guard. He'd get them both killed. Niamsha hurried after him to examine the carnage within. A maid huddled on a fine couch, her eyes wide and flustered. The baron's guard fell to the ground, clutching some piece of paper. And beside the couch, a side table held one of the delicate glass earrings Niamsha had last seen on Lady Saylina.

"Ya well?" Jarod knelt beside the maid, his blade already wiped clean.

Niamsha snatched the earring off the table, dangling it before her before she could answer. "Where'd they go?"

Another day she might have felt sorry for the woman. Not today. The Rogue Baron's servants chose his house, serving for a lifetime knowing what he was like.

"Who?" The maid blinked at Niamsha in confusion.

"The lady." Niamsha waved the earring again. "You ain't gonna tell me ya didn't know. Hard ta miss."

"Now, lass, be kind." Jarod rose as if to stop her, but the maid spoke before he could do more.

"On to tha dungeon, I think," she said. "With the baron's son."

Jarod scowled at her, no doubt realizing he'd saved a woman with no loyalty to High Lord Arkaen. With a muttered curse, he stalked out of the room. When Niamsha joined him, he pointed down the hall.

"Milord Phoenix said ta check there. You sure?"

She showed the earring again. "Lady's wearing this last I saw her."

He nodded and turned away. "Come on, then."

Following Jarod through the halls once more, Niamsha tried to note the layout. She'd need to find her way through here when the high lord's sister was safe. Somewhere, Nijel had Emrys here. But Jarod moved with the certainty of a man who'd walked these halls before. Too fast for her to take much note, and he quickly located the narrow stairs leading down from a servant's hall. Nobles never did like their prisons near their pleasures, she supposed.

They'd only gone down a few steps when voices drifted up to them. Two males, arguing, and a woman. Niamsha hurried on Jarod's heels as the room below came into view.

Lady Saylina stood in the center, her dress in tatters, once-pretty hair messy and soiled, chin raised in pride. Placing herself as a barrier between a pair of guards and the noble lady who hunched over Baron Rikkard's prone form.

"You'll have to go through me." Lady Saylina's voice shook as it hadn't when she'd defended Niamsha. And her lighter skin showed bruising even in the dim light. But there she stood.

As before, Jarod charged before Niamsha could make any decision. His speed knocked the first guard to the ground, slicing into the guard's gut. The second turned to face him, blade drawn, and they began the fight. Hurrying down the steps to help, Niamsha reached the foot just as the second guard fell. And for an instant a weight lifted from her shoulders. One thing she'd done right. Not her, exactly, but—a flash of movement from the floor.

"No!" Niamsha shouted before she thought to move, eyes fixed on the fallen guard's sword. Jarod knocked the blade aside before Niamsha's shock released her.

"Gotta be quicker'n that, lass." His gruff voice held no real condemnation despite the words.

"Niamsha!" Lady Saylina darted across the room, pulling her into a hug. "Gods, I thought you'd been killed for sure."

Niamsha pulled free, scowling at the woman. "I ain't—" But she'd been worried. A noble-born lady genuinely worried about her. "Made it, couldn't find ya."

"I can hardly blame you." Lady Saylina gestured at the fallen baron. "Oskari has been very cautious. Even with his son."

"My lady, I must object," Baron Rikkard said from the ground. "This is one of my father's scoundrels."

"I know who she is," Lady Saylina said. "What I don't know is how she got here." She turned back to Niamsha. "What happened?"

Niamsha nodded at the stairs. "Yer brother. He's challenging the baron on some noble thing. Successor's tribe."

"Oh, gods, no." Baron Rikkard's eyes went wide. "He invoked the Successor's Tribune?"

"You and your bride had better go, Rikkard," Lady Saylina said. "If the Tribune has started, your life is forfeit."

"But you—"

"I'm Sentarsin blood." She scowled. "And Arkaen has always been hot-headed. He probably didn't see a solution but throwing a weapon at it. If he plans to name me heir, I must be present for the Tribune."

"That ain't his plan." Niamsha shook her head. "He wanted me ta get you out."

"Then he'll be terribly surprised." Lady Saylina strode across the room. "Come on, Niamsha. My fool of a brother needs me."

"But…" She couldn't leave—Niamsha took a deep breath, forcing herself to think clearly. Lady Saylina had worried about her when Emrys left her to die. Lady Saylina deserved her help. And as weak as Lady Saylina was, she looked like she could use more help than just a guide.

"I'll find yer lad," Jarod said. "Go on."

Niamsha sighed. But she didn't have a choice. Again. With a nod, she led Lady Saylina back up the stairs.

Arkaen strode into the great hall, pain throbbing from the gash in his side. A dozen pairs of eyes turned toward him. Former guardsmen, a few commoners, even a minor noble or two who'd lost standing under Arkaen's rule. No one likely to support his claim that Oskari had broken the rules of the Successor's Tribune. But on the dais at the far end, Counts Tenison and Skianda flanked the lord's seat, Skianda muttering something with furious hand gestures. Deyvan had managed his end of the plan.

Oskari's eyes focused on Arkaen and he waved Count Skianda away. Arkaen smirked, pushing himself to maintain the confident swagger he'd adopted to reassure his flameguard.

"Why, if it isn't my former baron holding court." Arkaen paced forward, hoping his injury didn't reveal too much strain. "How is life as a commoner, Oskari?"

"I was born in House Weydert." Oskari rose, eyes narrowing. "To noble parents, with noble blood. And none can take that from me."

"Quite the contrary," Arkaen said. "I've already taken your title, and I've every intention of taking your blood. I might even make it quick. If you *release my sister.*"

He paused halfway down the length of the room, hands resting on his sword hilts. No fighting could be done on the dais anyway, so forcing his weakened body up the stairs to confront Oskari more directly could only risk his slim chances of success. Oskari stepped forward and froze at the steps, gaze dropping to Arkaen's bound side.

"Strong words from a man already wounded." He met Arkaen's eyes with a satisfied smile. "I'm sure there's no need for further bloodshed. Forfeit and I'll grant plenty of chance for you to find a comfortable home in exile."

Arkaen pulled his sabers, twisting his wrists in a quick flick to settle the grips properly. "I've taken my oath, Oskari. Take yours."

"High Lord!" Count Skianda stepped to the edge of the dais, pushing Oskari back. "You can't fight with that injury. The Successor's Tribune must be delayed."

"Impossible," Oskari snapped. "I'll not have my victory stolen because he challenged me in a sorry state."

Count Skianda spun to face Oskari, face red with anger. As if Oskari had any intentions of respecting traditions of honorable engagement. And Arkaen had no time for the argument. Every moment they talked, his strength waned.

"There is no such precedent," Arkaen called. "And I've not asked."

"My lord—" Count Skianda frowned at him.

"If you follow my rule, Brayden, you'll honor my decision."

Count Skianda stared, shaking his head as if to deny Arkaen's words. The hush of the room drew the moment into an eternity, Arkaen's focus blurring as exhaustion and injury ate at his calm. He gritted his teeth, digging into the last of his focus to maintain the illusion of confidence.

Finally, Count Skianda sighed. "I dislike it, but I will not betray my high lord."

"Then take his oath," Arkaen nodded at Oskari. "I'd rather hear it witnessed by a lord I trust."

Count Skianda nodded, turning to Oskari as he drew a slender knife. Arkaen scouted the room as Oskari's blood began to drip. Four pillars, too far apart to be used together. And cover would only draw the fight out. He needed a swift win.

The spectators backed themselves against the walls, but the central space was still small. Not much room to avoid a strike, and less to tire his opponent. The stairs could be of value, though. Arkaen started forming a plan. Draw Oskari back, run… one good trip over the edge of those stairs and Arkaen could even the battlefield. And on an even field, Arkaen's skill far exceeded Oskari's.

"…holding the weight of a defeat." Oskari hefted his shield and gave a few test swings of his longsword. The drips of blood under his feet were distinctly lacking. Count Skianda cast Arkaen a questioning glance, but Arkaen shook his head.

"I presume you're ready?" Arkaen took a step forward and shifted his weight to a stable balance. "Let's begin."

Oskari charged, offering no reply to give warning. Hoping to overpower Arkaen, no doubt. But Arkaen's injury hadn't stolen his speed. Yet. Arkaen counted the steps, spinning backward and away from the strike as Oskari closed. He deflected the slash of Oskari's blade with his off hand and the clash of steel rang through the room. Thrust his blade at Oskari's shoulder. A grunt and they parted. Red stained Oskari's tunic. Not much—too little to hinder him at all—but a start.

"Gods above, I thought you'd at least practice," Arkaen taunted. "You knew I'd challenge you."

"Why waste the time? You've always been weak." Oskari rotated his shoulder, shrugging the injury off.

Backing away, Arkaen led the fight toward one wall. Four, three, two more steps. He set his foot on the slight rim of the floor where his grandfather had set a decorative pattern on top of the older stone. The damned thing had tripped half the courtiers who visited the estate while his uncle reigned.

But Oskari was done running blindly. He stepped to the side, thrusting from behind the cover of his shield. Arkaen batted the sword away easily. Testing Arkaen's defense. Oskari was either too smart to be goaded, or aware of the danger. And he *had* lived here for several days.

"Now, just because you've never fought a war is no reason to be frightened." Arkaen slid to one side, leading with several strikes at the outer edge of Oskari's shield. "Let that shield down. See what a real blade can do."

Oskari followed, lips pressed into a tight line. Trusting his defense. Solid, comfortable in his technique. But not innovative. Arkaen threw a quick feint at the shield edge again. Ignored. Perfect.

Darting to the side, Arkaen swung his main hand in an arc at Oskari's exposed throat. Easy to block. Anyone skilled would have seen the feint, but Oskari swung his shield in place. And Arkaen dragged his sword down, across Oskari's sword guard, to slide inside his defense. A quick slash flicked more blood across the room. Enough, this time.

"Ouch." Arkaen stepped back. "That—"

Oskari's shield slammed into his shoulder and Arkaen stumbled further. Tripped on the damned decoration and caught his balance. Just in time, as Oskari's sword snaked forward. Arkaen stumbled away, to one side, as the longsword flashed past. A new sting from his arm, Oskari's sword tinted red.

The spectators gasped. Someone screamed.

"How's that for fear?" Oskari's voice had the sharp edges that could only speak of fury. But his movements were careful. Controlled. Better than Arkaen had planned for.

Arkaen backed away again. He needed distance, time to recover. But Oskari pressed the advantage, chasing him with swift steps as Arkaen dodged swipe after swipe. A twinge at Arkaen's side and the slightest tickle. He'd torn his wound open again. Fresh bleeding would drain him far more than the fight itself.

He slid behind one of the pillars, feinting to one side before darting the other way. Into another slam from Oskari's shield. Arkaen fell to one knee. Blocked the sword with one hand. Oskari's shield blocking any strike, pressure hard against his shoulder. This wasn't going to last long.

Reinforcing his defense with his spare blade, his dropped his arms just enough to pull Oskari's weight. And twisted out from under, climbing to his feet as Oskari stumbled into the pillar.

"Well," Arkaen said, pausing by the stairs. "Now that we're finally started. How's that new cut?"

Oskari spun to face him. "How's yours?" He crossed the floor with a confident stride. Set his shield in place. None the worse for the injury.

Not possible. That cut should be at least as bad as Arkaen's. But Oskari walked with the ease of a man just risen from a week's rest. This was going to be harder than he'd thought.

The Ancient Spirits speak through him. Let all the People heed Their words.

— from the prophecies of the Chosen of the Four Clans

Chapter 37

Kìlashà floated in the void, pain searing through the empty place where his mind should float free. Physical, mental. Pain to his very soul. The last concerned him, in the distant way of things reaching through the veil of the Seeker's power to remind him of the world beyond.

Physical pain, he knew. Scars, strain beyond what his human body could stand. And more recently, the poison. The mental pain spoke of too great a use of his power. The Ancient Spirits only granted so much, and to stretch too far held dangers even he could not ignore. Though he had. But the last... Visions flared in the void.

Kaen stumbled aside, the swish of Oskari's sword cutting through the air behind him. Gasps from onlookers as blood flew from the tip. Another cut. Minor, but Kaen's primary wound bled freely once more, and his strength waned. The fight would end too soon.

Kìlashà fought the calm that pulled the vision away. His kai'shien needed him. The Ancient Spirits demanded he serve Their will. And They needed Kaen as much as Kìlashà himself.

Raeky shook him, one hand gently shoving at his shoulder.

"Jayls, get up." The whisper spoke volumes of their father's temper. Not to be trifled with this day. "You have to get up."

His eyes snapped open, sensations flooding through him. Silk on his skin, fire in his veins, pounding in his head. Pounding of his heart. Kaen needed his help. Two quick blinks of his lids and the room focused. His own room at Kaen's palace, gold-tooled window shades drawn to dim the room for his rest. Four of Kaen's *Serr-Nyen* guards spread about the room, hands on weapons. For once, their caution not directed at him.

Kìlashà slid from the bed, his balance weak, and caught himself on the heavy oak side table. One of the guards turned.

"Lord Dragon."

A sigh of relief from four throats at once. But Kìlashà's lips curled back in a silent snarl.

"A relief to see you woken." The guard seemed ignorant of his anger. "But you should rest. Lord Phoenix should return soon."

Kìlashà dragged his tongue across achingly dry lips. Found his voice, weak and raspy. "Not if he dies."

All four guards started forward at once, grabbing a variety of tools. They cared far more for Kaen than Kìlashà. But at least he could agree on that point. One guard appeared by his side, reached forward. Hesitated. A flicker of Kìlashà's power explained the intent.

"My gratitude, but I can walk." Kìlashà pushed himself from the table, forcing several steps across the room. "Fight, perhaps not. But walk."

"We'll commandeer a steed, Lord Dragon," the guard replied.

At his nod, they escorted him from the room as another vision filled his mind.

Lady Saylina collapsed beside the body, hiding it from Kìlashà's view. A male, human. Her tears poured across reddened cheeks, her hands covered in blood. And the room fell silent. Each of the spectators bowed their heads and sank to their knees.

And Third, to act always brave and face enemies with blade in hand.

— Third of Aeduhm's Teachings

Chapter 38

Niamsha hurried down the hall as Lady Saylina led the way, walking the corridors as though she'd been raised here. And maybe she had. Nijel said it was the home of High Lord Arkaen's mother. Lady Saylina turned another corner and froze. More guards stood by a wide archway, arguing with a bulky man carrying a dozen knives.

"No one in, on baron's orders," the man insisted.

Lady Saylina backed away, pushing Niamsha in front of her. Niamsha slid her feet along the floors. Aeduhm grant her silence and enough time. But He had other ideas. One of the guards glanced over and pointed at them.

"There!"

All three men turned as Niamsha dragged Lady Saylina around the corner and started to run. They'd just reached the far end of the hall when Lady Saylina grabbed her arm.

"We can't just flee," she said. "I have to help Kaen."

"Ain't nothing gonna help him that way." Niamsha pulled away.

"But—"

"Stop!" Boots pounded on the stone, leaving her protest moot.

No time to run now, and only one chance of getting out without a fight. She stepped around Lady Saylina, throwing up a hand as if to ward the guards off by herself.

"I'm the baron's girl—"

"Don't waste your breath." The first guard shoved her aside.

Her back hit the wall with a hard jolt, sending faint lights dancing before her eyes. Niamsha blinked her vision clear, pushing away from the wall. The other guard glared at her, arms crossed.

"You." The first guard grabbed Lady Saylina by the arm. "Back to the dungeons." He glanced at his companion and waved at Niamsha. "Get her. Baron'll want to talk to her."

The second man grabbed for her, and Niamsha dashed forward, away from the man. She couldn't be taken aiding Lady Saylina. Not if she wanted to give Jarod a chance to find Emrys before Nijel's wrath. Though maybe Nijel wouldn't hurt him. He swore he was a man of his word, and she'd done what he asked. All he'd said was to poison the demon and bring the high lord here.

"Dammit, girl." The man chased her down the hall several steps.

A heavy thunk of something connecting with flesh and a shouted curse. Niamsha spun around, shaking with tension. The guard had stumbled into a wall, a wide blade stuck into his leg.

"Gods, what the—" The man grabbed the blade. "Hit the girl if you're gonna throw."

"Then get yer ass outta the way." The third man stalked down the hall, another dagger in hand.

No way she avoided the next throw. They had no value for her life. But Lady Saylina held value. Niamsha charged the first guard, knocking him back, allowing Lady Saylina to pull her arm free. For an instant time seemed to freeze, Lady Saylina standing alone and Niamsha tangled with the first guard. Then the third threw a second knife.

Niamsha's heart pounded as the blade flew, but Lady Saylina raced away, her heavy skirts flying. The blade clattered against a wall. Aeduhm's grace, but that had been close. Niamsha fought her way free of the guard. Not hard, as he turned on his companion with rage in his eyes.

"Keep the damned blades put away," the guard snapped. "You hurt the high lady, we're all in for it."

Niamsha grabbed Lady Saylina's arm, pulling her down the hall as the three argued. Only a few turns away, Lady Saylina dragged her to a halt again.

"In here." She grabbed a door and yanked it open to reveal a narrow, dusty hallway. "This will lead us to Kaen."

Niamsha nodded and stepped into the hall, pulling the door closed after them. Lady Saylina hurried down the corridor, passing several doors without pause. Finally, she paused by one more, peeked in, and slipped inside.

Niamsha scrambled into the room at Lady Saylina's heels, the ring of steel echoing off the walls to hide the sound of their entrance. The motley crowd didn't even glance their way. Lady Saylina pushed her way past a pair of men, opening an unrestricted view of the center of the room where High Lord Arkaen faced off against the Rogue Baron. The Rogue Baron lunged forward, thrusting his sword from behind the shield as High Lord Arkaen—ran.

There was no more dignified word for it. His feet scrambled on the polished stone, one of his twin blades slashing the Rogue Baron's sword aside. He twisted as he fled, keeping his back turned away from the baron and his swords raised.

"Oh, gods." Lady Saylina reached a hand back, grabbing Niamsha's arm in a tight squeeze. "How bad is that wound?"

Niamsha yanked her arm back, but Lady Saylina's grip tightened. She spun around, glaring at Niamsha as her fingers dug into skin. Another clash of steel.

"How bad?" Lady Saylina pointed at the fight. "He's walked into this thing injured. Kaen isn't stupid, but if he thought he didn't have a choice…" Her eyes closed, lips set in a tight clench of grief. "Please tell me he's all right."

"Wish I knew. I ain't seen it."

Niamsha peered around Lady Saylina and frowned at the makeshift bandage. Gray of his shirt stained with a growing blob of darker fluid, the belt that held his wound closed loosening with every twist. If Aeduhm had cursed the high lord's demon, He must have blessed the man himself. No other way High Lord Arkaen could stand with that cut.

But he wouldn't be standing for long. The swords met again, High Lord Arkaen throwing his weight into his crossed blades as the Rogue Baron smirked. He glanced to the side and Niamsha followed the look. To one of the Rendell boys, crossbow held at the ready. Aimed at High Lord Arkaen.

Arkaen twisted out of the hold, his final shove breaking Oskari's balance enough for him to back out of reach. For a moment. He forced three long, measured breaths through his lips. Focus and planning. No other way to win. His muscles relaxed into the confidence of battle. The lingering pain of his wounds faded to a dull sting as he evaluated his options.

The stairs, as he'd thought. But Oskari wasn't biting at his feints any longer. As if summoned by the thought, Oskari charged forward, his blade a blur. Arkaen braced, swords crossed for strength and angled to deflect. Oskari would expect another sidestep. A quick flurry of blades and Arkaen twisted away, earning another shallow cut.

"Heavens." Arkaen forced levity into his breathless voice. "I'm going to make a few tailors rich, I suppose."

Oskari snorted. Bad, when his levity didn't even warrant a response. They both knew Arkaen's strength was failing.

A flicker of movement caught his eye, and he circled around Oskari, scanning the crowd. Surely…

Niamsha threaded her way through the spectators, focused on something ahead. But if she was here, where was Sayli? The plan relied on Sayli safe and out of Oskari's hands.

Arkaen's heart pounded anew at the sight. He *needed* Sayli safe.

"Something wrong, High Lord?" Oskari's taunt rang with confidence. He couldn't know she was here. Could he?

New fear throbbed in his veins as Arkaen swept his gaze over the crowd. Countered a series of quick strikes and twisted away from a shield slam. There. Brown hair disheveled, green eyes wide with panic. A rush of relief and horror mingled into one. Damn the girl to every hell men had ever devised. She'd promised to get Sayli out.

Arkaen backed away again, spinning to locate Niamsha. A knot of bodies where she'd been, the figures caught in some form of struggle. A bow string sang as it released, his augmented hearing catching the sound. Gods damn it all. Foolish, to think Oskari wouldn't cheat here as much as anywhere.

Throwing himself to one side, Arkaen threw a hand up, palm flat and facing the dais to demand a formal reckoning. He caught Count Skianda's gaze. Just as Count Tenison stumbled back, the bolt deep in his chest. A rush of servants onto the dais swarmed over Count Tenison, holding Count Skianda back from the chance to call halt. Every breath in the room froze, waiting for word of his fate.

"You dare!" The click of Sayli's heels echoed through the silence. "Bring an *archer* to a Successor's Tribune."

Arkaen spun to face her. "Stand down, Sayli."

"I will not."

"Listen to your brother, girl." Oskari glared at her, his eyes darting to the dais and back in a nervous tick.

But if Oskari had one bowman, he had several. Arkaen crossed to Sayli, sweeping his gaze over the crowd in a hunt for any further sign of treachery. A handful of commoners and merchants cowering against the walls. Several guards looking around as well. The few nobles were far more interested in the dais and the wounded lord there.

"I'm not a delicate flower to be shielded, Kaen." Sayli stepped up beside him, arms crossed over her stained and torn formal dress. "And I've a score to settle with our former baron."

Oskari smirked. "Don't be stupid. I'll not be shedding any lady's blood." He strode forward, setting his shield in defense.

Arkaen stepped to one side, his breath coming in heavy gasps. No time to argue. By tradition, any interruption should demand a halt to resolve the dispute. But Count Skianda hadn't managed a formal call of respite and Oskari clearly had no intent of granting one. His side throbbed as he shifted his weight.

"You had no trouble shedding Niamsha's blood." Sayli's anger could have frozen a lake solid.

Gods. The revelation hit Arkaen like a boot in the gut. Oskari had forced her to *watch* as he beat another woman senseless? Oskari's response sounded as a jumbled protest.

Fury stirred in Arkaen's gut, pounding in his ears, shoving the pain and exhaustion to the back of his mind. He slid around Oskari's next thrust, batting the long blade aside. A woman's screams echoed in his ears, the stench of her seared flesh lingering in the hall. Fear, horror, and pain faded into the instinct of battle and the confidence of blades in his hand.

Oskari circled. Stilted, formulaic dueling. Arkaen could read his movements as clearly as if Lasha's powers had fallen on him instead. A step there, thrust here. Arkaen stepped aside, the blade flying harmlessly by his shoulder. Timed his counterstrike to the pause as Oskari adjusted his stance. Flick of Arkaen's sword, tear of cloth. Blood stained Oskari's shield arm.

Step, thrust, twist away, counter. Arkaen's blades sang with the rhythm of steel. Ring, rip, grunt. More blood, seeping down Oskari's leg. Slide, parry, back off. His foot settled on the top step of the stairs. Oskari wouldn't follow. He'd seen the ploy.

Arkaen launched himself off the step, the extra height leaving an opening above Oskari's shield. Feint. Clash of his blade on the upper edge of the shield. The momentum sent him spinning in a flashy, dangerous twist. He batted Oskari's sword away from his exposed back. Landed, the force jarring every scrape and cut in his body. Thrust his free blade deep into Oskari's exposed side.

Oskari's scream echoed through the room, an eerie parallel to the screams of Arkaen's memories. To the pounding, endless pain of Arkaen's wounds and a new, sharper sting across his shoulders. Sayli ran forward, skirts pulled high, heels pounding on the stone floor.

"Kaen!"

He'd deflected the blow. His blade still held Oskari's sword to the side. His enhanced senses focused on the click of a crossbow bolt locking into place. Another bowman. But he had no time to focus on that. Oskari pulled away, stumbling across the floor with one hand clapped to his side, shield discarded.

"Yield!" Oskari collapsed against a pillar. "House Weydert yields."

"Yield?" Arkaen rose, stalking across the room. "After defrauding my people, destabilizing my rule, abducting and *terrorizing* my sister, you want to yield?"

"High lord!" Count Skianda ran down the steps of the dais, catching Arkaen's arm. "A Successor's Tribune ends when one house is dead or one house yields. House Weydert yields."

Forfeit holding the weight of a defeat. A tradition established near a hundred years past to avoid the extermination of the noble houses during a heated dispute over the ruler of Sentar province. Arkaen glared over Count Skianda's shoulder at Oskari.

"House Sentarsin does not accept."

Arkaen pulled free of Count Skianda's grip, crossing the final steps to Oskari's slumped form. Oskari stared at him, eyes wide with terror, breaths labored.

"I challenge the refusal." Sayli, voice shrill with desperation. "The Sentarsin heir challenges the refusal. The line of high lords shows mercy to its subjects."

Arkaen set his blade on Oskari's throat. "By tradition. Not law."

"Rulers stand down, Kaen!" She was at his side, clinging to his sword arm. "Think of Rikkard. Of Kyli. They've done nothing."

He pulled the blade across, slashing Oskari's throat. Blood sprayed freely, pouring down Oskari's throat, several drops spattering on Arkaen's hand. And Sayli's, as she tried to pull his arm back. He met her eyes, anger still burning in his gut.

"Rikkard has the right to abdicate his place in the family. House Weydert is dead."

Sayli's lips hung open, eyes wide with terror. Of him. Not the brother she'd remembered, despite her protests to the contrary. The crossbow sang, bolt whistling through the air.

Arkaen spun around, dragging Sayli behind him. Screams rang through the room as a dark figure darted past. As if anything could stop this end. No time to move, even if he wasn't the only shield between Sayli and death. The bolt clattered into the stairs, Lasha crouched defensively over Niamsha's prone, trembling form.

Thank the gods. Lasha lived.

Tension, anger, fear drained from Arkaen in a rush, leaving him sagging against the pillar. But his eyes fell on Niamsha. Too stunned to object if he left now and he wasn't done. Nijel still needed a reckoning.

"Count Skianda." Arkaen pushed off the wall, turning toward the door. "Lady Saylina will resolve any further matters. I've a promise to keep."

On the fateful night of Emperor Laisia's assassination, the Serr-Nyen *rebels led an attack on an imperial outpost, but Lord Phoenix was nowhere to be seen. The mysterious Kumiho had vanished weeks prior, if* Serr-Nyen *accounts are to be believed. And all reports say a demon spawned from Eiliin's hell stole into the emperor's window, tearing his throat with wicked claws before vanishing into the morning mist.*

— *from* An Abridged History of the Sernien War

Chapter 39

Saylina watched Arkaen storm out of the room with growing dread. No one would follow him after he'd abandoned this mess. And Baron W—Oskari. The man who'd held her captive, beaten Niamsha, planned to kill Arkaen and Kyli and Count Skianda and anyone else who stood in his way. Maybe even Emperor Corliann. Oskari's body still oozed blood at her feet, soaking into the ruined fabric of her court shoes. Another horror to add to her ever-increasing collection.

"My lady." Count Skianda grabbed her elbow, pulling her away from the body with a grimace. "Are you well, Lady Saylina? We heard rumors of all sorts, and your brother was frantic."

"I imagine he was, my Lord Count, but I am well."

The words felt foreign on her lips, a smile crossing her face that she knew held all the feigned politeness she'd ever seen from Arkaen. Was this how he felt, watching the political backbiting of his peerage with the knowledge of blood and death in his heart? No wonder he cared so little for their concerns. Birthrights and underhanded insults couldn't truly matter in the face of such violence.

"My lady, your pardon for my callousness, but we must resolve the current matters." Count Skianda gestured to the dais. "Jussi is dead, House Weydert is declared dead with heirs and lands unsettled. May we speak, or shall we adjourn until you've rested?"

Saylina swept her gaze around the room. Kìlashà still guarded the young woman, Niamsha, who now struggled to rise. A knot of Arkaen's Sernien soldiers stood nearby, watching the room with the caution she'd expect them to turn on a rabid dog. A dozen or more retainers muttered behind their hands to their personal servants. Several of the lower lords who'd sworn loyalty to Oskari, faces stunned. Wealthy merchants already hunting new patrons. And Arkaen had all but abdicated his authority to her. If she didn't take control of this now, she'd have no unified peerage to rule when she felt ready.

"I'll see to the critical matters, Count Skianda." Saylina pushed herself to walk across the floor toward the dais, her feet mired in soggy, blood-covered shoes. "Perhaps the rest can wait until I've had a bath and a proper meal."

A grim, knowing smile crept across Count Skianda's face. "I'm sure that can be arranged."

He kept pace beside her, leading her away from the carnage toward the dais. Inappropriate, perhaps, for a count to lead the high lady, but she couldn't seem to focus on where to go next. Count Skianda leaned closer.

"Jussi's heirs and the fate of Rikkard need addressed now, my lady. The rest can wait."

His whisper would carry the sound, but not the words. Aeduhm's Mercy. She'd look like a puppet. The stairs seemed to slide under her feet, Count Skianda's hand steadying her footing. Count Tenison's limp body drew her gaze, and she started to shake. That could have been her. *Should* have been Arkaen.

Count Skianda's hand squeezed her elbow. "Just a few moments, my lady."

Her breath caught in her throat. She needed to make these rulings, but those eyes. Dead eyes that had so recently argued with her and Arkaen. Furious demands that had leaped from those dead lips.

"I can't." The whisper slipped out before she could think of the meaning.

Count Skianda stepped forward, placing himself between her and the body. His eyes caught her gaze. "You most certainly can, Lady Saylina. You've more of your brother in you than either of you know."

Once those words would have offended her. But there was no denying this was a compliment. Count Skianda lifted a hand, indicating the seat Oskari had used as a personal throne. Perverting her mother's home with his treason. Saylina straightened, her shock giving way to anger, and crossed the dais to sit in her makeshift throne. As if on cue, Kìlashà led Niamsha forward, her struggles futile. Arkaen's few remaining soldiers spread around her, a formal retinue lending Arkaen's strength to her standing.

"I ain't gonna—" Niamsha was shrill and desperate.

"Lady Niamsha," Saylina focused on the woman, pleading with what little she could allow to show. "Would you do me the honor of aiding me. You've more direct knowledge of Oskari's treason's than I."

Niamsha stared at her, eyes wide and lips parted before glancing around the room, seeming to realize for the first time that she stood among the remnants of Oskari's rebellion.

"Aye, lady." Niamsha bobbed her head in agreement and let herself be led to Saylina's side.

"My gratitude." Saylina turned to the rest of the hall, pitching her voice to carry through the room. "I take this seat as formal voice of my brother, High Lord Arkaen. Let us first resolve the matter of the blood feud between House Sentarsin and House Weydert. By my brother's decree, House Weydert is dead. The living son of Oskari is stripped of his titles and the barony held by his family gone to ground."

"My lady." Count Skianda stepped forward with a precise, formal bow. Confident, no doubt, that she would hear his opinion and follow it. "May I request the barony be re-bestowed upon the younger Weydert. We have no evidence Rikkard had any part in this quarrel."

Guilt hung heavy on her. Rikkard was innocent, but if she undermined Arkaen's orders now, she'd have no standing to demand obedience later.

"I must decline, Count Skianda."

Muttering flew through the room, heads bowed to plot amongst themselves. None of them would dare question Arkaen. Saylina threw up a hand for silence, counting slowly to herself the seconds until the court acknowledged it. At the count of fifteen, as the murmurs continued to grow, she stood.

"I rule in this hall!" Her voice cut through the room, silencing the crowd. She spun to face Count Skianda, the body behind him looming in her thoughts. "This *quarrel*, as you describe it Count Skianda, was *treason*. House Weydert conspired with a powerful band of thieves and abducted the heir to your throne. They plotted the murder of your ruler and the usurpation of High Emperor Corliann's seat in Whitfaern. Any who engaged in this treason will be stripped of their titles and removed from their posts, their assets seized by the crown."

Too late, she realized her mistake. Merchants edged toward the door, minor lords laid hands on weapons, searching the walls as if fearing assassins. Ultimatums bred rebellion.

"Unless," she shouted the word, praying to catch their attention once more. Like a gift from the gods, the room focused on her, all eyes desperate for her next words. "They can prove they were misled, deceived, or unaware of the events."

She spun to face Niamsha. "Lady Niamsha. Can you name any here you know to be deceived?"

Stepping forward, Niamsha shook like a dead leaf in a strong wind. But she scanned the crowd and finally pointed one man out.

"He ain't a true rebel," she said. "Marcas made him think ya brother meant harm."

"Of course." Saylina resumed her seat, knees shaky at the disaster she'd barely averted. "I'm certain similar stories are true of many. I'll offer a week to any involved. Bring proof of your innocence in these matters to the high lord's palace in that time, and you will be pardoned. Any who cannot do so are encouraged to leave these lands before that time is ended." She turned back to Count Skianda. "The same is offered to our peerage. If Rikkard can bring proof of his innocence to the high lord's palace, he will be pardoned, and his titles restored."

A figure shoved his way to the front, revealing himself as Arkaen's former captain of the guard. The captain stepped forward, almost to the steps of the dais, and swept a cursory bow.

"My lady, my family is owed recompense for the difficulties we've suffered. I've come to claim them."

"You've come to be executed, Captain." Saylina gestured at Count Skianda, who grabbed the man's arm before he could object. "You swore an oath to serve my family, but when my brother angered you, that oath meant nothing. You abandoned him, joined his enemy, and aided in the conspiracy toward his death."

"You don't understand," the captain insisted. "Your lord brother—"

"Is your ruler, Captain," Saylina said. "And has been for five years. It took one disagreement to turn your loyalty. *You* will find no mercy here."

Two of the Sernien guards strode forward, grabbing the captain. One of them slammed a hand to his chest in salute. "We'll see to his incarceration, Lady Saylina."

"Thank you." Saylina turned to Count Skianda as they led the captain away. "Count Skianda, you were concerned for the estate of our late Count Tenison. However, as I understand, he has only daughters and all are married. That puts his land under some contention. I'll send messengers to his blood heirs and any he may have considered beyond his blood. We'll resolve the matter upon receipt of their responses."

"Fair and rational, my lady," Count Skianda said. He offered a hand to lead her from the dais. "That should be all that needs immediate attention. May I escort you home?"

"I'm afraid there's one more matter." Saylina bit at her lip. "We had a confessed traitor against the empire in these lands recently. I heard while held captive that Kumiho had come to the province. Who is he?"

Count Skianda's eyebrows rose, his lips going slack in shock. He hadn't heard. Perhaps no one but Niamsha and Saylina herself knew. And Arkaen. There was no chance Arkaen's old war friend had come through and not spoken with Arkaen. She could feel Kìlashà's eyes boring into her from behind, reminding her of one more who must know the man's identity.

"May I ask what source told you of Kumiho's presence?" Count Skianda asked, finding his voice at last. "We'd heard that he vanished near four years ago, and no one has heard of him since."

Saylina waved at Niamsha. "Lady Niamsha. She said she met a man answering to Kumiho who spoke of my brother as a friend. We know my brother denounced the Sernien traitors upon taking his throne, but this man still has the potential to jeopardize our empire's peace. He must—"

"No, I—" Niamsha cut herself off, her face flushed. Something was wrong. "I may been wrong…"

Saylina frowned. She'd been sure in the thieves' home. What would make her change her story now?

"Pardon, lady." One of the remaining Sernien soldiers stepped forward. "I gotta say. Lord Kumiho ain't no danger to yer emperor."

"He led a rebellion against our emperor's uncle," she replied.

But the consistency of the protests gave her pause. And Kìlashà's gaze still tore at her focus, his intensity leaving her unsteady. Suddenly, the reason seemed clear. Kumiho. An old friend of Arkaen's, met during the war. Arkaen had known few outside the Sentarsi nobility when he went to war. And he'd returned a close confidante of High Emperor Corliann. She met Kìlashà's gaze, saw his recognition in the deep ebony of his eyes. He smiled.

"I'll speak to my brother on the matter when he's recovered." She turned away, praying her revelation didn't show in her posture. "Lord Kìlashà, will you and my brother's guards see to his well-being?"

"Always. Come along, Niamsha." Kìlashà strode from the room, two Sernien guards breaking from the group to position themselves on either side of her as the rest followed him and Niamsha from the room.

Pre-arranged by a fighting force she would never have control over. Saylina rose, pushing the trembling nerves aside long enough to take Count Skianda's arm.

"I think a rest would be valuable, my Lord Count." The Sernien guards followed her down the stairs. "Thank you for your aid."

"Where the hell is Jarod?" Arkaen muttered. Jarod should have escorted Niamsha and Sayli out. Instead she'd shown up in the hall with Sayli in tow. His feet stumbled at every turn, exhaustion pulling at his body. But he couldn't let Nijel loose, and he'd promised to find Niamsha's brother.

Arkaen glanced back as the door swung closed, giving a sigh of relief. Lasha stood watchful guard over Sayli, flanked by four of Arkaen's flameguard. At least he knew they were safe.

He wound his way deeper into the estate, toward the maze of guest suites where he'd played as a child. If Oskari had used these halls, he'd have used the servants' wing. Fewer twists and more clearly delineated, smaller rooms.

By the second hall, it was clear Oskari had used these quarters. Torches lined the halls, at least one door stood open. And the sound of metal clashing came from around a corner ahead. Arkaen pushed himself into a jog, his blood pounding in time with the aching head Lasha's tragyna brew always gave him when the effects faded.

Chaos filled the hallway as he approached, three soldiers flanking a pair in the middle, the young, stocky man sporting several minor injuries already, guarding a dark-haired woman—Rikkard, standing between his new bride Kyli and three of Oskari's guards. Arkaen darted forward, his blades sliding free once more. Two men turned, but Rikkard cut the third down before Arkaen had reached the battle. Better than his father with a blade.

Arkaen deflected a clumsy strike, running his free sword through the guard's gut. A grunt from further down the hall. Rikkard shoved the second guard aside, blade raised as he met Arkaen's eyes.

"I'll assume my father is dead?"

Arkaen yanked his own blade free, dropping his eyes. Damn it all. Of course he'd run into Rikkard. Why hadn't Rikkard left if he heard of the Tribune?

"House Weydert is dead." Arkaen wiped his blades clean on the guardsman's tunic. "I'd like to keep it that way without further bloodshed."

"My life is worth more than my name." Rikkard glanced back at Kyli. "But you can't…" He scowled. "As my high lord says."

Gods, he was right. Stripping Rikkard of his barony was worse than what Oskari had done to Kyli. Married, but not even noble any longer, and no chance to raise her station. Arkaen cursed. He needed a solution.

"See my sister," Arkaen said. "She has a barony to dispense, and as I recall, there are some laws around reclaiming titles gone to ground."

Rikkard nodded. Reluctant, but who could blame him. Nothing to be done now, though, and Arkaen had a promise to keep to Niamsha.

"Seen any of my guards?" Arkaen asked. "Preferably one a decade too old for fighting with a boy by his side?"

"The Sernien? Blond?" Rikkard asked.

"That's him. Jarod. Should have been this way looking for the boy."

Rikkard pointed back toward the guest halls. "He said the boy was that way. He was looking for someone else. A thief king or something."

"Dammit." But Arkaen couldn't blame Jarod for trying to find Nijel. Too smart and too loyal to risk Arkaen's death. "My thanks."

Arkaen forced a quick walk toward the guest wing he'd avoided before. The walls shifted from bare stone to wood paneled as he walked. And then the guest wing, all elegance and luxury decades old.

The tapestries draped along the walls of his mother's childhood home, faded and barely recognizable, did nothing to soothe his pains. Down a long corridor. Turn to the right. A sour stench started to permeate the walls as he walked. He stopped dead. A hint of sickly-sweet, roasted flesh teased at his nostrils. Memory. It had to be. No one would dare…

Arkaen pushed himself into a run, hands trembling and bile rising in his throat already. He could see the darkened cell, chains heavy around his wrists as she screamed for mercy from a throat so raw—he shook the memory free. No time. But that gods-damned reek wouldn't fade.

Haste nipping at his heels, Arkaen barreled around a corner and froze at an iron door. With a set of pan scales carved into the door. They'd perverted a holy temple, or what might have once been one. And there was no denying the stench came from behind that door. He froze, laying a hand on the metal as his body shook at the terror of what lay beyond that door. But someone had to look, and no one else should see. Arkaen twisted the door handle, pushing the door inward.

The rush of memory slammed into him, mixing with the released fumes, putrid smell of burnt hair, scorched flesh, and stale urine. He stumbled forward, stopping in the doorway with hands braced on either side. Not again. He couldn't step into that hell one more time.

Leaning over, his stomach churning and breath labored, Arkaen started to notice the flaws. Two bodies in the center. One chained and mangled, the other whole, armed, and posed in an attack. Jarod. But that meant the tortured boy could only be Niamsha's brother. Forcing his feet into motion, Arkaen strode into the room, spinning to examine the presentation.

Dark smears across the walls stank with a pungency he had no desire to examine further, his gaze skirting past the horror chained to the middle of the floor. No need to look to know what that was. Arkaen's throat, jaw, gut ached with the need to scream.

Manacles held a third bloody, beaten body to the wall, but leather straps attached the manacles to the stone wall instead of chains. His bonds had been chains. Arkaen crossed the room and checked the wrists. No sign of struggle. Dead before he was placed there. And no one he knew. His other guards had gotten free, only Jarod sacrificed to the horrors of this recreation.

He should be focusing on the scene. Finding the clues that would lead to Nijel. But Arkaen couldn't get the war out of his mind. How many hopeless battles had he won with Jarod's help? How many imperial loyalists turned through Jarod's gruff words?

Standing, Arkaen turned to the charred central body. Young, male. Not enough to identify from what little Arkaen knew, and the body was in tatters. Except the face—undamaged but for a deep slash to the throat, the blade still stuck in the skin. A clean, sure strike too familiar from his days at war. A mercy killing. Gods, the boy *had* been alive.

Arkaen forced himself closer to examine the body, kneeling to pick up the blade. Too much char and too few blisters. That was another flaw. Plus, most of Bloody Emperor Laisia's victims had been women. And this body had been set on fire instead of burned with pokers. Even if he'd been alive, the boy would have died from smoke long before the fire killed him.

He closed his eyes and forced a deep breath through his nose. The remnants of Lasha's damned tea left his senses just sharp enough, letting him separate the individual scents more than he'd been able to the first time he'd seen this. Urine, feces, blood, burnt skin. Smoke. Too much smoke. And no sweaty stink of fear. Footsteps beyond the door and he knew Lasha had arrived. His own personal savior.

Arkaen lifted a hand in greeting. "It's done all wrong."

The realization eased a deep-rooted fear. A foolish terror. He'd slit the throat of the sick bastard who'd tortured him with his own hand.

"Wrong?" Niamsha's shriek ate at his soul.

Gods damn it all. He snapped his eyes open, leaping to his feet to protest. But she was already backing away, horror twisting her face into a mask of fury and grief.

"How should ya do it?" she demanded. "What's the *right* way to… torture—" A sob choked her words off.

"Wait!" Arkaen stepped toward her. "That's not—"

Niamsha ran, his words lost to her sobs. Arkaen scrambled after her, catching himself on the doorway as his foot slid on the fouled stone. He stepped out and scanned the hall. No sign of her, no sound he could catch. The last thing she'd needed was to hear him criticize the brutality her brother had suffered. She'd headed left, he thought. But Lasha caught his arm.

"Kai'shien." Lasha's breathy voice cut at Arkaen's control.

"I have to find—"

"She will be well." Lasha shook his head, crossing to the doorway. "And her master is already gone. Your wounds cannot be ignored longer."

"Niamsha thinks I approve of this." Arkaen thrust a finger toward the horrors inside the room. "She thinks I did it."

Lasha's eyes narrowed. "Niamsha will endure. Saylina has returned to your palace. You will be abed months already. If I do not see to the wound, you may never fight again."

"You know I can't do that. I promised Deyvan we'd join him."

"Pardon, Milord Phoenix." One of the guards stepped forward, slamming a fist to his chest in salute. "You'll not want to cross the Lord Dragon on this. The flameguard'll see you home."

"I—"

Arkaen stared into their faces. Four guards determined to see him to bed with the force of Lasha's will behind them. He knew when he was beat. With a gesture at the room, he nodded.

"I need to know the intent of that mess."

Two of the guards stepped forward, gagging as they approached the doorway. But after a few breaths, they stepped inside. Soldiers before decent men. Anyone decent couldn't stomach that horror.

Lasha stalked behind him as Arkaen turned away. Too much blood for this day. A call from the room behind and one of the guards came running out.

"Found this, milord." The man handed a chain over and returned to his task.

Arkaen twisted the charred mass so he could see better. A silver ring hung from a plain copper chain. Arkaen rubbed the soot off the silver and examined the make of the piece. A noble's signet ring from the looks of it, and the crest was a strange, winged creature. He looked closer, rubbing again to remove more soot, and frowned. The winged beast was half lion, half eagle. A gryphon.

Arkaen looked up. Caught Lasha's gaze. "What does Griffon have to do with this?"

"She is dead, kai'shien," Lasha said. "She can have no part in today's events."

But Lasha's distant tone and ebony eyes betrayed his lie. The ring meant something. They just didn't know what.

Niamsha stumbled against the wall, the pain of holding back sobs choking her throat. Her lungs burned for air, but she couldn't force a breath through her trembling lips. He couldn't be gone. Not Emrys. Not her little brother. He couldn't be that... *thing.*

The reek of scorched hair and burnt flesh clung to her nose, tormenting her with the truth. Blinking against the tears blurring her vision, Niamsha set one hand on the wall, inching forward by feel more than sight. The stone corridor mocked her. So similar to her room in the baron's palace where she'd hoped to share luxury with Emrys. The same luxury now serving as a tomb for her brother's butchered corpse.

Get away. Just get away from it all. From the stench of what he'd done to Emrys. From the bastard high lord who dared to mock his death. *It's done all wrong.* As if there was a proper way to torture a boy to death. As if murder and desecration were commonplace. A thing one might learn with proper study. A skill the high lord knew.

Another corner, and another. One more to a door, or maybe three. The house became a maze under her hand, eyes too blurry to guide her and shoulders shaking in silent sobs. Her throat, shoulders, eyes, gut, *everything* ached with the need to endure. But why? What could possibly be left with Emrys gone? A door under her hand. No, there shouldn't be a door. Or was there? She couldn't remember, the maze a strange echo of the home she'd lived in.

The wood opened under her hand, and she stumbled into the room. Nijel stood by the door, a slight frown marring his smooth, pale skin.

"Nisha, dear, what's wrong?"

There was something in his voice. Something she couldn't place. A lilt of joy, or a hitch of surprise, or... something she hadn't heard before.

Niamsha shook her head. Choked on a sob. Backed away. Not Nijel. Nijel couldn't be trusted.

"Oh, good heavens." Nijel stepped forward, laying a hand on her shoulder. "Something's happened. Please, tell me. Where's Emrys?"

She couldn't tell Nijel. If she spoke, she'd cry, and Nijel would know she was weak. And if she was weak, Nijel would kill her. Niamsha blinked several times, her eyelids heavy with lingering tears as Nijel tilted her chin up to meet his eyes. Eyes of a sharp blue, softened now with a sympathy she'd never expected.

"Em…" The word slipped out, an admission of her sorrow to the one person she couldn't imagine would understand.

"Is he all right?" Nijel glanced down the hall. "Oh, no. Dear, don't tell me they found him. I'd asked our brother to stay hidden when I realized the high lord's dogs were loose."

"Dogs?"

"His guards from up north," Nijel said. "The ones in plain clothes. They're vicious, and so duplicitous. Why, they once convinced my mother… oh, but you don't need that now. Tell me what happened to dear Emrys."

"I… I thought he was trapped. Tried ta save 'im." Her voice broke on a sob. "And now he's *dead*!"

She closed her eyes against the sight of Nijel's sympathy, but the horror of that room lingered in the darkness. Emrys's death was her fault. She'd sent the guard to find him. If she'd done what Nijel asked, instead of trying to make her own plans. With the demon, and the high lord, and the high lord's guards. With the very bastard who had murdered her brother. Her throat closed, severing her breath with sobbing.

With Niamsha's help. None of it would have worked if she'd trusted Nijel. She dragged her eyes open again, cutting off the scene she couldn't stop seeing.

"Oh, gods, Nisha." Nijel held his arms out, offering comfort she hadn't seen since Papa had died. "You couldn't have known, and with you in the high lord's keep, I didn't know how to tell you without putting you in danger. It's my fault. I'm so sorry."

Niamsha hesitated. Nijel couldn't be trusted. He was brutal, conniving. And he'd always taken care of her. He'd protected her from Marcas. She stumbled forward into his embrace, burying her face in his shoulder as his arms closed around her. Her shoulders trembled as she poured her grief into the fine silk of his shirt, his hand stroking her hair.

"There, there, dear. It's not your fault," he murmured. "There's nothing you could have done."

"I coulda—if ain't sent him—"

"Oh, but who wouldn't try to help their brother?" Nijel pulled her into the room, guiding her to a soft couch and sitting her down. He sank down beside her, running a hand through her hair. "Anyone who would leave a brother to the whims of the world, unaided and alone. What a monster that would be. And you, dear, are far from that. You couldn't have guessed what the high lord would do."

Niamsha collapsed against him, shaking, tears pouring over her cheeks, her hands, his shoulders. Nijel simply sat with her, one hand stroking her hair in comfort as he mumbled soothing words she could no longer make out. Time lost meaning, her throat slowly losing the ache of repressed tears and growing raw from crying, her shoulders aching no longer from strain, but from the constant shake of her tears.

When her sobs finally subsided into quiet whimpers and her tears had slowed to occasional drips, Nijel leaned over and kissed her hair. With a final run of his fingers through her hair, he rose and crossed the room, returning a moment later with a glass of a deep red liquid.

"Here." He offered the cup. "It's a bit dry, but I've no other wine here, and you've got to be hurting. Take just a sip."

Niamsha reached a hesitant hand out, taking the cup from him. Heavy, more than the wine would account for. She spun the glass in her hand, examining the thickness, with intricate designs laced throughout that spoke of a master glasswright's work. At the bottom of the glass, just above the stem, she found a tiny stretch of etched initials. IP. Her mother's initials. It could be anyone, could stand for any name. But the glasswork was so exquisite.

"Papa made this."

"I was quite a fan of your father's work, Nisha." Nijel resumed his seat beside her. "When I found his children alone, on the street. And you, so devoted to caring for your brother. How could I do anything but take you in?"

A smile, bitter and cold, stole across her face. Four years in the Rendell house had been hell. But at least it hadn't been the streets. And Emrys had been safe. She took a sip, the bitter liquid harsh on her tongue, and her body shook, splashing the wine against the high sides of the glass. Nijel snatched the cup away.

"It is quite strong." He set the glass to one side. "Does that help? Tears can be so draining."

Niamsha nodded, and Nijel sighed, leaning back in his seat. She could feel his eyes on her, studying every breath she took as if trying to guess what she might do next. What could she possibly do next? She'd thrown her chance at stability away for a shot at freedom from her papa's debts. She'd lied to the high lord, and to his demon, and to Nijel. She'd led people to fight and kill.

She'd betrayed Holy Aeduhm by making a deal with a demon. And now He'd taken her brother's life for it. What more *could* she do?

"Come along, dear. No need to linger here." Nijel rose from his seat, offering her a hand. "I know this is hard. I mourn our brother as you do. But we must move on. Come north with me. I've some land once ruled by my family, now long abandoned. A perfect place to rest and recover from this tragedy."

"I can't—" Niamsha jerked her head up, her words frozen on her tongue. Couldn't what? Leave Emrys? He was already dead. Leave the town that had taken everything from her? She'd planned on that for weeks now. There was nothing left for her here. But Nijel offered nothing without a price. "What ya want from me?"

"What do I desire from you?" He smiled at her, teeth clenched in what she couldn't help but read as predatory glee. But he had no reason to harm her. Not if he planned to help her. "Don't be foolish. You're my sister. My sister's troubles are my own."

She hesitated. Nijel had been kind, but she knew better than to trust him without a reason. Even after this. He'd never given something for free.

"Ain't gonna take charity."

She might have, from someone she trusted. But she didn't have any of those left. Except maybe the lady. Lady Saylina seemed innocent of her brother's bloody deeds. But too devoted to be convinced of his crimes. And there was Emperor Deyvan. Kind, concerned for her well-being. He couldn't know who his friend really was. Neither would help her at High Lord Arkaen's expense.

Niamsha set her lips in a tight frown, looking up at Nijel. "I come with ya, we gonna have a deal. I owe in cash, but I need more. Need the high lord dead."

"A common goal, then, Nisha," Nijel said. "And I know the perfect use for your skills." He smiled at her again. "My dealings in Sernyii need a supervisor to ensure the security of our goods. You've a good head on you, Nisha. Be my Mistress of Keys. Underlings, resources to plan your revenge. We'll make an exceptional pair."

The title sent chills down her spine, too reminiscent of the woman who held sway over the whorehouse. But Nijel had never laid a finger on her. On anyone, to her knowledge. And she needed the support. Swallowing a lump of fear and lingering grief, Niamsha nodded.

"Perfect. I'll need to leave swiftly." Nijel crossed to the desk, stacking a collection of papers and sliding them into a satchel. "My business here is completed, and I'm afraid the high lord and his pet may be displeased with me should I linger."

Niamsha rose. No real choice. Except for once she had one. Stay and suffer under the man who'd tortured her brother or join Nijel. Learn the thieves' trade and gather allies to seek her justice. No reason to turn him down. Torsdell was no longer her home. This city had taken everything from her. Even her brother. And High Lord Arkaen had caused it all with his laws and his gods-damned demon. This city was a hell.

And High Lord Arkaen was her enemy.

Appendix of Notable Characters, Locations, and Religious Pantheons

Laisian Pantheon

Aeduhm—High God of the pantheon, known as the father of the Divine Children and the Steward of the Eternal Feast

Eiliin—Betrothed of Aeduhm, known as the mother of the Divine Children. Corrupted by her empathy for lost souls and banished to rule over Hell for eternity.

Satar—Brother of Aeduhm, God of War and Justice.

Istvan—Eldest son of Aeduhm and Eiliin, God of Merchants and Travel.

Marpaessa—Eldest daughter of Aeduhm and Eiliin, Goddess of Fields and Family.

Edros—Son of Aeduhm and Eiliin, God of the Day.

Thirena—Daughter of Aeduhm and Eiliin, Goddess of Love.

Ancient Spirits—Pantheon worshiped by Kìlashà and the mysterious Drae'gon clans.

Landed Nobles of Sentar Province

Sentarsin Bloodline

Johannus Sentarsin—Previous high lord, ruled Sentar province under the reign of High Emperor Caildenn Laisia. Cause of death unknown.

Katrivianne Istalli Sentarsin—Previous high lady, wife of Johannus Sentarsin. Died from ill health suffered while carrying a third child of poor disposition.

Arkaen Sentarsin—Ruling high lord, son of Johannus Sentarsin.

Saylina Sentarsin—daughter of Johannus Sentarsin, acting as presumptive high lady until her brother takes a wife.

Tenison Bloodline
Jussi Tenison—Count of the Tenison estate, known companion of Baron Oskari Weydert

Skianda Bloodline
Brayden Skianda—Count of the Skianda estate, long-time supporter of Sentarsin rule.
Arianne Skianda—sister of Brayden Skianda.

Lesser Nobles of Sentar Province
Andriole Bloodline
Viscount Andriole—Viscount of the Andriole grounds within the Tenison estate, granted as holders until such time as the Tenison family reclaims the land.
Kyli Andriole—Daughter of Viscount Andriole, formerly engaged to Baron Weydert's son.

Weydert Bloodline
Oskari Weydert—Baron of the Weydert manor in Torsdell. Adviser to the former high lord, Johannus Sentarsin.
Rikkard Weydert—heir to the Weydert manor, son of Oskari Weydert, formerly engaged to Kyli Andriole.
Camira Weydert—daughter of Oskari Weydert, engagement proposed to and rejected by Arkaen Sentarsin.

Imperial Bloodlines
Caildenn Laisia—Former high emperor of the Laisian Empire, killed in an assassination during the Sernien War.
Eevanna Corliann Laisia—First wife of Caildenn Laisia, mother of the imperial princes. Died while the princes were still young, believed to be at the hand of assassins from the former country of Sernyii.

Raekeen Laisia—Eldest son and presumptive heir of Caildenn Laisia, killed as a child by assassins from the former country of Sernyii.

Jaylen Laisia—Younger son of Caildenn Laisia, killed as a child by assassins from the former country of Sernyii.

Mikkal Corliann—Distant cousin of the imperial bloodline, brother to Eevanna Corliann Laisia, father of Deyvan Corliann. Ruled imperial holdings under Caildenn Laisia's reign. Current residence unknown.

Lizbetta Rainen Corliann—Wife of Mikkal Corliann, father of Deyvan Corliann. Current residence unknown.

Deyvan Corliann—Reigning High Emperor of the Laisian Empire, son of Mikkal and Lizbetta Corliann and nephew of the former high emperor, Caildenn Laisia. Named heir by Caildenn Laisia at the start of the Sernien War after the imperial princes were killed.

Other Notable Characters

Kìlashà san Draego de Mìtaran—Personal guard and lover of Arkaen, known to his mysterious people as the Chosen of the Four Clans of the Drae'gon.

Princess Prillani Kitorn—Adopted daughter of the reigning king of Osuvia.

Jarod—Leader of Arkaen's personal guard force, the *Serr-Nyen* flameguard.

Torsdell Commoners

Niamsha Pereyra—Daughter of a local glasswright, now working as a thief among the Rendell gang. Took her mother's name in honor of her heritage.

Emrys Pereyra—Son of a local glasswright, brother to Niamsha, merchant's apprentice at Istvan's temple. Took his mother's name by his sister's request.

Master Trieu—Father of Niamsha and Emrys Pereyra, well respected glasswright. Died of an unknown illness.

Caela—Personal servant to Lady Saylina Sentarsin, has been serving Saylina since they were both children.

Tressa—Niamsha's childhood friend, also the daughter of a local glasswright.

Master Ferndon—Former guildmaster of the glasswright's guild.

Janne Ferndon—Son of Master Ferndon, given a glasswright's apprenticeship previously promised to Niamsha.

Rendell Gang

Nijel Rendell—Leader of the Rendells, claims the other members of his gang as siblings.

Marcas Rendell—Nijel's chief lieutenant. Runs most of the jobs for the gang.

Eli—Rendell lookout and common scapegoat.

Locations

Serni province—Recently added province of the Laisian Empire and site of the Sernien War. Previously known as the kingdom of Sernyii.

Sentar province—Formerly the northernmost province of the Laisian Empire. Home of the Sentarsin family.

Torsdell—Capital city of Sentar province and location of the Sentarsin family estate.

Laisian Empire—Southern empire covering much of the continent of Myiratas. Was expanding until the recent Sernien War resulted in a shift in leadership.

Whitfaern—Capital city of the Laisian Empire and location of the imperial palace.

Osuvia—Northernmost kingdom on the continent of Myiratas. Frequently at war with Yllshana.

Yllshana—Northeastern kingdom on the continent of Myiratas. Historically reclusive and frequently at war with Osuvia.

Mindaine—Western kingdom on the continent of Myiratas. Close trade partner with the Laisian Empire.

Western Isles—Loosely allied bands of historically reclusive islanders. No recent trade with the Myiratas mainland.

Chelsea Harper is the author and publisher of Wake of the Phoenix, book one of the Artifice of Power Saga. She lives in Colorado with her husband, daughter, two dogs, one cat, and countless imaginary friends. When she isn't writing she enjoys games, from World of Warcraft to Elder Scrolls to tabletop RPGs and even the occasional board game.

Twitter: @chelsofharper

Blog: www.musingsmythosmagic.com